THE
GREATEST MAN
IN CEDAR HOLE

THE GREATEST MAN IN CEDAR HOLE

STEPHANIE DOYON

BLOOMSBURY

First published in Great Britain 2005

Copyright © 2005 by Stephanie Doyon

The moral right of the author has been asserted

Bloomsbury Publishing Plc, 38 Soho Square, London W1D 3HB

A CIP catalogue record for this book is available from the British Library

ISBN 0 7475 7989 x
ISBN-13 9780747579892

10 9 8 7 6 5 4 3 2 1

Printed in Great Britain by Clays Ltd, St Ives plc

All papers used by Bloomsbury are natural, recyclable products
made from wood grown in well-managed forests. The manufacturing
processes conform to the environmental regulations
of the country of origin.

www.bloomsbury.com/stephaniedoyon

To my grandmother, Evelyn—
we were more alike than I knew.

ACKNOWLEDGMENTS

I am forever indebted to the following people who started me on my path to writing: Ann Brashares, for giving me my first writing job; to Maja, Rosie, Amy, Al, and everyone at Writers House, my training ground for the publishing business and home of my wonderful agent, Simon Lipskar; and especially to Rick Russo for his instruction, advice, and staggering support when the most I had hoped for was a kind word or two.

Many thanks also to David Rosenthal and everyone at Simon & Schuster, especially my editor, Denise Roy, a story charmer who has a gift for coaxing the best out of a manuscript.

Finally, I am deeply grateful to my husband, family, and friends for their patience, encouragement, and love. I don't know if I would have had the stamina to finish this book if it hadn't been for your support.

PART ONE

~ Chapter One ~

BOTTOM *of the* BUCKET

On the first morning of the new school year, Miss Delia Pratt began the session by ignoring the collection of miserable little souls that made up her fourth-grade class. As they wandered in from the playground, she cracked open the newest issue of *True Detective* magazine and flipped directly to the exploits of Detective Nick Cabot, whom she followed faithfully every month. To the bumbling students in slickers and rain boots clotting the doorway, Delia raised an absent hand—the same way a cow might swat a cloud of flies circling her flank—but her full attention was paid to Cabot, who was clipping at the heels of the notorious jewel thief he had been trailing all summer. A flash of the badge, a click of the handcuffs, and the classroom dissolved; Delia's mind became broad and dense, the corners rounded and dulled to a blissful stupor. Her body took on the slogging consistency of pudding, allowing her head to wobble forward and her chin to sink down into the exposed chasm of her cleavage.

The students stared in horror as their teacher's eyelids flitted closed and the brass clasp holding her blond updo slid along the back of her neck. A single whimper rose up from the doorway. Beads of rainwater rolled down to the hem of the children's slickers, drip-drip-dripping onto the floor in monotonous rhythm. Lungs paused, afraid to breathe. Two students with compulsive tendencies checked and rechecked the name on the front door; upon confirming and reconfirming they were in the correct classroom, one proceeded to tap his fingers against the wall, five taps per finger, while the other mentally sang through a comforting, continuous loop of "Dixie." Among the more generous children, Miss Pratt seemed, at worst, curious and unhelpful—but to the majority she was sinister and cold and her profile, if viewed at the correct angle under certain light, was not unlike that of a witch.

"Maybe she had a heart attack," one of the children whispered. The offhand comment lightened the communal mood; more than a few spines tingled at the possibility of a dead teacher and class being canceled for the entire year.

"I think she's still breathing," another said. "Go poke her with a ruler."

"*You* do it."

"Uh-uh."

As the children debated their course of action, the sun elbowed its way into the classroom, cutting a diagonal swath from the back window to the chalkboard at the front of the room. There was cruelty in the timing of the sun's sudden, unobstructed appearance–from nearly the moment school let out in June to that very September morning, the sky had been a constant smear of gray and wet.

Cedar Hole was at a disadvantage, and not just because of the weather—the town seemed to exist almost by default. It was five miles of negative space, patched together from the discarded scraps of the surrounding hill towns of Palmdale and Mt. Etna, contained within a border so ragged and senseless it appeared to be drawn with the sole intent of shutting out every possible geographic feature of charm and beauty. The terrain was joyless; spreading out low and flat, prone to collecting runoff from the hillside, and trapping a thin fog that often didn't burn off until suppertime. The land was soggy even through summer, smelling of green rot well into the bleached heat of August.

Only the grass seemed to enjoy all the moisture. Cedar Hole lawns came up as thick as a carpet without the trouble of sprinklers or fertilizer or any of the other nonsense they had to deal with in other communities. In fact, the grass grew so quickly that constant mowing was required to keep the phenomenal growth at bay—depending on the rainfall, most people mowed upwards of three times a week. It was the first chore Cedar Hole parents passed off to their kids as soon as they were tall enough to reach the push bar, and during brief, dry periods, children hurried outside to trim the lawn before the weather turned wet again. Happy to finally get some fresh air and sunshine, they mowed with reckless speed and diffuse concentration. It was no coincidence, therefore, that Cedar Hole had the largest number of severed toes per capita in all of Gilford County.

As the sky broke for the first time in months, Miss Pratt's classroom became saturated in a teasing gold. The abrupt change in brightness roused Delia from her semi-coma; as she blinked in the glare and collected her oozing posture, her mind resumed its three dimensions. The room returned to her, bringing with it insipid paper leaves taped around the doorway and the aspirin smell of chalk dust. A dark mood was fermenting inside Delia. She took one last, longing look at Detective Cabot and slapped the magazine shut.

"Sit your asses down," she ordered.

In the doorway, the children jerked to attention. They scattered and thinned out along the wall of coat hooks, abandoning their rain boots and lunch bags along with any hopes of school being canceled. Movement brought a fleeting sense of relief, though as soon as they chose their seats and settled behind the rows of wobbly desks, relief gave way to an oppressive dread. The entire school year stretched out before them long and endless, paved by a woman whose temperament was as inhospitable as the Cedar Hole climate.

Delia rested her hands on her hips, her figure still unencumbered by the strains of motherhood or the comfortable slouch of marriage. "I don't want to be here, either, but unfortunately there are laws we have to obey." She leaned back against the front of her desk. "How many of you can already read and tell time?"

There was a smattering of raised hands.

"Make change?"

A few hands dropped away.

"That's good—looks like everyone's caught up on their learning. No matter what they tell you, everything else is just a waste of time. History and science are only helpful if you're going to be a contestant on *Twenty One*—and I think it's safe to say that none of you ever will." The sunbeam trespassed across the corner of Miss Pratt's desk. With a yank she pulled the window shades down to the edge of the sill, returning the room to a more manageable atmosphere of artificial light. "So I guess we'll just have to kill time until the school year is over. Anyone have any ideas?"

Another whimper rose up from the back.

"Last year, our teacher had us make name tags," a brave soul called out. "So you can learn our names."

"I suppose that's a fair idea," she sighed. "What do you need?"

"Cards and crayons."

Miss Pratt rifled through the supply closet at the back of the room, and to her surprise discovered the exact supplies she needed. She traipsed up and down the rows, distributing index cards, fistfuls of broken crayons, and strips of cellophane tape, all the while examining the face of each student. One or two of the kids, she noticed, were new to Cedar Hole. It was easy to spot newcomers. Aside from the obvious physical clues (rosy complexions, shiny hair, and other hallmarks of a superior gene pool), there was a restlessness behind the eyes, an almost wild panic. No one came to Cedar Hole by choice or accident—they were delivered only by the cruel hand of misfortune, dumped on the town's doorstep after all other prayers, favors, and bargains had been thoroughly exhausted.

"Welcome, dear, to Cedar Hole Elementary," Miss Pratt said to a plump brunette with pigtails. The girl wore a dotted Swiss party dress with a yellow sash tied around the waist that spoke of money but not necessarily taste. "What's your name?"

"Candace." The little girl smoothed a curl off her forehead.

"What brings you here, Candace?"

"We moved from Palmdale a few weeks ago."

"Who's 'we'?"

"My mother and my sisters."

Miss Pratt surveyed the prissy upturn of Candace's nose. "What about your father?"

Candace yawned and stretched her arms overhead, the sole survivor of a sinking ship. "He took his secretary to Hawaii."

Moments like these, Miss Pratt concluded, were what made teaching worthwhile. Ten-year-olds were keenly observant and wise to the workings of their households, and spoke faultlessly of their parents without the hindrance of discretion. One more year, Delia knew, and contempt for their families would slowly worm its way into their hearts along with a perverse loyalty that would eventually steel their mouths shut. But right now, she could find out everything.

"That's a nice story, Candace. We'll have to talk more about it later." Delia made a few notes in the grade book next to Candace's name, underlining both the words *Palmdale* and *Hawaii* to be remembered for discussion during lunch break in the teachers' lounge.

"If anyone brought chocolate chip cookies today for snack break, see me later," she announced to the class. "No nuts, please."

Miss Pratt resumed crayon duty, digging deep into the bucket. The brighter colors—the yellows and oranges and even some reds—were hardly used, while the drab colors were worn down to nubs. In her experience, the children of Cedar Hole did not like to draw rainbows or unicorns or other sappy, mystical things. Instead, they had a penchant for rocks and moss and other tedious signatures of their landscape, their palette running to a dismal spectrum of grays, browns, and greens.

"I'll take an orange," said a little boy in the front row. "If you have one."

The boy sat bolt upright in his chair with his hands folded neatly on the desktop. Delia paused. He was so shiny and well groomed that she automatically assumed he was also a newcomer who had suffered a fate similar to Candace's.

She handed him the crayon. "Interesting choice."

The boy immediately got to work on his name tag. His letters were bold and steady, evenly spaced and gently serifed, an unusual contrast against the feeble penmanship of his classmates. Even more unusual was the inclusion of a middle initial between his Christian and surnames, accompanied by a tiny star where one could have more predictably expected a dot. The boy's creativity was so undiluted that Delia suspected he couldn't have been in Cedar Hole for very long at all—a week, at most.

" 'Robert J. Cutler,' " she read aloud.

Miss Pratt had only said the name in passing—an absent play of the lips as her eyes scanned the tag, a habit from childhood that returned during unguarded moments—but Robert took it as a call to attention and stood beside his desk. The boy appeared tall for his age, though in truth he fell just below average. The illusion was created by the way he distributed weight within his slight frame—shoulders rolling back comfortably in their sockets, rib cage floating over the pelvis, chin and neck forming a confident ninety-degree arc. One hip bore the majority of his weight while the other sloped gently downward, which came across not as effeminate or arrogant but conveyed a maturity the other children in the class wouldn't reach for several more years, if ever. None of these subtleties registered with Miss Pratt, however, who was singularly taken with the boy's dress shirt and trousers. They had been pressed to a state of crispness that made her think of Sam Spade in *The Maltese Falcon*.

"What's the *J* for, Robert?"

"Jeremiah. After my paternal grandfather."

"Your *who?*"

"Paternal grandfather."

"We use regular words in this classroom, please," Miss Pratt scolded. "There are others who might not understand your fancy language."

"My father's father, then."

Miss Pratt sniffed the air and thought she noted the starchy scent of old money—Palmdale money for sure. "Am I supposed to call you Robert J., then, or just Robert?"

"You may call me anything you like, Miss Pratt," the boy said.

His answer pleased her. Robert's manners suggested to Delia that he was from a prominent family, one that must have experienced something tragic and irreversible for him to end up in Cedar Hole. It was undoubtedly a delicate, yet juicy situation. She drew closer, choosing her questions carefully.

"When did you move here, Robert?"

The boy shifted his weight to the other hip. The smooth skin of his forehead made a fair attempt at confusion, but produced only the barest suggestion of it. "Miss Pratt?"

"When did you get here? Over the summer?"

"I think you've been misinformed," he said, lacing his fingers behind his back. "I've always lived here."

"I mean Cedar Hole."

"I understand. I've always lived here."

A shallow breath caught in Delia's throat. "You *can't* be a Hellion."

"Pardon?"

Cedar Hellion was the less vulgar of the two pet names Miss Pratt had for Cedar Hole natives. Like the children who were currently inhabiting her classroom, most Hellions had doughy faces and demeanors marked by alternating moods of whininess and defeat. They were fond of postures that demonstrated a sort of collective lethargy, frequently running air through their vocal cords with each exhalation to produce a repetitive string of downhearted sighs. This shiny little boy was neither doughy nor tired nor pathetic. He was clearly carved from a much finer stock than the rest.

Delia sucked her teeth. "You must have been born somewhere else, then. You were born somewhere else and your parents brought you here when you were a baby."

Robert shook his head. "My mom and dad are from Cedar Hole. We've always lived here."

"So have I—and I don't know any Cutlers."

"William and Sissy?"

"What's your mother's maiden name?"

Delia searched the boy for the distinct facial features that ran in certain local families. There was the high, yellowed forehead of the Wellers, which sank back from a very pronounced, shelflike brow bone. Or the Hanson neck, a gangly, disjointed thing that always looked ready to buckle under the weight of a too-large head. And of course there was the pitiable Rendyak smile, an overgrown set of teeth housed in an otherwise small mouth—Rendyaks were recognizable by their strained lips and their constant need to lick their teeth to keep them from drying out. Occasionally, two members of these distinguished clans would marry and have offspring, which Delia thought produced an almost unparalleled homeliness worthy of Barnum & Bailey. Perhaps, just this once, it had produced a specimen as fine as Robert.

"Beaumont," he said.

"I've never heard of them."

"No, Miss Pratt," the boy answered, returning to his name tag. "I don't suppose you have."

Numbed and startled by this new information, Miss Pratt gave him a handful of the best crayons. "We'll talk more on this later."

Delia continued on down the row. By the time she reached the last desk, she had reached the bottom of the bucket, with only a few crayon crumbles remaining.

"Not much left for you," she said to the boy sitting there. She turned the bucket upside down and dumped a handful of burnt sienna chips onto the desktop.

The boy snaked his arm around the crayon pile and swept them in close to his chest, leaving a trail of brown streaks across the top of the desk.

"Hey, I know you," she said, looking down at him. "You're a Pinkham. You've got that little dimple at the end of your nose that they all have."

Most of the students turned to take a look, except for the entire left side of the room, which had melted into infectious puddles of sleep. Bathed in the dusk of the window shade, the contagion was now threatening to spread; other nearby students nestled into the crooks of their elbows, lulled by the warm, dark cave their bodies made against the desks.

The boy made no indication to the affirmative, but Delia knew he was a Pinkham. His eyes were that same flinty gray she had seen in all the Pinkhams—eyes that craved attention, then just as quickly deflected it. Pinkham lips were curled and brooding, perpetually sour-mouthed, and frequently engaged in the process of either eating or expectorating and often both at the same time. The skin was pale to the point of translucency, a milky sheath over prominent veins, quickly turning a pulpy red if provoked. Delia even recognized the sweater the boy was wearing; the front was covered with a hand-knit baby chick, once yellow, now a peaked yellow-green, hatching from a jagged gray shell. She had seen the same sweater on all the Pinkham girls, nine times over.

"Your parents certainly are *busy,*" Miss Pratt said with a leering wink. "How many more after you?"

"I'm the last," he said, curling in on himself, as though he half expected to crawl inside the chick's shell. If Robert was Cedar Hole at its best, the Pinkhams were the lowest of the low.

"And what did they name *you?*"

"Francis."

Miss Pratt snickered. "All those girls and they name you that."

The doughy boy sitting directly behind Francis raised his hand. "You can call him Spud—that's his nickname."

Miss Pratt knelt beside Francis's desk and leaned in close to his ear. "Don't worry, no one's expecting too much from you. If you're gonna take off, don't hang out in the hall where Principal Nelson can catch you—he's already on my case enough. Go out back in the woods—got it?"

Francis didn't answer. He picked up a piece of brown crayon and wrote SPUD on the index card.

"And another thing," she said, lowering her voice. "Any chance I could bum a smoke off you? I left mine at home."

Francis curled his upper lip, where a white crust of mucus had dried. "I don't have any."

"Sure. Well, if you see any of your sisters, tell them to meet me behind the Dumpster at lunch. Billie owes me half a pack by now. Okay?"

~ Chapter Two ~

The INAUSPICIOUS CONCEPTION *of* FRANCIS PINKHAM

The history of Cedar Hole is peppered with halfhearted undertakings and misguided efforts, none of which are worth mentioning here in any detail other than to note that they rarely had any meaningful impact. On occasion, however, whether through sheer stubbornness or blind chance, someone mustered enough ambition to inch himself above the bar of mediocrity, just high enough to manage an accomplishment or two. Success, as might be expected, was rarely welcome no matter how dubious the achievement, often viewed among the townsfolk as an unexpected jolt that threatened to upset the natural order. Right-minded people know that success for one is success for all; that in this dark world a little happiness in a single life is a victory for the common good. But in Cedar Hole, when a person rose above the lot, everyone else looked around and thought they were sinking. Balance had to be restored, and if fate didn't see to it, the citizens of Cedar Hole took it upon themselves to make sure that victory and defeat were served up in equal portions.

Such is the story of Francis Pinkham. Francis's story begins well before Miss Pratt's fourth grade, even before Robert J. Cutler, all the way back to a full fifteen years before his birth. It begins with his parents— Lawrence and Frances Pinkham—and his father's humble ambition to

have a son. As a young wife, Frances Pinkham wanted to make her husband happy, which included keeping his work clothes clean and pressed,
cooking rich meals, and making herself available in the bedroom. She
also wanted to give him children, but only a few—perhaps three or four
at most. Although larger families were popular at the time (just like the
old homesteaders who needed a brood to work the land, the women of
Cedar Hole often joked that they kept having babies just so they'd always
have someone to mow the grass), Franny didn't believe in cramming a
house full of unhappy, needy children who were starved for both food
and attention. She saw a future full of leisurely, abundant Sunday dinners
around the dining room table and Christmases with plenty of gifts for
everyone.

Larry, on the other hand, didn't care how many children they had—
just as long as one of them was a boy. He had been raised in a family of
four boys, his father was one of three, and his grandfather was the
youngest of five. Masculinity was prized among the Pinkhams; it not
only carried on the family name but the family business as well. For three
generations, the Pinkhams had been building and selling pine desks, bu-
reaus, headboards, and footstools, out of the barn behind the family
farmhouse. Larry dreamed of one day passing on the trade and family
business to his own sons. But as is often the case with worldly desires,
Larry and Franny's hopes didn't coincide with what nature had planned.
Their problem was not of fertility but of chromosomes—the Pinkhams,
as it turned out, were quite prolific breeders. Unfortunately, they were capable of making only baby girls.

Upon hearing that Franny was pregnant with their first child, Larry
ran down to the lumberyard and bought a piece of scrap maple. He
turned the wood on a lathe, shaving it into a lean cylinder that gradually
tapered from the middle toward one end, which he flared out into a flattened knob. Even though it was the first baseball bat Larry had ever
made, it turned out to be a fine specimen, with just the right balance and
weight, a solid swing, and a good, clean crack on contact. He sanded and
oiled the wood to a satin finish, his heart expanding with thoughts of his
future son working beside him and playing baseball with the neighbor-
hood kids in the field behind the barn. Larry would teach him everything
about pine and baseball and anything else a boy needed to know. With a

wood-burning tool and a sure hand, Larry carved the name JACK
PINKHAM into the shaft.

When he was finished, he showed the bat to Franny.

"Who on earth is Jack Pinkham?" she asked.

"Well, who do you think? It's our boy."

Franny, who at the time was canning strawberry preserves to put up
in the pantry, didn't break from the rhythm of filling her jam jars. "I didn't
know we'd settled on a name just yet."

"I thought of it while I was in the shop. It's a good name," he said. "A
good, tough name makes a good, tough boy."

Franny wiped down the jar rims with the corner of a damp flour-sack
towel. She had been with Larry long enough to recognize when he had
latched on to an idea, clinging with such a white-knuckle grip that disappointment was the only inevitable conclusion. In later years, she would
come to learn that leaving Larry to his delusions was the best way to handle him, but for now, when their marriage was still young, Franny was
compelled to shelter her husband from his own worst instincts.

"Have you given any thought that we might have a girl?"

Larry leaned the bat against the kitchen cabinet, turning it so that the
name was visible. The letters were still warm to the touch and smelled
faintly of smoke. "It's science, Franny. We Pinkhams only make boys."

"Well, your father and grandfather did—and maybe your brothers
have a couple—but that doesn't mean that's what's going to happen to
you."

Larry shook his head. "Look at the odds . . ." His voice trailed off.
"You can't argue with odds."

"Don't be so sure." Franny swatted his words away with a wave of her
hand. "When you're too sure, life has a way of making you a fool."

Larry took a seat at the kitchen table, shoulders hunched up to his
ears. He stared at her belly with a look of rabid fear. "I don't know why
you have to talk like that, Franny. It's science."

He looked so dejected that Franny wished she hadn't said anything
at all.

"Well, you know I don't know anything about science," she relented,
sawing off a thick slab of brown bread from a loaf that was cooling on the
table. "I wasn't very good with it in school." As a consolation, she handed

Larry the bread and set the jam pot on a folded towel right in front of him, so he could soak up the dregs of the preserves. He tore the slice in half and dove into the pot with both hands, mopping up every last bit.

"Don't burn yourself, now," she said.

That was the last time Franny ever challenged Larry's certainty about the sex of their baby, which only caused his fervor to return even more intensely than before. Larry painted the nursery a powder blue and made toy cars and a rocking horse out of scrap pine he had lying around the shop. He built a crib with JACK burned into the headboard and a changing table for Franny with a baseball diamond painted on the side. She thought it best to go along with him—after all, she reasoned, he had a fifty-fifty shot at being right, and time would settle the argument soon enough. She did her part by sewing little shirts with appliquéd baseballs and baseball bats, but used a loose stitch just in case he turned out to be wrong.

The baby arrived a week ahead of schedule. It was to Franny Pinkham's benefit that her first child was born at a time when husbands were not present during delivery—the experience was exhausting enough without the added drain of also having to console a disappointed husband.

"I'll go get Larry," Dr. Potts said, after the nurses had helped Franny transform herself into a fresh, glowing example of new motherhood. "I'm sure he's anxious to see his daughter."

"Please don't say anything about the baby being a girl," she said. "I'd like to tell him myself."

Franny had every intention of breaking the news to Larry right there in the hospital, but when he burst into the delivery room with a blue-banded cigar pinched between his teeth, she didn't have the heart. His happiness was so pure, so complete, it seemed wrong to spoil the moment.

"Hi, there, Jack! This is your dad," he shouted. "It's nice to finally meet you, son. You're a big guy, aren't you?"

The nurse who had attended to Franny gave Larry a look of alarm, but Franny brushed it off, saying, "The baby's healthy. That's what's most important."

Larry's joy seemed to ebb for a moment as a deep line creased his forehead. "Why is he wrapped up in a pink blanket? Are they trying to make my son a tinkerbell?"

"It's for warmth, Larry. Does the color really matter?"

"To my son it does," he said. "Jack hates pink. Don't you, boy?"

And so it went for the first few days of their daughter's life: little baby Pinkham slept in a blue room surrounded by toy cars, wore clothes with tiny baseballs on them, and twitched when called by the name of Jack. Larry puffed with pride more and more each day, while Franny grew more anxious. Treating a girl like a boy, she feared, might cause irreparable harm; yet she shrank with dread at the prospect of telling Larry the truth.

One afternoon, while Franny was changing the baby's diaper, Larry snuck up behind her, as he later put it, "to see if Jack was a Pinkham, through and through." She didn't know he had been standing there looking over her shoulder until she heard him gasp.

Franny worked quickly at the diaper pins, thanking the good Lord that the secret was finally out and that she was spared from having to tell him directly. "Don't be angry," she said, avoiding his eyes. "I didn't know how to tell you."

Larry stood still, his lips melting pale against his skin. His voice darkened. "We'll sue. When we're done with him, he won't have a pot to piss in." He kneaded his fist. "I have half a mind to go over there right now and try my baseball bat out on him."

Franny spun around. "Who are you talking about?"

"Dr. Potts!" Larry brushed her aside. Wincing, he pulled down the baby's diaper to take another look. "Sloppy bastard."

In every marriage, there are certain times that cause a spouse to reconsider her vows, and for Franny this was one of those moments. Suddenly she remembered being back in her parents' kitchen not even an hour before the wedding, watching her father sign a check he promised gladly to hand over if only she'd "ditch that dumb ox." It occurred to Franny, as she finished pinning the baby's diaper, that she had never even bothered to see how much the check was written out for.

"It's not a botched circumcision, Larry. Jack's a girl."

The limp relief of knowing his child was not disfigured helped Larry swallow the disappointment. In the abstract, a boy was ideal, but now that the baby was here it was hard not to love her all the same. Jack (whom they immediately started calling Jackie) had already won a place in his heart.

"We'll just have to have another baby, that's all," Larry decided.

Six months later, Franny was pregnant again.

This time they consulted Franny's grandmother, Pearl, who dangled a threaded needle above her belly. The needle swung in a straight line that, according to Grammy Pearl, was a definitive sign that it was a boy. People commented on Franny's broad belly and how she carried low, also signs, they insisted, that she was carrying a boy. These omens, in addition to Larry's sketchy knowledge of statistics and science ("Last time we had a fifty percent chance of a boy—but now that we already have a girl, it's a hundred percent"), were enough evidence for him to confidently name his unborn child George. They left the nursery blue and kept the toy cars in their rightful places. Franny even kept the baseball appliqués on all the clothes because she was so busy with baby Jackie she didn't think she'd have the energy to sew them on again once the new baby arrived.

Little George, however, turned out to be a little Georgie instead. Two babies were enough for Franny, but Larry became more determined than ever to have a son. Six months to the day after Georgie was born, Franny was pregnant again.

The cycle continued for the rest of the Pinkham girls—Charlie, Rickie, Rae, Teddie, Ronnie, Billie, and Larrie Jr.—and might have continued for another decade if an exhausted Franny had not put an end to it.

"You're only going to have daughters, Larry," she told him as he hauled out the old full-sized mattress from their bedroom to make room for a new set of twin beds. "It's time you made the best of it."

Larry Pinkham took his wife's advice to heart and brought up his daughters in the way that he imagined he might have raised a son: showing them how to split logs with an ax, teaching them the subtle artistry of making pine furniture, taking them to baseball games. The Pinkham girls grew up rugged and thick like their father, their hands toughened by hammers and sandpaper. As far as the domestic arts were concerned, Franny had little success with her attempts at getting the girls to cook and sew or even help clean the house. If they weren't at school or in the woodshop they were out on the back lawn playing baseball.

On their fifteenth anniversary, Larry treated Franny to dinner at Shorty's Diner. They were alone for the first time in as many years, and Franny was feeling sentimental. "You know, life hasn't turned out too bad for us. It could have been worse."

Larry leaned over his platter of meatloaf and mashed potatoes. "But think about how much better it could have been, you know, if things had gone the other way."

Franny Pinkham was not an oversensitive wife, like, say, Kitty Higgins, the town librarian, who colored everything her husband said with old arguments and unrelated contexts. Had she reacted in the same way, Franny might have noticed the timing of Larry's comment (being their anniversary) and decided he was unhappy with their marriage. But Franny knew her husband was a straight shooter. He didn't have a mind for hidden agendas and subtlety.

"You wanted a boy, but you got nine tomboys instead," she said. "Not too bad a trade."

"I suppose. But I keep thinking about when they grow up, though. They're all going to get married and have kids and not one of them is going to be a Pinkham in name."

"It's not like the Pinkhams have done anything to make the name so important. We're not the Rockefellers."

"What about the store? That's something." Larry fell silent and mopped up the gravy on his plate with a flaccid dinner roll. It wasn't sadness that Franny felt coming off him, so much as defeat—as though he had failed not only his whole family, but also every Pinkham that had ever come before.

"It will always be Pinkham's Furniture, even if the girls run it," Franny said. "I don't understand the problem."

Larry was quiet for the rest of the dinner, even when Shorty graciously brought them a complimentary slice of blueberry cream pie to share. He didn't say a word during the ride home, either. Franny thought her husband's continued attachment to having a son was disgraceful, considering that they had been blessed with nine healthy girls, while others, like Kitty Higgins, couldn't have any children at all. Still, she hated to see Larry so sullen, so full of regret. When they returned home from dinner that night, Franny threw back the covers of her bed and sighed.

"I'll give you one more shot," she said.

Nine months later, they had a son.

By the time Francis came along, Larry had run out of good, tough names and decided to name the boy after his mother. The Pinkhams were overjoyed by Francis's arrival; Franny felt as though she had come to the end of a long, arduous journey and Larry was finally able to relax, having fulfilled his biological imperative.

Regardless what effort is required to obtain a hard-won goal, the novelty of achievement quickly fades—and the birth of baby Francis was no different. Within a matter of weeks, the boy went from being the pride of the Pinkhams to just another mouth to feed. Franny found that her energy level had dropped dramatically since the birth of her last baby, Larrie Jr., and that caring for ten children was exponentially more difficult than nine. She managed to save the tiny baseball shirts she had so lovingly sewed, though after nine babies they were stained and threadbare, and the appliqués had fallen off. She often thought about sewing new ones, but there never seemed to be enough time in the day for anything beyond the constant cycle of cleaning and feeding.

As busy as Franny was, Larry had a tougher time of it. He had expected to feel a special bond with his son that he didn't share with the girls, but in reality he felt no different about this baby than he did about any of the others. For years he had dreamed of teaching his son how to build a table or throw a curveball, but now it occurred to him that he had already done those things with the girls, nine times over. Although he never would have dared to say anything to Franny, Larry came to the guilty conclusion that he had no desire to go through it all again.

Being the only boy, and the youngest, one might have expected the girls to fawn over their baby brother, but Francis was absorbed into the Pinkham fold without any particular interest or consideration. The younger girls viewed him with a mild indifference, the same way they regarded floral skirts or bone china; it was something they knew they were supposed to like but couldn't find much use for. The older girls, especially Jackie, approached him with open hostility. They snapped the wheels off the toy cars and pulled their beds away from the walls and lined them up in the middle of the room like cots in triage, so Franny couldn't fit the crib in their room. The other girls followed, until Franny was forced to move him to the only space left in the house—a slanted alcove beneath the first-floor staircase. When their mother's back was turned, the girls would lean into the crib and tighten up their faces into pruny, eye-bulging scowls until Francis started to cry.

WHEN FRANCIS was old enough to crawl in and out of the crib, Franny knew it was time to finally give him a room of his own. She had been avoiding the problem of where to put him for some time. The girls had their own ideas.

"Stick him down in the basement," said Jackie, who already spent most nights sleeping on the parlor sofa because the bedroom was so crowded. "Let him sleep with the goblins."

Francis was only three and didn't know what goblins were, but figured if they were in the basement and Jackie knew about them, they couldn't be good. He turned a pleading glance toward his mother, who spoke about him in a hushed voice as if he were under the staircase taking a nap instead of sitting right there in the middle of her lap. "We can't do that to him—it's cold and damp down there."

"A little cold never hurt anyone—not even the goblins." Jackie pinched the baby fat on the sole of Francis's foot hard enough to make his eyes fill up, but he didn't squirm or cry out. Even at such an early age, he quickly learned that the best way to get along, especially around Jackie, was to keep quiet and not call too much attention to yourself. "You can swim, can't you, Francis? Maybe I should take you down to Beaver Creek and throw you in, just to be sure."

"What about the woodshop?" Larry asked. "The woodstove's plenty hot—it should be warm enough in there."

"He's only a baby," Franny said. "We can't leave him all by himself with a hot stove and room full of saw blades."

Jackie shrugged. "Why not?"

"Dump him off at an orphanage," Billie said. "We can leave him on the front steps in a basket."

"Or a pine box," Jackie added.

The girls clapped their hands together with enthusiastic approval.

Franny sighed absently. "I guess the only spot left is the pantry."

The pantry was narrow and windowless, just wide enough to accommodate a small Murphy bed that tilted up into the wall during the day so that Franny still had access to the jars of pickles and jam and potted meat that lined the shelves. Over the years, the pine had absorbed the smells of the pantry—most notably the scent of vinegar brine—and on Francis's first night in his new bed the odor was so bright and pungent it made his eyes water. But it wasn't the smell that had him yearning for his old spot under the stairs. What bothered him more was the one-inch gap between the pantry door and the doorframe that permitted light from the kitchen. The light cast ominous shadows over the shelves, turning quarts of dilly beans into the tentacles of menacing sea creatures and illuminating ten-pound flour sacks until they glowed like ghosts. He didn't know what a goblin looked like, but if he had to guess, it resembled the lumpy sack of potatoes slouched on the shelf right above his head.

Even more frightening than the monsters inside the pantry were the ones that lurked outside of it. The girls, whose appetites were rarely satisfied, were prowling the kitchen at all hours of the night, burrowing through the icebox for leftovers. Their pounding feet rocked the floorboards beneath Francis's bed, shaking him out of sleep. He'd wake to the flicker of their dark forms passing in front of the light, to the smacking of sucked bones, and to the leering, singsong rasp of lips pressed to the crack in the door.

"*Fran-cis,*" they sang. "*We're gonna get you.*"

FRANNY's successful handling of the bedroom situation filled her with a newfound sense of authority over the girls, who had developed the bad habit of listening only to their father. Larry was soft; he never gave them a chore without a qualifying "if you want to" or "see how much you can do." He never raised his voice or hand to them, and as a result, the girls ran around the house doing anything and everything they pleased without fear of punishment. They spat at each other and wrestled on the parlor floor; swore liberally at the dinner table and chewed with their mouths open; skipped classes and got sent home regularly from the library for unruly behavior. In short, Franny saw that the girls were getting more and more out of control, and instead of waiting for Larry to do something about it, she finally decided to take care of it herself.

"From now on, you'll each take turns hanging out clothes to dry. Every night, two of you will help me with dinner," Franny announced in the kitchen one afternoon during the girls' after-school refrigerator raid. "Tonight it's Georgie and Rae's turn."

Rae folded her arms across the bib of her overalls. Despite the good many dresses Franny had sewn for Rae and her sisters, the girls still insisted on dressing like boys. "Where's Dad?"

"Never mind your father. You heard me. Set the table."

Ever since Jackie tested her father's new wood plane on Grammy Pearl's mahogany china cabinet, Franny forbade the family to use the dining room—even on holidays. Instead, they ate in the kitchen on a picnic table and benches Larry built to accommodate everyone. Jackie, Georgie, Charlie, and Rickie took up one side, their barrel bodies and rounded elbows jockeying for space, while the five younger girls squeezed together on the opposite bench. Two chairs flanked either end for their parents, with Francis's high chair pulled up beside Franny.

The girls grumbled obscenities as they set plates and silverware. Georgie took Francis's high chair out of the pantry and left it in the corner, as far from the table as possible while still keeping it in the same room.

"Don't bother with the high chair tonight," Franny told Georgie. "Francis is big enough to have a grown-up chair now."

Taking a chair from the dining room, Georgie tried to find a place for it at the table. "Where's it s'pose to go?"

Rae pulled a screwdriver from her tool belt and started taking apart the faucet, despite the fact it wasn't leaking. Unlike the other members of the family, Rae's interests were in plumbing, not wood.

"Rae—stop fiddling with that. Go into the pantry and get me some potatoes." Franny ordered. "I don't know, Georgie—give him my place. I'll eat later."

Rae dragged her feet and yanked open the door to the pantry. Though it was difficult to speculate the exact reason for her mother's sudden bossiness, Rae figured that Francis was probably somehow to blame. Jackie had told her right from the beginning that every man (with their father being the only minor exception) was evil—and that Francis was one of the devil's minions. Rae didn't believe her at first, until Jackie dragged her into the pantry one night after they raided the refrigerator.

"Touch his head," Jackie had whispered as they stood over Francis's bed, wedging themselves in the narrow space between the shelves. "Right on top but kind of off to the side—a few inches above the ears."

Rae wriggled her fingers into Francis's brown curls. His eyes were closed but he hardly seemed to be breathing. She thought she could almost feel his scalp twitch beneath her fingertips.

"I don't feel anything."

"You're in the wrong spot—down more," Jackie snorted. "There's one on each side. They're small right now, just little bumps. But in a few years, they'll turn into horns."

Rae swallowed hard. Francis stirred and she felt her heart pounding in her throat. "It's smooth."

Jackie sneered and grabbed her hand. "Over *here,*" she said, directing her. Francis lay completely still, like a sleeping demon. "See that?"

There was a disturbing change of topography—the slightest rise, the beginning of something. Rae's squeamish stomach buckled and she yanked her hand out of Jackie's grip before she could feel the rest of it. Nobody ever questioned Jackie's authority in any matter, and Rae had no intention of being the first.

"Evil little turd," Rae muttered, remembering with a shudder as she walked into the pantry to fetch the potatoes. The brown burlap sack was on a high shelf barely an inch out of her reach. She stepped on one of the lower shelves to gain a little height, but the wood groaned under her weight, threatening to snap. Rae lowered Francis's bed down from the wall and stood up on it, grinding the heel of her work boot into his pillow. She ripped open the burlap potato bag with the screwdriver and speared a dozen potatoes, dropping them into the bib of her overalls. When she was finished, Rae left the potato bag hanging open on the shelf above, dusting Francis's bedsheets with a speckled film of dirt.

At dinner, Francis was terrified to discover that he had been upgraded from a high chair to a big-boy chair (with the help of a dictionary and a pillow) and that he no longer had the protection of his mother sitting beside him. From Francis's new perspective, his sisters looked like two lines of hungry bulldogs—jaws set, beady red eyes challenging one another across the table, snarling snorts between breaths. With utensils planted in tight fists, no one dared flinch before the food was set down on the table. The last time someone jumped the gun, Billie ended up with a fork stuck in the back of her hand.

"Be careful, now, there's bones." Franny approached the table with a platter of roast chicken. She set the platter in the center of the picnic table, jerking her hands out of the way just in time before the bulldogs attacked their dinner. Francis pushed himself back against his chair as far as he could possibly go.

"Slow down, girls. There's plenty enough for everyone."

Franny put out bowls of mashed potatoes and rutabaga, dilly beans and cottage cheese; plates of roasted carrots and boiled onions; two baskets of buttered rolls and a lemonade pitcher full of gravy. Every new dish was met with an ambush of greasy hands. Franny barely cracked open a quart of pickled beets before someone had her fingers in the jar, fishing around for the biggest one.

"Say something to your daughters, Larry," Franny said, taking a damp towel to the spray of beet juice that stained her apron. "They eat like mongrels."

Larry leaned back in his chair, fingers folded on his paunch, waiting for the furor to die down before it was safe to fill his own plate. "Not much I can say about it, Mother. The girls are hungry."

Francis watched as the chicken was stripped down to its carcass, his own plate still empty. His belly ached for a spoonful of potatoes or even a beet, both of which were almost gone. For a moment he entertained the thought of standing on his chair and reaching over the table to snatch a bowl of applesauce, but was curbed by the fear that if he got too close to his sisters' greedy paws, he, too, would be picked clean.

Larrie Jr., who sat next to Francis on the younger side of the picnic table and was the closest thing to an ally that he had in the house, shook her head at his empty plate. "Don't just sit there, Francis. You gotta get in there and dig in."

Francis eyed the nearly empty bowl of mashed potatoes just out of arm's reach and leaned toward it. Billie caught his gaze. Despite the heaping plate of food piled in front of her, she pulled the mashed potato bowl against her chest and ate directly from the bowl, flashing him an oily grin. Crushed, Francis sank into the chair and sucked on his small, meaty fist.

Larrie Jr. sighed at Francis's weak attempt. "I'm only going to do this once," she said, scraping half of her meal onto his plate. "Next time, you're on your own."

Later that night, when the girls had retired to their rooms and the thuds and creaks from upstairs settled into an even quiet, Francis sank into a heavy, dreamless sleep. Suspended above his head was the burlap potato sack Rae had left open before dinner. Throughout the evening, its contents had been slowly yielding to the strains of gravity, and now, while Francis slept, the bag's gaping mouth bent down toward his pillow. A few minutes past midnight, a mottled spud near the opening of the bag finally lost its purchase, dropping next to Francis's ear. Its momentum was just enough to disturb the remaining contents of the bag, and soon a rolling avalanche of potatoes came tumbling down onto the boy's head.

Francis's screech pierced through the upstairs floorboards and bolted the Pinkham sisters upright in their beds.

"What in the hell is that?" Billie asked, pulling the covers over her head.

Georgie rolled over and closed her eyes. "It sounds like one of the barn cats next door."

The sound was so sharp that the glass globe on the hallway light fixture rattled. Jackie grabbed the baseball bat from under her bed. "No cat squeals like that. It's a demon."

The cry was of a particular frequency that cut through the white noise of Larry's snores and alerted Franny. Even though the girls had trouble recognizing the source, Franny knew immediately the sound as coming from one of her own, and more specifically, from Francis down in the pantry. She flew out of bed and raced down the stairs.

"What's the matter, baby?" The moment Franny flicked on the light switch, her heart turned cold. Francis's eyes, cheeks, and mouth were buried under a mound of potatoes. Every part of his face was covered except the nose, which poked out of the heap like a white button mushroom pushing up through a pile of manure.

Franny jumped on the bed and frantically dismantled the pile, pushing the potatoes out toward the edges of the bed. "It's Mommy, baby. I'm here, don't you worry."

The sudden burst of light and the soothing efficiency of his mother's hands calmed Francis down. The screech vaporized in his throat.

"What's his problem?"

Francis brushed the dirt from his eyelids and looked up at the pantry doorway, where Jackie stood holding a baseball bat. The other girls were there, too, crowded around behind her, craning their necks to get a good look inside.

Franny glared at the bat. "For God's sake, Jackie, just what do you plan on doing with that thing?"

"We thought it was a wild animal. He sure screeches like one."

The girls laughed.

Francis nestled his head deeper into the pillow, the potatoes fanning around him like a crown. He could not remember a moment in his young life when so many eyes were fixed upon him at the same time. Francis drew from the bottom of his lungs and let it rip again, reasserting his newfound power.

"Shut it, you twerp!" Charlie yelled, covering her ears.

"Shhh." Franny stroked Francis's forehead until he was quiet again. "He's had a scare." She looked pointedly at Rae, who stared down at the floor and shrank to the back of the group.

Rickie, who possessed the closest thing to a sense of humor that the Pinkhams ever got, struggled to keep a straight face. "Maybe instead of Francis we should call him Spud from now on."

"Spud Pinkham," Georgie said, trying it out.

"Don't you dare," Franny scolded, even though the girls were already nodding in such complete agreement that she knew it had already stuck. While she never would have admitted aloud that Spud was a good name, it somehow seemed reasonable, even appropriate. It was a good, tough name that was likely to take her son farther than Francis ever would.

"Tomorrow, you're all going to empty the pantry shelves so this doesn't happen again," Franny said.

Jackie's laughter died. "Oh yeah? And where are we supposed to put all this stuff?"

"For now, in the bottom of your closets."

One by one, in a chorus of groans, the girls headed back to bed. Only Jackie remained, tapping the baseball bat against her open palm. "Thanks a lot, Spud."

"Leave him alone, Jackie," Franny warned. "Go to bed."

As his sister turned to leave, Francis dug deep, howling from his toes all the way to the crown of his head. He shook the bed and clattered the glass jars above, his skin turning from red to purple, howling until he had nothing left.

Chapter Three

CEDAR HOLE'S
FIRST VOLUNTEER

Children, up to a certain age, have no real accomplishments to set themselves apart from the masses and therefore must go about distinguishing themselves in other ways or else risk disappearing into the herd. They could, perhaps, rely on personality, but that, too, is unformed and flat at such an early age, a kind of mirror that only reflects the light around them while creating little of its own. Distinction lies solely in action, and from there a small-town child is nestled into a comfortable, identifiable compartment where he will sit for the remainder of his life, sinking in deeper and more comfortably until he fully inhabits his space. Tell a joke and you become the class clown. Hit a double in gym and you are the jock. Every class has their pet, their baby, their hypochondriac, their tattletale, and so on. There is only one label for each, and any kid who catches on to the game too late must search out another way to be identified—even if that label doesn't, at the outset, fit quite as snugly.

In Miss Pratt's fourth grade, the position of teacher's pet and all-round good kid went unquestioningly to Robert Cutler, who established his domain over the classroom as early as kindergarten. Among the teachers of Cedar Hole, he was widely described as the greatest student the school had ever seen, even though by no means was he the smartest. No child in recent memory, not even the occasional newcomer, carried himself with such optimism and fervor, such calm and sensitivity. Robert welcomed homework with an almost appalling level of energy, often doing more work than the assignment called for. He was last to leave the classroom at recess and the first to raise his hand when the teacher asked a question—and, unlike most children his age, he had a peculiar love of public speaking. Whenever the mood struck, Robert would stand at the front of the class, arms tucked neatly behind his back, and talk at length about any subject that was of particular interest to him. Robert's love of learning was a constant source of hilarity and wonder among his teachers, including Miss Pratt. She thought that if she had been one of his peers, she would have been tempted to stick him in the ribs with the tip of her pencil, but as his teacher, she welcomed his outstanding effort. The more Robert did for himself, the less she had to do for him.

If Robert hadn't arrived at his station first and had not so perfectly filled the role, and if the teachers had been able to put aside their prejudices toward the Pinkhams, it is not impossible to think that Francis could have just as easily become the teacher's pet. Although he was not a star pupil, he was reasonably intelligent, pulling in above-average scores on his exams. He was withdrawn enough to be considered well behaved and never resorted to the whining and sniveling that was popular among his classmates. If Robert wasn't so good, Francis might have been the standout, but as it was, Robert played his character with such exhausting energy that Francis knew it would have been foolish to try imitating him. Any attempt would have undoubtedly fallen short.

By the time Francis reached Miss Pratt's fourth grade, he had decided his method of distinction was to become a bully, an inheritance as natural as one of his sisters' sweaters and just as ill-fitting. Being a Pinkham made intimidation almost too easy to execute among the submissive population of Cedar Hole. No threat needed to be spoken, just a hard stare (a look he modeled after Jackie or Rae) and the imps would crumble and hand over their snacks and whatever else it was they held dear, even if it was safely stowed out of sight in the pockets of their jackets. If only they had resisted he would have left them alone—he had no interest in punches or wedgies or any of the other methods of coercion his sisters relied on. Despite the amount of good loot he gathered, Francis couldn't help feeling disappointed every time someone handed over a brand-new pencil or a cookie without any resistance. Bullies, even fake ones, want their victims to fight back just a little.

At morning recess, Francis scanned the edges of the playground with his friends Henny and Allen, looking for the ding-toed, loose-necked losers that cowered in the hidden nooks behind the gym or in the thicket of pine trees that bordered the playing field. They waited until the snacks came out—their eyes picking up glints of tinfoil, their ears straining for the dull crinkle of wax paper—before descending in a humorless, foraging pack, usually out of boredom or hunger, since Jackie or Rae often jumped them for their own snacks on the way to school.

"Pair of oatmeal cookies, twelve o'clock," Henny called out from his perch atop the slide. "And near the monkey bars I think I see a slice of sugar bread."

"Who's got the cookies?" Allen asked.

"Mary Ann."

Mary Ann Meadows was a jaundiced, bug-eyed girl who was susceptible to frequent bouts of pneumonia and spent weeks of every school year in a hospital bed looking up all the correct answers to her make-up exams.

"Leave her alone," Francis said, even though the thought of cookies made his stomach rumble. "She'll probably pass out if she doesn't eat. What about the sugar bread?"

"It's Robert's," Henny said.

Allen and Francis groaned.

"I don't see much else that looks good—carrot sticks, raisins, an apple . . ."

"Aw, hell, I'm hungry," Allen said. "I say we get it. I don't care if it's his."

Henny skidded to the bottom of the slide, his rubber boots squealing all the way down. Francis, the designated leader, started first toward the monkey bars, his heels dragging against the gravel. Robert was sitting on the lowest bar, one hand gripped to the bar above for balance, neatly biting the crust off a thick slice of bread. The sun was high and warm, still holding steady, bouncing off the bars that surrounded Robert so that he looked as though he were sitting inside a shiny silver box. The sleeves of Francis's slicker felt sticky and tight, but he zipped up his raincoat anyway, to cover up the baby chick on the front of his sweater.

"Whatcha got there, Roo-bert?" Francis kept his throat low and loose, trying to sound like Jackie.

Robert swallowed, then brushed off a few errant sugar crystals from the corners of his mouth. "It's bread with butter and sugar on it. Want some?"

Henny sighed loudly, then turned on his heel and stalked off back toward the slide. Francis, feeling equally reduced, shoved his hands in his pockets. "Nah. Never mind."

"Yeah, we do." Allen stepped forward. "Hand it over."

"Help yourselves." Robert hooked his ankles around the vertical bars for stability, and reaching out with both hands offered up the slab of bread.

Allen sniffed and bowed his head. His fingers snatched greedily at the wax paper, but as soon as he touched the crust, he paused. His shoulders sank, and instead of taking the whole piece, he tore it gently in two, leaving one half on the wax paper. He cradled his portion in his open palm, then ripped it in three equal pieces—one for Francis, one for Henny, and one for himself.

"Hope you like it," Robert said.

Allen sniffed as he hurried away. "Aw, stuff it."

MRS. KITTY HIGGINS had known Robert since he was six years old—when he was just a little peanut of a thing who came to the library with a satchel that hung from his shoulder all the way down to his knees. He visited the library every afternoon, spending hours drawing on his sketch pad or reading, smoothing down the pages with his little hands (the sign of a true book lover, Kitty thought). He was always quiet, never demanding, and approached everything he did with reverence and an unmitigated sense of purpose.

Because Robert was so well behaved, Kitty was willing to overlook the fact that he was alone, despite her cardinal rule that children were not allowed in the library without adult supervision. Too many Cedar Hole parents had a habit of treating the library as though it were a day-care center, picking up their children hours after school let out, dropping them off early on a summer morning and abandoning them there until dinnertime. Kitty did not have the nerves for discipline (the precise argument her husband Norm used as to why they should not have a baby) and could not bring herself to raise her voice even if she caught the children mixing reference books in with the fiction or shoving whole rolls of bathroom tissue down the toilet. To do so would be to admit that all her years of studying library science added up to little more than a career in babysitting. Instead, Kitty enforced her rule with a quiet dignity—she allowed three consecutive violations before sitting at her old pine desk to type curt (but polite) letters to the offending families, informing them that their children were not to return without adult supervision (expressly defined therein as a parent or legal guardian and *not* a slightly older but equally rambunctious sibling).

Kitty's first direct interaction with Robert happened nearly four years previous, on the third day of Christmas break, a date she remembered distinctly because of the pile of curt letters she was typing to send home with a group of older teenagers who, for the third day in a row, had kicked off their winter boots and were taking turns sliding up and down the aisle between the stacks in their socks—a spot they had smugly named "Sock Alley." The old floor varnish beneath their feet was beginning to rub away, revealing thin veins of wood grain that were surfacing above the finish. Kitty could see a hideous chain of destruction sprouting—snow melting off boots and hitting the exposed wood, water seeping deep into the boards, rot and mold chewing at the floor. Foresight can be a terrible burden, especially when others do not share the same vision, and this discrepancy of observation brought Kitty no end of psychological discomfort. Most things were in steady decline and most people, she noticed, did little to prevent the decay if not outright hasten it. Didn't they see? Or was it that they simply didn't care?

Kitty glared at the teenagers. She took the assault on the floorboards, on the library—*her* library—quite personally and stifled a boiling urge to point out to the children the eventual rot that would come about because of their foolishness. Scolding, she knew, would have no effect; adolescents, though insecure on their own, drew great reserves of confidence in

a group. Conversely, the larger the group of kids, the more Kitty felt diminished, intrusive—an invisible, nagging splinter. So instead of repri-
manding them, she vented her frustration into the typewriter, her ears
tuned for a possible yelp, in hopes that someone's foot would catch the
edge of an exposed nail head.

In fairness, it is important to note here that Kitty was in this particular mind-set when Robert spoke to her for the first time, which explains
her uncharacteristic bitterness. She was in the middle of typing an especially curt letter to the Pinkhams, the family that produced the majority of the library's troublemakers. Jackie Pinkham was the instigator of
the three-day sock-sliding event, a hefty brute of a girl who had stayed
back so many times at Cedar Hole High that she was nearly as old as
some of the new teachers. Because Jackie was an adult (in the legal
sense), Kitty believed that she was entitled to a curt letter of her own.
It had taken Kitty nearly an hour to strike just the right pitch (author-
itative without being condescending, firm yet not totally unlikable), and
at some point during that time, Robert rose from his seat and stood by
her desk. How long he had been standing there waiting, she had no way
of knowing. He could have stood there for a much longer time if her
typewriter ribbon hadn't run dry. As Kitty swiveled in her chair to retrieve a bottle of ink from the supply cabinet she saw him, hands tucked
patiently into the pockets of his wool trousers, mouth open in an eager
half smile.

"WHAT?" (Kitty would carry the guilt of this reaction for the rest of
her life, not so much for the word choice as the tone in which it was spoken—abrupt, shrill, startlingly loud—all the shades of expression she de-
spised.)

Robert, however, was not shaken. "I want to help," he said.

The boy's eyes, Mrs. Higgins noticed, were the same warm caramel
brown as the leather ink blotter on her desk. Kitty realized at that instant
that she rarely noticed the color of children's eyes—they never stood still
long enough for her to get a fair look.

"I'm busy right now," she said, thawing slightly. "Go read a book."

The plastic cap of the ink bottle she was holding cracked between her
fingers as she gave it a turn, leaking ink onto Jackie's letter and blacking
out entire phrases with the thoroughness of an overzealous military cen-

sor. Kitty ripped the ruined letter from the typewriter carriage, her hands speckled with ink, and threw it into the wastepaper basket.

The boy left for a moment, which was fortunate, for Kitty teetered so close to her snapping point that she could have easily lashed out at him simply for being nearby. He reappeared a moment later with a damp towel from the kitchen and a bar of soap. "To help you clean up," he said. "My name is Robert."

"Thank you, Robert," she said, taking the towel. "Now *please,* go sit down."

Just then, the library door opened wide, bringing in a blast of bitter December cold and, along with it, a runny-nosed Francis Pinkham. The brother of Jackie, six-year-old Francis was the youngest of the sprawling Pinkham clan and the most benign, though no one—not even Kitty— was naïve enough to declare any Pinkham harmless. Unlike his sisters, Francis was an introvert. He had the tendency to curl in on himself like an egg, and always carried with him the bracing odor of vinegar. He had a perpetually startled, pouting look, as though he had been scared awake from a deep sleep, then shoved out into the cold without breakfast. His winter coat, a threadbare hand-me-down with an inside lining that sagged below the hem, was a creamy, girly-colored mint with fake white fur trim encircling the hood and running vertically alongside loose mother-of-pearl buttons. Kitty had seen that same coat several times before on Francis's sisters, and remembered the fur being much longer at one time; now it was cut down into a spotty fuzz reminiscent of dirty cotton batting. A wool cap pasted his brown bangs to his forehead and was knit in an assertively boyish navy yarn with the letters F-R-A-N-C-I-S cross-stitched in white thread across the cuff. Kitty knew that Francis had plenty of legitimate reasons for being ill-tempered—namely being the most oddly dressed and frequently ignored of the ten Pinkham children—yet for some reason it wasn't enough to rouse her compassion or even her pity. The only feeling Kitty could manage toward the boy was disdain, plus an overwhelming desire to buy him a box of clean handkerchiefs.

Francis stopped in the middle of the threshold to unlace his boots. Through the open doorway, Kitty saw three of the older Pinkham girls rolling in the snow near the library steps, packing snowballs with their bare hands to throw at passing cars. Suddenly, a gust of wind kicked up and blew into the building, swirling around the circulation desk and giving flight to the stack of typed letters that had avoided the spray of Kitty's ink bottle. For several seconds, the pages tumbled on the current of air, then floated to the floor, landing among the slushy pile of winter boots.

"FRANCIS!" Kitty yelled. "CLOSE THE DOOR!"

Francis stared at her numbly, his upper lip slick with mucus. He dragged the sleeve of his coat across his face, leaving a thin wet trail from wrist to elbow. This appeared to have the effect of not only clearing Francis's nose but his mind as well; he took a deep breath and blinked several times. As he turned to reach for the doorknob, a snowball came flying through the entrance, smacking him squarely on the forehead before shattering on impact. Laughter erupted from behind the stacks, with Jackie's unabashed snort drowning out all the others.

Robert reached for the red welt on his classmate's forehead with two fingertips. "Are you all right, Francis?"

"Piss off," Francis said, backing away before Robert could make contact.

Kitty sank to her knees and gathered the papers, which, like Jackie's letter, were ruined. They were covered in a mist of snowball spray and slush, giving each word a fuzzy, crystalline appearance as the ink bled into the water droplets. She reminded herself that those in a position of authority, especially librarians, had a duty not to show weakness—but the tears came anyway. Kitty remembered keeping her head bowed down over the letters and biting the insides of her cheeks.

A small hand touched her shoulder. It was Robert. "I'll go get the mop."

From that moment on, Robert became indispensable. Every day after school, he asked to help. Kitty resisted at first—after all, the boy was only six and barely tall enough to reach above the third shelf—but little by little she found simple projects for him, such as pasting on library pockets and running to the Superette across the street for coffee. When Robert turned eight she let him shelve books. At nine she taught him how to catalog. By the age of ten, she had taught him everything there was to know about the Cedar Hole Library. He fixed typewriter jams, read through the moldy volumes of discarded encyclopedias packed away in the basement, and had used every stale spice in the kitchen to season his tuna sand-wiches. He knew just how to jiggle the toilet handle to keep it from run-ning, how to process a new acquisition from label to shelf, and had even typed up a few curt letters of his own (though his wording had substan-tially less bite than Kitty's and often alluded to the possibility of forgive-ness). For such a young boy, he seemed to have a respect for order and an understanding of the nature of decay, and when he looked at her, his eyes were devoid of hostility. For the first time ever, Kitty Higgins had an ally.

Summers brought both the mixed blessing of having Robert by her side for the entire day, along with the every other kid in the neighbor-hood. By September, she craved a return to stillness, but regretted that Robert had to go back to school. She thought of him frequently through-out the day, setting aside a small pile of work for him to do when school let out. At two-thirty, she found herself looking out the window, an im-patient hen awaiting the return of her hatchling. When he walked through the door, the silence lifted. There was movement and purpose and a warm surge pulsing beneath her breast.

"There's a cup of cocoa for you in the kitchen. You'd better drink it down before the others get here." She helped Robert out of his slicker. "How was school?"

"Good. We made name tags today." Robert went immediately to the kitchen to drink his cocoa, with Kitty trailing closely behind.

"And Miss Pratt? How was she?"

"She's funny—she thought I was new here. She'd never heard of my mom and dad."

"I'm sure your dad and Miss Pratt don't travel in the same circles, and your mother . . ." Kitty's voice trailed off. "So what did she look like?"

Robert took a seat at the small vinyl-covered table in the corner of the kitchen. "You've never seen Miss Pratt?"

"Of course I have." Kitty poured herself a cup of coffee. "But I've only seen her outside the classroom—I was just wondering how she dresses for school."

"She had on a gray skirt and a fluffy sweater—kind of like the yellow one you have. And her hair was pinned up."

"Did she look pretty?"

Robert took a sip of cocoa as he considered the question, then nodded.

"That's nice," Kitty said, smiling weakly. "It's nice to have a pretty teacher."

"Am I shelving today?"

"You can if you like—we have a couple of returns. First, there's something I want to show you." Kitty opened the cupboard and took down from the top shelf a small metal filing box. "I wanted to wait to show you until you were old enough to appreciate it. I think you're ready." Kitty nudged him to open it.

Robert lifted the hinged lid. The box was mostly empty, except for a few scraps of paper that covered the bottom.

"There isn't much," Kitty laughed. "I guess I was being optimistic."

Inside, there was a photograph of Main Street at the turn of the century, a recipe for apple cake scrawled on the back of a napkin from Shorty's Diner, grocery lists, and old coupons. A novena card, with a picture of St. Jude on the front, showed his fingers clutching a walking staff and a pink tongue of fire burning at the crown of his head. There was also a crumbling wrist corsage of dried red carnations pressed flat, and a few newspaper articles clipped from the *Gilford Gazette* about Marcus Griffin, the founder of Cedar Hole.

"I discovered some of the clippings in old book donations—I couldn't seem to throw them out, so I put them in here. I kind of think of them as snapshot of life here—a historical document. That apple cake recipe, by the way, is very good." Kitty picked up a newspaper ad showing a picture of the inside of the Superette, and her husband, Norm Higgins, standing behind the meat counter, posing with a rump roast. "Other things—things that had to do with Cedar Hole directly—I clipped out of the newspaper myself. Sometimes I even jotted down a thing or two that seemed good or important. Things that seemed worth remembering."

Robert dug further into the box and pulled out an index card printed with Kitty's surgical handwriting. There was a series of dates listed with his name written next to them.

" 'Robert earns straight A's on his report card,' " he read aloud.

" 'Robert runs to Superette for cocoa—returns with receipt AND correct change.' "

Kitty's cheeks flushed. "A few of your accomplishments."

" 'Robert J. Cutler—Cedar Hole's first volunteer.' " He looked at her. "That's not true."

"It could be. You're the first volunteer since I've been here. People only come by to drop off their kids or skim magazines. Hardly anyone reads a book and they certainly don't volunteer to help out." Feeling her edges fraying, Kitty quickly gathered herself up again. "But you're different. Sometimes you see people, Robert, and you can tell, just by looking at them, that they're destined for great things. You're one of those people." Kitty put the index card back in the box and closed the lid. "When you're off seeing the world, I want to remember the good things you did right here."

"You don't have to worry about that," Robert said, draining the last of his cocoa. "I'm not going anywhere."

"There's nothing for you here. When you get a little older, you'll see that."

The sound of the heavy front doors creaking open echoed all the way back to the kitchen, followed by the trampling of a dozen demanding feet. "I'd better get out there," Kitty said, "before they dump the card catalog again."

Robert cleared his throat. "Mrs. Higgins? When I said Miss Pratt was pretty, I didn't mean to say that you weren't. I think you're very pretty. I think you're even prettier."

"That's kind of you, Robert," Kitty said as she put the metal box back in the cupboard, "but it's not a competition."

OFFICER HARVEY COMSTOCK was in the middle of his Monday night shift (a meaningless term, since he was Cedar Hole's only police officer) when Delia walked in. He disliked personal visits, even if they were from Delia, as they disrupted his cultivated air of professionalism.

"What's the nature of your business, ma'am?"

"Cut it out, Harvey. Take me somewhere."

"I can't. I'm working."

"It's Monday night. Nothing happens on Mondays. Everyone's home watching TV."

"There could be an emergency—a car accident. I need to be here."

The radio scanner sitting on Harvey's desk crackled white static. The large coat closet he converted into a holding cell several years ago stood fresh and unused, almost begging to be reverted to its former incarnation. The walls were painted a soft gray, which under the harsh lighting turned more toward lavender than concrete. A long padded bench flanked the wall. Harvey wanted to install a toilet and sink, but the town refused to put up the money, so instead he put a chamber pot in the corner, which he hid behind a striped privacy curtain.

"We'll call it your supper break," Delia said, tossing her raincoat in the cell. "You'll be back in twenty minutes. If anyone gets smashed up, I'm sure they can hang on until you get back."

As usual, Harvey needed little provocation. He drove to their usual rendezvous, the entrance to the town landfill just off Webber Road, the only place in Cedar Hole where he thought they wouldn't be spotted.

"How's school going?" he asked.

"I've got another Pinkham—the last of them, thank God. Some people just don't know when to stop breeding."

"The last one's a boy, right?"

"Aren't they all?" Delia snorted.

In routine silence they climbed into the backseat of the police car, where Harvey pressed his considerable bulk on top of Delia and fumbled around her like a blind man in search of lost pocket change. She lit a cigarette, using the drags and exhales to disguise her yawns.

"Harvey, have you ever heard of William and Sissy Cutler?"

A roll of neck fat bulged at the back of Harvey's close-cropped head as he burrowed into the crinolines of her skirt. He took a wrong turn somewhere between the layers of tulle and found himself on an unexpected detour that brought him in intimate contact with a seat belt buckle.

"I'm lost," he said. "You've got to help me out again."

"Don't make it so tough, Harvey." Delia stifled another yawn and stamped out her cigarette against the armrest. Detective Cabot, she imagined, would never get lost. "You act like you're returning a stolen wallet. Think *bank robbery*."

Harvey closed his eyes for several long seconds, and when he opened them again Delia could see that the image had been planted—however fleetingly—in his mind. "Okay," he said, reaching for her skirt again.

"Hold on a second—" Delia pushed Harvey off her and propped herself up against the car door. "Tell me about the Cutlers first. There's this kid in my class—he says he's from around here, but there's just no way. I think the little shit is lying."

"Oh, I don't know much." Harvey steered himself upright and pressed his knees against the back of the driver's seat. His badge—which Delia thought was by far Harvey's best feature—shone in the fading evening light.

"So you've heard of them."

"Yeah, they live on Thornberry Lane—right behind Shorty's."

"They been there long?"

"As long as I can remember." Harvey reached for her skirt again.

"Wait a second," she said, slapping him off. "What else?"

"I never seen them for sure. Only the name on their mailbox."

She sighed. "Never mind what you've seen—what have you *heard*?"

Harvey scratched the top of his head. "Nothing much. I guess they're the types that keep things to themselves."

She cracked open the window to let in some fresh air but the atmosphere was just as stagnant outside as it was in. Overhead, seagulls were circling above the landfill, so far inland that dinner became a competitive dive among the trash dunes. "You're not helping at all."

"Well, I can ask Shorty if you really want. He probably knows a few things."

"He doesn't need to know I'm asking questions about the Cutlers," she said. "Don't bother."

"Hey, it's up to you. Why do you want to know, anyway?"

"It's no big deal," she said. "Never mind."

Harvey closed his eyes again, imagining, Delia presumed, armed bandits storming Mt. Etna Banking & Trust. "Are you all set now?" he asked. " 'Cause I'm supposed to be back at the station in ten minutes."

Delia slid back down on the seat, her own thoughts drifting to Detective Cabot muscling the jewel thief into the back of his squad car. "Yeah, all right," she said, lighting another cigarette. "Go ahead."

~ Chapter Four ~

A VISIT

"Our town has a proud history," Robert began, fingers laced behind his back. "Contrary to popular belief, Cedar Hole was *not* founded as a penal colony."

Aside from the requisite snickers elicited from the use of the word *penal,* the malnourished minds of Cedar Hole Elementary's fourth grade came to life the moment Robert stepped up to the front of the class and began to speak. Even a casual observer would be able to note the changes quite clearly—the newcomers fell still, the wildness in their eyes swept away by calm, as though they had recovered something familiar and lost, while the Hellions half roused themselves from droolly naps into a nearly upright position. Even though they had been hearing Robert's speeches since the first grade, his words were an endless novelty, a curious fix, an entertaining break from an afternoon otherwise filled with broad stretches of boredom and the maddening tick of the clock's second hand.

"We did not descend from murders and thugs, like others want us to believe." Robert was not one to name names, though he was obviously referring to the residents of neighboring Palmdale and Mt. Etna, who made Cedar Hole the punch line to all their favorite jokes. He was quick to point out that only one of Cedar Hole's original founders was an ex-con and it was unfair to lump the rest of the settlers in with him. "The only crime Marcus Griffin was ever charged with was stealing a horse— a skinny, unkempt horse that was most likely being abused. He pled guilty and paid his debt to society by spending a week in the Gilford

County Jail. I'm happy to report that the horse recovered nicely, thanks to Griffin, and went on to lead a happy, prosperous life."

"Excuse me, Robert," Miss Pratt interrupted, looking up from her magazine. "Just where did you get your facts?"

"The library."

"Did Mrs. Higgins help you, by any chance?"

"She was helpful, as always," Robert said.

"Hmmph." Delia curled her upper lip and sniffed. "Keep going."

Unruffled, Robert continued. "Marcus Griffin settled here because he found it to be a 'tranquil parcel of land, ripe with opportunity.' When he saw the green grass, he nicknamed Cedar Hole his 'little emerald gem.'"

"I don't think so," Miss Pratt interrupted again. "I don't know a lot about history, but you can be pretty sure that Marcus Griffin and his band of thieves didn't pick this spot on purpose. They got lost, they were hungry, and when they looked up at the hills of Palmdale and Mt. Etna they realized it was too tough a climb."

"I'm sure Marcus could have climbed up to Palmdale, if he really wanted," Robert said. "But he wanted to stay, instead. He had found his right place in the world."

Delia shook her head. "Trust me, he didn't choose this place—he gave up. You can tell *that* to your Mrs. Higgins."

Francis Pinkham could not have cared one way or another whether Cedar Hole was founded by determination or resignation, and laid his head on his desk, pressing his arms against his ears to dampen the bright cadence of Robert's voice. He opened one eye and peeked out over the rise of his elbow to see Allen sleeping with his legs stretched straight out and his shoulders and head thrown back, a faint snore zipping up and down his throat. Right behind Allen, Henny was awake, but his head nestled deeply against his arm and his thumb was plugged firmly in his mouth. Henny's eyes and attention were firmly trained on Robert. Francis sneered at the betrayal.

"... Whatever Marcus Griffin's motivation was for settling here, we owe him a great deal. ..."

Francis sat upright, and then quietly, gently eased out of his seat and made for the door. Even though Miss Pratt had given him permission to come and go as he pleased, Francis still felt compelled to play innocent. He hesitated for a split second at the coat rack. It had been pouring all morning and he knew he would need his slicker, but he left it on the hook. When he closed the door behind him, he took a right turn toward the boys' bathroom, on the off chance that one of his classmates saw him leave.

Outside, the rain was cool. Fat drops splattered on the top of Francis's head, then ran in eager rivers along his scalp, curving around the bump he got the day before from Teddie when she knocked him off the couch because he wouldn't make room for her. A steam vent just above the cafeteria kitchen spewed greasy orange smells. He darted off toward the woods, the rain whipping pinpricks against his face, feeling so light that for a moment he wondered if he might have turned to vapor.

It would have been easy to get caught on the streets, either by his father on his way to the lumberyard or by Officer Comstock, so Francis walked along the thickly forested tracks of the Metropolitan Rail. Francis had never seen the train—it stopped running the year before Larrie Jr. was born—though he had heard enough stories about it that he could almost imagine the sleek outline of the engine car rolling toward him down the track. At its peak, the train ran twice daily from the city to Gilford County and back, stopping at Harris, Chester, Royalton, Grandview, Macon, Rowley, Kentwood, New Trumbull, Burnsville, Mt. Etna, Palmdale, and lastly, Cedar Hole. For those who remembered the Metropolitan Rail, it remained a dusty thumbprint of failure; a bureaucratic miscalculation by the stuffed shirts of the Gilford County Board of Transportation, who assumed the residents of Cedar Hole would be just as inclined to make the hour-and-a-half trek to the city as their Palmdale and Mt. Etna neighbors. They extended the line and built a stunning depot in the center of town, running parallel to Main Street just south of Thornberry Lane. The building was constructed in an oval shape, the narrower end serving as the ticket window, while the broader portion contained the waiting room. Since the Gilford County Board of Transportation could not afford actual bricks, the building was painted brick red instead, to which the Metropolitan Rail Service added decorative moldings and black signage lettered in gold. A handsome Roman numeral clock hung off a filigree bracket on the rail side of the building.

The depot, in its brief heyday, was the most elegant building in town—a proud, shining egg.

What the board failed to realize was that most Cedar Hole residents considered the world outside their perimeter to be an untrustworthy and dangerous place. Any interest there might have been in the train or the city was quickly squelched by stories of stolen wallets and lost children, shoddy merchandise and con artists ready to prey upon unsuspecting country folk the moment they walked onto the platform. Everyone knew someone whose friend's cousin's sister was just minding her own business when she was suddenly tricked out of her life savings. The stories took hold and train after train rolled out of Cedar Hole empty. It didn't take long for the Metropolitan Rail Service to get the hint. The Cedar Hole stop was shut down within less than a year and from then on, Palmdale became the official end of the line.

Francis knelt down by the tracks and pressed his ear to the rail. Even though service was suspended past Palmdale, the rails were still intact; which stood to reason that even though the trains weren't *supposed* to enter Cedar Hole, theoretically, they *could.* This was his safety valve, the out that kept him going when Robert Cutler rambled on and on in class or when Jackie made him take the blame for something he didn't do. As long as there were tracks, there was always the chance of brake failure or a conductor falling asleep on the job, and that meant that there was always the possibility that the train could return. And if it came back, it would just as surely have to leave again—the most glorious possibility of all, because Francis had every intention of being on it.

The rail was cold and silent, save for the pitter of rain that rang in a toneless chime. He dragged himself to his feet, the rain dripping down into the gap between his neck and collar, and the high, tight wheeze of hunger pulling at his stomach. He thought about the half of a peanut butter sandwich he and Allen and Henny had taken from the new rich girl that morning, and how it sat warm and dry, still tucked into the pocket of his slicker back at school. Francis snapped off a blade of spear grass growing in a patch alongside the railroad bed and chomped on the end, sucking the essence through his teeth.

"I think I hear somebody . . ." a voice whispered.

"Shhh."

Francis whipped around and stared at the thicket of raspberry bushes just behind him. He froze, his eyes flitting from one damp cluster of leaves to the next, looking for movement. The bushes were still. Carefully, he inched behind a nearby oak and, curving his body around the other side, strained for a better look.

"Did you hear *that*?" The voice was female and unfamiliar.

"I don't hear nothing."

Francis knew the second voice for sure—it was Jackie. The moment of recognition nearly made his heart stop. Through the leaves he saw a patch of blue denim. Slowly, he slid his arm back behind the oak, and pressed his lips to the bark to still his breathing.

"Get off me, for cripes' sake. There's someone over there," the first voice said.

"If you don't shut your trap, I swear I'll throttle you." There was a heavy grunt and the rustling of leaves. Francis pressed himself tighter and smaller against the trunk. "If anyone's out there nosing around, you'd better start prayin', 'cause I'll come after you. And if I get a hol' of you you're dead."

Francis bit his teeth into the bark to stifle a whimper rolling in the back of his throat. He clamped his eyes shut as a warm river coursed down the leg of his pants. And then he did pray, thanking God for the rain and for the fact that his pants were already soaked through, and if anyone saw him they'd never know the difference.

"See?" Jackie said. "I told you there's nobody around. You're just jumpy."

Francis took one last, musty inhalation and, upon opening his eyes, backed away from the tree. His stomach lurched at the exposure, but he kept a silent steady line all the way up to the curve of the rail bed, his eyes fixed on the raspberry bushes. It was then that his heel hit the edge of the rail. The momentum kept Francis reeling backward, his arms swatting the air for balance, a yelp of surprise on his tongue. Panic clanged in his limbs. He torqued his body in the direction of the tracks and landed on his free foot with a plodding bounce. As soon as he gained his balance, Francis took off like a shot, running all the way to town.

•   •   •

HE HID OUT in the depot for the rest of the afternoon. The building was no longer a glorious egg but a boarded-up eyesore, the embodiment of unrealistic expectations and dashed hopes. The clock no longer worked, its face having long since been smashed by vandals. Patches of silvery weathered wood showed through the peeling red paint, and a bench, which had been placed beneath the shady overhang of the depot's eave, had fallen prey to bird droppings and the vulgar carvings of local teenagers. The golden letters of CEDAR HOLE were cracked and speckled with black mold.

The deterioration only made the building more attractive to boys like Francis, who saw the depot as an elaborate play fort that begged to be explored. He gained entry through a window above the bench. Time and trespassers had sufficiently loosened the plywood that boarded the window to the point where it remained attached only at the top two corners, allowing him to pull it open like a hinged cat door. Once inside, he scampered up and over the windowsill, the board slapping back against the window behind him.

The waiting room was not much larger than his father's woodshop. Gaps between the plywood and the windowsills let in shards of light, made visible by the clouds of dust Francis stirred up as he scuffed his shoes against the cement floor. The interior of the depot was an ever-changing landscape of beer bottles and cigarette butts, with the waiting room benches constantly being moved in various configurations. Once he found them in an open square, with one bench in the middle that had been chopped down into kindling to fuel a small bonfire. Another time, the benches were pushed flat against the walls and Francis found a pair of abandoned metal roller skates. He tried to slip them on over his shoes, but they were too big and the owner, it seemed, still had the key.

Francis rummaged through the deserted treasure of the ticket office, which housed rolls of train tickets, rusted clips, dried-up ink pads, and rubber stamps. He revived the ink pads with a few drops of beer from the near-empty beer bottles, which worked beautifully for inking the rubber stamps until they dried out again and took on a bitter, stale smell that reminded him of Jackie's car. He stamped the walls PAID and CANCELED until it looked like wallpaper, and pushed himself around the floor on the old wooden desk chair with wheels. When he grew tired, he took a nap on one of the benches, listening to the rain tapping on the roof.

Francis woke midafternoon to the sound of children playing. School was out. He lifted the plywood and slipped out the window to look for Henny and Allen. As usual, he found them at the penny candy counter of the Superette.

"Give me a nickel," Allen was saying to Henny. He was holding a root beer candy stick and five pieces of Bazooka. "I don't have enough."

Henny rolled his eyes. "Then put something back. I gave you money yesterday."

"Two cents."

"So?"

"Screw you."

"Screw *you*."

"Screw both of you, you little bastards," Arnie Hanson said, smacking a dry hand on the counter. "Either buy something or get out. I don't need your dirty hands all over my candy."

Allen brightened when he saw Francis. "Spud, loan me a nickel, will ya?"

Francis shrugged. "I don't have anything."

Allen groaned and put back the root beer stick. Arnie carefully counted out the number of Bazookas in his hand and made sure it corresponded exactly with the number of pennies Allen paid him. "Next time, don't touch unless you have the money."

Outside, Allen tossed Francis a piece of bubble gum. "So where'd you go today?"

"Nowhere. Out."

"You should've told us. We would've skipped out, too, you know."

"You were sleeping. And *you*," Francis said to Henny, "you liked the speech. I saw you."

"Did not."

"Uh-huh. You listened to every word. I bet you didn't even see me leave."

Henny stuffed a piece of chocolate in his mouth. "I was sleeping with my eyes open."

Allen flipped a piece of gum in his mouth. "You like that freak."

"Do not," Henny protested.

"Sure you do—you didn't want to take his sugar bread last week."

"That's 'cause he was giving it to us. It's no fun if he gives it to us."

Francis kicked a fallen twig into the street and watched it get swept away by the current of rainwater speeding toward the storm drain. "I'm sick of hearing him talk. All he does is yak yak yak about stupid stuff. He thinks he's the teacher."

"He's probably a Martian dressed up to look human," Allen said. "He's trying to bore us to death so he can take our bodies back home and do experiments."

Henny laughed. "I heard his mom is a rhino."

"Who said that?"

"My brother's friend Tim—he washes dishes at Shorty's. He can see their house out the back window."

"Yeah, right," Francis said.

"It's true, I swear. She's as big as a house—*bigger*. Imagine ten Jackies sideways and you're getting close."

Francis gave Henny's shoulder a hard smack. "Don't talk about Jackie."

"I'm just saying. She's *big*. Like a whale."

"I don't believe it." Allen popped the rest of the Bazookas and worked them into an enormous wad. "Cutler's the smallest kid around."

Henny shook his head. "I'm telling you, Tim wouldn't lie."

"There's only one way to know for sure," Allen said, snapping his gum. "Let's go take a look."

DELIA was not in the habit of thinking about her students outside of school, but Robert and his origins were such a riddle that thoughts of him began to intrude on her free time. The mysteries of the Cutler household seeped into her consciousness at inopportune moments— during the warm Sunday morning slip between dreaming and waking; in the bank line on payday; while Harvey pawed her in the dark with the finesse of a golden retriever puppy. Judging from the way Robert turned out, Delia assumed that Mrs. Cutler was the kind of woman who

starched her bed linens and kept decorated cakes in the freezer for unexpected celebrations. Mr. Cutler probably read four newspapers every
morning before heading to the office, tipped generously in restaurants,
and could hold a conversation with anyone about anything. These people
had to be educated, articulate, fancy to produce a son of Robert's cal-
iber—not the sort you found in Cedar Hole, or anywhere in Gilford
County, for that matter, but sophisticated city people. And yet they were
incomprehensibly from Cedar Hole. The disparity was a grain of sand in
Delia's oyster shell, a minor irritation that she worked over and over until
it grew into a pearl too large to contain, until she finally decided she had
to meet the boy's parents. It was the only way to purge the Cutlers from
her system.

"I'm coming over to visit your mother," Miss Pratt told Robert after
school. "Tell her I'll be over at four."

The address listed in Robert's file was 14 Thornberry Lane—a clue
that ought to have been enough to convince Delia that her perfect vision
of the Cutlers was mistaken. Thornberry was a residential street sandwiched between the defunct railroad tracks of the Metropolitan Rail and
Main Street, home to a dreary strip of peeling clapboard houses that
looked out onto the back lots of Mt. Etna Banking & Trust, Shorty's
Diner, and Hanson's Superette. The properties themselves were no worse
than any others in Cedar Hole—the houses were just as neglected, the
lawns just as thick and shaggy-edged—and yet the view of Shorty's
garbage cans lined up on one side of the street and the abandoned railroad tracks running behind were universally considered distasteful
among the town's residents. By most accounts, Thornberry was the slum
of Cedar Hole.

After school, Delia pinned her hair back into a prim bun and but-
toned up the front of her blouse before heading out to the Cutlers'. By
the time she reached Main Street, however, she began to lose her nerve.
It was hard enough to follow a conversation with Robert—how did she
plan on keeping up with his parents? Delia rifled through her purse for a
cigarette, only to find the pack empty. She remembered sucking down a
few by the Dumpster during Robert's speech, when a couple of the
Pinkham girls came around and hit her up for a couple of smokes. She'd
told them to buzz off but they threatened to tell the principal and so she

caved in. Delia wished to God she had had the courage to do what she'd really wanted to do—which was to stamp out her lit cigarette in the eye of smarmy Rae Pinkham.

She ducked into the Superette for a fresh pack and a moment to regain her composure. Arnie Hanson grunted behind the cash register, counting and recounting the bills in the money drawer, while his son, Hinckley—a kinder, scrubbed version of his old man—faced off a shelf of canned tomatoes. Delia had adored Hinckley since first grade. When they were growing up, he seemed permanently suspended in a bubble of hope; half the time Delia didn't know whether to hug him or burst him with her claws. A few years back, when the train was still running, he had married a city girl—an artist—who did a good job of bursting him for her. Hinckley seemed weightier now, not quite as buoyant. Then again, maybe a failed marriage wasn't the only thing that had crushed his spirit—waiting for your stingy father to kick the bucket so you can take over his store was no doubt just as draining.

"Good afternoon, Delia," Hinckley said. "What can I get for you today?"

"My usual." While Hinckley stepped behind the counter to get her cigarettes, Delia noticed a bucket of daisies at the end of the counter. Bright and fresh, they were just the kind of flower she imagined Mrs. Cutler arranging into a centerpiece. "How about some of those daisies, too?"

"Special occasion?"

"I'm meeting someone."

He nodded. "I have some nice paper in the stockroom to wrap these in. I'll be right back."

Rather than make conversation with grumpy old Arnie, who by this time had counted his bills three, four times over, Delia strolled down the side aisle, past barrels of yellow onions and roasted peanuts, past shelves of canned ham and jars of pickle relish. Just beyond the dairy case was the meat counter, where Norm Higgins was up to his elbows in a plastic tub of meatloaf mix. He pushed deep into the tub, squeezing the ground meat through his fingers, then scooped up the entire mass and turned it over.

"It looks like you've got your hands full," Delia purred.

Norm gave her a wink. "I said the same thing to your fella when he was in here the other day."

"And what did he say to that?" Delia pressed one hip against the meat cooler and leaned luxuriously in the vicinity of a pork tenderloin.

"He just stared at me. He didn't seem to know what I was talking about."

"That's Harvey for you," she sighed. "Not the brightest bulb in the box."

Norm kneaded the meat with an assertiveness that almost had Delia envying his mouse of a wife, Kitty Higgins. "I suppose if he was, he would have married you by now."

She pretended to brush off the compliment by examining a package of chicken thighs. "It's not like he hasn't tried," she said casually, as if it were the truth.

"It's that way, is it?" He eyed her. "Well, when you've had enough of him, let me know. Maybe we can work something out."

"I'd watch it if I were you—one of these days I'm going to say yes and then you're going to have to do something about it."

Norm grinned. "That's what I'm counting on."

Hinckley called Delia from the front of the store to tell her the bouquet was ready. She shot Norm a puckered grin, then turned on her heel and swayed down the aisle, leaving him to his meatloaf mix.

"I DON'T KNOW about this," Henny whispered. "There's a truck right there. Someone's gonna see us."

"We're not doing anything wrong. We're just looking," Allen said.

The boys hid on the edge of the rail bed behind the Cutlers', which was further hidden behind a stand of birch trees. While Henny and Allen cased the house, Francis kept looking over his shoulder, terrified of running into Jackie again.

"The windows are too high—Spud, you're gonna have to climb on my shoulders," Allen said.

"I'm staying here," Henny said.

Allen rolled his eyes. "Fine, be a baby."

"You need a lookout, don't you?"

Allen ignored him. "You in, Spud?"

"Sure."

"On the count of three, we'll run up to that window and I'll give you a lift, got it?" He gave his gum a snap, then spit the wad into his hand. "Hold this for me," he told Henny.

"No way."

Allen rolled his eyes again and pressed the wad to the papery bark of one of the birches. "Okay—one, two, three!"

Francis cut through the brush and ran across the back lawn to the small square window on the left side of the house. It was only a foot or two above his head. Allen laced his fingers; Francis stepped one foot into his open palms and hopped up to the sill. He held himself in the air for several seconds, his entire torso in full view of the window as Allen pushed him up and onto his shoulders.

"What do you see?"

"Nothing yet. Move closer."

Allen wobbled nearer to the window as Francis tipped his weight forward and pressed his brow to the glass. A shade was pulled halfway down and the room was dark. He squinted hard but could only make out the lines of a couch and the antenna of a radio.

"Nothing here," he said. "Can't see a thing."

"We'll try another."

A sharp whistle pierced the air around them. They turned to the birches, where Henny was waving frantically. A truck door slammed.

Francis panicked. "Let me down."

"Are you gonna be a baby, too?"

Chapter Five

The REMARKABLE SELF-REARING *of* ROBERT J. CUTLER

Robert told his mother about Miss Pratt's impending visit before he went to the library. Delia might never have met Sissy Cutler had it not been that she happened to be passing by the front door at the exact moment Delia knocked. Sissy rarely saw the front of the house; her world was confined to a dark sitting room off the kitchen, where she spent all of her time napping or listening to the radio with the volume turned just loud enough to buffer the outside. An urgent knock or persistent ring of the doorbell was unlikely to penetrate Sissy's cloister, but even if it had, she would have ignored the call rather than go through the trouble of walking all the way to the front of the house to answer it.

Sissy Cutler was not physically ill—simply tired. Her father died when she was eight years old, forcing Sissy and her eight siblings to leave school for jobs at the Wear-Tex Factory. She worked in stitching, where she sewed undershirts at the blinding rate of four pieces per minute, a pace that quickly earned her the ironic nickname of Sissy Slow-Hands. She wasn't the straightest stitch, but her prolific output made her a star.

At sixteen, Sissy crossed paths with William Cutler. The war ended just before Will was old enough to be shipped out, so he stayed on at the factory packing large boxes of underwear to be loaded onto trucks for delivery. Even though he was only a year older than Sissy, his experiences were worldly by comparison, though they were limited to bars and the trouble that frequently accompanies them. She often saw him in the break room, nursing his hangovers and black eyes with coffee and ice packs. Will spoke to her in lulling tones. She liked the feel of his arm around her shoulders when he told her about different people he'd run into the night before. It was the first time Sissy thought of anything beyond the factory, her family, or the tedium of stitches and seams.

On her eighteenth birthday, Sissy convinced Will to take her to his favorite watering hole right on the edge of the town line, called the Left Hand Club. The bar was a dark-paneled cave on the bottom floor of a three-story apartment building. It was not a club in the traditional sense, in that there were no formal memberships or dues to be paid; the only rule was that all patrons were required to drink using only their left hands. Anyone caught breaking the rule had to pay a nickel fine to the bartender, who rolled the cash into the weekly betting pool. Sissy was already left-handed and had no trouble avoiding the fine while she sipped her seltzer water. Will, however, spent a good portion of the evening paying the bartender, returning to their booth after each violation with a fresh pint in hand. The more he drank, the more fines he paid, though his carelessness turned out to be Sissy's good fortune. After three pints, he said she was beautiful; after eight, he proposed. Both phrases came easily to Will when he drank, and he passed them around to all the girls in the club as frequently as he paid his fines. Sissy was unaware of this behavior, though if she had been it might not have made much of a difference. Unlike the other girls in the club who brushed him off, Sissy took him at his word.

Will bought a small clapboard house on Thornberry Lane for his new bride and planted a plum tree in the backyard as a wedding present. After Sissy became pregnant, she left her job at the Wear-Tex Factory as soon as her belly grew too large to work behind the sewing machine. While she had been quite suited to stitching undershirts, Sissy discovered after several months away from the factory that she was even better suited to a life of leisure. When their son Robert was born, Sissy declared herself permanently retired from sewing of any kind, even sending out popped buttons to the seamstress down the street. Gradually, she abdicated herself from all other household responsibilities—sweeping, dusting, laundry, cooking—until there was nothing left for her to do. By the time Robert was old enough to feed and bathe himself, Sissy's list of approved activities had been reduced to lounging and slow, nonrepetitive movements. As her waistline grew, Will spent more and more time at the club, drinking beer and pinching waitresses with his left hand.

Drinking was the only time Will was able to forget about his shut-in wife and his goody-two-shoes kid, who strutted around town dressed like a politician. At ten years old, Robert was already showing signs of being a better man than Will ever hoped to be, and instead of being proud of his son he was just plain embarrassed. When he looked at Robert, Will could not find even the faintest glimmer of a reflection staring back, not even the barest thread of a Cutler trait woven through him. He could not lay claim to any of Robert's goodness, any more than Sissy could, and at times (usually in the middle of a good bender) Will considered challenging the boy's paternity. He might have done it, too, if common sense hadn't prevailed; Will knew that Sissy was no more inclined to have an extramarital affair than she was to get her ass off the couch.

On the particular afternoon of Miss Pratt's visit, Will managed to lure his wife from her room the only way that still worked—by giving her a present. He left the gift on the radiator in the dining room.

"Got you something," he called from the kitchen, raising his voice above the crackle of Sissy's radio. A warm, stale funk was growing in her room, and Will held his breath within a two-foot perimeter of her door to keep the nausea from crawling up his throat.

Sissy turned off her radio. "WHAT?"

"I bought you a present. Come out here and see."

Will's purpose was twofold: first, to get Sissy moving enough so that she might reconsider her pledge to laziness, and second, to distract her so he could slip unnoticed out the back door and get away for a few hours. They had been together long enough that he was well past the point of needing to ask Sissy's permission to go out with the boys, but he liked to keep his departures quiet just to avoid the assault of questions a trip to the bar was likely to prompt. Once in a while he considered making up a story—saying he was going to the hardware store or the landfill—but he still hadn't quite developed the stomach for flat out lying to Sissy. Instead, he settled on giving her a dusty box of chocolates from the Superette, a nebulous gesture that fell somewhere between a diversion and a bribe.

"IS ROBBIE HOME?"

"Not yet. Come on out here."

Sissy pulled her shrunken Wear-Tex smock around her and leaned against the doorframe, her breath quickening. "Well, where is it?"

"Over there. In the dining room."

Surveying the distance from where she was standing to the dining room, Sissy frowned. "Why'd you have to leave it all the way on the other side of the house? Bring it here."

"Go get it yourself."

Sissy frowned. "You do something nice, and then you have to go and ruin it." With a tentative step, she moved away from the door and leaned against the kitchen wall. Her chest heaved. "It looks like a box of candy."

"Chocolates—the filled ones you like," Will said. "Hurry up—if you leave them on the radiator too long the cream will melt right out."

A rosy flush colored Sissy's cheeks and lips, making her look almost pretty again. "You bought me chocolates?"

Will smiled in spite of himself. "Go on, now. They don't have legs."

Sissy hardly heard the back door slam as she ambled across the kitchen toward the dining room. The box was dusty but undented, and when she opened it, all the chocolates were unbroken and in their rightful places. Sissy's throat swelled. She couldn't wait to tell Robbie.

AND SO IT was at that very moment, as Sissy sat on the dining room radiator nibbling a Vermont maple cream, Delia Pratt knocked on the Cutlers' front door. Cradling the daisies in her arm, Delia ran her tongue over her front teeth to catch traces of lipstick, and smiled expectantly at the unopened door.

Sissy answered the knock with the box of chocolates propped against her hip and her mouth full of maple cream. Delia took one look at the Wear-Tex smock and assumed the woman standing before her, licking chocolate off her fingers, was the maid.

"Hello, I'm Miss Pratt—Robert's teacher," she said. "I'm here to see Mrs. Cutler."

"Well, you're looking right at her." Sissy showed her the box. "Would you like some chocolate? My husband bought it for me."

Delia's mouth retracted its smile. Already, she regretted letting her curiosity get the best of her. She thrust the bouquet at Mrs. Cutler, throwing up a barrier between her and the chocolate box. "I brought these for you."

Sissy's eyes widened. She set the chocolates back on the radiator and hugged the bouquet to her chest, rocking from side to side. "Is there a special occasion I don't know about?"

Delia backed down a step. "It was nice meeting you. You have a nice evening, now."

"Wait," Sissy said, clamping her fingers around Delia's wrist. "Don't run off. Come sit awhile."

They sat in the parlor, a room that hadn't seen company since Robert's birth, on a green vinyl sofa that squeaked under Mrs. Cutler's weight. The room was spare; not at all the fussy, doily-filled cream puff Delia imagined it would be. The sofa was flanked on one side by a matching vinyl armchair and ottoman, and on the other side by a low end table and candlestick lamp. A curio cabinet in the corner of the room housed a collection of chair-shaped pincushions, each upholstered in a different calico and trimmed with lace and seed pearls. Once, Delia had seen a woman making the very same pincushions at the St. Joe's Christmas fair. Even though Delia didn't sew, the chairs were cute and feminine and for half a second she thought about buying one—that is, until she saw what they were really made of. The woman peeled away the layers of cloth and cotton batting to show Delia that the frame was an empty tuna fish can with its lid still attached and bent up to form the seat back. The woman arched her eyebrows as if she expected applause for being so clever, but Delia skulked away, feeling like the butt of some inside joke.

Sissy balanced the chocolate box across the solid span of her thighs and steadily worked her way through the top tray.

"Robert says you've lived in Cedar Hole your whole life." Delia said this only as a formality, as a final punctuation on the reason for her visit, though she needed only to watch Sissy suck the center of a buttercream to know that Robert had been telling the truth.

"Both Will and I were born here."

"Was Robert born here, too?"

Sissy frowned. "Where else would he come from?"

"I was wondering if he was adopted."

Sissy nodded. " 'Cause he's so different." She unwrapped the gold foil from a cherry cordial. Delia averted her eyes from Mrs. Cutler's mouth as cherry syrup slowly leaked out of the corners, distracting herself with alternate thoughts of Detective Cabot and Norm Higgins. "No—he's all ours. My husband thinks he's weird—thinks he's got a mental defect. He says Robbie has a screw missing upstairs."

"I don't know if he's missing anything—it's more like he has too much of something."

"Well, he tries too hard, you know? He wants to do everything and I keep telling him that he doesn't have to—that's why there are other people in the world. We have no idea where Robbie gets any of it. Did you know that on Sunday mornings he gets up real early, dresses up in a suit, then goes to church all by himself? That gnaws on Will's nerves something fierce."

"Which church does he go to?"

"All of 'em. He takes turns."

Sissy offered Delia the box again, as if it were an apology for Robert's defective personality. This time, she took two pieces. "I hardly have to ask him to do anything in class. He always does twice as much as he needs to."

"It's like me at the factory," Sissy said, pointing to the Wear-Tex logo on her smock. "You should've seen me on the machine. I could stitch together a shirt faster than you can blink—didn't get me anywhere, did it? As soon as you've finished one, there's always another one right behind it. I mean, what's the point? When does it end?"

"What about your other children? Are they like Robert?"

"We don't have any others. Robbie's more than enough to handle."

Delia Pratt smiled through her disappointment. It would have been nice to have a whole line of Cutlers working their way through Cedar

Hole Elementary, one right after the other, taking her all the way up to retirement.

"I worry about him," Sissy said. "He's always thinking. There's always something going on in that head. It's like me—I sewed four shirts a minute, eight hours a day, for ten years. You think about that a minute. A person can only sew so many shirts before they can't take it anymore. I used to get into bed at night and close my eyes, and all I could see was stitches."

"I can imagine." Delia bit into a peppermint cream and felt the sweet coolness melt on her tongue. "You know about the funny little talks he gives?"

"Oh yes! I bet they're just precious. He does them for me here, some-times, but it must be cute in front of the class, with all the other kids watching."

"He gave one today on Cedar Hole. It's not something I care much about, but he was so serious. I should just sit back and let him teach the class. He knows a hell of a lot more than I do."

"That would be so precious!" Sissy sighed. "My Robbie—a teacher!"

"Although he would probably spend all of his time talking about Cedar Hole."

"He loves this town. Always did."

The back door opened and Robert came in through the kitchen with a book satchel slung over his shoulder. "Mom?"

"I'M IN THE PARLOR," she called, "WITH YOUR TEACHER." The words sounded strange to the ears of both women, sending Delia and Sissy into a fit of giggles.

Robert appeared in the doorway, as genial and fresh as ever. "Hello, Miss Pratt."

Mrs. Cutler waved the yellow box at her son. "Robbie, look what your father bought me today!" She removed the empty top tray, revealing a new layer of chocolates below. "Here—take one up to your room."

Robert disregarded the box and gave his mother a warm kiss on the cheek. "But it's almost time to eat."

"See, Miss Pratt? This is the kind of thing I'm talking about—always thinking." Sissy beamed. "Did you tell your teacher about the Train Festival? Robert's signed up to be in the Lawn Rodeo this year."

Delia nodded, impressed. "You don't say. I bet you could do real well with that."

"I'll try my best."

"He's been practicing every night after dinner—haven't you been, Robbie?"

"A little."

"You'd better watch those toes," Delia snickered.

Robert smiled politely. "I'm going to do some laundry before I make dinner. Do you have anything you need washed, Mom?"

"Oh no, I'm just fine."

"Maybe we ought to freshen up that smock," he said, helping her out of it. Underneath, she was wearing the largest Wear-Tex undershirt Delia had ever seen. "It's time we changed your bed linens, too."

"Whatever you say, Robbie." Sissy patted him on the back of the head. "He's good to me, that one."

Delia crossed her legs. "Tell you what, Robert, I'll go get my dirty laundry at home and you can do that, too."

Sissy threw her head back and belted out a hearty, knee-slapping laugh.

He nodded humorlessly. "Okay, Miss Pratt."

"Your teacher brought me some lovely daisies. Why don't you go find a vase for them?"

With his mother's smock in one hand and the flowers in the other, Robert slipped back through the doorway into the kitchen. Now that Delia had met his mother, the boy was more of a puzzle than ever; it was one thing to imitate the quirky habits of one's parents, and entirely another to follow one's own moral compass instead, especially one that seemed mysteriously calibrated toward what was right and true. Delia felt an ebb in her heart as he left the room, as though he had somehow let her down, but she couldn't exactly pinpoint how.

"Robert?" she called to him, shuffling through her purse.

The boy reappeared in the doorway. "Miss Pratt?"

"I have something for you, too." Delia opened the pack of cigarettes she bought at the Superette and held it out toward him. "Take one."

Robert looked sideways at his mother.

"Go on, now," Sissy said, shrugging. "Listen to your teacher."

He stepped forward and took one from the pack. Robert stared hard at the cigarette, as though he could see through the paper. He rolled it back and forth between his fingertips.

"Have you ever tried one before?"

"No, miss." Robert curled his upper lip and balanced the cigarette beneath his nose like a mustache. The prop seemed to provide comic inspiration—he began circling the room with the stiff-jointed march of a toy soldier, keeping the cigarette steady across his top lip.

"Would you look at him?" Sissy laughed, clapping her hands in time to his steps. "He's such a goof sometimes."

Delia shook her head. "You light it, see?" She demonstrated with her own cigarette and a book of Superette matches that Hinckley had thrown in for free. "And then you breathe in."

Robert removed the unlit cigarette from beneath his nose and placed it between his lips, puffing imaginary clouds of smoke with a clownish exaggeration that had Sissy collapsing into a fit of giggles.

"That is the most precious thing I've ever seen!" she cried. "Oh, I wish we had a camera, Robbie. I keep telling your father to buy one but he never does."

"Come here," Delia said, striking a second match. "It doesn't work without this."

Robert removed the cigarette from his lips. "Thank you, Miss Pratt, but I have to go make dinner now."

"Light it and you can take it with you."

He held the cigarette out to her. "You can have it back."

"No, no, I gave it to you—it's yours," she said, pushing it away. "Save it for later."

Robert shrugged and put the cigarette on the end table, where Delia knew it would remain untouched. She frowned and stuffed it back into her purse.

Sissy picked up one of the ruffled paper cups inside the box and licked off a bit of melted chocolate. "Robbie, would you be a sweetheart and make some mashed potatoes for dinner?" she asked. "I've been in a mashed potato mood all day."

• • •

AFTER the truck had pulled out of the driveway, Allen and Francis sneaked around toward the front of the house. They stayed low, against the side of the porch, where a peeling, gray lattice covered the three-foot gap between the floor of the porch and the ground. Allen wanted to climb the front steps and peek into the windows from there, but Francis held him back, cautioned by the sound of approaching footsteps. The boys kept close to the lattice as the footsteps drew closer, feeling, at last, the vibration from above.

While Francis stayed crouched, Allen raised himself just high enough to peek over the edge. He stole a quick look, then fell back down beside Francis.

"You won't believe who's standing there at the door," he whispered. "It's *Miss Pratt*."

"Come on."

"It's her—I swear. Go see."

Francis straightened up. He was sure that Allen was lying just to get him to look. But there she was—their teacher, looking unusually neat and proper and carrying, of all things, a bouquet of daisies. Francis hardly got more than a three-second glance before Allen tugged him down again.

"Are you sure we're at the right house?" Francis whispered.

"It said Cutler on the mailbox."

The boys leaned soberly against the lattice. They felt as though they had stumbled upon something private and odd, something that would have been better to remain unknown.

"Well, what do you suppose she's here for?" Francis asked.

Allen shrugged. "Who knows?"

They heard the latch of the screen door release. Words were exchanged, though the syllables were muffled and distorted. Miss Pratt's voice, which was normally leathery and clipped, had slackened into a strangely soft, undulating cadence.

As soon as the door closed, Allen popped up again. "Let's go."

Francis stayed close as Allen crawled around the corner to the front of the porch, then slowly climbed the steps on all fours. He shimmied across the floor of the porch on his belly. Francis followed, his movements less quick and more stilted, and joined Allen at the window. He stayed flat against the floor, while Allen ventured a look.

"Is she big?" Francis whispered.

"Like a cow—Henny was right."

Satisfied that proof had finally been obtained, Francis started wiggling back to the edge of the porch.

"Hey—" Allen grabbed the cuff of his jeans. "Where are you going? Don't you want to see?"

Francis's heart pounded heavily in his chest. "Let's just go."

"No one can see us. Take a look."

He raised his head a few inches above the sill. There she was, Mrs. Cutler, sitting on the sofa with a box of chocolates in her lap. She was huge, with a jellied neck that creased over the top of her chest. The boys had expected a feeling of victory, but Miss Pratt's visit had dampened their findings.

"She's eating some of Mrs. Cutler's chocolate," Allen said.

"What do you suppose they're talking about?"

"Probably Robert, of course."

A nail from one of the porch boards had begun to work itself loose and was digging into Francis's knee. He shifted irritably. "Maybe she's mad that Robert talks all the time. Maybe she wants his ma to punish him."

"Maybe, but then why would she bring flowers?"

The boys watched in silence as the two women talked and laughed and ate. Francis had seen enough. He wanted to leave, but Allen was transfixed.

"There's Robert—he must've gone in through the back," Allen said.

Francis winced when he saw him kiss his mother. "He's a mama's boy."

"Miss Pratt's not mad at all—look, she's smiling at him."

"Henny's probably wondering where we went. We should go back."

"Now she's laughing. She likes him. Miss Pratt actually likes one of us." Allen leaned closer to the window. "His mom sure is huge. She looks like she swallowed a hot-air balloon."

"So what—Henny's mom is fat, too, and he doesn't mind."

"I'll tell him you said that."

"Don't you dare."

Francis watched as Robert tenderly helped his mother out of her housecoat. Mrs. Cutler looked at him with a look of pride and awe that twisted Francis's gut. He leaned over and pretended to lace his sneaker. "Do you think he's got any older brothers or sisters?"

"Nah. I think he's the only one."

Francis left Allen at the window and climbed over the porch railing, with two new reasons to hate Robert Cutler.

"Don't you dare step foot in this house," Franny said as soon as Francis approached the kitchen door. "You're full of mud. What did you do? Roll around in a pigpen all afternoon?"

Jackie, who was snapping pole beans as if they were live chicken necks, glared at him through the screen. "Ma, Spud skipped school today."

A hot film of sweat broke over Francis's upper lip.

Franny wiped her soapy hands on a dish rag. "And how would you know? Were you skipping, too? For God's sake, Jackie, don't you think it's time you buckled down and graduated already?"

Jackie gritted her teeth. "It was a *joke*."

"You stay right there, Francis. I'll get you a towel and some fresh pants," Franny said. "You take off those sneakers, too."

As soon as Franny disappeared, Jackie was on him. Francis slapped his hand up against the screen door and leaned hard against it. He might not be able to hold Jackie back forever, but maybe he could do it long enough for his mom to return.

She pressed her face against the screen. "I saw you running away, you little sneak," she snarled, pushing at the door. "Were you following me?"

Francis locked his elbow. "What do you mean? I was in school all day."

"Bullshit. I saw you at the tracks—don't you lie to me."

"Someone was in the bushes. I didn't know it was you."

Jackie pushed harder, until Francis thought his arm would snap like the pole beans on the kitchen table. "I swear," he said.

"What did you see?"

"Nothing," he said, keeping his hand in place. "I didn't get close enough."

Jackie backed off. Her eyes probed darkly at him. "You're lucky, 'cause if you did, you'd be dead right now."

"I swear. I don't know anything."

"We were just having a smoke, is all," she said. "Me and my friend May. If you tell Mom, I swear I'll go into your room and smother you in your sleep. Got it?"

Jackie returned to her pole beans just as Franny entered the kitchen with a hand towel and a pair of jeans. Francis kicked off his sneakers and peeled down to his underpants.

"I'm behind on laundry," Franny said. "You'll have to wear your sister's."

∼ Chapter Six ∼

The TRAIN FESTIVAL

The very first Train Festival was a propaganda campaign waged by the Metropolitan Rail in an attempt to drum up interest in the failing Cedar Hole station. Conductors served hot dogs at the depot, made balloon animals for the kids, and offered free round-trip train tickets to the city. The hot dogs were a rousing success, the balloons less so—the children were confounded by the purpose of giraffe-shaped balloons that didn't float. They piled them up in the stairwell of the engine car and waved good-bye to the menagerie as the train pulled out of the station, still without a single human passenger.

Even without the train, the residents of Cedar Hole continued the festival on their own year after year, with the same hangdog resignation one usually reserves for the indulgence of an unshakable habit. The second year, Shorty sold hot dogs and hamburgers at the depot while kids played hopscotch in the parking lot. The next year, Arnie Hanson seized the opportunity to make some money and sold Popsicles from an ice chest. By the fourth year, the Ladies' Auxiliary put together a tag sale fund-raiser, lining up card tables full of cracked dishes and knickknacks all along the railroad tracks. And so it evolved; year after year, different groups and businesses added to the muddle, until a full-blown festival was born.

Among the most popular events of the Train Festival was the Lawn Rodeo. The competition was open to anyone age ten and up, and consisted of three separate heats; the Start-n-Go, the Obstacle Course, and the Quarter-Acre Mowdown. The rodeo took place on the back playing field of Cedar Hole Elementary, where the groundskeeper happily let the grass grow out for three weeks. In the Start-n-Go participants competed in a series of elimination trials by running across the field to their speci-fied lawnmower, starting the engine, and racing back to the finish line. The top five competitors then moved on to the Obstacle Course, where they negotiated a swath of grass for time, careful to avoid large hidden stones and pieces of wood.

The grand finale of the rodeo was the Quarter-Acre Mowdown, where the top two competitors from the Obstacle Course each had their own roped-off quarter acre of grass to mow. The winner again was the person with the fastest time, though sloppiness was discouraged—any missed tufts of grass carried stiff time penalties. Principal Nelson, who acted as timekeeper, was a ruthless judge; there was the integrity of the Left Hand Club pool to consider, plus the numerous side bets placed by his staff and faculty.

Unlike most people in town, Francis couldn't have cared less about the Train Festival in general and the Lawn Rodeo in particular; his sole interest at the moment was to keep breathing. He had spent most of the night wide awake, thinking about Jackie snapping pole beans, deathly afraid she might reverse her thoughts of mercy and decide to smother him anyway. Despite his best efforts to stay on guard through the night, Francis drifted off toward the light of morning, sleeping through the noise of breakfast, past the jumbled exodus of the Pinkham clan heading off to the festival. He woke with a start on the soft side of noon, as if he had forgotten to breathe.

The house was eerily still as he emerged from the pantry. Bowls and spoons were piled high in the kitchen sink, and the remnants of a pot of oatmeal on the stove was left to harden—perhaps the one day of the year that Franny allowed her housekeeping to slip. Francis padded across the floor and stuck his finger in the pot, to see if there was anything left to salvage.

Upstairs, he heard the toilet flush. The sudden hiss of the pipes made him jump back from the stove and bite down hard on the tip of his finger. Who was still around? He held his breath still in his chest until he heard further movement, and suddenly there it was—the clunk of work boots overhead. It could have been any of the five oldest girls, but there was a certain lazy, ominous quality to the walk that made Francis shudder. He dropped the pot on the stove with a bang and bolted to the pantry, jumping into the first pair of jeans he laid his hands on.

"You up, Spud?" Jackie called, her heavy steps plodding down the stairs. "I've been waitin' for you."

Panting, Francis pulled a T-shirt over his head and jammed his arms through the sleeves.

"Want some eggs? I'll make you some."

His mouth watered. He froze behind the pantry door, his mind clicking. Why was she being so nice? Was she still afraid he might tell on her? An impatient growl rumbled in his belly. He opened the pantry door and saw Jackie standing by the stove, a cast-iron frying pan in her hand.

Despite the civil tone of her voice, her eyes were stone. "I could make pancakes, instead."

The thought of refusing breakfast nearly brought him to tears, but he didn't trust her. "No, thanks," he said, staying close to the wall as he made a quick break for the back door. He let the screen door slap behind him as he jumped off the back steps and sprinted across the yard.

"Yeah," Jackie called, "you'd better run."

ROBERT arrived at the Lawn Rodeo a half hour early to give himself plenty of time to acclimate to the competitive atmosphere. Before he left, Sissy told him how sorry she was that she couldn't be there, and gave him her smock to wear as a good-luck charm. Robert slipped it on graciously and smiled, even though the arm holes came down to his waist and the hem grazed his ankles.

"I guess it's a mite too big," Sissy sighed. "That's too bad."

Robert snapped up the front. "I can still wear it."

"You'll look silly, running around out there. Besides, you could trip. We don't need you getting hurt."

He took off the smock and handed it back to his mother. She flipped back the front of the smock and found a loose thread behind her embroidered name. She snapped off the excess thread. "Put that in your pocket," she said, giving it to him. "I guess that'll have to do."

Robert tucked it into the tiny coin pocket of his jeans.

"What's the big prize, anyhow?"

"A Superette gift certificate."

"Oooh! That sounds nice. We could get some nice things with that—maybe some potpies?"

"Whatever you want, Ma. I have to win first, though."

"Oh, you will, Robbie. I just know it." Sissy looked out the window. "You're father's not back yet from his weekly dump run?"

Robbie shook his head.

"You'd better head off on your own, then—don't be waiting for him. You know how he gets hung up. I'm sure he'll get there just in time."

At the rodeo, Robert checked the roster at the judges' table—he counted twenty-five competitors in all—then did a few deep knee bends to warm his muscles. He was the only one on the school field, save a few loitering teachers and the groundskeeper, who was lining up mowers on one end of the field and setting up orange pylons. An ambulance was stationed at the corner of the field, just in case someone caught a piece of debris in the eye, or severed a toe, which happened every fifth year or so. Everyone else was perusing the white elephant table at the Ladies' Auxiliary tag sale and stuffing themselves full with Shorty's chili dogs.

Robert circled the school parking lot three times in search of his father's black pickup, but it was nowhere to be found. All the spaces were taken, which filled him with a niggling worry—where would he park when he eventually got here? Would he keep circling the lot until someone left, or would he just give up and go home?

Deciding not to waste his energy on circuits around the building, Robert returned to the field and sat high on the bleachers, so he could rest while he watched over most of the lot from above. Miss Pratt waved to him from the judges' table as she poured lemonade into a paper cup. She was wearing a floppy sun hat with a bright red bow, despite the light drizzle and stubborn fog that clung to the sky. Robert waved back and smiled. Encouraged, Miss Pratt approached the bleachers.

"Why you hidin' up there for?" she said, making the precarious climb in her wedge sandals. "You haven't dropped out, have you?"

"I'm looking for my father. He'll be here any minute."

"Come down on the field. He'll know where to find you."

"He's not going to know where to park," Robert said. "All the spots are full."

Miss Pratt hummed. She clamped a manicured hand onto the top of her hat and scanned the lot. Her red nails matched the sash perfectly. "What about that spot in front of the Dumpster?"

"It says NO PARKING."

"Can't say that's stopped me before," she laughed. "Come here—let's see what we can do."

Robert followed Miss Pratt down the bleachers and back across the field to the table, where Principal Nelson was drawing up the heat brackets on a clipboard.

"Give me a piece of paper, Dickie," Delia cooed, "and I'll take that marker when you're done."

Principal Nelson handed over both. "I hope you're not thinking of stirring up some trouble, Delia."

"You just mind your own business," she said with a smooth smirk. Delia laid the paper flat on the table and wrote on it in big, bold letters. She then tore four pieces of masking tape off a roll, careful not to ruin her manicure.

Robert followed her to the Dumpster, where she taped the piece of paper over the NO PARKING sign. It read: SAVED FOR ROBERT CUTLER'S DAD.

"What do you think?"

He nodded. "I think it's beautiful."

FRANCIS arrived at the depot, panting. He knew Jackie hadn't taken off after him—not in the physical sense, anyway—but he felt her spite behind him the whole way, a rabid dog snapping at his flanks. He leaned against the ticket window to catch his breath and spotted a dime on the ground next to his feet, and with it bought himself a root beer. Francis downed the soda in a series of desperate gulps, ending in a full, sated burp.

"Took you long enough," Allen said, sucking on a cherry Popsicle. "The rodeo's already started. Henny's going to be pissed if we don't get over there to watch him."

"You didn't have to wait."

"Nah, I don't want to watch the whole thing—it's too damn boring."

The boys sprinted down to the tracks, weaving in and out of tag sale tables, and cut through a worn path between a cluster of raspberry bushes to the edge of the school playing field on the other side. The Start-n-Go was already under way. As they followed the perimeter to the bleachers, they watched five contestants dash across the field to their individual mowers. Hinckley was one of the older contestants and started his mower with a single rip of the rope. The younger, less beefy contestants were struck with panic as their ropes unwound without so much as a sputter.

Henny was waiting for them on the sidelines, his flushed cheeks puffing. "I made it to the Obstacle Course," he said. "So far, I've got the second best time."

"Way to go, Hen," Francis said.

Allen sniffed the air. "Who's first?"

"Cutler."

"No shit. He's so small."

"Yeah, but he's fast. You should've seen him fly across that finish line. The whole crowd was cheering."

Principal Nelson recorded the finishing times on his clipboard and showed them to his secretary, who seemed to be comparing them against the previous times. He then raised a megaphone to his mouth and called out the final five contestants, while the groundskeeper returned the mowers to their starting positions halfway across the field.

"I'd better get going," Henny said. "The heat's almost over."

"Good luck," Francis said.

Allen nodded. "Give Cutler hell."

The bleachers were already packed full, so Francis and Allen sat in the grass near the sidelines. Principal Nelson sounded an air horn and the mowers were off, tearing across to the other side of the field. Francis didn't know any of the contestants, they were all high school age or older, and though he had no doubt that many of them were classmates of his sisters, by simply being male they were automatically not friends but objects of scorn. Frequently, he looked over his shoulder to see if Jackie was sneaking up behind him—a nervous habit he'd begun to pick up as of late—and was continually surprised to find she wasn't there. He took a sidelong glance at Allen, leaning back on his spindly arms, and wondered if he'd be willing to take his side if Jackie showed up. If asked, Allen was likely to be assuring, but the look of self-serving independence that lodged itself in the corners of his mouth made no promises.

When Principal Nelson called the top five names, Henny was number five and Robert Cutler was number two, just behind Hinckley Hanson.

"They shouldn't let him in," Allen said, flinging a rock in the direction of the judges' table. "His dad's the one giving the prize."

"If Hinckley wins, then he won't have to give the money to anyone else."

"Well, no kidding, Einstein. It stinks."

Francis and Allen moved down to the middle of the field, where the Obstacle Course was set up. There were ten individual lanes about three feet wide marked off with cones and rope. At the sound of the horn, the competitors started their mowers and raced through their own alleys, trying to avoid hidden rocks and twigs and the occasional metal pipe buried in the grass by the groundskeeper. Unlike the smooth, whining hum of the Start-n-Go, the Obstacle Course was fraught with the grinding of overtaxed motors, the splintering crack of snapped branches, and the shuddering ring of rocks hitting the blade. It was a head-splitting chorus the crowd loved and yearned for all year long, when they could hunker down on the bleachers with their shoulders up to their ears, teeth bared, dulled nerves finally on an anticipatory edge. Then, after the sounds had been endured with excruciating delight, they could spend the rest of the afternoon commiserating about how awful it had been, how reprehensible it was to damage good mowers, and how they were sure that their ears would continue to ring for days.

Like all boys, Allen and Francis had an unabashed love for loud noises, and as much as they thought the whole rodeo was cornball, the Obstacle Course pumped them with giddy comfort and a lustful yearning. Allen's family was too poor for a motorized lawnmower. He was used to using one of the old-fashioned rotary-style mowers that made no sound at all, climbing over twigs and rocks instead of trapping them noisily in its cage. Francis's father had a real mower, but Francis never had the opportunity to use it, since the older girls were always taking turns mowing. It was such a small, normal thing, but just once he wanted to know what it felt like to pull the rope and feel that engine roar.

"I can't believe that son-of-a-bitch is winning," Allen muttered as Hinckley Hanson rounded the top of his lane and started heading back toward the finish line. So far, he managed to avoid all the hidden obstacles and was moving toward an imminent victory. "It's like he knows where all the rocks are."

"Maybe they forgot to put them in his lane," Francis said.

"Forgot—yeah, I'll bet."

Arnie Hanson suddenly appeared near the judges' table, having wheeled his ice-cream cart from the depot to the school field, where all the action was taking place. As Hinckley drew closer to the finish line, Arnie hobbled farther and farther away from his cart, too distracted by his son's glorious run to notice that he had left the top hatch open, exposing his precious inventory to the melting effects of the midday air. His consciousness never left the money apron tied around his waist, however—his fists were buried deep in the pockets, clutching, Francis thought, the bills between his fingers.

"Check this out," Allen said, nudging Francis. He stood up and slinked over to the cart, reaching his hands deep into the opening, pulling out a brazen handful of squishy ice-cream sandwiches. No one seemed to notice—least of all Arnie—or if they did, they didn't seem to care. Allen gave Francis two, which he scarfed down without even the slightest flicker of guilt.

On the other side of the field, Henny was having trouble. He still hadn't made the turn at the top of the row, and his mower was bucking away from him as though it had suddenly come to life and was trying to make a desperate break. A toothy, grunting noise came from the engine, spitting dark puffs of smoke and debris. Henny's knees buckled and turned toward one another, while his elbows splayed east and west. His head bobbed as he wrestled the machine, until with one last, violent snarl, the mower erupted in a spew of wood chips and the engine stalled.

"He killed it," Allen sighed, slinging his balled-up ice-cream sandwich wrapper onto the field. "I could see that frigging log from over *here*."

By now Hinckley Hanson had crossed the finish line and was bent over with his hands on his kneecaps as he tried to catch his breath. A smattering of polite applause broke over the crowd. Arnie gave his son a gleeful smack on the back and then pushed his cart back and forth in front of the bleachers, hoping someone had a taste for ice cream.

But no one seemed to notice, because all eyes were trained on the soon-to-be second-place finisher, Robert Cutler. Even Allen and Francis turned their attention away from Henny, who had flipped over his stalled mower and was now accompanied by the groundskeeper as they assessed the damage. Far more compelling was the sight of the small, glowing boy, whose head just cleared the push bar, weaving through the obstacles with absolute surety, dodging all foreign debris with an almost uncanny sense of confidence. Robert zigzagged and zipped his way back down the field without the slightest hesitation, his eyes clear and singularly focused on the finish line, blowing easily past boys twice his age and triple his size.

Allen was so still, Francis wondered if he was holding his breath. As soon as Robert sailed across the finish, Allen exhaled loudly. "Shit—did you see that?"

Francis shrugged, though a hot fire of envy was flaring in his stomach, torching the remains of his ice cream. "He was lucky."

"That wasn't luck," Allen scoffed. "That was—hell, I don't know *what* that was."

Principal Nelson sounded the air horn. "The Quarter-Acre Mowdown will be between Hinckley Hanson and Robert Cutler," he announced through the megaphone. The groundskeeper pushed Henny's mower back to the judges' table, with Henny dragging behind, red-cheeked and close to tears. "We also have a permanent disqualification. Henny Perkins is banned for life from the rodeo for bending a blade."

Francis and Allen cheered and whistled loudly for Henny, who bolted toward where they were sitting and buried his face in the crook of his elbow.

"You'd better not be crying," Allen warned. "If there's one thing I can't stand, it's a sissy."

THE BOYS stuck around for the Mowdown even though Henny begged to go. Allen said he wasn't about to leave the only exciting thing that was going on in town, and Francis, despite his burning jealousy, couldn't look away. He watched Robert do his odd little stretch routine, pace the parking lot, and talk to Miss Pratt. Francis watched him with a throbbing fascination as Miss Pratt licked the corner of her lace handkerchief to wipe the errant blades of grass that stuck to his forehead.

"That's better," Miss Pratt said, tucking the handkerchief into the pocket of her skirt. "Can't have you going into the Mowdown looking all scroungy."

Robert smiled and looked over again at the empty parking space in front of the Dumpster. "He's still not here. Maybe his truck broke down. Maybe we should drive around and look for him on the side of the road."

"You can't leave now, honey. It's about to start."

"I don't want to go if he's not here. Can they postpone it until later? Just until he gets here?"

Delia laughed. "Of course not—don't be silly. You just go ahead and do what you're supposed to and you can tell your father all about it when you get home."

Robert's heart sank. Fortunately, it was blessed with an unusually buoyant property; as soon as it fell to the depths of disappointment it quickly floated to the surface again, taking in a fresh breath of optimism. "There's still time," he said. "Maybe he'll show up just as I'm crossing the finish line."

"That's a way to think about it," Delia chirped.

Allen snorted at the way Miss Pratt was fawning all over Robert. "I can't believe she still likes him—especially after meeting his mother."

Francis said nothing. He studied Robert's straight-spined posture and his broad smile and wondered what it was that made him so likable. Was it the full upturn of his mouth, or the wide set of his eyes? What exactly was it that made him so mesmerizing? The inability to pinpoint such an elusive quality was even more maddening than its existence. Certainly, if he knew what it was, Francis could copy it and take it for his own. Maybe he could do it even better.

The crowd was clapping impatiently as the groundskeeper moved the mowers to the two roped-off sections of the field. Henny rolled over, planting his face in the grass.

"C'mon. Let's just go over to my house," he moaned. "I'll let you guys play with my dad's gun lighter."

"Are you kidding me?" Allen snickered. "Don't you want to see Cutler get his ass kicked?"

Francis felt himself brighten. As tempting as the gun lighter sounded, there was no way he was leaving now. Even Henny sat up, sniffling away the last of his tears.

"It's time for our last event of the Lawn Rodeo—the Quarter-Acre Mowdown!" Principal Nelson shouted through his megaphone. The crowd, which was growing more and more awake each minute, was buzzing. "Today's grand prize is a twenty-five-dollar gift certificate to Hanson's Superette. Contestants, please take your places."

Robert turned to the crowd and waved, sending up a cheer through the bleachers as he jogged to his square of grass. Hinckley's father, Arnie, escorted his son to his position with one hand clamping him firmly by the scruff of the neck and the other gripping his upper arm. Arnie was leaning in, talking into Hinckley's ear. Francis had never seen the two in such close proximity to one another.

When Hinckley and Robert were ready, Principal Nelson sounded the horn. Both started the engine on their first shot and took off at a dead run. Hinckley mowed to the end of his square and made a tight pivot, continuing right next to the mowed strip, like every other Mowdown contestant before him. Robert arrived a beat or two later, but instead of turning 180 degrees, he made a quick right-angle turn, following the outer edge of the square. For a minute, Francis's heart leapt into his throat. Robert, it seemed, had made a fatal error.

"What the hell is he doing?" Allen yelped. "He can't go that way! Henny? Doesn't it say in the rules that you have to go row by row?"

Henny shook his head. "I don't think it says anything. I think you can do it any way you want."

Francis's throat prickled with panic. "Just 'cause he's doing it different doesn't mean it's better. I mean, everyone's been doing it the other way for a reason, right?"

This seemed to calm Allen down somewhat. "I don't know. I guess. He thought he'd do something different, but it's probably a dumb idea."

No sooner had these words been spoken than Robert made his second corner, starting down the third outer wall of the boundary. He was still a beat behind Hinckley, who had made his second pivot, but there was a sense that maybe Robert was clearly on to something. His turns took only half as much time as Hinckley's full pivots. They both reached their fourth row at exactly the same time.

"Look," Henny said, pointing, "Cutler's rows are getting smaller every time."

Hinckley, too, seemed to be withering in his own skin. Francis wasn't sure if Robert's method was superior, but Arnie's presence on the sidelines definitely seemed to be affecting the competition. On all the odd rows, as Hinckley mowed toward the crowd, Arnie was standing there facing him, shouting and purple-faced, waving his fist in the air. He seemed to slow down on the opposite stretches, when he didn't have to look at his father.

Robert, on the other hand, gained speed with each turn. His rows turned in on themselves, almost like a square snail's shell. The crowd jumped to its feet, marveling at the innovative pattern, and began shouting, "Rob-ert, Rob-ert," in various syncopated rhythms.

Allen beat his fist into the ground. "This is crap."

As Robert neared the center of his square, queasiness burned bright in Francis's stomach. He jumped to his feet and ran toward the school gym, but the door was locked. A cool sweat broke over his upper lip and forehead. Francis staggered toward the empty parking space in front of the Dumpster and leaned against the green metal monster, waiting for the nausea to pass. The air horn sounded and the crowd roared. Francis felt his stomach seize, and made a silent promise to himself never to eat ice-cream sandwiches for breakfast again.

Chapter Seven

The MOUSE DISCOVERS *His* CALLING

Francis skipped school the next morning. At breakfast, he was too tired to wrestle Larrie Jr. for the last of the oatmeal pot. Instead, he tucked a jam biscuit in the waistband of his pants and sneaked out the front door while his sisters were still busy eating, getting a good twenty-minute start on most of the walkers. He passed School Street and continued down on Main, turning west when he neared the depot.

Inside, the waiting room was dark and cold. Francis broke off half the biscuit and ate it in slow, nibbling bites—a luxury in the absence of Georgie and Rae. The other half he left on the bench for later, content to know that it would still be there whenever he wanted it.

In the ticket office, Francis sat behind the desk and helped himself to the bright orange roll he found stashed on a high shelf. He spent the morning selling train tickets to imaginary passengers—one of his all-time favorite games—cramming orange slips under the brass window bars and through a half-inch gap in the plywood, where they disappeared to the outside. Francis liked to imagine that he was the owner of the railroad—a rich, important man who raked in so much cash that his sisters screamed with jealousy. He had big plans for the money. First he'd buy some new clothes that weren't girlish or smelling of vinegar; then he'd get a roller skate key and a bucket of penny candy at the Superette for Henny and Allen. He'd share some of his fortune with his mother and father and none with his sisters—unless, or course, they were really sorry for hitting him and ignoring him and promised to save him some food at dinner from now on. Maybe he'd even buy them presents at Christmas if they let him play baseball with them just once.

Francis was in the middle of determining his sisters' possible share when a clinking sound came from the exterior window. He put down the rubber stamp and looked up to see a quarter sitting in the brass coin tray.

"One, please," a man's voice said through the crack. "Round trip."

Pressing his face to the bars, Francis peered through the plywood gap and saw a patch of white broadcloth. His breath was still in his chest as he took the quarter from the dish. He ripped a ticket off the roll and stamped it paid. Unlike the other tickets, which he had shoved out the window, Francis gently slid it under the bars.

"Well, would you look at that," the man said, taking the ticket. "That's the smartest mouse I ever saw."

Francis jumped out of the chair and pressed his face up to the opening. "I'm not a mouse."

"He talks, too! Wait till my wife hears about this—a mouse smart enough to talk."

"I'm not a mouse, really," Francis said. "I'm a boy."

The man stuck his finger through the crack in the plywood. "Don't try to trick me, Mr. Mouse. No boy could fit through a hole that small."

"I didn't go through there!" Francis protested. "Wait a second—I'll show you."

He ran into the waiting room and climbed up on the windowsill, pushing out the loose plywood board and landing on the outside bench. "See?"

The man looked ancient to Francis, though in actuality he was only in his early sixties. He had white and gray hair that was thin enough to show a tight pink scalp underneath. "I guess you're right, then. You certainly don't look like a mouse—your ears are far too big and you're missing a tail," he said, rubbing the white stubble of his chin with his thumb and forefinger. "On the other hand, I don't see why a boy would be crawling around a dirty old train station when he should be in school."

"I was home sick, see, and I saw a three-legged cat go by the window." The man smiled as though he had seen many three-legged cats in his day, giving Francis the courage to continue. "He looked hungry and I wanted to feed him but he ran. I chased him in here."

The man pointed to the pile of orange train stubs Francis had shoved out the window that were now scattered all over the ground. "I imagine the cat is the one responsible for this mess. Like I've always said, you can never trust a cat—especially those sneaky three-legged versions. If you happen to find the beast, I'd appreciate it if you'd tell him to pick the tickets off the ground."

Francis fell to his knees and scrambled to pick up the orange slips. "He's not around anymore. You scared him off—but I can do it for him."

"Good boy." The man stood by as Francis shoved the tickets into the pockets of his blue jeans. "I suppose we ought to let your mother know your whereabouts so she doesn't worry—especially since you're in such a delicate condition."

"What's my condition?"

"Well, I don't know—you didn't say. But apparently it's grave enough for you to miss school."

Francis felt a prickle at the base of his spine. "We don't need to tell her—she knows I'm all right," he said. "Besides, I'm feeling much better now."

"What wonderful news, Mouse! You had us all worried sick. We ought to celebrate your recovery." The man scratched the top of his pink scalp. "Tell you what—my wife, Mrs. Mullen, made a cake this morning and it came out too big. Great big fright of a thing. Perhaps you could do us the favor of coming over to eat some before it takes over the kitchen?"

It just so happened that Francis was in the mood for some cake, so he followed the man to a little white Cape-style house on the other side of Elm Street. The house sat on a rise, a rare hilly spot in Cedar Hole, with a steep driveway that gained sharply before taking a hard left. Just behind the house was a barn, with weathered gray shingles that still clung to flakes of red paint. The lawn was overgrown with dandelion weeds and knotted grasses almost too thick to mow. Francis had seen grass grow that thick behind the barn at his own house, so long and tough his father needed a scythe to cut it down. Jackie once got Francis to hide in the grass when their father was working, saying it would be funny to jump out of the grass and spook him, but Larrie Jr. pulled Francis from his hiding spot before their father got there, telling him that Jackie only meant it as a joke.

At the bottom of the hill, near the start of Mr. Mullen's driveway, was a mailbox built to look like a miniature, newer version of the barn out back. Francis had never seen anything quite like it, not even among the endless parade of furniture his father and sisters were constantly churning out. It was constructed out of wood, with a gambrel roof and a tiny, vented cupola made out of slender dowels and toothpicks. The box was appropriately red with a black roof and white trim, and various handpainted barnyard animals loitering about the perimeter. A horse stuck its head out of the open door to feed on a feathery haystack, while a cow grazed nearby, swatting flies with its tail. Chickens scratched and pecked at the dirt, and a plump hen, startled by a sheepdog, flapped its wings in the air, feathers flying. The animals were painted with such life that Francis lost himself in the scene, the action nearly playing out right in front of him instead of being frozen at a precise moment. As great as the animals were, the best part of the mailbox was the crowning touch—a single piece of wire cleverly bent into the suggestion of a rooster, swiveling freely on the cupola like a weather vane.

"This is real nice," Francis said, spinning the rooster around. "Did you make it?"

"My son did. When he was twenty."

"How old is he now?"

"He's gone." The man said this in such a way that Francis knew *gone* meant dead, and whatever happened must have happened a long time ago.

"Do you have any other kids?"

"No—just the one."

Francis stopped playing with the weather vane and ran his fingers along the side of the barn where the name MULLEN was painted in black letters. "Well, it's real nice anyhow."

Mr. Mullen nodded. "I think so."

When they walked inside the house, Mrs. Mullen was in the kitchen. She was a warm, wobbly woman, who teetered across the floor at a sluggish pace even though her smile betrayed no difficulty. As soon as he saw her, Francis closed the door quickly behind him, afraid that if a gust of wind blew in it might knock her over.

"I caught myself a mouse by the train station, Lila," Mr. Mullen said to his wife. "I thought he might help us eat that monstrous cake."

"I'm a boy, not a mouse—and my name is Francis," he said. "My sisters call me Spud."

Mrs. Mullen beamed at Francis. "You're not the little Pinkham boy, are you? You look just like Franny—doesn't he, Walter?"

Mr. Mullen pushed back the lace curtains that hung in the kitchen and pressed his face so close to the window that his breath fogged the glass. "Dammit—the mail's here. I swear he watches me from Hanson's parking lot. He waits 'til I'm inside and then he decides to deliver it. I'll be right back," he said, going out again.

"Take a seat at the table, Francis," Mrs. Mullen said. "I'll bring you over a nice piece of cake. It's still warm."

The Mullens' kitchen table was small and round, surrounded by four ladder-back chairs. The circular shape seemed marvelously democratic compared to the Pinkhams' long picnic table, with each seat being equal to all others. Francis mentally circled the table a half dozen times before picking a place to sit.

"You know my mom?" Francis asked.

"Not directly. I've been to the furniture shop a few times." She sliced the cake and poured a glass of milk with surprising dexterity and speed, then carried the tray across the kitchen so slowly that Francis's stomach nearly cried out in frustration. "How's your dad's business?"

"I don't know. Good, I guess." He kicked his feet against the chair in an impatient rhythm. "I was sick today. In case you're wondering why I wasn't in school."

"I didn't think of it, but thank you for telling me, Francis."

The cake was a good, dark slab of gingerbread with blueberries and whipped cream, and when it finally arrived at the table Francis could hardly restrain himself. He ignored the fork Mrs. Mullen set out for him and shoved half the cake in his mouth with his fingers.

"Take it easy, now, there's plenty. Have only as much as your stomach can hold."

Francis's chest tightened as Mrs. Mullen watched him eat. Her eyes were soft and pleased, following every bite. Being the object of close attention was unusual for Francis, and while he enjoyed it, he also found it unnerving.

Mr. Mullen returned with an open letter pinched between his dry fingers. "Shady Acres is having a half-price sale on all their burial plots," he read. "I've already got one foot in the grave and they're trying to kick the other one out from underneath me."

"Hush, now," Mrs. Mullen said. "Have some cake."

"I'm going to take that parcel of land we got on the other side of town and turn it into a graveyard," he said, cutting a healthy slab. "Apparently burying bones is good business."

"That's enough—you'll scare the boy."

But Francis was too distracted to care. What had him really spooked was a wall clock in the shape of a black cat hanging right next to the telephone. The cat's eyes were bulging, with rhinestones around the slitted pupils, shifting from side to side in time with his pendulous tail. The cat's mouth was open in a wide grin—big enough, Francis suspected, to swallow an entire piece of Mrs. Mullen's gingerbread whole, or to devour an unsuspecting mouse that just happened to be scurrying by.

Next to the clock was a framed, sepia-toned photograph of a man in uniform. The man looked about the same age as Jackie. Francis wondered if he was the one who had made the mailbox. The man's eyes were round and steady, unlike the sly tempo of the cat, but Francis noticed if he stared at the cat for a solid ten seconds, then quickly glanced over at the man in the photograph, he could almost swear he saw the eyes move.

"You wouldn't happen to mow lawns, by any chance," Mr. Mullen said, snapping Francis's attention away from the photograph.

"For God's sake, Walter—he's too young," Mrs. Mullen cut in. "He could hurt himself."

"Only a dink gets his toes cut off mowing the lawn," Walter answered. "You're not a dink, are you, Francis?"

Francis shook his head, even though he wasn't quite sure what a dink was, or if, with any certainty, he could truly deny being one.

Mrs. Mullen added another slice to Francis's empty plate. "That's all I need, some poor ten-year-old boy losing his fingers and toes on my front lawn."

Francis took a sip of milk and swallowed his cake. "Robert Cutler's only ten, and he won the Lawn Rodeo."

"Fair enough," Mrs. Mullen sighed, "but Robert's a rather exceptional example."

"Hogwash!" Walter shouted so loud that Francis flinched. "Robert Cutler's no better than this boy sitting right here. Isn't that right?"

Francis was unsure, but gave him a feeble nod anyway.

Walter winked at Francis. "You up for earning a little pocket money, Mouse?"

Francis nodded again, more vigorously this time.

"I don't know. School's not out yet. Suppose Harvey Comstock catches him playing hooky?" Mrs. Mullen said.

"Harvey is the King of Dinks and I'll have no problem telling him so right to his face if he makes any inquiries."

"I'd button up that lip if I were you—he's probably just waiting for someone to mouth off so he can fill that empty jail cell of his."

"Come on, Mouse," Mr. Mullen said, wiping his mouth on a napkin. "Finish up that cake. I want to show you something."

Unlike his father's barn, which was regularly swept out and had the astringent smells of pine and varnish, the interior of Mr. Mullen's barn was a dark, oily mess. The horse stalls held a lifetime of accumulation; an old icebox, a bathroom sink, the bedspring of a horsehair mattress, a set of caned chairs with all the seats broken through, boxes of *Life* magazines and encyclopedia volumes whose pages had become swollen with moisture. Bicycle parts intermingled with car parts that were strewn among children's board games and hidden behind a Hoosier cabinet filled with bolts and glass bottles. Everything seemed to have acquired either thin silken cobwebs or a bright orange film of rust.

"Here's the baby," Mr. Mullen said, wheeling a dusty Toro lawnmower from behind an oak bureau that had three missing drawers. It wasn't as polished as the mowers at the rodeo, but it had a well-worn dignity, much like Mr. Mullen himself. He opened the icebox and pulled out a gas can and funnel, then unscrewed the gas cap on the mower and poured the fuel in, spilling a liberal amount on the barn's spongy floorboards. "She's thirsty. Let's give her some juice."

When the Toro had her fill, Mr. Mullen wheeled the mower outside to the driveway. "Work in a straight line, and watch out for rocks—they'll wreck the blade," he said. "And don't ever get your hands or feet near it unless you want your bones to fertilize the lawn. Got it?"

Francis nodded.

"I don't have to tell *you* that—you're no dink."

Mr. Mullen took a length of rope with a knot at one end and a wooden T-handle at the other and slipped the knot into a groove on the mower's pulley. He wrapped the rope around and around the pulley until it strangled it like a snake. "Step back," he said.

Francis moved back and watched as Mr. Mullen put one foot on the mower to steady it, then gave it a hearty yank with the wooden handle. The rope uncoiled with a violent whip, but otherwise, nothing else happened.

"Sometimes you've got to do it a few times to get it going," he said, giving the rope another wind. "Why don't you give it a try?"

Francis propped one foot on the mower, like Mr. Mullen had, being sure to keep the other foot far behind, out of harm's way. He grasped the wooden T with one hand and pulled his arm back. The pulley gave far more resistance than he had imagined, and the rope unwound limply, a soggy noodle at his foot.

"It may be a little hard for you just yet," Mr. Mullen said, taking the handle back from him and winding the rope again. He gave the rope three, four, five stiff jerks until finally the motor coughed and sputtered. He let out the choke until it chugged to life. Stepping back, he motioned for Francis to take the helm, and as soon as the boy wrapped his fingers around the push handle he felt the exhilarating strangeness of vibration buzzing right down to his marrow, shifting his insides and loosening the fiber of his muscles. He waited for Mr. Mullen to step aside, and then he pushed.

The grass, which had grown too long and dense, proved too much for the engine, which immediately stalled out with a sudden jolt. Francis yelped—his arms and shoulders still vibrating from their all-too-brief moment of lawnmowing glory.

"I broke it," he said, his throat thickening.

"No, no. I let the grass get too high." Mr. Mullen rubbed the silver bristles of his beard. "You're going to have to tilt her back and lower the blade down on it." Mr. Mullen demonstrated the technique. "Once it's short enough, you can go over it again, keeping it level."

Mr. Mullen started the engine again and watched Francis for a few minutes. The mower throbbed with violence and power as he chewed through the tangled lawn, spitting out grass with the force of a tornado. At last, he understood Billie's smug smile when she snatched the last chicken leg off the platter or Jackie's laughter when she had him squeezed in a headlock. It was a feeling of victory, of having conquered. He tilted and turned and pushed the mower, until the lawn bent to his will.

"I'LL BE INSIDE," Mr. Mullen shouted. "COME IN WHEN YOU'RE DONE AND I'LL PAY YOU."

But Francis couldn't hear a word above the engine's whine. He pushed on through the afternoon, into the fading light of early evening. His bones buzzed, hot as smoke.

PART TWO

~ Chapter One ~

STAR *of the* RODEO

Francis "Spud" Pinkham met his future wife, Anita Reynolds, on his first day of high school. Due to an error in the main office, Spud (as everyone called him now, though mercifully his sisters had just enough Pinkham loyalty to keep the nickname's origin to themselves) was accidentally placed in the advanced Algebra II class instead of Algebra I. He let the error play out rather than go through the trouble of correcting it, having developed, at fifteen, a certain fatalistic attitude toward whatever was going on around him. Life happened, Francis noticed, whether he was involved or not.

It had been a summer of upheaval at the Pinkham house. After a great deal of nudging, Franny convinced Jackie to find a place of her own. At twenty-eight, the oldest Pinkham child had more than overstayed her welcome—inviting her rowdy friends to the house at all hours, then demanding, rather belligerently, that her family keep quiet during the day while she slept. Tired of making furniture, she started a carpentry business of her own, restoring the interiors of old houses in Palmdale, and convinced several of her sisters to abandon the furniture shop and work for her instead. Even though her business brought in nearly triple what her father made, Jackie saw no reason to contribute to the household expenses.

Franny saw things differently, and while she often made circular attempts at the topics of independence and responsibility, the truth was that Jackie flat out intimidated her. Barefooted, Jackie stood a head's

height above her mother, though she often wore heeled work boots even in the house to exaggerate the difference. One night, though, in the middle of July, Franny neared her breaking point as Jackie invited half the town of Cedar Hole over for a huge bonfire in the backyard, fueled by some of Larry's handmade furniture.

"Talk to your daughter," Franny hissed in the dark as she watched the glow of the bonfire from their bedroom window. "Call Harvey if you have to."

Larry rolled over and groaned. "Let her be. It'll only make things worse."

"For God's sake, Larry, she's pulling out the garden bench you made yesterday."

"The corners didn't square up. I was going to have to take the whole thing apart, anyway."

"She's too old to get away with these things. It's criminal."

"She's just young at heart," Larry said. "Let her be."

Even if Larry didn't want to do anything about the situation, Franny had had enough. The next day, she informed Jackie of what exactly was expected of her. "If you're going to live in this house, it's time you paid rent."

"You can't charge me rent—I'm your daughter," Jackie barked. "What are you going to do, throw me out?"

When it came to a shouting match with one of the girls, there was no winning. Franny found it was better for her to lower her voice to just above a whisper so they were forced to listen, though sometimes they just yelled over her.

"You're an adult now. It's time you took on some responsibility."

On the rare occasion when Franny had the courage to confront her eldest born directly, Jackie had a tendency to bolt. She'd tear out of the house red-faced, hiding out in the back woods until the steam hissed out of her, or until she felt that the situation had blown over enough so that no one would hassle her about it again. It was for this reason that Franny positioned herself between Jackie and the back door, bracing one hand against the sink and the other against the kitchen table, to block her escape.

Jackie's eyes grew hard and her nostrils flared. She made a quick bull charge at Franny but stopped short.

"Not just yet," Franny said, holding firm. "I'm not done."

But Jackie was. She lengthened her spine to its fullest expression, then seemed to expand sideways, inflating with fury. Grunting, she knocked into her mother, breaking Franny's grip on the table, and shoved past her. The momentum of Jackie's push swung Franny back into the cupboards, where she lost her footing, and smacked her head against the edge of the counter on her limp descent to the floor.

Jackie, who already had her hand on the screen door, whirled around. "Ma?"

The worst of it had been her teeth, which clacked together on impact; a strange bone-on-bone collision that made her shiver. Otherwise, there was a small throbbing and a wetness at the base of her skull. She was bleeding, though the injury hardly felt like more than a scratch. Franny had enough experience to know the smallest of head wounds could produce copious amounts of blood—but Jackie didn't.

"God, Ma—are you okay?" Jackie sank to her knees, cradling Franny's head in her hands. She looked at her palms, slick with red, and grabbed a kitchen towel to press against the wound. "I didn't do anything . . . you fell."

"You pushed me."

"Oh God . . . it was an accident. You know it was an accident, right?"

Franny watched her daughter's eyes soften, fascinated that they were still capable of tears. She suddenly found herself thinking back to when Jackie was a toddler and had finally grown too heavy for Franny's arms to carry and how it broke her heart to let her go. Jackie seemed content enough to climb around on her own, but Franny wanted more than anything to let her daughter know that it wasn't her choice. If she had been able, she would have been happy to carry her forever.

"What do I do?" Jackie cried. "I don't know what to do."

By this time, Franny felt well enough to sit upright, even to stand on her own, but she didn't move, captivated by the sudden attention that Jackie was giving her—respect that apparently could only be earned with blood.

"I want you to gather your things and go live on your own," Franny said.

"I'm talking about your head. You're *bleeding.*"

Franny tilted her chin down toward her chest so that when she looked up at her daughter, it would seem as though her eyes were rolling back in her head. "It's time you took on your own responsibilities. There's too many of you to take care of—I'm tired, Jackie."

Jackie nodded, her lower lip quivering. "I didn't mean it, though. It was just an accident."

Franny eased upright and took the towel from her. "I want you to pack up and go before your father gets home. I'll tell him I slipped on a puddle of water."

"Don't be mad at me. You forgive me, right?"

"Get along now. There's a lot to do."

Franny drove herself to the doctor, less than a mile a way, where a nurse cleaned the wound and declared the cut too shallow for stitches. When she returned home, Jackie had emptied her closet and had taken Georgie and Charlie with her. There was a note on the kitchen table, saying they were staying at a girlfriend's place until they found an apartment together and that they'd be back later for the rest of their things. Franny went to the Superette and asked Norm Higgins to wrap up a few of his best steaks for dinner.

With three of the girls out of the house, the rest of the Pinkhams reveled in their newfound breathing room. Franny decided she wanted her pantry back, so Francis was moved to the empty bedroom upstairs, and the exiled cans of vegetables and jarred pickles were pulled out of the closets and returned to their rightful places on the pantry shelves.

Francis laid awake the entire first night in his new bedroom. Jackie had picked the room clean of all its comforts, leaving only one bed and a dented metal desk whose drawers had been locked and the key summarily lost. In a larger bed, Francis felt vulnerable. He kicked the sheets loose and slid down, until he felt the familiar posture of his feet dangling off the edge of the bed.

By the fifth night, Francis walked into his new room and found that the strangeness had dissolved, that the lines of the bed and desk no longer spoke of his sisters but whispered for him instead. With Jackie,

Georgie, and Charlie gone, his life improved dramatically. He was finally able to move from the end of the dinner table to the side, where he could eat his fill without fear of being stabbed every time he reached for a chicken leg. Without their ringleader, the other girls had toned down their antics. They still sneered at him when he took too long in the bathroom and still excluded him from their baseball games, but in general they left him alone. Whenever they were looking for a fight, Francis had the luxury of closing the door to his room and locking them out.

ONE LATE AFTERNOON in September, when the sun made one of its rare appearances, Henny swiped a bottle of beer from the delivery truck behind the Superette. Allen and Francis were on lookout from the alley, watching the deliveryman through the gaps in the fence and waving Henny on when the coast was clear. The boys had expected Henny to make off with at least a six-pack, maybe two, but Henny, ever the pragmatist, took only one bottle. "That way, if we don't like it, the rest won't go to waste," he said.

Allen frowned. "You should've taken the rest anyway—we could've sold it off." He took a drink and passed the bottle around. Francis tilted it back just enough to get his lips wet, hoping to make the beer last all afternoon. He rubbed his fingers over the gold label. It was the same brand he had seen piled up in the back of Jackie's wagon.

Allen and Henny plunked down in the middle of the railroad tracks, but the idea of it made Francis skittish. He took a seat on the rail instead, the sun-warmed iron searing through the seat of his jeans. He curled the toes of his sneakers beneath him. When the train came, he'd be ready to run.

"It's not coming, Spud," Allen said, as though he could read his mind.

Francis touched his fingers to the hot rail, feeling for vibrations. "It has to—sometime."

Allen shook his head. He was only a couple of months older than Henny and Francis, but he acted as if he had been around years longer and knew everything there was to know. "No, it doesn't."

Henny lined up six quarters on top of the rail, side by side, to be flattened, just in case. "Why would somebody want to come here, anyway?"

"Ask that twit Robbie Cutler," Allen snickered. "I bet he could give you a million reasons."

"Free beer." Henny pulled off his sneaker and slipped off his sock. His toes were long and elegant for such a round body, all except the second toe of his right foot, which had been clipped by a lawnmower blade just over a year ago. Ever since the accident, Henny suffered from a phantom itch in his missing tip, which he often scratched at until his skin bled. Francis never had Henny pegged as a dink, but apparently he was one after all.

"Let's just say for a second that it did come through. Would you get on it?" Francis asked.

Henny shook his head. "No way. There's nothing out there for me."

"How would you know if you've never been anywhere?"

He shrugged. "I just know. I'm here and that's it."

"You're a pussy," Allen said. "I'd be on it in a second. As soon as we graduate, I'm gone. I'm gonna drive all the way to the West Coast." He passed the bottle to Francis. "You in?"

"Sure. Hell, I'd leave now if we could drive."

"No, you wouldn't," Henny said, stacking his quarters like poker chips.

"Sure I would," Francis said. "Nothing worth staying here for."

Henny dropped the stack on the rail and slipped his sneaker back on. While he tied his laces, Allen grabbed the quarters.

"Give 'em back!" Henny whined.

"I'll pay you back Friday," he said, slipping them into his pocket.

Francis stood up, wiping dirt off the front of his jeans. "Look, I gotta head out. I got a lawn to mow," he said, shoving a stick of peppermint gum in his mouth. "Might as well get to it before dinner."

"Aw, come on—that old fart doesn't know how high his grass is," Allen said. "Do it tomorrow."

"He owes me some money. If he doesn't fork it over, I'm going to whack him in the knees with his cane." Francis swung his arms for the purpose of illustration and bravado, and wondered if he looked convincing. Allen and Henny didn't need to know that he looked forward to mowing the Mullens' lawn; there seemed to be no good way of explaining that sitting around with old people seemed like a better thing to do than to hang out by the tracks all afternoon sipping stolen beer. He wasn't even sure himself what compelled him to keep visiting. When he sat there, at their kitchen table, a feeling came over him that was hard to identify. It wasn't quite accurate to say that he felt that he belonged there—the cat clock with its shifting eyes and the tart, stale smells made him nervous—it was more that he felt visible. Justified. His blurred edges had a way of pulling themselves together. And from what he could tell, Mr. and Mrs. Mullen seemed glad to see him, too.

"Listen," Henny said. "You sign up for the Lawn Rodeo? Me and Allen were thinking you ought to give it a shot."

"Like I give a crap about that corny thing."

"Think about it. Cutler's won the last four years in a row. You might be the only one around here who could give him a run for his money."

Allen snickered. "The kid's never lost a thing in his life. Could you imagine the look on his face if you whipped his ass in front of everybody?"

Francis smirked. "It would be kind of good, I guess."

"Good? It would be the fucking upset of the century!" Allen threw his hands up in the air and a golden arc of beer launched from the bottle, landing in the bushes behind him. "You gotta do it."

"You don't even have to win," Henny said. "Just give him a hard time."

Allen slapped the back of Henny's head. "Whaddya mean, he doesn't have to win? Of course he has to win! That's the whole frigging point."

"I'm just saying—"

"Never mind him," Allen said, brushing Henny aside. "Are you in, Spud? Are you ready to take Cutler down?"

By FALL, Mr. Mullen's health had begun to deteriorate; emphysema prevented him from being as active as he once was. Francis rearranged the Mullens' living room furniture to help him get around, moving their hardly used brocade couch and turning Mr. Mullen's recliner at an angle that allowed him to look at the television and out the picture window at the same time, so he could keep his eye on the mailbox outside.

"The cow's tail got hit by a pine cone and it chipped a little," Mr. Mullen said as Francis hung his coat on the hall tree next to the front door. "I saw the whole thing. Just happened to be looking out at the right time. I don't think I've ever seen a pine cone fall before—never paid much notice."

"Let me take the box off the post and bring it inside," Francis said. "So you can see it better. I'll put up a regular metal one."

"Leave it alone. It's just where it belongs."

Through the doorway, Francis saw Mrs. Mullen coming toward them with a tray of apple pie and two cups of coffee. He met her three-quarters of the way on her slow journey and relieved her of the tray.

"You're a sweet one, Francis," she said, patting the side of his head.

He brought the tray into the living room and set it down on the side table next to Mr. Mullen's recliner. The top was clear except for the base of a brass table lamp, but the lower shelves housed starched lace doilies and porcelain figurines of a blue jay, a hummingbird, and a cardinal. Mr. Mullen released the footrest and leaned forward.

"Look at that pie. That's a thing of beauty, right there."

Francis helped himself to a slice. He wasn't the kind of person who liked to look too far into the future—a day or two, maybe a week at most—but every time he bit into Mrs. Mullen's tender pie crust, he found himself looking ahead to a time when Mrs. Mullen wouldn't be there and neither would her pies. He couldn't imagine a world without either.

"You make sure you get yourself a wife like that, who cooks and takes care of the house. Don't go for any of that women's lib business—it ruins them."

Francis thought about his sisters, who seemed as liberated as girls could be, and decided that Mr. Mullen's pronouncement had to be correct.

"There *is* someone I like," Francis found himself saying. The ease with which this declaration came out startled him; he hadn't even said a word about it to Allen or Henny. "She's in my algebra class."

"What's her name?"

"Anita Reynolds."

"I think that's Bob and Judy's daughter." Mr. Mullen threw back his head and yelled toward the kitchen. "LILA? DO BOB AND JUDY HAVE A DAUGHTER?"

"Anita," Mrs. Mullen called back with significantly less volume. "Pretty girl."

"She's not a damn feminist, is she?" he asked Francis.

"I don't think so. I don't know."

"Well if she is, you do yourself a favor—turn right around and run. You don't need that kind of trouble."

Francis couldn't imagine Anita being anything close to trouble. Sitting behind her in algebra, he marveled at the softness of her blond ponytail, the curls that dipped and bounced into the nape of her neck when she moved her head. Her loafers captivated him, too, legs crossed neatly at the ankle; they tapped a nervous beat against the leg of her chair. Most wondrous of all was the small bump of her bra strap that antagonized him every time she huddled over her notebook. It was a detail so intimate that staring seemed crude, and yet Francis could not find the strength to look away.

One morning, before algebra, he found himself tapping her on the back, just three or four vertebrae above that elusive bra strap.

"I'm Spud Pinkham," he'd said.

Anita had turned her head and given him an odd look, though it wasn't unkind. "Of course you are."

Francis's heart lurched. "You know me?"

"Well, for one, you sit behind me every day. Secondly, you're a Pinkham."

"I'm not like them, though. My sisters, I mean."

"I should hope not. They're girls."

"I'm nicer."

Anita smiled. "I'm glad to know that, Spud."

Francis relayed the entire exchange to Mr. Mullen, hoping that he, too, could bear witness to her charms and offer some valuable advice as to how he should proceed.

"She sounds a little mouthy," Mr. Mullen grunted when Francis was done.

"It's just because she's smart. I didn't get it right. Her tone was real sweet."

"That's how they usually do it—they twist the knife in you with a smile on their face," he said. "But it doesn't matter what I say. You're already gone."

Francis felt himself blush deeply.

"You've got that poor, sorry dink look about you."

"I'm no dink," Francis said, stirring his coffee.

"No, I suppose you're not." Mr. Mullen wiped his face with his handkerchief. "But you're gone, and that means you're past the point where you can just turn around and set your sights on the next pretty thing that walks by. Now you're stuck. Now you're going to have to do something about it."

"Like what?"

"Ask her out for a sarsaparilla."

The blush left his cheeks. "Oh, I don't know about that."

"What? Is she too good to go to the soda fountain with you?" Mr. Mullen snorted.

"It's not that," Francis said. "She doesn't know me very well. It would seem kind of—quick."

Mr. Mullen pursed his lips. "So you haven't talked much."

Francis shook his head.

"Well, Mouse, it's clear to me that your biggest problem is confidence. You've got her so high in your mind, you think she's looking down at you. You need to do a little something to pump yourself up, to feel worthy of her."

"Like what?"

"It could be just about anything, as long as it's something you're proud of. What about that rodeo coming up? What if you did that?"

"I've thought about it, but I don't know. Robert Cutler's won the last four years in a row—I don't want to look like a jerk."

Walter sighed. "For Pete's sake, never mind about him. Despite outward appearances, there's not a soul on this planet who doesn't break from time to time. In my experience, the perfect ones have just as many cracks as the rest of us—they're just better at spackling."

Francis considered this for a moment. "But nobody can beat him. Not even Hinckley."

"Hinckley doesn't even want to be there—he's there because of his father," the old man said. "Maybe no one's beaten Robert Cutler because you've never tried. Maybe you're the greatest lawn mower in all of Cedar Hole."

Francis laughed. "Yeah, right."

"It'd be a shame not to find out." Mr. Mullen kicked in the footrest of his recliner. "Say, when was the last time I paid you?"

"A few weeks ago."

The old man reached for his wallet and pulled out a five-dollar bill. "Here's half—I'll give you the rest next time you come. And take this, too," he said, giving him a second five-dollar bill. "Spend it on your girl."

"She's not mine yet."

"She will be when you win that rodeo. That'll impress her."

"Thank you, Mr. Mullen."

"All I ask is that you stay out of trouble," he said. "Don't let her get the best of you. Make her work for it a little."

IN FRONT OF Henny and Allen, taking on Robert Cutler in the Lawn Rodeo was a gaff, a goof. It was something they laughed at when there was nothing left to talk about. Francis laughed loudest of all, shrugged off any mention of Robert, and even pretended he forgot about the whole thing sometimes. What he kept to himself was the fact that over the next few weeks he had managed to slash in half the time it took to cut Mr. Mullen's lawn, that he sometimes wheeled his father's mower out into the back field late at night to practice silent turns, and that he kept a calendar under his mattress counting down the days.

"We should get drunk first," Allen said on the morning of the rodeo. They were standing outside the depot at the curve of the ticket window. "Hanson's only got one cashier working the store. He's so worried about his damn ice-cream cart, he wouldn't know if someone snuck in the back and made off with a six-pack."

"You want me to win, don't you? I'd be all over the field," Francis said.

Henny nodded knowingly. "He could cut a toe off."

Allen rolled his eyes. "Don't be so serious. I'm just saying it would be funny, is all."

Francis coughed up a stifled laugh, but his throat felt as though it were stuffed with straw. He leaned his head back and tapped it absently against the plywood, hoping it could shake loose the thick soup that was swimming around inside his skull. Allen and Henny each propped one foot on the wall behind them—Allen first, then Henny following close behind—and shoved their fists into the pocket of their blue jeans. Their eyes focused on a middle distance in a cool detachment they'd been perfecting all summer. Allen had the look down cold while Henny struggled, repeatedly falling into his natural state of engaged interest, before trying once again.

While the two boys withdrew from the surroundings, Francis looked deep into the scattered throngs of people, looking for one of the few things in life that captured his interest. He found her strolling along the railroad tracks, running her fingers along the edge of the Library Association's bake sale table.

Despite Allen's seeming disinterest, he still didn't miss a thing. "Got a thing for Anita Reynolds, huh?"

Francis gave him a sour look. "No."

"You couldn't get her anyway."

"Says who?"

Allen smirked. "Just look at her. She's from *Palmdale*, for chrissakes."

"Well . . . she's here now."

"And you're a Pinkham, don't forget."

"Shut up, Allen."

Henny snickered. "Yeah, shut up, Allen."

The edges of Allen's mouth drew tight. "Five bucks says that if you go over there right now, she won't even talk to you."

Francis was about to protest, saying he spent all his money on notebooks and pencils for school, when he remembered the five-dollar bill still in his back pocket that Mr. Mullen had given him to spend on Anita. He had come to regard it as a talisman, a precious hope, but the possibility of watching Allen eat his words was far too tempting.

"I'll do it," Francis said, feeling both foolish and brave at the same time.

Allen kicked himself off the wall. "All right." The coolness had melted and his game face was on. His limbs jittered. "Go talk to her—but she has to say something back. And hi doesn't count. And if she gets mad at you, that doesn't count, either."

"Not a problem." Francis reached into his back pocket and touched the five-dollar bill for good luck. He strode over to the bake sale table, his torso throbbing, grateful that he had never told Allen or Henny that Anita was in his class and that he'd spoken to her before. But even Francis, who had absolutely no experience with girls, knew that talking in school and talking outside of school were two entirely different things.

Anita studied the plates of cookies and brownies and pulled her ponytail over her left shoulder, rubbing the end between her fingers, the same way she did during a pop quiz. She seemed so deep in thought that Francis was terrified of scaring her; instead of coming up straight behind, he swerved to the left and sidled up to her.

"Hi, Anita."

She snapped out of her daze and smiled. "Hi, Spud."

"Buying some brownies?"

Anita laughed. "Just looking."

Francis took a surreptitious glance over his shoulder. Henny was nodding vigorously; Allen drew an imaginary knife across his throat.

"If you see something you want, I'll buy it for you," he blurted.

Anita blanched. "That's very nice, but you don't have to."

"No, no—it's okay. I've got some money." He took the bill out of his back pocket. "See? You can have anything on the table you want for five dollars."

A visible giggle vibrated her throat. Francis felt himself melting into the dirt between the rails. He wished he knew what was so funny. "Maybe later," she said. "I'm not really hungry right now."

"Oh, okay." He stuffed the bill back in his pocket. "Are you going to the rodeo later?"

"I don't know. Maybe."

Francis swallowed. "Well, I'm gonna be in it. I've been practicing."

"Is that so?"

"I don't know that I have much of a chance, but it's worth a shot."

"Now, don't go saying that—I'm sure you'll do well."

Francis felt himself blush. Back at the depot, Allen was kicking the
side of the building. "Well, if you decide to go, keep an eye out for me."

"I will. Good luck to you."

BY THE TIME the rodeo started, gravity no longer had a hold on Francis.
All evidence suggested he had moved from the depot to the playing field
under his own power, but neither his senses nor his memory could provide proof. One minute he had been looking in Anita's eyes, and the next
he was lined up with the other contestants waiting for the whine of Principal Nelson's air horn. Blood flowed warmly through his chest. His
pocket was now five dollars richer.

It was a warm and humid day for the Lawn Rodeo, and the sun made
vague threats of appearing between broken clouds. Both the heat and the
sunshine were likely to have an adverse affect on many of the contestants.
Ever since the rodeo that Hinckley Hanson nearly won at the gruff urg-
ing of his father, it was declared that the grand prize needed to come
from a nonprofit source to avoid a conflict of interest. This year's prize of
fifty dollars was provided by the Left Hand Club, which donated two
weeks' worth of nickels from their fine jar. Many of this year's rodeo contestants were Left Hand Club patrons who dragged themselves out of
the bar just in time to compete, hoping to win back some of the fines they
had contributed. Francis stared down the line at his competition, with
their slumping postures and gray skin, sweating and blinking, unaccus-
tomed to the light of day.

Will Cutler was not among them. He was still at the club, unable to
pull himself away from his barstool, even though the bartender cut him
off early.

"Go on," the bartender said. "Go see your kid. He's won the last four
years in a row."

"He does just fine without me," Will said. "If I show up, it'll probably
jinx him."

Just as Will assumed, Robert was doing well. He had woken up early
and had noticed that the gray sky had grown thick and craggy, like
smooth cobblestones, and thought that maybe there was a chance of
clearing. He rummaged through the top drawer of the sideboard in the

dining room and came upon an old pair of his father's sunglasses. The lenses were oval and too large for his face, but Robert put them on anyway, securing them in the back with a spare piece of twine. Now, as the rodeo was about to begin, he was thankful for the glasses, which seemed to give him an edge over all the squinters around him.

Francis couldn't have cared less if he saw anything at all. Dead ahead, about five hundred feet, was his mower, on loan to the rodeo by Mr. Etna Hardware, looking buffed and shiny in the brightening light. All of his nervousness had been quelled. He no longer cared about the rodeo, about Robert Cutler, about Jackie, or even about the crowd watching. All he wanted to do was drop to the ground at the sound of the air horn and yell Anita's name to the sky, just to hear the sound of it in his throat.

Henny offered a last-minute bit of encouragement. "Don't look at anyone else—just keep pushing ahead."

Francis nodded numbly.

"Kill Cutler," Allen said, giving him a slap on the back. The hit was hard enough to leave a sting so sharp that Francis could mentally trace the imprint of his hand. The burn was a welcome snap to attention; Francis crawled out of his comfortable daze and took an alert survey of the line of people beside him. Robert was on the end, looking ridiculous in a pair of oversized sunglasses. The crowd on the bleachers began clapping and chanting, "ROB-ERT, ROB-ERT," as Principal Nelson raised the air horn over his head. Francis leaned forward and pumped his fists. Just before the horn sounded, he wondered if Anita was in the crowd, and if she, too, was chanting Robert's name.

The second the shrill split the air, Francis was off. His vision was singular, focused solely on the mower ahead of him. In his mind, he could see himself from the stands, the way Anita would be seeing him. *Watch me,* he thought. *Look how fast I am.* He was on the mower in seconds, pulling the rope. He ripped it hard. The engine was nothing like the Toro, turning over slick and smooth. He barely let out the choke before he was pushing back toward the edge of the field. As he crossed the finish line, the cheers from the bleachers dissolved. When Francis looked up, he realized he was the first one across. Robert followed a full three seconds behind.

"Did I forget to do something?" he wheezed, trying to catch his breath.

Henny shook his head. "You were just plain fast."

Through the remainder of the Start-n-Go trials, Francis's time held. Several of the Left Hand Club patrons were disqualified for forgetting to start their motors or running out of their lanes and into each other. While he sat on the sidelines waiting, Francis looked back at the bleachers to try to find Anita in the crowd.

"Do you see her anywhere?"

Allen plucked a long blade of spear grass and sucked on the meaty end. "Listen. This is the tough one right here. We know you're fast, but you've got to be able to get around all that crap they have hidden in the grass. Try to look for uneven spots. If you can make this, you're guaranteed golden."

"I know all that. Do you see Anita anywhere?"

"Would you never mind about her? You've got Cutler right where you want him."

Francis relented and tried to concentrate on the next heat. The other four contestants to make it to the Obstacle Course were Robert, as expected, Hinckley Hanson, and two male patrons of the Left Hand Club. Hinckley Hanson always made a strong showing at the rodeo, but this time the heat and sun seemed to liquefy him, with giant sweat rings darkening the underarms and back of his blue shirt. The Club members didn't seem much of a threat, either, patting one another on the back in an endless chain of sloppy congratulations. Robert, on the other hand, seemed focused as ever, looking stony behind his sunglasses.

As soon as Principal Nelson gave the signal, Francis ripped the motor again. The buzz deadened his nerves, though above all the vibration he could still feel his heart pounding in his chest. He entered the course cautiously, knowing care was almost as important as speed. To his right, he noticed an odd swell in the grass, so he made a sharp left. He switched back to the other side, noticing the brown nub of a tree limb. He fought on, steady, quelling the urge to push too hard or too fast. The urge only became stronger as, out of the corner of his eye, Francis caught the speeding figures of the two Club members zooming ahead. Alarm bells clanged in his head. He was losing.

Just as Francis made it to the top of his lane, there was a crunch, a sputtering sound, and then a yelp just off to his left. He didn't dare look over, for fear of hitting a stone. The return trip was much easier—he just had to follow the path he had made on the way up, allowing for the slight differences in the contours of the mower on either side. Francis's heart quickened.

Principal Nelson held the megaphone to his lips. "Could we please get the paramedics on the field?"

As Francis crossed the finish line, he saw no sign of Hinckley or the Club members. A yellow burst of joy melted his insides. At the end of the line, Robert was already sitting down, drinking a paper cup of water that Miss Pratt had given him. So what if Robert came in first, Francis told himself. At least he was in the Mowdown.

He had expected Henny and Allen to come running over to congratulate him, but the two were frozen on the sidelines, mesmerized by what was happening on the field. Francis turned around and saw the two Club members and their mowers in a tangle; one of them apparently had crossed his rope barrier and had smashed into the other. There was a splash of blood on the pant leg of one of the men. Hinckley, who had stopped mowing, was stumbling in his own lane, before succumbing to the scene and passing out on the grass.

Two paramedics ran onto the field with a stretcher. One of them signaled the judges' table by holding up three fingers. Principal Nelson resumed talking on his megaphone.

"As you may have noticed, we've had a little mishap this afternoon. It seems as though one of our contestants has lost three toes. Unfortunately, with the grass as high as it is, it's hard to find them. If I could have five volunteers on the field to help in the search, it would be greatly appreciated."

Everyone on the four lowest benches of the stands sprinted onto the field, with Allen and Henny leading the pack.

"And another announcement," Principal Nelson said. "Robert Cutler and Spud Pinkham will be our two finalists for the Mowdown. We'll get to that as soon as the mess is cleaned up."

In the end, only two of the three toes were found, though Allen and Henny continued to comb the area for the rest of the afternoon, just to be sure. The field was quickly cleared of the two members and of Hinckley, who regained consciousness after a few stiff slaps from his father.

The Mowdown was on just before Francis was starting to lose his nerve. It was the only event that Robert had never lost. Francis wasn't sure if it was because he was fast or because he had a better method. For some reason, every single contestant used the exact same pattern as Hinckley, the same unimaginative row-by-row method, while Robert continued with his spiraling box. It seemed to Francis that to have any chance at all of beating Robert, he'd have to mow the same way.

Robert left his mower and walked up to Francis, his hand extended. "I just wanted to say good luck, and whatever happens, it's for the best."

Francis didn't want to touch him, but the thought that Anita might be somewhere in the crowd watching made him offer a limp shake. "Yeah, okay."

"Are the contestants ready?" Principal Nelson called as Robert took his place. "On your mark, get set, GO!"

Francis pounced. The air around him seemed clouded, except for the mower and the patch of land directly in front of him, which burned bright and vivid. He raced to the first stake and took the quarter turn, just like he had watched Robert do year after year, starting down the second wall of the box. There was an almost maddening, gruesome delight in running down the snarling grass, beheading the wild purple chive blossoms that Francis pictured as soft-shrunken Robert-heads, being chewed up and spit out the side, then feeling the short velvet carpet underfoot in its wake.

Another stake, another turn. He was facing Robert's square now. The desire to look was too great and he raised his head, allowing the smoke to clear beyond his immediate space. Robert was just a beat or two behind, just reaching the third stake as Francis zipped down toward the fourth. He dropped his head and refocused. It was okay now—he was ahead. He wouldn't need to look again.

The crowd was clapping and cheering. There were a few chants of "ROB-ERT, ROB-ERT," but nothing urgent and organized, and certainly not enough to break Francis's will. He quickened his step as the pattern began to curl in on itself. His lungs felt clear and unburdened. He could see the prize in his mind—the glass pickled egg jar filled with rolled nickels. They belonged to him, to Anita. When this was all over, he would find her and buy her something. He'd even buy the entire bake sale, table and all, if that's what she wanted.

The turns came quicker now, the world spinning beyond his line of vision. He spiraled in, faster and faster, coiling tighter and tighter, closing his eyes to keep from getting dizzy. Of all the times he had tried to do anything in his life, this, by far, was the easiest. This, he thought, was what it must feel like to be Robert.

When at last he came to the final patch, Francis pushed the mower away from his body and threw his hands up in the air. He had yet to even look and see if he was truly the winner, but he needed no confirmation. He knew he had won.

It wasn't until Principal Nelson sounded the air horn that Francis had the courage to look over at Robert. Just as he thought, Robert was still mowing his square. Henny and Allen abandoned their severed toe search and skipped over to Francis, yelling and screaming the entire way.

"You won, you won!" Henny ripped a two-fingered whistle. "I saw Anita here."

"Where?" Francis couldn't hold back a broad smile.

"She was standing by the bleachers. I don't see her now."

Francis pressed his wrist to his forehead and tried to look into the crowd, but the sun was too bright to see.

Allen gave Francis's shoulder a hard punch. "Whatcha gonna buy me, huh?"

"I don't know—maybe a Bazooka," Francis joked.

"Better be more than that." Allen looked over at Robert. "The dummy is still mowing. I don't even think he knows he lost yet."

The crowd appeared to be thinking the same thing, for they had grown silent, all eyes fixed on Robert as he continued to mow his square. Something was decidedly off, Francis thought, for instead of the usual snail-box, Robert was mowing in an entirely different way. His angles seemed sharper and more frequent, almost ziggy-zaggy. Curious, the boys moved down to the other end of the field to see what was going on.

"Would you look at that, folks," Principal Nelson announced. "It looks like we have an artist among us."

Francis, Allen, and Henny walked back up the embankment to a higher spot to get a better view. Robert mowed the last bit of grass and cut the engine. When he was done, he was standing in the center of a five-pointed star.

"Good Lord," Henny said.

Francis could hardly breathe. The star was perfectly proportioned, and inside was a series of nesting stars, each smaller than the next, finally culminating with Robert himself. He lifted up his sunglasses and placed them on top of his head. The crowd roared.

"In all my years at the rodeo, I have to say I've never seen anything like this," the principal said. "What do you all think of Mr. Cutler's star?"

The crowd cheered again. The back of Francis's neck prickled. He looked at the nickel jar and felt it slipping away.

"Unfortunately, he didn't finish first."

There was a collective sigh of disappointment and then a low mumble as they talked about the strange turn of events.

"Now, let's all settle down. We can work this out," Principal Nelson said. "We'll take a vote and see who you think should win. Robert, come on up here a second."

Robert crossed the field to an explosion of applause.

"Robert, why should we make you the winner?" He handed the megaphone off to him.

"I don't know that you should," the boy said. Delia Pratt stepped forward and mopped his forehead with a handkerchief. "But I always try my best. That's what I want for Cedar Hole, that we always try our best, no matter what."

The cheers grew louder. Principal Nelson handed the megaphone to Francis. "Go ahead, son. What do you have to say?"

The crowd fell silent.

Francis's arm was shaking, making the megaphone wobble a quarter inch on either side of his mouth. His mind was white and vast and slippery, with no coherent thought words could attach themselves to. He cleared his throat, which echoed gently in the air, then said:

"I got nothin'."

Francis's arm dropped suddenly and Principal Nelson grabbed the megaphone before it crashed against the table. "All right, you've heard them both. Those of you who think Spud Pinkham should be the winner of the rodeo and the fifty dollars' worth of nickels sitting right here in this jar, let's hear your applause."

Henny and Allen whistled and hooted and stomped their feet, goading the crowd to follow. Only about half the crowd responded, their claps being polite at best, apathetic at worst. Francis felt a searing pain down the inside of his throat, as though he had just swallowed the mower blade whole.

"Now, if you think Robert is the winner, let's hear it!"

The crowd was suddenly on its feet. They erupted in a thunderous explosion. Principal Nelson grabbed Robert by the wrist and lifted it high in the air.

Allen kicked the ground. "That is such bullshit."

THE NEXT MORNING, before the first bell, Francis waited by the front doors of the school with Mr. Mullen's five-dollar bill tucked in his back pocket. The rain was heavy, and despite taking shelter beneath the overhang, he was wet from the wind, which blew the rain in at a deep angle. Francis's jeans were drenched from the knee down and the insoles of his sneakers squished as he shifted his weight, but his fragile optimism remained high. His intention was to catch Anita as soon as she got off the bus. He would say hello and open the door for her, make some comment about the rodeo and try to spark a conversation. He'd play it cool and friendly. They'd talk again before class and if he still felt confident at lunch, maybe he'd ask her out then. Or later, before she caught the bus home. Francis didn't want to push too soon but the question crackled hot in his brain, snapping off fiery little impulses that jolted his nerve endings and left him jazzed but also drained. It was going to be a long day.

When the 47-A bus finally arrived, an electric hum reverberated from the base of his heels all the way up to the back of his skull. He wiggled his toes inside his sneakers to alleviate the mounting pressure, then checked and rechecked the five-dollar bill in his pocket. It was still dry. He rubbed the money between his fingers, the crisp texture offering an intangible measure of comfort.

He felt her even before he saw her appear in the stairwell of the bus. It was wondrous to sense her approach—the heightening, the keying up, the fine-tuning of attention, the thousand downy antennae seeking out her static. He stood a little straighter as she descended the stairs. She was wearing a green slicker—unlike Cedar Hole natives, who by the time they reached high school became impervious to the elements—but still raised a single notebook above her head as a makeshift shelter from the rain. As she stepped down, he caught a glimpse of leg between the hem of her skirt and her ankle, ruddy from the raw air. His mind clouded. Francis took a deep breath to push away the fog. Clearing his throat, he took a step forward, out into the rain. The distance from the bus to the entrance was too long. He'd meet her halfway.

A red umbrella approached from the road, edging into his peripheral vision but not yet scraping the fringes of his consciousness. Francis worked his way forward through the throng of bus goers, sidestepping feet and puddles until he found an open spot toward the outer rim of the path. The umbrella drew closer, its bright color eventually registering in Francis's brain, which ultimately deemed it inconsequential and thus it was quickly disregarded. More important and entirely absorbing was Anita's palm, turned upward to catch the rain, and the cascade of drops that ran down the inside of her lovely wrist.

Francis was only three strides away when the umbrella, more insistent than before, intruded on his vision; it sidled up toward Anita and absorbed her beneath its red dome. A strangled yelp formed in his throat and quickly died. She lowered the notebook by her side. All Francis saw of her companion was a pair of brown tweed trousers and a pair of shiny loafers, but it was enough. Together, they walked right by him.

"Hi, Spud," Anita said as they passed.

"Good morning, Francis," Robert added, tilting back the umbrella to make eye contact.

With words unavailable to him, Francis raised a heavy hand and waved.

~ Chapter Two ~

A DEPARTURE

Cedar Hole loved hard-luck cases, and earlier that summer, Will Cutler was drinking so heavily he quickly became everyone's favorite cause. It started when he lost his job at Wear-Tex by accidentally setting fire to a box of undershirts with a burning cigarette butt. It was precisely the kind of screwup his supervisor had been waiting for—something public, dramatic, potentially dangerous—to get rid of a once-productive employee who now spent more time in the bathroom nipping a flask of whiskey than he spent on the job.

Everyone, it seemed, was willing to give Will a shot at turning his life around. The manager of the Left Hand Club hired him as the afternoon bartender, but Will drank a shot for every two he poured. At the Superette, Hinckley Hanson let him stock shelves at night, though the beer cooler, too, proved to be a temptation. Shorty hired on Will at the diner to bus tables, but the early schedule didn't agree with him.

"I hate to do it to you, Will, but morning's my busiest time. I need someone who can be here at five, ready to go," Shorty said. The counter only came up to the middle of Shorty's chest, which made Will, in his perpetual state of inebriation, see his boss not as a person but as a talking head in a children's puppet show. Shorty's pointy, bald head, antenna ears, and bulbous nose went a long way to support Will's delusion. He could hardly look at the man without snickering.

Shorty, who understood the effect his height had on people, grabbed a child's booster seat and stood on it. "Look, I know you've got a family to feed, and I want to help you out. The town's looking for a few construction workers to do some roadwork. The fresh air would be good for you." Shorty gave Will the number and a dime for the pay phone. "Give them a call."

As it turned out, Will and his drinking habit were perfectly suited to construction work. His job was to hold the SLOW sign to oncoming traffic, and as long as he kept the sign upright, the foreman didn't seem to care much how he held it. He enjoyed being outside, despite the rain, and found the steady stream of cars soothing. After a long night at the bar he could prop his arms and forehead on the sign and lean into it for support, close his eyes and listen to the *whoosh* of the passing cars. Sometimes the gentle noise lulled him to sleep. The other guys in the crew were good to Will, keeping an eye on him as they worked. When he started to tip a little, they nudged him awake with the butt of their shovels so he could prop himself up again.

Still, construction didn't pay nearly as well as Wear-Tex did. At home, money was tight. Whatever Will didn't drink went directly into the mouths of Sissy and Robert.

"YOU COULD BRING US A STEAK ONCE IN A WHILE," Sissy called from the back room, turning up her nose at the frozen dinners Will brought back from the Superette. "OR A NICE PIE."

"If you don't like it, don't it eat."

"THAT'S NOT WHAT I'M SAYING. IT'D BE NICE TO HAVE SOMETHING DIFFERENT. ROBERT'S A GROWING BOY—HE NEEDS NUTRITION."

Robert, it seemed to Will, was more than healthy. His cheeks held good color and he never complained about headaches or stomach pains. He sat at the kitchen table as though he were in the middle of a four-star restaurant and ate his creamed chipped beef in slow, elegant forkfuls. "This is good," he said, no matter what slop Will put in front of him.

"No, it's not—it looks like puke." Will unscrewed the top of his hip flask and spiked a mug of cold coffee left over from the morning. He caught the boy staring at him, his eyes groveling and expectant, like a hungry mutt. "What?"

"Thank you."

"For what?"

"Dinner," the boy said. "For paying the bills. For taking care of us."

Will took a hard swallow of coffee and closed his eyes. He longed for the support of a construction sign pushing against his weight or the cool surety of a pint glass in his left hand. These were the things he understood.

"I know you work hard." Robert lowered his voice. "Mom knows it, too. She just can't say it."

"WILL? DO WE HAVE ANY KETCHUP?" Sissy shouted from her room.

"What do YOU think?" he shouted back.

"BRING ME SOME."

Will took the ketchup bottle from the refrigerator door and bowled it across the kitchen floor, through the doorway of Sissy's room.

"HOW AM I SUPPOSED TO REACH THAT? I'M NOT AN ACROBAT."

"I thought you might need to know," Robert continued. "We're grateful."

The backs of Will's eyeballs felt bruised. He stared out the screen door at the old plum tree in the backyard. The limbs were dry and twisted, stretching out to him like beggars' hands. The nursery where he bought it promised fruit after three years, but it had been fifteen now and still nothing.

"Dad?"

"All right, all right. Just shut up and eat."

One Monday afternoon in late fall, two weeks after Robert's Lawn Rodeo victory, the foreman gathered all the construction workers together during their break to make an announcement.

"Looks like we're all done here 'til spring," he told them. "The town doesn't have enough money in the budget to finish the rest of the repairs. I'm afraid I'm going to have to let you all go."

Most of the men took the dismissal in stride, knowing all along that it was a short-term gig. Will, however, took the news hard—he complained to his coworkers about his wife, his strange boy, and the bleakness of his future over several rounds of beer at the club.

"Don't they need people to hold signs in the winter? I could hold one of those FROST HEAVE signs if they'll let me."

"You'd freeze, Buddy," one of his coworkers said. "Besides, they've got those handy little tripods to keep them in place."

"Get your truck license," said another. "You can drive a sanding truck. Or better yet, head south. I hear there's a ton of construction jobs in Florida."

"Nice weather down there," the bartender agreed.

Will shook his head. "I can't even get the wife out of her room anymore. How am I supposed to get her to go to Florida?"

The men fell quiet. He drank the last of his pint and stuck a dollar bill in the fine jar.

Will returned home at midnight, his wallet empty and his belly full of beer. As he turned into the driveway, the headlights of his pickup swept across the front of his property and illuminated the mailbox staked on the corner of the lot. As soon as he saw the box he hit the brakes. The door was open, hanging by a hinge, while the remainder of the box was bashed into a knob of scrap metal, sitting on top of the post like a crumpled beer can. He staggered out of the truck and tried to jam his hand inside, though the crushed opening proved too narrow for his broad fingers. Through the slit he could see, just beyond his reach, the bent corner of an envelope that bore the town seal. His last paycheck.

Will looked down the dark alley of Thornberry Lane, scanning the rows of perfectly whole, untouched mailboxes that lined both sides of the street. It took a moment for the singularity of the incident to penetrate his slushy mind, but when it finally did, the message rang clear.

Many unfavorable things have been said about Will Cutler over the years, but one of his better and often overlooked traits was that, in essence, he was an optimist. While it seemed that Robert's positive outlook came down from the stars, in truth it was a quality he inherited from his father, who in his own small way possessed a kind of wondrous longing often attached to dreamers, who held in his heart the tiniest seed of hope against life's calamities. It was optimism that always made him reach for another drink, certain that this would be the one that would finally fill him and that he'd never have to drink again. It was optimism that made him think every morning that maybe this was the day that Sissy would get out of bed and make breakfast on her own, renouncing her life of leisure. And it was optimism once again that made him see his crushed mailbox not as a personal attack but as a sign; a divine message delivered by an unseen hand. Cedar Hole was a leech that gulped down Will's lifeblood with barefaced delight, but now it seemed that it was letting him go. He no longer had to stay just to have his blood drained, or his mailbox crushed, or to be the recurring punch line in some sorry joke. He was free. Cedar Hole didn't want him anymore.

Will kicked the mailbox post with the heel of his boot and pulled it out of the ground, tossing the whole mess into the back of his truck.

He stumbled up the stairs to his bedroom with the superfluous bumps and knocks a drunk makes when he's trying extra hard to be quiet. Without turning on the light, he yanked open bureau drawers and stuffed some clothes into a paper grocery bag along with a toothbrush, comb, and a bottle of aftershave he found underneath the bathroom sink. He went down to the kitchen and boiled a pot of coffee, which he poured into a thermos, and then sandwiched pieces of salami between the slices of an entire loaf of white bread, gently sliding the whole loaf back into the bag and knotting it at the top.

Sissy slept the entire time. Will kept an ear tuned to the rhythm of her breathing, the grumbled pitch and fade of her snores, and when her beat was steady and deep he found himself nudging open the door of her room. The stagnant, oniony air wrenched his stomach, bringing him no farther than the doorway. Sissy slept with her back toward the door, her face nearly pressed to the wall, the same way she slept when they had still shared a bed years ago. She always insisted on having one side of the bed flush against the wall and her body right up to the edge, pinned in, secure. He remembered how sweet she used to look in her sleep, eyelashes lying against her cheeks, lips slightly open. He was glad that all he could see now was the dark mat of the back of her head and the loose slab of her upper arm.

Will's body suddenly began to move independent of thought, with an intention all its own. His torso turned against the doorjamb and his arm reached across his chest, his hand gliding along the inside wall. He felt around in the dark until his fingers found their desire—Sissy's portable radio. He wiggled the plug loose from the outlet and collapsed the antenna, then tucked the radio under his arm.

"Dad? What's going on?"

Robert was standing by the kitchen window in his pajamas and socks. The boy's hair was parted perfectly down the side, as though he had taken the time to comb it before coming downstairs. The thought mortified Will, even more than getting caught stealing his wife's radio.

"Go to bed," he said. "You'll wake your mother."

"What are you doing?"

"Never mind. Go to bed."

The boy glanced over at the coffee thermos and the sack of sandwiches. "Someone smashed our mailbox tonight."

"I know. I saw."

"I heard it and woke up, but by the time I got to the window, they were gone. I didn't know what to do—I didn't know if I should call the police or something."

"Nah, that's all right. Harvey couldn't do nothing about it."

They stood together for what seemed like a long time—Will, with the radio tucked under his arm and his trip provisions a maddening three feet away, and Robert, with the clean toes of his socks drawing aimless circles on the dirty kitchen floor.

"So where you going?" he finally asked.

"Florida." The truth seemed irrelevant now and it just eased out of him without the slightest prompting. "I can get work down there."

"How long?"

"Don't know."

"When are you coming back?"

He shook his head.

Robert drew himself up, locking his joints. Will hardly paid attention to his son's height in the past, but now he saw that the boy would probably always fall on the puny side, far short of his own six-foot-plus frame.

"I suppose they don't have radios in Florida," Robert said.

The surface of Will's skin burned as he pulled the radio tight against his ribs. "She'll have the house."

Robert went to the sideboard in the dining room and opened the top drawer, pulling out a fifty-dollar bill. He returned to the kitchen and handed it to his father. "Would this make a difference?"

"Where'd you get that?"

"It's my winnings from the rodeo. I didn't want to give you a bunch of nickels, so I cashed it in."

Will patted the back of his son's head. "You keep it." He seized the bag of sandwiches, the thermos, and the paper bag full of clothes. "You'll be all right."

Will jumped into the cab of his truck, while Robert watched from the kitchen door. He never looked up but felt the boy's watching eyes crawl up the back of his neck. Will drove straight on through the night and into the next day, not stopping until he hit Florida.

~ Chapter Three ~

PINKHAM BASEBALL

Jackie, Georgie, and Charlie rented a two-story house overlooking the Cedar Hole Elementary baseball diamond, and though Francis had never been invited over, Billie and Larrie Jr. said the place was a dump. The building itself was in good condition—a sturdy shingled cottage—but the girls had apparently made a mess of the interior. There was no garage, so Jackie kept all their tools and lumber on the floor of the living room. Charlie put the table saw in the dining room and the interior of the kitchen cupboards more closely resembled the shelves of Cedar Hole Hardware than Franny's pantry. Every spare surface of the apartment was coated in a beige film of sawdust, the air being so saturated with wood particles that sunbeams coming through the windows looked solid enough to touch. By all accounts, the girls seemed quite happy with the new arrangement.

Francis, however, wasn't as free from his older sisters as he had hoped. They dropped by frequently, usually for a meal or when they needed something. Jackie, who had a violent aversion to shopping, used the Pinkham home as her own personal commissary, pilfering shelves and cupboards when no one was around to stop her. It was not unusual for Larry to discover, in the most vulnerable of moments, that the toilet paper had been stolen, or for Franny, in a hurry to put dinner together, to find that her pantry had been ransacked. Even Francis had come home on more than a few occasions to find the sheets taken off his bed, pencils missing from his desk, a wool jacket (*and* its hanger) gone from his closet. Everyone else seemed fine with their losses—in their minds, it was an even swap for having a little more time in the bathroom in the morning and not having to crawl over jars of pickles to find your shoes— but Francis never quite grew into the free-flowing attitude of communal sharing. In heavy black marker he began to label everything he owned, writing SPUD in bold letters on the soles of his winter boots, the headboard of his bed, the tags of his clothes, the lamp on his desk. The mere act of labeling seemed to keep his belongings safe—Francis knew that just the sight of his name was enough to taint anything the girls had designs on.

One evening, after Jackie stopped by the house for dinner, she grabbed Francis by the front of his shirt just as he was leaving the table and dragged him into the hallway.

"You want to play a little baseball with us, Spud?" Jackie twisted Francis's shirt in her fist, pulling it tight under his arms.

"I dunno." It wasn't exactly the most attractive of invitations, but one he'd been hoping for his whole life. Francis stared up at his sister, whose mouth wrinkled at the corners as though she were trying to conjure a burp. "Who's going?"

"Charlie, Georgie, Billie—maybe Rickie. Does it matter?"

"Maybe, I guess."

Jackie released Francis from her grip and poked a finger at his chest. "You used to whine all the time that we never took you anywhere. Now's your chance."

"How come?"

"How come what?"

"How come you're asking me now? You've never asked me before." A damp heat sucked at his eyeballs as he tried to ignore the pointed tip of his sister's finger drilling into his breastplate. He focused his attention on Jackie's thick, tree-stump neck and mentally noted the multitude of ways it differed from Anita's delicate form.

"I'm loading up the car," she said with a smirk. "Be outside in five minutes."

Francis ran upstairs to grab a pair of sneakers, which he had newly tagged SPUDSPUDSPUDSPUDSPUDSPUDSPUD around the edge of the soles. Larrie Jr. appeared in the doorway of his room, an unlit cigarette hanging from her lips.

"It's your turn—finally," she said, smiling. "I'm sure it was the rodeo. They think you're ready."

"For what?"

Larrie Jr. ignored the question. "You'll have fun. I did mine last year. Jackie takes the whole initiation thing very seriously."

Francis tied his laces in double knots—the last thing he wanted was to trip on the field and give his sisters even more reasons to ridicule him. "What do you mean, last year? You've been playing baseball with them for years."

Larrie Jr. slid open the window and sat on the sill. She propped her bare feet on Francis's desk and lit the cigarette from her pocket lighter. She traced the SPUD Francis had painted on the base of his table lamp with the tip of her big toe. The letters were pink and frosty; marker ink didn't take, so he had to use their mother's nail polish instead.

"You like girls, don't you, Spud?" she asked.

The hair on the back of Francis's neck bristled. "Well, yeah."

"Just checking." Larry took a conspiratorial drag from her cigarette— a sort of side-mouthed draw that looked as though she were coaxing a secret from it. "I'm glad she convinced you to go. You need to get out of this room. You're always moping in here."

"I get out."

She flicked ash on his desk. "Not much. How come you're always avoiding us? Are we really so bad?"

Francis didn't answer.

"They've been rough on me, too, you know. It's just their way," she said. "It starts with Jackie and the shit gets passed down the ranks—too bad you're the end of the line. It all sort of piles up on you."

"So it's nothing personal."

"Well, you *are* a boy, and we all know how she feels about them." Larrie yawned. "I'm glad you're here, though. Otherwise it would all end up on me."

Francis smiled. He pulled at a bare thread hanging from the quilt at the end of his bed. This moment was rare and real and he wanted to contribute to the exchange by offering her something equally personal. "Hey, do you know Mr. Mullen? He's this old guy that lives near the train depot."

Larrie stared at him blankly.

"He lives in that white house with the really steep driveway."

"Okay—I guess I've probably seen it before." She ground her cigarette into the windowsill.

"He had a son who died in the war. His name was Jasper and he liked to paint things. There's a picture of him hanging in the kitchen next to this crazy cat clock with eyes that move back and forth."

"So?"

"And Mr. Mullen's wife likes to bake these cakes, except she makes them too big and they can never eat it all by themselves."

"Are those your friends? A couple of old farts?" Larrie started to laugh.

He had misjudged her. Sensing his mistake, Francis pulled back, hoping it wasn't too late to save himself. "It was Henny's idea," he found himself saying. "He dared me to grease down their front step with Crisco, you know, for a gag." The lie rolled itself out so boldly and without hesitation that he had no choice but to follow. "But old man Mullen caught me. I was on my knees with this huge scoop of grease in my hand when he opened the door."

Larrie hugged her knees to her chest and curled her toes on the edge of the windowsill. She clearly liked where this was going.

"So there I am, with the Crisco and everything, and he's staring down at me like he wants to bury his boot in my ass—and Henny and Allen, who were supposed to keep watch from the side of the house, are booking it down the street."

"So what did you do?"

"I told him I was a Boy Scout selling Crisco door-to-door so I could earn enough money to get to Jamboree."

"Nuh-uh."

"Sure did," Francis said. "And he believed me, too. He even invited me into the house for some cake."

Larrie laughed so hard she folded her arms across her belly and fell back against the window screen. Francis leaned forward, prepared to grab for her ankles should the metal mesh let go. "Oh man! What I wouldn't have given to see that."

"That's not even the best part." Francis felt revved up now. Cocky. "He actually bought the Crisco off me for two bucks."

Larrie's laughter gave way to a full-bellied Pinkham guffaw—a deep-throated phenomenon free of pretense and mystery, fueled by violent snorts of air. Outside, Jackie's car horn blared.

"You'd better get going, Spud," she said, catching her breath. "You don't want to keep her waiting. And don't you dare chicken out."

Francis stood up. "If this is going to be bad, tell me now."

"They're not going to hurt you. I promise."

"You'd tell me, right?"

"Don't be such a whiner," she said, punching him in the thigh. "Just go."

JACKIE DROVE. Georgie was in the passenger's seat of the wagon, while Francis was crammed in the backseat between Charlie and Billie. The baseball bat their father had made for them was pinned upright between Charlie's knees.

"I'm glad you're the last one, Spud, because I'm definitely getting too old for this," Jackie said, eyeballing him in the rearview mirror.

Francis stared at the bat. On its surface, all of the girls' names had been burned into the wood.

"Yours will be on there tomorrow," she said. "How about that?"

Francis didn't answer.

Georgie turned around and snarled. "Larrie Jr. told you, didn't she? I saw her in the window. She better keep her trap shut."

"Don't get your panties in a wad," Charlie said. "No one's going to find out anything. Are they, Spud?"

"Better not." Georgie faced front again, but the menacing look she had given Francis remained cold and deep in his marrow. Billie jutted her elbow against his side, jabbing him in the ribs every time Jackie raced over a bump. Francis clenched his teeth, letting the yelps dissolve silently in his throat.

By now the sun had been forgotten and dusk was asserting its blue grip.

There were no field lights at the Cedar Hole Elementary diamond—the town could barely afford just to mow the field—and soon, Francis knew, it would be too dark to see the baseball glove in front of his face, let alone one of Jackie's curveballs. Billie rolled down the window and stuck her torso through the opening, hollering and waving her arms at the sky. The heavy aroma of old sweat muted the balmy air that blasted into the car.

Charlie grimaced. "Shit, Billie, you stink!"

Billie pulled back into the car. "Who the fuck asked you?"

The car turned down Webber Road, the main thoroughfare connecting Cedar Hole to Palmdale, with the town line drawn somewhere near the midpoint. On the Cedar Hole side, Webber was a lane of broken pavement and loose gravel as slippery as ice if you hit the gas too hard, with sloping shoulders and a ravine on both sides perfect for giving a reckless car a good roll. On the Palmdale side, however, Webber abruptly turned into a pristine blacktop with painted lines, the ravine filled in to a solid shoulder. In the winter, the Palmdale Public Works Department plowed and sanded Webber all the way up the town line, while Cedar Hole's side accumulated several layers of snow and ice that remained neglected until rain melted it away in the spring.

A Superette bag was wedged between Georgie and Jackie in the front seat. Georgie opened the bag and pulled out a beer, popping off the bottle cap with her teeth. "Where we hitting tonight?"

"Wherever we feel like it," Jackie said. "We'll just ride around until we see something good."

Francis pulled himself forward and tucked his face in the gap between the two front seats. "I thought we were going to the school."

Jackie laughed. "Georgie—get Spud a beer. It's his consolation prize for not winning the rodeo."

Georgie complied, cleanly biting off the top, then spitting it onto the dashboard.

"Make him squeal for it," Billie said, imitating the unearthly howl Francis discovered while beneath a pile of potatoes in the pantry.

"Shut your trap!" Georgie handed Francis the beer without demanding a performance. "Drink up, Spud."

"You never said nothing about entering the rodeo," Jackie was saying. "You sure do like to keep things to yourself."

Up ahead was the railroad crossing, thoughtlessly built along an old frost heave. Underneath the sign declaring the crossing exempt, was the understated warning of BUMP AHEAD, situated a scant one hundred feet from the heave—undoubtedly a bone-jarring surprise for lost, lead-footed out-of-towners who found themselves on Webber after sundown.

"We never thought you'd make it past the Start-n-Go," Billie snorted. "We thought you musta rigged up something to make the mower go faster."

"Either that or he put water in the other mowers to mess with the engine," Charlie said.

"I didn't do nothin' like that," Francis said. "I played it fair."

Jackie glared at him in the mirror. "Of course you did. Too bad they didn't play it fair on you."

"I know." Francis sank deep against the seat, soothed by the unexpected vindication.

"But you couldn't have been surprised," she continued. "You knew they were going to make Robert win no matter what, right?"

"What do you mean?"

The girls burst out laughing.

"What do you mean?" he repeated, to an even louder chorus of laughs. "What's so funny?"

The persistent thought that dogged most of his childhood came to the surface once again, that his sisters hated him and he didn't know why.

"When are you gonna to wake up, Spud?" Jackie said, glaring back at him. "Cutler is one of those people who will always win everything. And you're the kind that will always drag along behind, picking up the scraps."

Francis looked over his shoulder at the back of the wagon and noticed that there were no baseball gloves, not even a baseball or any other sports equipment at all. Just piles and piles of empty beer bottles. His chest tightened, feeling as leaden as if Jackie were sitting on it. Her invitation seemed less surprising now. He silently cursed Larrie Jr. Whatever it was he now found himself involved in, she had delivered him up to it completely and without conscience.

They drove aimlessly until dark. By then the beer had slackened

Francis's joints and thought processes, though conversely it only seemed to wind up the girls even more. The wagon rocked on its springs as they bounced up and down in their seats, shrilling over one another with snorts and insults.

"I want to go first!" Billie shouted, wrenching the bat away from Charlie. "Go to that place right over there—the white house over there."

Jackie turned down a residential street in one of Palmdale's pricier neighborhoods, a generous grid of picket fences and showy properties. The house Billie pointed to was triple the size of the average Cedar Hole residence—a three-story whitewashed Colonial with a broad half-round porch. Billie's eyes brimmed with injustice and disgust, and somewhere in there Francis thought he saw envy, too.

"Make sure you get close enough," Billie told Jackie. She pulled her upper body out the window, as she had done before, this time with bat in hand. Fear clawed distantly at Francis, though the beer kept it from taking hold. He took another swig just to be sure.

Jackie backed up the road a couple hundred feet, then stomped on the brake. "Ready?"

From where he sat, Francis could hardly see anything except his sister's rear end as she leaned out the window. The bat was now above his line of vision, poised, he assumed, for a swing.

Jackie hit the gas hard enough to throw Charlie and Francis back in their seats. She steered the wagon close to the edge of the road as they approached the house, nearly clipping the black metal mailbox mounted on a wrought-iron post. As soon as Billie was close enough, she swung, cracking the bat against the side of the mailbox with a tinny thud.

Jackie put the car in reverse to survey the damage. There was a good-sized dent in the side of the box, but the door looked as though it could still be opened. "I'd say that's about a double."

A laughed rippled up from Francis's belly. Whacking mailboxes—that's all it was. He had expected something more criminal from his sisters, like robbing houses or torturing stray animals. This was nothing. This was something he could do.

"What's so damn funny?" Billie asked, gouging him in the ribs. "You think you can do better?"

"I know I can."

"Not yet," Charlie said, grabbing the bat and crawling over the both of them. "I'm next."

Georgie pointed to a prim Victorian across the street with swirls of gingerbread trim. "Wait a second—I think I just saw a light go on," she said. "We'd better get moving."

The tires squealed as Jackie took the corner hard to line Charlie up perfectly with the first mailbox in their path. Francis soon discovered that such precision was merely a warm-up; once the girls got in a few solid hits, Jackie made it tougher for them by swerving the car away from the box at the last second or throwing off their timing by hitting the gas. Georgie had the best swing of the three, denting the rim of the boxes so hard the doors usually flew open, and, if her reflexes were quick enough, knocking the doors clean off with the upswing. But once Jackie started weaving and putting her foot to the floor, even Georgie had a hard time—her arms and the bat wobbling willy-nilly in the wind.

Francis did not volunteer a turn at bat, but sat back instead and watched his sisters as they left a trail of crumpled mailboxes all over Palmdale. In the warm golden rush that swam in Francis's head, what they did seemed right—almost noble. While Robert Frigging Cutler had his futile obsession with elevating Cedar Hole to the rest of Gilford County, the Pinkhams had a much better idea—knock everyone else down. A few whacks and things suddenly became a little less lopsided, a little more fair.

Georgie leaned halfway out of the car, with Jackie holding on to the cuff of her jeans to keep her from falling out the window. The leverage helped Georgie knock three boxes in a row right off their posts. "Here, Spud," she said, sliding breathlessly back into the car. She handed him the bat. "Your turn."

"Let him sit up front so I can guide him," Jackie said.

Georgie crawled over the seat and tumbled into the laps of her sisters, her squeal of pain dissolving into hysterical laughter. Francis slid head first down the front of the seat, planting his face into the vinyl. Jackie righted him by grabbing the scruff of his neck.

"Get ready," she said. "I think I see a good one."

Just as Francis started to pull himself out of the window, the flashing blue bubble of Palmdale police lights lit up the neighborhood.

"The pigs are out!" Billie hooted.

From the passenger-side mirror, Francis saw the police car's radiator and headlights gaining on the wagon's bumper. Charlie, Billie, and Georgie collectively slid down low in their seats.

Jackie pushed Francis's head to the floor. "Don't get up until I say so."

Cramped in the foot well, Francis hugged his knees to his chest. Jackie made another hard turn and the back of the wagon swung in a wide arc, smacking his head against the glove box. Sirens blared behind them and the blue lights flashed on the ceiling of the car as Jackie stomped the gas pedal all the way to the floor. Francis bit his teeth into the knees of his jeans, a countermeasure against the stinging in his eyes, and braced for one of the only two eventualities he could imagine; prison or death.

A jerky, guttural laugh broke from Jackie's throat and then the front end of the car seemed to rise up slightly, coming down hard in a bone-jarring thunk. Francis's front teeth hit his kneecap and upon impact seemed to be driven up inside his skull, but when he pressed the tips of his fingers to his mouth nothing seemed to be missing or misplaced. The sawing vibration that ripped up through the floorboards told him they were on a rougher surface. They had reached the town line.

"It's all clear," Jackie yelled to the girls in the backseat.

Francis sat up. He looked back at the line where Palmdale's smooth black top met Cedar Hole's craggy road and saw the police car turn around and head back toward town. Even after all the damage they had done, apparently they weren't worth the hassle of pursuit—all that seemed to matter was that they stayed on their side of the line. Jackie kept her foot hard on the gas, correcting for every fishtail the car made as its tires struggled to find friction on the loose gravel. They sailed over the railroad tracks, making Francis's stomach flip. As they landed, he stared down at the soft shoulder—only inches away from the tires—and the gully beyond.

"You barely made it out of there alive, Spud." Jackie reached over and tousled Francis's hair. She smiled then, a genuine smile that crept up into her eyes. He noticed that one of her bottom teeth was missing. He wondered if she lost it opening beer bottles the same way Georgie did.

"It was fun," he said, sinking back into his seat. He felt his defenses letting go and he closed his eyes for the first time in Jackie's presence, trusting that the days of sucker punches and headlocks were over.

"Don't go to sleep on us just yet," Jackie said. "You still haven't had your turn."

Francis opened his eyes. "You're not going back there—"

"We'll do it in Cedar Hole."

"But someone might recognize us."

"You think that lard-ass Harvey Comstock would do anything about it? Besides, everyone's either asleep or passed out in front of their TV sets right now." Jackie chucked her empty beer bottle out the window.

"Let's bust Miss Pratt's," Billie suggested.

Georgie shook her head. "We should go after Mrs. Higgins for all those times she kicked us out of the library."

Francis, however, had someone else in mind.

Monday night was probably the only night of the week that it was safe to play Pinkham baseball on Thornberry Lane. Shorty closed the diner on Mondays, so there was no fear of being spotted by one of the dishwashers hanging out back, and Hanson's biggest delivery day was Tuesday, making the back lot to the Superette empty.

As soon as Francis saw the Cutler mailbox, blood starting pumping fast into his limbs. He thought about Robert sleeping soundly in his bed, dreaming about puffy clouds or whatever sugary make-believe stuff rattled around in that abnormal brain of his. He thought about Miss Pratt's adoration, and the adoration of every teacher they'd ever had. He thought about luck, which was heaped on only a chosen few, leaving the rest to scratch the dirt. But mostly he thought about Anita underneath that umbrella, swallowed up before he even had a chance to get to her.

The mailbox was a small thing, a harmless thing. Francis brushed his fingers against the smooth bare patch in the center of the bat, where tomorrow his name would be burned. It was an act of justice in an unfair world.

"So you got a thing against Creepy Cutler?" Charlie called from the backseat. "What did he do to you?"

"He's alive, isn't that enough?" Billie snorted.

Jackie pulled up alongside the mailbox and put the wagon in park.

"I'll give you a free one—we'll just stay right here and you can pound on it all you want. Make it quick, though. Hit it hard."

Francis pulled himself out of the window and half sat on the edge for balance. His breath came short and shallow but the bat was a seamless extension of his arms—weighty, unyielding, powerful. He cocked his elbows and raised the bat to his ear, as though he were waiting for a pitch. When his grip was sure and his mind steady, he swung.

On the first try, the mailbox rejected his swing—the bat bounced off without making so much as a scratch. The recoil took Francis by surprise; he lost his grip and the bat dropped against the side of the wagon, leaving a dent in the door.

"Watch it!" Jackie yelled, pinching him on the back of his calf.

Billie laughed. "Way to go, champ."

"Give it another go," Jackie said. "But *hard* this time."

Heat burned Francis's neck and down his spine. The bat grew slick in his hands. He raised it again and swung, holding firm. This time he made a shallow impression on the top of the box, about the size of his fist.

"Not bad!" Jackie shouted. "I'd say that's a single."

Francis swung again. And again. The mailbox resisted even less the third time, and the fourth, and the fifth. The side of the box was caving in, the front and the back slanting up toward the sky, the door falling open and hanging by a single hinge. Francis grunted with each impact, his stomach fluttering as the metal surrendered to his power. He raised the bat overhead and bashed in the top of the box, the side, the front.

Jackie put the car into drive and they rolled forward, with Francis still hanging out the window and the bat fused to his hands. The air was chilling to his damp skin; his teeth began to chatter, his muscles twitched with nervous energy. He pictured Robert, on his way to school in the morning, stopping to look at the mangled wreckage of what was once his family's mailbox, his throbbing heart unable to comprehend such an act of violence. It made him laugh out loud.

"You just missed four boxes in a row!" Jackie shouted. "What are you waiting for? Swing!"

Francis swung, scoring a double and triple, respectively, to the cheers of his sisters. Jackie turned toward the train depot and Francis hit every box down one side of Elm and halfway up the other.

"You knocked that one clean off!" Georgie said.

With every swing of the bat his blows grew more vicious and random until he was swinging wildly, blindly.

"Feels good, don't it?" Jackie slowed the car. "Look at that one up ahead. Would you get a load of that?" Had Francis not been so high on adrenaline, he might have been conscious of the fact that his joy was already fading, long before he saw the mailbox. Somehow he had managed to ignore this eventuality by tucking it in some inaccessible recess of his mind, but here they were. Right in front of Mr. Mullen's house.

"I've never seen a barn one before," Charlie said, staring out the window. "It has cows, chickens, everything."

Georgie leaned over her sister's lap to get a good look. "It looks like someone painted it by hand. They did a real pretty job."

"That's nothing," Jackie snorted. "I could do that blindfolded."

Francis pulled himself back through the window and into the passenger's seat. "Man, Jackie, I am so beat. Let's call it."

"Get this last one and we'll go home."

"Why don't we just go home now? I've hit my share." He panted hard and threw his head back against the seat. "It was real fun, though. Thanks for taking me along."

"What's your problem?" Jackie watched him for a long moment, then narrowed her eyes. "Is the box too pretty?"

Charlie, Georgie, and Billie were silent now. The fun they'd all been having just a few minutes before seemed so distant it was as if it had never happened. Francis felt himself oozing, sliding back down to resume his place at the bottom of the Pinkham dung heap.

"I don't want to do it," he said. "Let's just go."

Jackie backed up the car. "One more, Spud. Then we can go."

"I'm done."

She picked the bat off the floor and handed it to him. "I *said* one more."

Francis looked at the mailbox and swore to himself, wishing Mr. Mullen had let him bring it inside the house. Aside from the weather-beaten paint that was flaking off in patches, a few nails had been working loose over time and the whole structure of the box leaned slightly, like a real barn on the verge of collapse.

Jackie backed up the car and steered close to the edge of the street. Francis's stomach lurched.

"The other boxes aren't a big deal 'cause they can go and get another one at the hardware store no sweat," Francis pleaded. "But this one's one-of-a-kind. It wouldn't be fair to wreck it."

"What's the big deal? It's just a crummy mailbox—those chickens look more like pigeons, if you ask me," Billie said. She kicked the back of his seat so hard that he felt the force of it in his kidneys.

"It's falling apart anyway," Jackie said. "Seems to me we'd be doing them a favor. You could just blow on it and the thing would fall over."

Francis spoke up again, this time with a softer voice. "Just because it looks bad to us doesn't mean they don't like it."

Jackie put the car in park and gunned the engine. "Are you going to sit around all night telling me how pretty it is or are you going to get out there and hit it?"

"Come on, Spud. Hit it and we'll put your name on the bat tomorrow," Charlie said.

Francis slumped against the seat. "Please don't make me do this."

"I would just sideswipe it," Jackie said. "Give it a good tap and it should go down."

A groan buzzed from his throat all the way down to his belly as Francis took his perch on the edge of the car door. He wanted it over. Quick.

Jackie put the car in gear and hit the gas. Francis held the bat up to his ear and watched as the mailbox came into sharper and sharper focus. There was time enough, it seemed, to study every paint stroke, to recount every piece of mail he had brought in and remember every loving word Mr. Mullen had said about his son. Francis's throat burned hot and dry and the car's engine roared in his ear. When he was close enough to see the eyes of the cow, he swung.

The bat remained level until the last possible second, when its weight, responding to the apprehension in Francis's heart and hands, surrendered to gravity. The swing dipped suddenly, scooping the air beneath the mailbox and missing it completely. Francis's eyes bulged as he caught his breath.

Jackie slammed on the brakes. Francis lurched and gripped the window molding to stop himself from tumbling down onto the pavement.

Jackie grabbed the belt loop on the back of his jeans and jerked him back into the car.

"What the hell was that?" she yelled.

He shrugged. "I missed."

"You are such a waste." She backed up the car to its original starting position. "You'd better hit it this time."

"Jackie—"

"What? Are you a pussy?"

"Francis the pussy," Billie sang. "He loves fancy mailboxes with cows and pigeons."

"SHUT UP!" he yelled. The backseat fell dead silent.

Jackie glared at him, her voice low and cold. "How'd you get so damn soft, Spud? I thought you were supposed to be a tough guy—you little snot, you punk. No wonder Dad never talks to you. His only son is a big, fucking pansy freak."

Francis clenched his jaw until he felt the throb of his head leak down into the roots of his teeth. Silently, he hoisted himself out the car window and sat on the ledge, the bat cocked and ready behind his ear, his heart hardened against what he was about to do.

"This is your last chance," she said. "You'd better make it good."

This time, when Jackie stepped on the gas, Francis held firm. The mailbox dissolved into a bleary patchwork of gray, indistinguishable from the rest of the passing landscape. He gave the bat a clean swing and closed his eyes to imminent disgrace.

∽ Chapter Four ∽

The MOUSE SUSPECTS HE MIGHT BE *a* DINK

Jackie burst into Francis's room the next morning and presented the bat as though she were awarding him a polished bowling trophy. "There you go, Spud. You can keep it for a week, but after that it's mine."

He'd expected her to burn his name in the middle of the bat, in the blank space that his sisters' names orbited; the space he had assumed was his birthright. Instead she'd put it on the handle, in small, tight letters, away from everyone else's. Francis ran his thumb along the dark grooves of the engraving, his stomach a sour mixture of accomplishment and nausea.

"You spelled my name wrong," he said, holding up the bat for her to see. "You forgot the 'S.'"

"Right—PUD," Jackie laughed. "My burning tool has a short in it. It conked out before I was done."

"But it's the first letter."

"I like to burn backward—is that a problem, twit? Give me the damn thing and I'll fix it." Jackie jerked the bat out of his hands. With an angry grunt, she dove into his closet and helped herself to a brand-new thermal undershirt Francis's mother had bought him for school. She examined the tag with the name SPUD written in permanent marker and shrugged. "I'm going to borrow this for a couple of days."

Francis let her take it, knowing full well there would be a drought in Cedar Hole before he ever saw that shirt again.

"Jackie! Come downstairs, please," Franny called. "Officer Comstock's here and he'd like to have a word with you."

"Shit." Jackie tied the shirt around her waist and threw open the window. "Tell her I left a while ago," she said, popping out the screen.

Francis watched as she swung one leg out onto the roof, then the other. "If you run, he'll know we did it."

"That idiot doesn't know nothing."

"Probably not—but it'll look bad," Francis said. "Just talk to him."

Jackie groaned and swung her legs back inside. "If he takes me away, I'll tell him you were there, too."

"Jackie!" Franny called again. "He's waiting!"

"Shut your trap!" she hollered back. "I'm coming down, dammit!"

Francis listened for Jackie's lumbering boots to smack the downstairs floor before he followed, taking a seat on the fourth step down from the top of the staircase. If he angled his body tight against the banister, he could see through the hall to the front door, where Officer Comstock stood.

"Good morning, Miss Pinkham," he said.

"I don't see nothing good about it."

"Jackie—don't be rude," Franny scolded. "I'm sorry, Harvey."

"That's all right. I know the sight of a uniformed officer can bother some people," he said.

"It don't bother me none," Jackie said. "I could break you over my knee like a twig."

"Jackie! Honestly, she is so grouchy in the morning."

Harvey laughed, but from where Francis was sitting, it looked like his smile was tight.

"If you don't mind, Mrs. Pinkham, I'd like to talk to your daughter alone. It's procedure."

Franny hesitated. "If you could just tell me what the problem is—"

"Some mailboxes around town were busted last night. Jackie knows a lot of people, and I was wondering if she heard any talk about who could have done it."

Franny turned to Jackie. "Do you know anything about this?"

"Buzz off, Ma. He wants to talk to me."

"You watch your mouth." Franny's voice was strained. "We have a guest."

"I didn't ask him over."

Franny wiped her hands on the front of her apron. "I'll be in the kitchen. If she gives you any trouble, Harvey, you let me know."

"I don't suspect she will," he said, taking a notebook from his belt.

Francis pressed his face against the spindles and watched his mother withdraw. Jackie widened her stance; the spread between her feet was as broad as her shoulders. Her arms bowed out from her sides as a large intake of air broadened her back, puffing her into a menacing balloon. Officer Comstock took a noticeable step back toward the door.

"You look tired, Jackie. Out late last night?"

"Why do you care?"

He tipped his hat back and sighed. "Someone saw a wagon that looks just like yours riding around town busting mailboxes, that's why. Got a report from Palmdale saying the same thing was happening over there."

"I ain't the only one with a car like that."

"Given your history of mischief, you can understand why I thought of checking with you first. Who was with you?"

Jackie took a step toward him, her hands pumping into fists. "Are you trying to be tricky? I didn't SAY I was OUT."

"Lower your voice, please."

"Is everything all right, Harvey?" Franny called from the kitchen.

"We're fine, Mrs. Pinkham." The tips of Officer Comstock's ears turned scarlet. His voice dropped so low that Francis had to strain to hear. "Look, I've let you go on a bunch of things, Jackie, but this time people are upset. I gotta give them something."

Francis's throat ached. Tears came the moment he imagined Mr. Mullen waking up to find his mailbox smashed off its post, his eyes squinting in disbelief, his voice panicked and shaky as he called to his wife. Francis wiped his eyes on the sleeve of his T-shirt and rested his head against his arm. His head was too full. As soon as they got home last night he bolted from the car and got sick behind the barn, gutted with shame and the thought of Mr. Mullen finding out. In between spasms, Francis had stretched out in the cool grass, and as the pain in his stomach eased he noticed a light, mortifying flicker of pride. It was confusing and contrary but unmistakably present, fueled by the echoing cheers of his sisters and the residual smart of Jackie's congratulatory smack.

"You need to own up to this one," Officer Comstock was saying. "I'm not going to send you to jail or anything like that. I won't even put it on your record. Not that I couldn't do it, I'm just giving you my word I won't. Say you're sorry to the people and pay for the mailboxes and we'll call it even."

Francis's stomach turned again and he pressed his mouth hard against his arm, taking in fast, shallow wisps of air through his nose. Jackie said nothing, rocking from one foot to the other as if she were weighing her options.

"Did anyone see me break those boxes?"

"I know you did it. Or maybe your sisters did, but you're their ring-leader and I'm holding you responsible," he said. "You can't go around doing whatever you want to other people's property. I know it was you who spray-painted the side of the school gym last year and scratched up the benches outside the library. You don't think I'm smart enough to fig-ure it out, but I know."

"You sure are some detective, Harvey. What gave it away—the fact that I painted my *name*?"

"All I'm saying is, it's one thing to mess up things around town, and it's another to wreck stuff that belongs to people. I can't let it slide—peo-ple are asking questions."

Jackie crossed her arms. "If no one saw me do it, then I didn't do it."

"I told you what you need to do. If you're not going to play nice, I'll take you in and we can sort this out another way."

"It's not my job to cover your ass, Harvey."

He hooked his thumbs through his belt. "Watch yourself, now."

"If you'd been watching over things like you're supposed to, you would have saw who did it—but you were probably out by the landfill, boning Delia Pratt in your squad car like always."

Officer Comstock's lips twitched. Francis forgot the knot in his stomach as he watched purple-red roses blossom on the policeman's cheeks. "Careful, young lady. I can still arrest you if I want to."

"Don't you even try it." Jackie took a step toward him. "You know I'll make you sorry."

Harvey shrank back across the threshold. He flipped his notebook closed and tucked it into his belt. "I might be able to hold them off this time, but people remember. You can only let things slide so long."

"Nobody has a better memory than me, Harvey."

SINCE scandal was rare at Cedar Hole High School, most rumors were born purely from fiction. If a story had contained even the smallest speck of reality it might have come alive, but without any truth at all a rumor made only an anemic ripple through the student population before petering out. One can only imagine the excitement, then, as two full-blooded rumors made the rounds on the exact same day. And no one was more pleased about it than Francis Pinkham.

"Did you hear about the mailboxes all over town?" Candace Montgomery wheezed, having just returned to school after a lengthy bout of mono.

Francis bristled. "Yeah, I heard something about it," he said, opening his locker.

"I heard that Officer Comstock knows who did it."

Hot alarm raced up his scalp. "Oh yeah?"

Candace nodded damply. "It was a bunch of football players from Palmdale High. It's a threat for the football game on Saturday."

As relief swept over him, Francis started to laugh, despite the quizzical look on Candace's face. Henny and Allen came out of the boys' bathroom and joined them outside home room.

"What's so funny?" Allen said.

"I was telling Spud about the football players smashing mailboxes, and he thinks it's funny," Candace said. "Our team's talking about going up to Palmdale and smashing their boxes the night before the game."

Allen sneered. "Who cares about that crap?"

Candace gave Allen a sulky sniffle and turned on her heel.

Henny leaned against the bank of gray lockers and stared at Francis, wide-eyed. "Did you hear about Robert's dad?"

"No—what?"

"He took off."

Francis swallowed hard. "What do you mean, he took off?"

"For California, in the middle of the night. Robert drove him so crazy talking all the time that instead of killing him, he just took off."

"He tried to strangle him before," Allen said with authority. "Two times."

"He'd already been in jail once—for murder," Henny added. "He said he didn't want to go back."

"No way."

Henny crossed his fingers over his heart. "I swear—it's true."

Despite the fact that the mailbox rumor was totally false, Francis wanted to believe that maybe there was justice in the world and that this was Robert's payback for unfairly winning the rodeo. The crowd of students in the hallway waiting for the morning bell suddenly parted and Robert ambled his way through, books hugged tightly to his chest, his face uncharacteristically sullen. The boys stared at him as he trudged by.

"See?" Henny whispered as he passed. "I told you it was true."

Francis was overwhelmed. The timing of both stories struck him as more than a coincidence, until he had almost convinced himself that with the bat he had indeed restored nature's balance. Though he would voice his theory to no one—not even Henny or Allen, whom he hadn't even told the truth about the mailboxes—Francis wondered if he had indeed turned fate's approving eye away from Robert and directed it toward himself instead.

Nearly convinced that Luck was now beginning to intervene on his behalf, Francis walked into algebra class confident enough to again tap Anita on the back.

She glanced at him over her shoulder. "What's up, Spud?"

"I wanted to ask you something."

"I don't show my homework around, if that's what you want to know."

"No—no—" he stammered. His stomach caved. "It's not that. I was wondering if you were going to the football game Saturday."

"Do you need a ride? We have plenty of room."

"Actually, I was wondering if you wanted to go with me."

"Yeah, okay."

Francis's mouth went dry; his tongue made an embarrassing clucking noise as he peeled it off the roof of his mouth. "You sure?"

Anita laughed. "Yeah, I'm sure."

"What about Robbie—do you think he'll mind?"

"Why would he?"

"I thought you two were going out."

She smiled and wrinkled her nose. "What made you think that?"

"Well, I saw you two walking together a few days after the rodeo."

Anita dropped her pencil and turned to look directly at him. "You know, I didn't think that was fair at all. The rodeo I mean. You finished first—you should have won."

AT THE GAME, Francis bought Anita a bag of cotton candy with some of the money Mr. Mullen had given him. They ate it while watching from the sidelines, the drizzly rain melting the fluff on contact, studding it with dark pink speckles. At halftime they found shelter by sitting cross-legged underneath the bleachers, knees touching. It was there that he told Anita the origin of his nickname. He had expected her to laugh, but she didn't.

"Do you like it?" she asked.

"I don't know. I haven't really thought that hard about it."

"But it's kind of mean, don't you think?"

He shrugged. "It's just a name."

Anita reached out and touched the back of his neck, her fingers sticky from the candy, the inside of her elbow smelling of sugar and talcum powder. "From now on I think I'll just call you Francis."

Francis put his own hand behind her neck in a sort of awkward imitation and they sat like that for a long time, while bits of popcorn and paper napkins rained down on them from the seats above. He was afraid to breathe, afraid that if he moved Anita might take her hand away, or worse, snap out of whatever hallucination she was having that made her want to be with him. He looked down at the ground, afraid she'd somehow see through him. He didn't want her to know he was weak enough to be bullied by his sisters and spineless enough to do whatever horrible thing they asked.

One afternoon, after school, Francis brought Anita to the train depot. It had been years since he'd returned, though the plywood was just as loose as he remembered, and except for a few bottles of beer on the floor, the rest of the place seemed largely undisturbed. They chased each other around the waiting room with rubber stamps, trying to give each other ink marks.

When they were tired of running, Anita sat on his lap and nestled herself against him, the faint tang of salt rising off the hollow of her throat. "Have you ever been on a train?" she asked.

"Never."

"My aunt used to take me into the city once a year for my birthday. We'd go to see a show and then have tea." Anita spoke of the outing plainly, as though it were something everyone did, something even Francis could do if he wanted. He loved her faith in him, her blind assumption that even though she was from a small family and had spent most of her childhood in Palmdale, they were not all that different. But they were. Anita didn't know what it was like to sleep in a pantry or to have your sisters pummel you for looking at them the wrong way or to have to write your name on your belongings to keep them from being stolen— but she had known her share of trouble. Her father had been a resident at Mt. Etna General when a patient died while he was drawing blood. While it was later determined that he was not negligent, Dr. Reynolds was nevertheless fined and transferred to Cedar Hole Family Practice. Even though he eventually fulfilled his dream of becoming a doctor, the pay wasn't nearly as good and the family had to sell their white-columned Palmdale house for a Cedar Hole split-level.

"I loved tea," Anita said. "The cups were real china, trimmed in gold and almost as thin as eggshells. I remember sipping carefully, hardly touching my lips to the rim because I was scared I might press too hard and break it."

"What's the city like?"

"You've never been?"

"Why would I? My parents don't go anywhere."

Anita leaned her head against his shoulder. "It's great. There's always something to do—not like here."

"Henny says that city people will smile at you right in the face while they pick your pocket clean. All you have to do is ask the wrong person for directions and you can get kidnapped."

"That's not true!"

"It happened to one of his cousin's friends."

Anita shook her head. "I don't believe that for a minute. Has he ever been to the city?"

"I don't think so." Francis held her tight against him, trying to keep her warm from the damp air that whistled between the cracks in the plywood.

"Most people who say things like that have never been there. They don't know what it's really like," she said. "People are so afraid of anything different. When I first moved here, hardly anyone talked to me."

"I'm not afraid," Francis said. "I can't wait to leave here."

"We're the same, aren't we?"

Francis opened the desk drawer and took out a felt-tip pen. The nib was dry and brittle, but he moistened it with a few drops of rainwater that had collected in the brass pass-through underneath the ticket window. "Give me your hand."

She opened her fist to him without so much as a word or a questioning glance. Francis kissed her palm. He pressed the tip of the pen against her hand and wrote, in clear block letters, SPUD.

IT WAS Francis's budding romance with Anita and his overwhelming guilt about the mailbox that kept him away from Mr. Mullen for as long as possible. He waited until the lawn took on the same wild tangle it had the first time he visited and would have liked to stay away forever, but every time he passed by the house and saw the box missing from its post and a few errant splinters on the sidewalk, his chest clenched so tight he thought he was being strangled from the inside out. He missed the steady, patient drag of Mrs. Mullen's feet across the kitchen floorboards as she carried her tray to the living room. He missed Mr. Mullen's firm grasp of the workings of Cedar Hole and the world in general, and his desire to share them. He missed the tingle that danced up and down his arms after several hours of mowing, the velvet sheen of the grass after it had been cut down to one uniform height, and the feeling of having money in his pocket for doing something worthwhile. And when the longings finally bore down harder than the guilt, Francis walked up the steep driveway to the barn, wheeled out the old Toro, and mowed the lawn.

When he cut the engine, Mrs. Mullen was standing at the screen door, waving for him to come inside. Francis wondered how long she'd been standing there watching him.

"Walter wants to see you," she said.

Francis took a bandanna from the back pocket of his jeans, wiped down his hot neck and forehead, and kicked off his grass-stained sneakers next to the hall tree by the front door. It was approaching suppertime, and the kitchen smelled of roasting chicken. Mrs. Mullen, who had barely made it to the kitchen by the time Francis was inside, did not greet him but turned her focus instead to the table and the two place settings she was arranging.

Francis teetered in the living room doorway, suddenly unsure of his place. He had strode into that room hundreds of times before, seating himself on the old brocade couch as easily if it were his very own, but this time he felt as though he were intruding.

"Did you get up close to the side of the barn?" Mr. Mullen's beard had grown in a little more than its usual prickly stubble, looking as soft as white feathers. "The weeds were getting pretty tall." His gray eyes latched on to Francis in a way that terrified him.

Francis looked away. "Yeah, I got 'em," he answered, then fell silent. The missing mailbox out front was a conspicuous topic of conversation and his failure to mention it seemed to Francis to be as good as a full-blown confession. He couldn't ask what had happened to it because he already knew, and all other angles he turned over in his mind to prompt Mr. Mullen into talking about it would require some form of acting Francis was simply not capable of.

"It looks like it might rain later tonight," Francis finally said, leaning back against the wall.

"What's the weather to you? You're young—you've got other things to think about."

"I'm thinking I might have to mow twice this week."

Mr. Mullen pulled a handkerchief from his back pocket and blew his nose with a high-pitched snort that Francis thought rivaled the Toro when she hit a particularly thick tuft of crabgrass. "Are you going sit down or are you just going to stand there holding up the wall?"

Francis shuffled across the room and sat on the couch. He kept his feet flat on the floor and his hands on his knees.

"How are things with your girl?"

"Pretty good, I guess." The mere mention of Anita eased the pressure building in his temples. "She's real sweet."

"Well, that's good. A good woman will keep you on the straight path," Mr. Mullen said, nodding. "You see her every day?"

"Practically." Through the doorway he could see the cat clock in the kitchen, with its eyes and tail shifting in relentless rhythm, his heart thumping double-time in between the beats. In a sort of masochistic penance he forced himself to look at the photograph of Jasper on the wall right next to the clock. The soldier seemed so much younger to him now, not a man but a kid like himself. The heavy look in his eyes had no connection to the broad smile on his face. For the first time, Francis could see that he was frightened.

A tickle ran up the back of his throat and his eyes stung. "I'm sorry about letting the grass go so long," he said with a hard swallow. There was relief in saying sorry, even if it was for the wrong reason.

Mr. Mullen nodded slowly. "You've got bigger concerns now. More on your mind."

"It's not like I forgot about it—I could see it growing every time I walked by—but I kept putting it off, you know?"

"If you didn't get to it, the winter would have killed it eventually," he said. "The point is, you cut it. There's not a lot of sense in fretting about something that's over and done with."

Francis pinched the smooth skin of his inner cheek between his teeth and bit down until he tasted the tinny flavor of blood. "Right."

"I think it's time you forgot about the lawn, anyway. You need to spend more time with people your own age. I hired a landscaper from Mt. Etna—an old friend of my son's—who's going to start coming once a week."

"You didn't have to do that," he squeaked. "I can keep mowing for you. Really. I don't mind at all."

"I think we both know, Francis, that it's time you moved on." Mr. Mullen leafed through his wallet and pulled out a twenty-dollar bill. "I still owe you half for last time, plus there's a little extra in there for your girl."

Mr. Mullen held out the money, but Francis didn't take it. "I can do other things besides mowing, you know," he said, his voice thickening. "If there's anything you have that needs fixing—"

"You'll be good, won't you? And stay out of trouble?"

Francis nodded. With limp resignation, he took the money.

Mr. Mullen raised a frail hand and patted him roughly on the shoulder. "Go on, now."

Francis made his way to the front door by memory rather than sight, his vision having become a limpid blur. He made it as far as the hall tree, where Mr. Mullen's musty windbreaker hung, before he felt the firm grip of bony fingers on his wrist. He smiled at Mrs. Mullen with a wilting embarrassment, and wiped his eyes with the shoulder of his T-shirt.

"Take this with you," she said, pressing a piece of wax-paper-wrapped gingerbread into his hand. Gently, she touched his cheek. "My boy."

He nodded. When she finally turned away, Francis slipped the twenty-dollar bill into the pocket of Mr. Mullen's jacket, and left.

~ Chapter Five ~

The INTERVIEW

It wasn't the silence that clued Sissy Cutler in to her husband's departure. All summer long, Will's morning sounds—the tramping of steel-toed boots across the kitchen floor, the clang of the cast-iron fry pan against the stovetop, the bugle buzz of his nose blowing into a handkerchief—had grown so infrequent that the few times he *was* home, the mere sound of him clearing his throat was enough to make her jump clear out of her smock. Nevertheless, when Sissy awoke the morning after Will left to find his fortune in Florida, there was an uncomfortable stillness that had curled itself at the foot of her door. She opened her eyes to the sly intruder and noticed that her radio was gone. It was then that she realized beyond all doubt that Will had left for good.

Sissy's face was red and swollen when Robert brought in her breakfast tray. "What else did he take?"

"Just some clothes. Some food."

"My cookies—he didn't take those cookies up in the cupboard, did he? You know how I love my cookies with a nice cup of tea."

"I don't think so, but if he did I can get you more."

"My radio," she sobbed. "He wanted to get me and he got me good."

Robert sat down on the green vinyl hassock at his mother's feet. "Maybe he knew he was going to miss you, so he wanted to have something to remember you by."

This quieted Sissy. She took a bite of toast. "Do you think he'll be back in a few weeks?"

"Anything is possible."

"You're such a good boy. I don't know what I'd do without you." Sissy smiled through a sniffle. "You're not going to leave me, too, are you?"

"Where would I go?"

"To find your father. Or away to college."

At the tender age of fourteen, when others, like Francis, were beginning to dream of their eventual exodus from town, Robert had no such inclination. Although he had the temperament to become a great traveler (owing to his compassionate nature and easy way with people), he did not desire a wide, scattered sampling of life across the globe; to him it was much more appealing to know one place as intimately as possible, perhaps better than anyone else ever could. Do not misunderstand— Robert was not one of those small-town people who spend their entire lives with their noses pressed up against the world, near enough to see some of its texture and color, but far too close to have any sense of its scale and scope. No, Robert had a fair grasp of life beyond Cedar Hole through his reading and discussions with Mrs. Higgins. He might not have seen what he was missing, but he certainly understood it.

"I'm not going anywhere, Ma." Robert propped pillows behind his mother's back to help her sit upright. "Don't worry."

Sissy pulled him to her bosom and hugged him tight. "It's so quiet in here without the radio," she said, her voice vibrating through her chest. "Robbie, be a good boy and sing us a song."

ROBERT had no opinion one way or another about his father leaving; it was, to his mind, just something that happened. He did not believe for a moment, as a lesser developed child might have, that he was in any way to blame for his father's departure, since, aside from paying the household bills, Robert had never required anything of him. Likewise, he did not blame his mother for pushing her husband away, for he was too young to understand the dynamics of marriage and had no concept of emotional abandonment. More importantly, though, Robert did not hold a grudge against his father. It seemed to him that Will was a troubled soul, and if an opportunity for happiness existed elsewhere, then he should follow it.

This is not to say that Will's absence didn't cause hardship. In the weeks following his departure, the cupboards slowly emptied, Sissy needed a new radio, and the electric company threatened twice to cut off the power. It was these problems for which Robert felt responsible.

"Maybe you could take a little time off from school," Sissy suggested. "Just until we get on our feet. I could probably get you an appointment with the head of stitching at Wear-Tex," she said. "You'd make a fine stitcher. It's in your blood."

WHEN ROBERT mentioned the appointment to Mrs. Higgins, Kitty's face turned red and her fingers anxiously kneaded the sleeves of her cardigan. "You are NOT going there," she said, loading her typewriter with a crisp sheet of paper. "Do you hear me?"

"I have to take care of her."

"She's supposed to take care of YOU," Kitty said, punching the keys. When she was finished with the letter, she sealed it in an envelope. "Give this to your mother."

Robert delivered the letter to his mother that evening, and although he had not read it, the wording was apparently so curt that Sissy began to cry. "She's right. You never mind what I said about the appointment, Robbie."

"I'll do whatever you want."

"You stay in school for now."

At the not-so-gentle suggestion of Kitty Higgins, Sissy took the appointment herself. When she emerged from the sanctuary of her stuffy little room, she was alarmed to discover that she had to turn her body slightly to the side to fit through the doorway. The kitchen seemed cavernous by comparison—exposed and overwhelming. Robert ran a hot bath (her first proper bath since his birth) and washed her Wear-Tex smock, while Sissy slowly made her way through the house, staying close to the walls.

Seeing the old factory for the first time in nearly fifteen years did not fill Sissy with the feeling of dread that she had imagined. The smells of bleached cotton and machine oil brought her right back to the comfort of her girlhood and to Will, with his quiet ways and promise of adventure.

"They used to call me 'Sissy Slow-Hands,' " she told the supervisor, her cheeks rosy with pride. "It was a joke because I could stitch so fast. Four shirts a minute."

"With the new machines we have now, we can go twice that fast," he said. "Who gave you that smock?"

"It's mine from when I worked here before."

"Right," he said, making notes on his clipboard. "That's an old logo. If we hire you, you're going to have to wear one of the newer ones, in a better-fitting size."

Sissy tugged at the edges of her smock, straining to pull the front snaps toward each other. She managed to bring them a full three inches closer, but as soon as she took a seat in front of the sewing machine the smock sprang open again, thrusting forward her voluminous belly.

After briefing Sissy on the new features of the machine, the foreman took a step back. "Show me what you can do."

It came back to her with startling ease. She remembered not with her mind but with her hands. One . . . two . . . three . . . shirts zipped through her machine with an effortless grace.

"Very nice," the foreman said, examining her stitches. "A little crooked, but quick."

Sissy beamed. Four . . . five . . . if only Robbie could see her now! Or even Will. She knew he'd be sorry for taking her radio, for making her walk halfway across the house for a box of chocolates. Six . . . she knew he'd be proud. He'd be sorry he left.

On the seventh shirt, the thread ran out. "Do you know what to do?" the foreman asked.

Sissy nodded. Threading was something she had done thousands of times, and the girls on her shift looked forward to it as a welcome break from repetition. She opened the small narrow drawer beneath the machine where a supply of thread spools and spare needles was kept, along with a laminated diagram showing how to thread the machine. Sissy took to the task quickly, guiding the thread through an obstacle course of hooks, loops, and springs.

"You seem to remember a lot," the foreman said, making more notes on his clipboard. "That's good."

At the very last was the eye of the needle. Sissy leaned in close to the machine and closed one eye as she attempted to feed the thread through the tiny hole. In her youth, her fingers were thin and nimble and could complete the delicate procedure in one try. But now, after years of TV dinners and copious amounts of rest, her fingers had swelled blunt and thick. Sissy's neck flushed red—the creases between the folds paled to a stark white.

"Is there a problem?"

Sissy shook her head and licked the end of the thread, twirling it to a tight point. She tried to pass the thread through again and again, her fingers becoming slicker and more awkward with each successive attempt. She blinked hard, yearning for the cocoon of her bed and the murmur of her old radio.

The foreman leaned in closer. "If this is going to be a problem . . . Well, it just can't be a problem."

Sissy pulled the thread out and aimed for the needle hole again, but the thickness of her fingers obscured the view. "Maybe some kind soul would be willing to thread it for me."

"I can't have people stop their machines to help you out," he said. "It will hold up the line too much. I'm sorry."

Sissy gathered her smock around her as best she could. "That's all right," she said, standing up to leave. "I'm tired, anyway. I think I'll go home now and take a nap."

As WORD spread to the far edges of Gilford County about Robert's unusual win at the Lawn Rodeo, he received a phone call from Mr. Holtz, the editor of the *Gilford Gazette*.

"I'll be straight with you, Robert," Mr. Holtz grunted into the phone. "I could give a hoot what you folks do down there in Cedar Hole, but I'm running short on space this week. Where can I meet you?"

"The finest place in town," Robert answered. "The library."

"And see if you can get that boy who placed second to be there, too."

When Kitty Higgins called Francis about the *Gazette* article, she said nothing about Robert—only that the editor asked to interview him about the rodeo. "Be sure to wear something clean," she said rather brusquely. "And leave your sisters at home."

Francis didn't even bother to ask the reason for the interview. In his mind, the answer was clear—someone had taken notice that he had been robbed of the win. Finally, there was a chance for justice. It is easy to imagine, then, the shock Francis felt when he stepped through the doors of the library, only to find the newspaper editor sitting at a reading table with Robert.

"Hi, Francis," Robert said with a cloying smile.

Mrs. Higgins took a nervous step forward and pulled out a chair for him. "Have a seat."

Mr. Holtz, who was jotting down notes on a yellow legal pad, hardly looked up. When he was done, he tugged at the belt of his high-waisted brown slacks. "You must be the runner-up."

Francis nodded.

"Speak up, Francis," Kitty said, hovering behind his seat.

"Yes."

"Mr. Cutler over here put on quite a show, didn't he?" Mr. Holtz said.

Francis was silent.

"Francis did really well, too," Robert added. "He beat out all the rest of the contestants."

"My name is Spud Pinkham," Francis said directly to Mr. Holtz. "Don't call me Francis."

"Spud? As in a potato?" Mr. Holtz gave Francis a skewed look, then jotted down the name on his pad.

Kitty cleared her throat. "Would anyone like some water? Or some cookies? I could run across the street."

No one acknowledged her, except for Robert. "I think we're all fine for now, Mrs. Higgins."

Inside, Francis fumed. His joints felt itchy, cramped, ready to bolt.

"So I take it you don't have an opinion on Mr. Cutler's performance."

"Oh, I have an opinion, all right," Francis said. "I think it stunk."

Kitty gripped his shoulder. "Francis, please! Mr. Holtz, I'm sorry—I should have warned you this was a bad idea. He comes from a rowdy family."

Robert paled, seemingly too stunned to speak. Mr. Holtz regarded Francis with suspicion. "I think we've got a sore loser here."

Indignation ached in his throat. "It was supposed to be based on time. He didn't follow the rules—"

"As I understand it, your Principal Nelson put the crowd to a vote and they were overwhelmingly in favor of Mr. Cutler," Mr. Holtz said. "Are you saying the whole town was wrong?"

"Yes," Francis blurted, knowing instinctively that what he was about to say would never make it to print. "They said one thing and they did something else."

"Honestly, Francis . . ." Kitty's voiced trailed.

Robert looked stricken. "I was only trying to do something different. If you think you should have the prize, Francis, I'd be happy to give it to you."

"No, you won't!" Kitty shouted. "You need that money to eat."

"Really," Robert insisted, "it's all right."

Francis sighed, his anger and indignation instantly diffused by Robert's senseless act of generosity. "Never mind," he said, heading for the door. "Just forget it."

~ Chapter Six ~

BIG NEWS

Mr. Holtz had been so impressed with Robert's deportment during the rodeo interview that shortly after he offered him a job at the newspaper. "I can't imagine anything worth a hoot goes on down there, but you seemed to be under the misconception that there is," he said. "Come up with five hundred words about something, *anything*, and maybe I'll make you my Cedar Hole correspondent."

The articles in the *Gazette* centered mainly on Palmdale and Mt. Etna, with a begrudging nod to outlying towns in a one-page section the paper called "Elsewhere." One half of the page was sold to advertisers, leaving just enough room for a list of calendar events and one short article of human interest that usually involved a Girl Scout cookie sale or a soapbox derby. Holtz's reporters had to be kicked, coaxed, and bribed to cover anything outside of the two major towns, often leaving Holtz scrambling to fill space. After Robert submitting a satisfactory article on Kitty Higgins, Mr. Holtz hired him on, assigning him to produce one article every six weeks.

"Too much happens in six weeks," Robert said, turning in a stack of articles on his first deadline. He defended his case with an appropriate amount of vigor but with no lack of respect. "I can't pick just one thing to cover."

"You don't have to," Mr. Holtz said. "I'm the editor. That's *my* job."

"You're doing the people of Cedar Hole a disservice. We need our own page."

Mr. Holtz thumbed through the stack. Somehow, Robert managed to dredge up enough material to start up a paper of his own, though much of it was pointless and, to Mr. Holtz, boring. "The Knights of Columbus had a bean supper on Saturday night—who in God's name cares?"

"Money was raised for a worthy charity—and Mrs. Kitty Higgins donated four of her delicious apple cakes."

"And that's another thing . . ." Holtz took his pen to Robert's neatly typed page. "Don't stick your opinion in where it doesn't belong. 'Mrs. Kitty Higgins donated four apple cakes,' period. Whether they were delicious or not is conjecture."

"I wasn't assuming—I had a piece and it was great."

"Keep it clean, Cutler," he sighed. "You can think that piss-hole town of yours is the best place on earth, but you can't put it in print."

Undaunted, Robert set out to prove to Mr. Holtz that Cedar Hole deserved its own weekly section and covered every possible happening he deemed newsworthy. He interviewed Hinckley Hanson, Miss Pratt, Principal Nelson, and even Shorty on how to make a proper milkshake. He spent a night in the Cedar Hole jail cell (much to the delight of Harvey Comstock) and declared the accommodations to be snug but quite comfortable. He learned about the finer points of library science from Kitty Higgins and even tried to interview his mother about her old days at Wear-Tex.

"What's the point, Robbie?" Sissy banished her smock to the back of her closet and had taken to drawing an old afghan around her shoulders for comfort instead. "That's all over with now."

"People should know what the factory was like back then. It provides context." He sat on the hassock near his mother's feet with Mr. Holtz's camera on his lap, listening to her labored breathing. Since her failed interview, Sissy's weight had ballooned to well over three hundred pounds.

"Find out from someone else."

"Your picture will be in the county paper."

Sissy pressed her hands to her face. "You're not taking my picture. I'll break the camera."

"We can take it together. You always said you wanted to get a camera and take pictures."

She shook her head.

"Come on," he said, tugging at the afghan. "You'll be famous."

"What do I care about being famous for? I've got no one to impress anymore."

"You never know," Robert said. "He might still come back."

"I wish that was true." Sissy sank deep against her pillow. "How do you always manage to stay on the bright side, Robbie?"

Robert didn't take his mother's picture but he did write the story, recalling bits she had previously told him and making up the rest to fill in the gaps. He handed in the story to Mr. Holtz along with five others, like he did every week.

"You can't have a whole page," Mr. Holtz sighed, after being sufficiently worn out by Robert's enthusiasm, "but I'll give you three inches on the back page next to the hot lunch menus. From now on, I only want to see one story a week or you're fired."

ANITA was four months pregnant when she graduated from high school. She and Francis married that spring at the county courthouse, with both Henny and Allen serving as best men. Francis would have preferred Henny to stand up for him alone (Allen's disapproval of the marriage was transparent; he openly referred to Anita as "the old ball and chain" and joked that instead of wedding rings, she ought to have SPUD branded on her "ample rump"), but Anita insisted Allen be there to spare any hard feelings. There were plenty of hard feelings on Francis's side, however, and though he grinned through all the jokes and teasing, he decided that his and Allen's friendship had finally run its course.

Anita's diplomacy included the maid of honor as well, choosing Larrie Jr. over her own sister as a way of extending herself toward the Pinkhams. Franny was pleased by the gesture, and so was Larrie Jr. (who marveled almost daily that Francis really was a heterosexual, and apparently potent), though Jackie was predictably pissed about it. Anita apologized for the oversight, saying she didn't think Jackie had any interest in wearing a robin's-egg-blue dress and a crown of daisies, and after giving it some thought, Jackie reluctantly conceded that Anita was right.

As a wedding gift, Anita's parents gave the couple a check big enough for the down payment on a leaky three-bedroom Cape at the bottom of a steep slope just off Webber Road. Larry Sr. had been pleased with his gift of a kitchen table and a set of four bow-back chairs—until he saw the Reynoldses' check—after which he blurted that a dining room set was also forthcoming, then spent the remainder of the year putting it together. Franny gave them a quilt in the Double Wedding Ring pattern, which she had been stitching by hand off and on for the last ten years, figuring that sooner or later at least one of the girls would eventually get married. So far, it had yet to happen, and with every passing year the possibility seemed more and more unlikely. The girls dated sporadically and with little interest—usually scaring off any potential beaus with their gruff manners and aggressive behavior. Larrie Jr., the most feminine one of the bunch, tended to snag the greatest number of prospects, though she had a flair for getting herself entangled with men who were otherwise spoken for.

Despite the girls' ambivalence toward love, they were nonetheless touched by Francis's marital union (or, at the very least, his moving out of the house and away from the family), and in a rare spirit of cooperative generosity, the sisters worked together to seal the leaks in the basement of the new house and paint the interior walls a fresh white.

"Don't think this was for free," Jackie told Francis. "You owe us a lot of meals to make up for this one."

Francis took a job delivering groceries for the Superette, which basically amounted to bringing TV dinners to shut-ins and tubes of hemorrhoid cream to people too embarrassed to pay for it in person. Arnie Hanson let Francis work solely for tips but gave him use of the Superette van as long as he paid for the gas and changed the oil. He supplemented his income by mowing lawns after cleaning up an old mower he found at a garage sale. The rains were heavy that year, and business was as abundant as the grass, which was growing so fast Francis swore he could almost see the blades straining up through the earth. It was good to smell the green, smoky mix of lawnmower exhaust and cut grass, to feel the lulling vibration of the motor humming in his bones. Francis charged his customers only slightly more than Mr. Mullen had paid him a few years back, not knowing that most Palmdale landscaping companies were charging double that price. Word got around and soon, between both jobs, he was making enough money to get by.

When school resumed in the fall, Francis told Anita that he would go back in October, after the first frost.

"There's no sense losing a month and a half of work," he told her. "We need the money."

"We need you to graduate," Anita said. Her belly was round and taut and so disproportionately large to her tiny frame that Francis often found himself trailing behind her, just in case she suddenly lost her balance and tumbled over.

"I'll make up the tests. A few weeks won't make any difference."

But as soon as the cutting season ended, Anita's due date was near. Francis decided to postpone school until the baby arrived.

ACCORDING TO THE DOCTOR, little Martin Pinkham came into the world not kicking and crying, but with a smirk. Francis couldn't tell if the doctor was kidding, exaggerating, or worse, being completely honest. If it was a joke, Francis didn't want the quack touching his son. If it was true—that little Marty had indeed entered the world with a grin instead of tears—Francis was terrified this meant his son was a dink.

"Relax—he's just fine," Franny told Francis. She had fallen instantly in love with her new grandson, experiencing for the first time the rush of joy a child can bring without the crushing burden of responsibility. "He's a beautiful, healthy boy."

The word 'boy' made Larry Sr.'s forehead wrinkle into an accordion. He spent a good portion of his hospital visit in the corridor, sulking. It was hard not to be at least mildly resentful that his teenage son had success right out of the starting gate.

"Boy, girl, it doesn't matter," Larry grumbled. "They'll both break your heart."

Francis couldn't imagine that someone so small and helpless, with Anita's soft mouth and big eyes, could ever break his heart. When they returned home, he took pride in having a quiet room for his son to sleep in, free of canned goods and the smell of vinegar. It wasn't until later, between piles of dirty diapers and hungry screams piercing his sleep, that Francis began to admit to himself that heartbreak was, at the very least, a possibility.

The teachers of Cedar Hole High welcomed Francis back to school in late November, right after Thanksgiving break. Had he lived in Palmdale or Mt. Etna, they wouldn't have let him back until the following year, noting that he had missed far too many tests and lessons to ever catch up before graduation. Though the Cedar Hole teachers felt no differently regarding Francis's ability to make up the work, they thought it would be entertaining to watch a Pinkham struggle (especially since he was already grappling with a shotgun marriage and new baby who, rumor had it, was mildly retarded) before ultimately collapsing under the stress.

At a meeting addressing this particular topic, the school secretary took bets as to how long Francis would last. "I give him a month, tops," she said.

Principal Nelson passed around a Cedar Hole Mules baseball cap to collect dollar bills. "I'll bring this over to the Left Hand Club tonight," he said. "We'll add it to the weekly pool."

Unaware of the opposition, Francis began to see school as a refuge. Though he loved Anita and the baby, it was hard not to favor the drone of a history lecture over the cries of a fickle baby, or the barking of a bitter old English teacher to Anita's hormonal shifts. Even the cafeteria, with its sticky, slop-house smell, was preferable to the sour tang of baby spit. And best of all, he still got to see his friends.

"You coming out with us tonight?" Henny asked while they waited in the lunch line. "We're going to the movies."

"Nah, I better stay home," Francis said. "Anita hasn't had much sleep."

Allen rolled his eyes. "Look at this guy—he's barely eighteen and his life's practically over."

Henny frowned. "Come on—he ain't got it so bad."

"I'm just saying. He's already married and has a kid. I mean, what else are you gonna do?" Allen took his comb out of his back pocket and ran it through the cowlick that sprang up in the middle of his bangs. "Me, on the other hand, I'm free. As soon as I save enough for a good set of tires, I'm heading out West."

"No, you're not," Henny said. "You'll wait 'til graduation."

"Maybe—maybe not. What I'm saying is, I can go anywhere I want. I'm free."

"I'm free, too," Francis finally piped up. "I mean, I'm with Anita and the baby, but we're not gonna stay around here forever. As soon as we save up enough, we're buying a house in Palmdale."

"You're going to have to mow a hell of a lot of lawns to get there, my friend."

Henny's girlfriend, Dixie, waved madly from the head of the lunch line for him to join her.

"I gotta go," Henny sighed. "See you in study hall."

Allen snickered as Henny trudged ahead and picked up a tray, silverware, and a carton of milk for her, while she stood by watching with her arms crossed and her long brown hair tossed over one shoulder.

"I say she breaks it off with him after New Year's. Come on, I'll bet you five bucks," Allen whispered. "January second."

"I don't have that kind of money to throw around."

He snickered. "That's 'cause you know I'm right."

Allen was sore, Francis knew, because he was a senior and he still didn't have a girlfriend. In Cedar Hole, most people found their mates in high school, and those who didn't had a fair shot at being single for the rest of their lives. Beneath Allen's swagger, Francis detected a very real panic mixed with honest bewilderment. It should have been easier for Allen; he had all the fundamental qualities girls were supposed to find attractive—confidence and wit, baby-blond hair and cornflower eyes, a square jaw and straight teeth. Even though, individually, the pieces were right, they seemed to come together all wrong. There was a hard set to his jaw that made it seem as though he were baring his teeth whenever he tried to smile, and his eyes, despite being a soft blue, were judgmental and slightly opaque. Even his humor was liberally sprinkled with sarcasm and mean-spiritedness, which only became heavier each time he was rejected.

"So, how much did you bet on me and Anita breaking up?"

Allen started to laugh but stopped short. "That's not a bad idea—I didn't think of that one."

"Like hell you didn't."

"You'll never leave her—you didn't have anything before her and you won't have anything without her. The one to watch out for is Anita. She's used to having better."

Francis had sense enough to know the mind-set this was coming from, but Allen still managed to snap the filament-thin tethers that held his sense of security in place. Had he not already felt shell-shocked from a lack of sleep, Francis was sure he would have defended his wife's loyalty, but his need to be with the guys precluded him from telling Allen what he really thought of his crackpot theories, his senior cockiness, and, for that matter, his overcoiffed hair.

At the front of the line, Henny was balancing a tray in each hand like a waiter, while Dixie gossiped with her circle of girlfriends.

"See how Dixie makes Henny dance? Eventually, Anita's going to do that to you, but not as bad," Allen said. "I mean, Anita's a better girl. She's not going to lead you by the nose just for the hell of it. But she's going to want things, and you're going to have to do the dance to keep her happy."

Francis shook his head. "It's probably that way with any girl."

"Sure, but it's worse with Palmdale girls. No matter how long they've been here, they'll always be Palmdale girls."

ROBERT continued to work at the *Gazette* through high school, and by his senior year, his articles caught the attention of the local colleges. Mt. Etna Community College offered him a full scholarship and Palmdale University gave him a large enough grant to get him through the first two years without having to get a job off-campus. Kitty Higgins was so excited that she became deaf to the normal library hullabaloo and let the troublemakers who were smearing their sweaty palms all over acid-sensitive book pages spend an extra two days entrenched between the stacks.

"If you think you can swing it, Palmdale U. is the better choice," she said, examining the course catalog. "You can study journalism—they even have internship programs at the city papers."

Robert didn't share in Mrs. Higgins's excitement. "Why would I study for something I'm already doing?"

"You can't work at the *Gazette* forever. Onward and upward."

"I like working there."

"Because you're comfortable. You need to challenge yourself." She closed the catalog and slid it across the desk toward him.

Robert stared at it, but didn't pick it up. "I want to stay and take care of her."

Kitty pressed her ink-stained fingers to her lips and swallowed hard, her eyes taking on a glassy sheen as though she might cry. "Please don't do this to me, Robert. All this time I've been grooming you for something better."

"She can't do anything for herself. I promised I'd stay."

"Commute to school, then. Or get a nurse."

"I'd still be gone all the time." Robert stared down at his hands as he said this, keenly aware of the proximity of Kitty's arm next to his own and the likely chance that she might brush against him by accident. "There are things I like here. Things I would miss."

"You don't even know what's out there for you."

But Robert held fast to his promise. Many years later, on a particular night when he would have been out celebrating his college graduation, he'd stand in front of the refrigerator at midnight, no more than a few steps from where he last saw his father, and hear an abrupt, strangulated sound coming from Sissy's room. Opening the door, he'd find her with the sheet tucked up under her chin and her lungs unnaturally still. Later, he'd tell Kitty that his mother had a placid look on her face—that he thought she even looked pleased. Dying suited her, Robert would think. It didn't seem to take any effort at all.

PART THREE

$\sim$ Chapter One $\sim$

BERNADETTE IGNORES HER BETTER JUDGMENT

Nadine Cutler's only true memory of her father was on the morning of his death, standing at the bathroom sink with toothpaste foam sliding down his chin. She had been three years old at the time, and despite repeated attempts to recall some earlier fragment of their history together, Nadine's mind was shut with uncompromising resistance. Everything that happened before was locked in the nebulous orb of memory; whenever she skimmed the surface she was inevitably led back to the same starting point. There was nothing but darkness—leaden, impenetrable—and then the sudden colorful burst of her little red step stool, the green of the fiberglass sink, the white vortex of water and foam as they tangoed down the drain.

He had been showing her how to brush her teeth.

"When you're done, spit out the toothpaste like this—" he mumbled, leaning over the sink.

While spitting might be a natural tendency for many toddlers, Nadine's instinct was to do the exact opposite. She remembered staring up at her father, cheeks puffed full of toothpaste foam, wavering between the desire to please her father and the impulse to swallow.

He sensed her struggle. "Let me show you again." With a fresh bead of paste, he brushed until he built up a considerable froth, then, opening his mouth, let the toothpaste cascade over his lower lip and down his chin. "See?"

Her father's foaming mouth reminded Nadine of Hoagie, the neighbor's basset hound, who ran around the yard with threads of saliva dripping from his jowls. The resemblance made her eyes water with laughter, her giggles muffled by a mouthful of toothpaste. He must have thought of the dog, too, for he stuck his tongue out and let it loll fatly out of his mouth, just like Hoagie.

"Don't hold it," he said. "Let it come out."

Nadine tilted her head forward and peeled her lips apart, waiting to see the foam fall into the sink. It was then that she remembered breathing, taking in air with a force that sucked the toothpaste back and down her throat, as cleanly as a vacuum hose.

"I'm sorry, Daddy," she said as he toweled her face.

"Not a problem, baby girl. We'll try again later."

He picked her up and carried her downstairs to the kitchen. Small and delicate for her age, Nadine preferred to be carried than to get around by her own power, fully willing to surrender control over her destination for the view it afforded her. From above, everything seemed kinder. The framed photo of Grammy Cutler at the top of the staircase came into sharp focus, her gaze tenderly meeting Nadine's instead of staring out into the ether floating over her head. The stairs, as they descended, rolled beneath them in a series of quiet undulations. She anchored her arm around the back of her father's neck, her cheek finding comfort in the shelter of his collarbone. He nuzzled the crown of her head.

Her mother, Bernadette, was standing at the sink scrubbing the breakfast dishes—or was she at the stove scrambling eggs? The action changed every time she thought of it, though its essence remained the same. Nadine seemed to remember a series of quick, agitated arm movements, the contagious burden of a heavy sigh.

"We need a glass of milk over here," he said.

Bernadette dropped either the spatula or the nylon scrubber—whichever it was that she had been holding—and glared at Nadine. "Did you swallow the toothpaste again?"

Nadine leaned into her father. His chin smelled of sugary mint.

"She gave it a real good try this time," he said. "We're getting there."

"Robert, if she doesn't get it right soon, I'm going to have to take her to the doctor." She poured some milk into a juice glass imprinted with sliced oranges. "I can't even get her to blow her nose. She keeps sucking it down."

"Give her a little more time. I'll pick up a bottle of soap bubbles while I'm in the city." He set Nadine down on a stool at the breakfast bar. "Maybe it'll get her to think *out* instead of *in.*"

A gust of wind lashed rain against the kitchen window. Outside, the old plum tree's branches whipped in the air. The house creaked and moaned. Nadine clutched at her father's arms and begged him to pick her up again.

"It's just the wind," he said, pulling away. "Drink your milk, baby girl."

Bernadette's voice was tight, her words clipped. "I still don't understand why you're doing this." She resumed her scrubbing or scrambling with violent fervor.

"She was counting on the new library. It's been an awful blow," he said. "She looks depressed."

"I understand that, but why do we have to be the ones to buy it?"

"If the Library Association's not going to do it, who will?"

Bernie pursed her lips. "She's done all right so far. Kitty's an efficient woman—I'm sure she'll figure out some way to get what she wants."

"Come on, Nadine. Drink your milk." He tilted the glass up to her lips.

That was as much as she could remember—the cacophonous tastes of milk and mint, the howl and slap of rain against the window, the unnecessary cup of her father's hand beneath her chin, poised to catch dribbles. There was a kiss and a hug and then he was gone.

EVERYTHING else Nadine knew of Robert J. Cutler had been told to her so frequently and from so many different sources that the memories played in her mind as vividly as if they were her own. People in Cedar Hole still talked about her father constantly, in reverential tones, even a decade after his death. They swapped stories and shook their heads, the loss of him apparently still fresh. A less well-adjusted person might have been bitter hearing about what a great man her father was—the greatest in Cedar Hole, by many accounts—considering that she would never experience such greatness firsthand. But Nadine was her father's daughter, if not by direct example, then at least by genetics, and therefore felt nothing but gratitude for any scrap of him anyone was kind enough to offer. It was better to remember her father by proxy, Nadine decided, than to be forever stuck with the single image of toothpaste foam rolling down his chin.

"Your father had great potential," Kitty Higgins often told her. "He was too good for this place."

"But he liked it here," Nadine said.

"He *made* himself like it. He saw a rotten situation and made the best of it. It's not wise to sacrifice your life to please others." Kitty didn't seem aware of the irony of her words. Somehow, it seemed to completely escape her that in the end Robert *had* sacrificed himself, in the most literal sense, for her. "I hope you'll do better than he did."

Nadine relayed Kitty's comments to Bernadette. "I wish you wouldn't listen to that nitwit—but she does have a point. He stayed around for his mother, and after she died, he was so comfortable he never bothered to go anywhere else. *That* was his big mistake," she said. "Why did he have to stick around here and ruin everything?"

"But if Dad had gone away, you two never would have met."

"That's precisely what I'm talking about."

If Bernie Cutler hurt Nadine's feelings by inadvertently suggesting her daughter's existence was the result of poor choices, that certainly was not her intention. Bernie never, for a moment, regretted having Nadine (after all, she thought, what kind of mother *would?*), but she did regret marrying Robert, and saw no point in pretending otherwise. As someone who rarely took things personally, she favored truth over spared feelings. The truth was useful; feelings had a way of mucking things up.

Sensitivity, according to Bernie, was Robert's greatest flaw. From the moment they met, she saw weakness in him—the desire to please. Bernie had been fired from her job as head server for the Palmdale Elementary hot lunch program (for refusing to serve the children freezer-burned hamburger patties, then telling the head cook where, in her person, she could shove said patties) and had just transferred to Cedar Hole Elementary. When Bernie first arrived, the kitchen at Cedar Hole was a disaster—potato peelings and lettuce leaves were piled in corners where the cooks had swept aside debris instead of picking it up; pests of various species crawled and swarmed around the grain bins; heavy-duty appliances sat unused, simply because no one seemed to know how to operate them.

But Bernie knew. She knew how to work all the equipment from her time at Palmdale and taught the cooks how to use them. She also showed them how to work in assembly line fashion. The workers became so efficient that there was plenty of time left over to keep the kitchen up to Bernie's rigorous standards of cleanliness. She threw out all the infested grains, devised new recipes and menus, and yelled at the deliveryman when he tried to unload crates of produce that were well past their prime and that had most likely had been rejected by every other school in the county.

"You're not going to get away with that anymore," Bernie warned him. "Forget Palmdale. Next time, you stop *here* first."

Bernie quickly became the star of the lunch program. Hot lunch at Cedar Hole Elementary improved so much under Bernie's supervision that word got around the county and to the Gilford *Gazette*, where Robert worked. The story had two elements that Robert found irresistible—Cedar Hole and improvement—so he scheduled a visit to the school cafeteria. He envisioned a two-part story: a serious culinary review of the day's offerings, and a hard-hitting interview with the woman who had turned things around.

Bernie was not nervous about the interview—nervousness, in her estimation, was reserved for people who had something to hide. Nevertheless, she wanted to present well, and stayed late the day before to make sure every exposed surface in the kitchen was polished. She selected one of her best menus—tuna pea wiggle on toast points, mashed potatoes (real, not instant), carrot coins, and pineapple upside-down cake. She even went to Nickerson's Department Store in Mt. Etna and bought herself a new dress.

There was a lot of fuss at the school surrounding Robert J. Cutler's visit, more than Bernie would have expected for a local news reporter.

The children in Delia Pratt's fourth grade drew pictures of him and hung them on the wall near the lunch line. The band practiced a Sousa march in his honor. Principal Nelson personally decorated the teachers' lounge with crepe paper streamers and balloons.

"Honestly, why all the fuss?"

Deedee Cross, who was in charge of desserts for the lunch program, was so stunned by Bernie's comment that she nearly dropped a five-pound can of pineapple rings on her pinky toe. "You don't know Robert Cutler? He writes for the *Gazette* every single week."

"I can't say that I've ever considered the *Gazette* required reading," Bernie said.

"He's one of our own," Louise Riley said, elbow-deep in carrot coins. "Went through here as a child. He still lives in Cedar Hole to this day."

"He's practically famous," Deedee said.

Bernie had her doubts that a real celebrity was living in Cedar Hole. Palmdale was right next door—wouldn't she have heard of him? "Well, besides the paper, what else has he done?"

Louise and Deedee exchanged glances, as though Bernie were being unnaturally dense. "Anything important that happens around here is because of him," Louise said.

Deedee nodded. "You'll know him when you see him."

As it turned out, she was partially right.

The first time Bernie saw Robert J. Cutler was in the lunch line. She usually didn't work the line, but in honor of Mr. Cutler's arrival she thought it was appropriate. After checking her hairnet, Bernie put a clean plastic apron over her new dress and took her station at the head of the serving line. She would scoop potatoes with her right hand and lay down toast points for the tuna pea wiggle with her left.

"We're ready," Bernie told Principal Nelson, who was holding back the children so Mr. Cutler could be first in line. Mr. Jacobs, the music teacher, climbed onto one of the cafeteria tables and tooted a few bleary notes of welcome on his trumpet.

Bernie stood on tiptoes so she could look over the sneeze guard at Mr. Cutler. She was shocked by his age—she had expected someone wiry and weathered, even gentrified, but Cutler was fresh-faced and energetic. Bernie thought they must have been the same age, or in the near vicinity, somewhere in the early twenties. His hands were white and soft, and he clapped them together loudly when the music teacher finished his earsplitting performance.

"I remember your father's eyes—they were so wide," Bernadette told her daughter. "He looked so easily impressed."

Delia Pratt was Mr. Cutler's self-appointed escort, handing him a speckled lunch tray and draping herself on his arm. She walked him to the front of the line, whispering intimately in his ear with the familiarity of a former lover. Even though the age gap had closed considerably between teacher and student (Delia had not yet reached forty), Bernie still found Miss Pratt's actions to be particularly sad and even more desperate than usual.

Louise snickered. "Get a load of *her.*"

"You go up to the window and put your tray *here,*" Delia said. Robert nodded and gave Delia a grateful smile, as though it were his first time.

"Good day, Mr. Cutler." Bernie arranged the toast points in the large compartment of his tray the way she had seen it done in her *Betty Crocker Cookbook.* "Welcome back to Cedar Hole Elementary."

"Are you Bernadette?" he asked.

Delia Pratt hugged Robert's arm against her chest. "Oh, I'm sorry—this is Bernadette Walker, the head of the lunch department."

"Nice to meet you, Bernadette. Everything smells delicious." Robert had a way of looking into her eyes that made Bernie regret her hairnet and plastic apron.

"It's nothing special, just what we cook every day." She gave him an extra scoop of mashed potatoes. While Bernie had never seen this supposedly famous man before, Deedee was right. Somehow, you could just look at Robert and you felt that you knew him. Even more incredibly, she felt that he already knew her, too.

"I think we'd all be fortunate to eat like this every day," Robert said. Delia frowned and nudged him down the line to the next server. He moved on without resistance, even though his eyes were still on Bernadette. "I look forward to our interview."

After lunch, Bernie went to the teachers' washroom to fluff her curls and touch up her lipstick. She was glad she had done so, because Robert ended up taking several pictures of her in the kitchen—standing next to the heavy-duty mixer, posed with a pyramid of creamed corn cans, art-fully decorating squares of pineapple cake with dollops of whipped top-ping. Bernie could hear herself talking on and on, with little prompting. Robert didn't take any notes during the entire interview; he just sat and listened.

"I think about lunch menus all the time. Sometimes I make them up while I'm driving to school or late at night when I can't fall asleep. It's not as easy as it may seem—you have to consider color, texture, nutrition, cost—and you have to think about the kids, what they like to eat."

"You remind me of someone—do you know Kitty Higgins, the li-brarian?"

Bernie shook her head. "I'm from Palmdale." She looked at Robert's fingers, folded on his knee. "I'm wondering how you can remember all of this—shouldn't you be writing something down?"

"No need," Robert answered, tapping his temple with his forefinger. "I'll remember."

"How can you possibly remember everything I've said? I've been bab-bling on and on."

Robert smiled. "I'm more concerned about capturing the spirit of the lunch program than simply listing facts."

A week later, the *Gilford Gazette* ran a full-page piece on Bernie and her staff, in which Robert declared her "chicken à la king" a "culinary miracle." He also stated that Bernie single-handedly elevated the Cedar Hole Elementary lunch program to a level on par with "Gilford County's best restaurants." Robert concluded that Bernie's efforts were "a prime example of Cedar Hole diligence and pride." Bernie had to admit the photo of her standing next to the mixer was one of the best pictures she had ever taken.

"He liked you," Deedee said. "I can tell."

No matter how flattering the article was, Bernie could not let the in-accuracies stand. She was immediately on the phone with the *Gazette*. "We have never served chicken à la king at Cedar Hole Elementary," she told Robert.

"I'm sorry," Robert said. "I'm not always good with proper names."

"And your review seemed slightly overblown." Bernie almost hated herself for sounding ungrateful, but once a thought came to the surface, it took nothing short of the Metropolitan Rail to stop her from saying it. "Memory has a way of making things seem better than they were. You should have taken notes."

"I think I captured the experience accurately," Robert insisted. "It was wonderful."

Robert's praise, though it seemed sincere, felt hollow to Bernie. How could she take a compliment seriously from a man who applauded a sloppy trumpet solo, who let Delia Pratt lead him around by the arm without a struggle, who was enamored with a town that had absolutely nothing going for it? To Bernie, Robert Cutler seemed to be a man who found glory in the mundane, who loved everyone and everything equally, regardless of merit.

"Go out with me, Bernie." His voice was so soft, so melted around the edges that Bernie wasn't sure she'd heard right.

"Where?"

"Anywhere," he said. "We'll have dinner."

Although she was an attractive woman, Bernie had never been the object of many suitors. There had been a few knock-kneed attempts by staff members of both schools she had worked at, but Bernie didn't like timidity and curtailed the offers midquestion to spare them both the dual pain of rejecting and being rejected. Robert, however, was not asking her out, but telling her—a tack that was certainly not timid, but that Bernie nevertheless found equally offensive.

"I don't think so," she said.

"Really? Why not?"

"You're too easy."

"By 'easy' I assume you mean agreeable."

"I mean you like everyone and everything." (Upon hearing the story, Nadine was mortified that her mother would say such a thing, and wondered why her father continued his pursuit after being insulted.) "You're the type that gets a crush on every girl that crosses your path—and I have no intention of being a member of your herd."

"I understand," Robert said. "Forgive me for asking."

There was a pause that lasted several long beats. She'd expected him to hang up, but he stayed on. "All right, then," Bernie heard herself say.

"You have a nice day."

"You, too."

They suffered through another pause, and then Bernie said, "How do you feel about pigs in a blanket?"

"They've always been a favorite."

"We're having them for lunch on Thursday," she said. "Knock on the back door near the Dumpster at one o'clock and I'll let you in."

Bernie hung up the phone before he had a chance to say anything else.

That Thursday, Robert showed up with a bouquet of wildflowers ("Sweet, but perhaps a touch overeager," Bernie recalled). They ate in the storage room on overturned milk crates, a bottle of ketchup between them. Robert said something about the gray-green color of her eyes. Bernie wrapped a few of Deedee's cookies for him to take home.

From then on, Robert came by every Thursday for lunch. Bernie opened a line of revolving credit at Nickerson's and hovered around the back door of the cafeteria, pacing the floor and smoothing the bodice of her new dress minutes before his arrival. He was prompt, cordial, thoughtful—and despite his apparent sensitivities, extravagant optimism, and ability to be seduced by the mundane, he seemed to be a good man.

Bernie waited until the end of the school year to make tuna pea wiggle again. After cleaning his tray of seconds, Robert got down on one knee.

"Marry me, Bernie."

Bernie knew there were dozens of good reasons to refuse him, but at that moment, she couldn't think of a single one.

Chapter Two

PINKHAM BOYS

The Pinkhams squeaked by nicely for the first couple of years until Flynn came along—a cyclone of a child who didn't double Francis's burden, but seemed to quadruple it. Flynn had a knack for breaking things, though it didn't seem intentional as much as it was the result of poor timing or unusual coincidence. For example, there was the branch of the sturdy old elm on the front lawn that Marty, who was roughly twice his size, had been swinging on for years that snapped the moment Flynn reached for it. Toys in Flynn's custody were dismembered, lost, or crushed within five minutes of playing, even though he appeared to treat them no differently than any other child, and often seemed more careful. Kitchen chairs came unglued when he sat on them; glasses of milk tipped themselves over in deference whenever he was near. Francis knew nothing of physics, but Flynn's entropic energy underscored a natural law that he had sensed in his heart—there was only one way for something to be whole and a million ways for it to fall apart.

Occasionally, Flynn's accidents were dangerous. Like the time he put his head through a plate-glass window in the living room. Francis was behind the house when it happened, cutting down the old holly bush near the back steps because he was afraid Flynn would somehow manage to ingest the berries, even though he had been told repeatedly they were poisonous. Anita was gone grocery shopping and the boys were in the house playing by themselves. At ten, Marty was serious for his age and seemed mature enough to take care of his six-year-old brother, though perhaps both Francis and Anita had underestimated Flynn's ability to get into trouble even in the presence of others. Francis was lost in the rhythm of his pruning shears when he heard a loud crack.

His first thought was that another sparrow had flown into the living room window. Anita kept her windows spotless, and many birds, drunk on fermented berries, had ascended the spiritual ladder by trying to fly into the house. The deaths were becoming so frequent that Francis stopped pruning the front hedges; partly because the overgrown shrubs covered a portion of the window, and partly because he couldn't stomach the sight of all those birds nestled in the hedges with their necks broken.

"Dad!" Marty came to the back door, yelling. "Flynn's head's stuck in the window!"

Francis couldn't even imagine how he made it inside the house, but somehow his legs carried him. He had expected to see chaos, but the living room was as neat and straight as if Anita had just cleaned for company. The only incongruent bit was Flynn at the window, bent forward at the waist, his head pushed through to the outside and staring down at the shrubs. While the window remained largely intact, a jagged circle of glass teeth surrounded his neck.

"How did he manage this?" Francis asked.

"How should I know?" Marty said. "I was in my room."

"You were supposed to be keeping an eye on your brother."

Francis approached Flynn slowly and from the side, so as not to startle him. "We're gonna get you out of there," he said. "Just keep your head still. Can you do that?"

"Yes, Pop."

"Good boy."

"It's funny," Marty said. "The hole looks smaller than his head."

He was right. Francis looked at the opening, which hardly seemed an inch larger than the circumference of the boy's neck, and suddenly felt his knees give out beneath him. He reached for the back of a nearby easy chair to keep himself upright.

"I'm not quite sure about this one," Francis said, scratching his scalp.

"You could break the bottom." Marty approached the window and pointed to the cracks just above the sill. "And he could slide his head out."

"The glass—it'll get in his eyes."

"We'll cover them up with this." Marty reached behind his father and snatched the handkerchief from his back pocket. "You need one of those big cartoon hammers, with the soft top."

"A mallet? I think I have one of those in my toolbox." Francis rested his hands on his knees. Even though Marty had laid out a game plan for him, Francis still didn't feel steady enough to trust his own legs. "Go out to the garage and see if you can find the hammer you're talking about. Go, quick."

Marty dashed out the front door, the tip of his tongue darting purposefully out of the corner of his mouth. The tendons in Flynn's neck strained to keep his head aloft, though the expression on his face remained relaxed.

Francis took a deep, uneasy breath. "You hang on there, boy," he said, lightly patting Flynn's hand. "Prop your hands against the still if you need to."

"I'm all right, Pop. Maybe you could get a towel and put it underneath me, just in case I can't hold out."

Finding strength in his legs, Francis darted to the bathroom to retrieve a towel. Flynn was always calm during his accidents, but Francis couldn't help but think that a little fear was helpful, that it might stop him from getting into bad situations in the first place. The time Flynn was almost clocked by the elm branch, Francis sat the boy down and tried to give him a lesson about the nature of cause and effect.

"If that branch had hit you on the head you could've been killed," he had said, hoping his son understood enough about death to avoid launching into that whole discussion. "Or ended up stupid for the rest of your life."

"It touched my back," Flynn had answered.

"But it could've hit your head, see? It came real close."

"It didn't hit me, though."

The conversation went around and around in spirals as Francis tried to make the boy understand the meaning of "almost." By the time he gave up, he was no closer. Flynn was firm in his belief that things either happened or they didn't. There was no such thing as almost.

Anita's sedan came rolling down the street, and as soon as the car's nose turned down the edge of the driveway it came to a jerking stop.

Anita left the car door open and headed toward the house at a dead run. "Flynn! Are you all right, baby? Say something!"

Francis found himself standing on the front lawn, meeting her halfway. "Don't scare him, now. Everything's fine."

"What are you standing here talking to me for?" Anita screamed. "Get him out of there!"

With Marty, Anita had been a confident mother. With Flynn, however, she wasn't so relaxed. His accidents turned Anita from a calm parent to a nervous one, her mind constantly racing ahead to forestall any future catastrophes while she dealt with current ones. She spent most of the time with her heart in her throat, nerves steeled against a world of impossible and infinite danger. Francis thought it would have been enough to prepare her for every eventuality, but each time Flynn was in a tight spot, Anita fell apart.

"Just hold on. Marty's gone to look for a hammer," Francis said. "We're going to break him loose."

"I'm fine, Mom," Flynn said.

"Call an ambulance, for Pete's sake!"

Francis squeezed her arm firmly. "Don't scare the kid," he whispered. "As soon as Marty brings the hammer we'll get him loose. If it doesn't work, we'll call Harvey Comstock."

"Harvey? What does he know?" Anita stroked Flynn's sandy hair, her fingers delicate and shaking. "Tell me, baby, how did you do this one?"

"I was reading a book," Flynn said.

Francis and Anita both nodded, as though the progression from reading to having your head caught in a picture window were a perfectly natural one.

Marty opened the front door, holding a big rubber mallet in his hand. "This should do it."

Francis took the mallet and headed back into the house.

"You might want to do it out here," Marty called.

Francis stopped in the doorway. "How's that?"

"Well, if you knock the glass from the inside out, you have a better chance of hitting him. But if you do it *outside in*, you'll be knocking it away from his face."

"He'll be getting glass on him no matter how I do it."

"Yeah, but this way's safer. He won't get any in his eyes."

While Francis had never thought himself an intelligent man, he figured he had enough smarts to get by and enough common sense to stay out of trouble. Never would he have dreamed though, that he could be so easily upstaged by his young children. They endlessly tested the boundaries of his will and strength, and seemed to prove almost daily what a fool he was. At five, Flynn started pointing out things that had somehow sneaked by Francis during his twenty-eight years on earth—like the way the bridge of his nose set slightly off-center. Every damn morning, for who knows how many years, he stood in front of the mirror shaving or brushing his teeth and not once did he notice that his nose was crooked, and then Flynn, with one look, could see the irregularity of line and make Francis doubt everything he ever thought he knew.

But of the two boys, Marty scared him the most. There was not a secret that could be kept from him. All he had to do was look in your eyes and read it right off you, as though it were written in ink on your forehead. He liked to sneak, padding around the house so quiet you didn't know he was there until he was right on top of you. He was fond of tricks, too, like hiding keys in places Francis would never think to look and would probably never find if he didn't yell loud enough to make Marty fess up. At Christmas, he named every gift before he unwrapped it, a smart-ass habit that Anita found funny but made Francis's mood turn south. "These must be my socks," he'd say, or "I think I'll unwrap the blue V-neck sweater vest next."

Francis squeezed the mallet in his fist. "Let me take care of this my own way."

"Marty's right," Anita said taking the handkerchief Marty gave her and tying it around Flynn's head like he was about to face a firing squad. "Getting glass in his eyes would be the worst thing."

"It seems to me we can't win either way we do it."

Marty tucked his hands in the back pockets of his jeans. "Do what you want, Pop, but it's the best way."

"Just hurry up—I can't take this," Anita said. "Put a pillowcase or something down so we don't get glass all over the living room rug."

Francis dropped the mallet and put on his pruning gloves, breaking off the shards of glass with his hands.

•   •   •

As soon as Flynn was freed, Anita wrapped him in a quilt and made him lie down on the couch, where she spoon-fed him hot chicken soup and cottage cheese, even though he had backed out of the window without so much as a scratch. Francis cleaned up the glass and taped sheet plastic over the hole. He contacted two Mt. Etna glaziers for price quotes before heading out to the Superette for his afternoon round of deliveries.

"I'll be back for dinner. Need anything from the store?"

"Get a package of chocolate pudding. Our little boy here needs a treat," she said.

Francis parked behind the store, in the very same lot where he and Allen used to keep a lookout for Henny when he swiped bottles from the back of the beer truck. He and Allen no longer spoke, other than to swap awkward pleasantries whenever they ran into each other on Main Street, though Francis often left the exchange feeling like Allen wanted to resume some sort of camaraderie that may never have been there in the first place. When he dropped out of high school, Francis used it as an excuse to let their friendship wither, though living in the same town made it difficult for the relationship to die completely. He knew that Allen graduated from high school with honors, that he worked at the Wear-Tex Factory, and that he had yet to find a woman who wanted to marry him.

Henny, on the other hand, was still a good friend. Francis often met him at Shorty's for morning coffee and sometimes they even went dancing with their wives on Saturday nights at the Legion Hall. Despite Allen's faithless prediction, Dixie never did break up with him—they ended up getting married six months after graduation. Henny had grown soft in the middle and in the eyes, worn down by two hyperactive kids and a wife who kept him running in circles. He made a living doing automotive bodywork out of his garage, while Dixie was a cashier at the Superette. He was a good man, chugging along, slow and steady, no matter what potholes life threw in front of him. Francis was not one who often voiced praise, but he admired the hell out of him for it.

The rear door to the store was open. Hinckley Hanson was standing by the Dumpster, breaking down a pile of cardboard boxes.

"Afternoon, Spud."

"Nice one, isn't it? Been dry all morning."

"Better enjoy it now. S'pose to start back up this afternoon."

"Can't catch a break, can we?"

"Not for long, anyhow," Hinckley said.

"Your father around?"

"You know he is. He's upstairs watching his money."

"Hang in there," Francis said, negotiating his way around the pile of empty boxes. "One of these days he'll get tired and hand over the kingdom."

Hinckley shook his head. "I've long since given up on that."

Debilitating arthritis made it impractical for Arnie to run the Superette from the floor, so he held court from his second-floor apartment, watching everything through a one-way mirror that ran along an adjacent wall at the back of the store. From his roost, Arnie had a bird's-eye view of everything—from the vegetable bins against the left wall to the dairy case on the right; behind the meat counter and deli in the back, all the way to the two cash registers up front. A pair of strong binoculars and an array of convex mirrors anchored high in the corners helped him get a good look around the ends of the aisles and at the cashiers as they counted out change. When he caught a shoplifter in action or witnessed a cashier making a mistake, Hanson called down to the floor by way of a buzzer and a telephone he rigged to work like an intercom system. In the ten years he'd been running the store from his apartment, not one item had been stolen and the cashiers' drawers were always balanced. No other store in the county, not even the big supermarket in Mt. Etna, could boast such a record.

Inside the store, Francis moved through the labyrinth of sadistic-looking butcher's saws, past the piles of bone-dust shavings that coated the floor of the hallway behind the meat department, up dark stairs leading to Arnie's apartment. The door was always open a crack. Francis gave it a firm knock and let himself in.

"Mr. Hanson?"

Arnie sat in his fusty armchair, binoculars pressed to his eyes. Behind him, the yellow-brown walls looked as though they had been brushed with several layers of tobacco juice. "Took you long enough," he murmured.

"Sorry—we had an emergency at home. My youngest put his head through the living room window this morning."

Arnie dropped his binoculars and picked up the black phone on the end table next to his chair. He pressed the intercom buzzer three times, the signal for whoever was in the deli at the time to pick up the phone.

"Norm—is my good-for-nothing son around? He was supposed to bring my lunch a half hour ago." Arnie paused. "Tell him when he's done with the boxes to bring me up a roast beef sandwich. And no stinking potato salad. I've had it up to my eyeballs with that crap."

Arnie slammed down the phone and picked up his binoculars again. He leaned forward until the edges of the lenses nearly touched the one-way mirror, grunting softly to himself.

Francis cleared his throat.

"I know you're there, Pinkham. What do you want?"

"The delivery list, sir."

"You know where it is—get it yourself."

Francis found the spiral notebook Arnie kept by the phone and ripped off the top page. "This is it? Just three?"

"Stop and fill the gas tank on your way back. It's almost empty."

"But I just filled it yesterday."

"I don't care when you filled it—it's empty now. If you're gonna drive all over town in my van, you're sure as hell gonna pay for it."

Francis slipped out the door and down the stairs, grabbing an empty box along the way to collect the orders. There was the daily order of three boxes of sugared donuts for Shorty, along with the weekly order for Mrs. Mullen. Her orders always contained a single, small item of insignificance—a box of toothpicks, a bag of pink mints, a book of stamps—nothing that ever seemed worthy of a delivery. Today, she wanted a pack of sewing needles.

"Hey, Norm—where's the sewing needles?"

Norm Higgins stepped out from behind the meat counter, his white apron freshly covered with smears of pink fat and dark blood. "I don't even know if we have any. Check that pegboard behind you."

Among the dusty measuring spoons, pairs of scissors, and bags of screws, Francis found a travel sewing kit with a mini spool of thread and a single needle stuck into a sponge. "Guess this'll have to do."

"How many deliveries you got today?" Norm asked.

"Just a few."

"Think you'll be back in a half hour or so?"

Francis shrugged. "Give or take."

"Good." Norm looked around and let his voice drop low. "Let me know when you get back, will ya? I need to run home with the van. I've been letting the garbage pile up in our garage and Kitty's going to have a fit if I don't get over to the landfill today."

Francis considered the perpetually drained gas tank, but decided to let the issue go for the moment. "Sure, Norm. I'll let you know."

Norm's mouth creased into a smarmy grin. "Good man."

After picking up a rump roast and a bottle of cough syrup for Bernie Cutler, Francis brought the deliveries to the front of the store, where Dixie rang them up. Francis slid behind the counter and bagged.

"Anita wanted me to ask if you and Henny were planning on going to the Legion this Saturday night. That swing band she likes is playing."

"It's only Wednesday. I'll have to see if Henny's up to it."

"Just thought I'd put a bug in your ear in case you didn't have plans."

Dixie nodded. She neatly folded the top of each bag and stapled their respective receipts. "Is that everything?"

"And this." Francis grabbed a chocolate bar from the candy shelf and held it up for both her—and Arnie—to see.

"You and your sweet tooth," she said, adding it to the total. "That comes to fourteen sixty-five."

Francis opened his wallet to find only a ten-dollar bill. "I forgot to bring a check. We had a bit of an emergency this morning."

"Everything okay?"

"Yeah, it's just one of those Flynn episodes. I'm sure Anita can't wait to tell you all about it," he said. "Spot me 'til I get back?"

Dixie frowned, her eyes glancing up at the mirror overhead. "Can't. My shift's almost up and the drawer will be off. I'm gonna have to add it to your tab. Sorry, Spud—you know how he wants his money up front."

Francis sighed and dropped the bags into the box. He turned his back on the mirror, knowing that Arnie could read lips. "It's a shame to be treated like a criminal by your own boss."

"Can't say I always blame him," Dixie said. "You never know what people might do."

Mrs. Mullen was already outside sitting on the front steps when Francis arrived. She asked that he never drive the van up to the house, but park on Elm instead. As he climbed the steep driveway, Francis noticed the lawn had been cut recently. There were no clippings, a sign that it had been a professional job.

"He's napping," Mrs. Mullen whispered, pressing a bill in his hand that encompassed both the cost of the delivery and an enormous tip. "But I'm afraid he might wake soon."

"It's too much," Francis said, trying to give the money back. He opened the bag. "They didn't even have what you wanted. They only had a sewing kit."

Mrs. Mullen shooed the money away and completely disregarded the bag. "How's everything at home?"

"All right, considering. My boy had a little accident, but he's fine. No harm done but a broken window."

"Flynn?"

He nodded.

"Oh dear—do be careful with that one."

"He's all right. He'll be just fine." Francis opened his wallet and pulled out two tiny photos. "Both boys got their pictures taken at school."

"Aren't they darlings," Mrs. Mullen said. "Is it possible they're so big already?"

"It sure goes fast."

"It certainly does."

"Sometime, maybe I could bring them over so you could meet them."

Mrs. Mullen hesitated. "You know I'd like that very much—but I don't think it would be such a good idea. Because of Walter."

Francis tucked the pictures back into his wallet. "I suppose it's my own fault."

"Don't take it hard. He's just stubborn." She touched the side of his face with a papery hand. "You look good. Anita must be feeding you well."

Francis didn't hear the compliment. "There has to be something I can do. Maybe I should talk to him," he said. "It's been going on long enough."

"He's weak, Mouse. We don't want him excited."

"I must've thought about building another mailbox hundreds of times."

"It wasn't just the box," she said. "He was disappointed."

To Francis's embarrassment, tears sprang quickly to his eyes. He looked down at the ground. "Please let him know I'm sorry."

"You were a child. God help us if we can't forgive a child's mistakes."

He handed her the bag. "I guess I'll see you next week."

"Wait. Before you go—I have something." She reached into the pocket of her apron and retrieved a neat, plastic-wrapped parcel of brownies. "For the boys."

WHILE PARKED in the Cutlers' driveway, Francis tore the receipt off the paper bag and jammed it in his pocket. He had saved Bernie's delivery for last, as a way of trying to avoid the inevitable. From the outside, the house always struck him as sullen, defeated—overrun with ghosts.

Francis tucked the candy bar inside the paper bag and knocked on the kitchen door. Ever since Robert died, it took Bernie a long time to answer the door. Francis pretended not to notice the sly parting of the lace curtains in the window off to his right or the paranoid series of clicks as Bernie unbolted the locks.

"Sorry to make you bring that, Francis," Bernie said, opening the screen door with a sudden rush. "It's ridiculous to have you deliver when the store's nearly in my front yard, but Nadine's been coughing all day, and sometimes I'm just not in the mood to see anyone."

"No reason to be sorry. I know what you're talking about." Francis handed her the bag and took an unconscious step back.

"Well, I appreciate it, anyway. How much do I owe you?"

"Seven dollars even."

Bernie's brow wrinkled. "That's an odd number. You sure? The roast has to be at least five, and last time I checked, they weren't giving cough medicine away."

"It just so happens we're having a sale on both today."

"Talk about luck," she laughed, but the lines at the corners of her eyes still looked sad. She gave him eight dollars. "A little something for your trouble."

"The cough—is it dry or wet?"

"Wet. She picked up something at preschool."

"You might want to put her over some steam. That's what Anita does for the boys."

"That's a good idea, thanks." Bernie peered into the bag. "I don't remember ordering chocolate."

Francis scratched his head. "Dixie must've put that in by mistake. Don't worry, you weren't charged for it."

Bernie took the bar out of the bag. "Here."

"No, no—you keep it," he said. No sense trying to undo what's already done. "Give that to your little girl when she feels better."

~ Chapter Three ~

THE DESK

A year after Bernie and Robert were married, Nadine was born. Like most new brides, Bernie entered the marriage with certain expectations. Her desires were not extravagant, but grounded firmly in the limitations of a reporter's salary. She didn't expect Robert to buy her a large house or fancy dresses, only that he provide a warm, comfortable home, good food, and sturdy clothing. Beyond that, Bernie also expected Robert to be an attentive spouse, spending most of his free time at home. The home was already provided for—he had inherited the house on Thornberry Lane from his parents—and the rest, she thought, should have been easy enough to manage.

Life with Robert, however, became an endless parade of bureaucratic projects and big ideas. Soon after their wedding and for the next several years, Robert's single obsession became the refurbishment of Main Street, starting with the renovation of the Cedar Hole Library. At first, Bernie had no issue with her husband's passion for bettering the town— it was, after all, the very same passion that had attracted her in the first place—but after Nadine was born Bernie came to realize that Robert was the kind of man who was capable of allowing only one thing to fully oc- cupy his heart and mind at a time. And he chose the library.

"For years, we've allowed this glorious building, this bastion of knowledge, to fall into neglect. For years, we've refused to purchase up- dated materials and provide proper maintenance. What kind of message are we sending to the young people of Cedar Hole if we fail to preserve one of our most sacred institutions?" Robert posed this question in front of the Cedar Hole Library Association during one of their monthly meetings. Kitty's eyes sparkled as Robert spread his carefully detailed plans across the top of the table. "I would like to present the new Cedar Hole Library."

A half dozen pairs of bifocals slid down various committee members' noses as they pulled in close to examine the drawings. The library's original façade remained largely the same, though a stone fountain was added to the front walk. Two new additions flanked both sides of the original building—sloped, sprawling wings like the flying buttresses on a Gothic cathedral. A bell tower crowned the very top, tall and proud enough to compete with surrounding church spires. The committee members blinked and breathed, equally stunned and stimulated, unsure of how to proceed. It had been years since anyone had brought a serious proposal before the association. Most meetings usually consisted of gossip and refreshments, and rarely accomplished anything of true import.

"That's quite a drawing you have there," the chairman said. "It looks like a complicated project."

"I've spoken with several contractors. They assure me it's feasible."

"What do we need the additions for?" one of the members asked. "If it's space we need, couldn't we just rearrange the furniture?"

"We need room for newer materials," Robert said. "The left wing will be an audiovisual room for music, and films, and books on tape. The right wing will be the children's reading room. If you'll notice the floor plan, I've included French doors that will allow Mrs. Higgins to visually supervise the children without having to be disturbed by unnecessary noise."

More than a few low grumbles circulated the table. Several were the oral kind, expressing keen displeasure at this unexpected call to action; most, however, were gastric in origin, wondering when the cookies would be served.

Kitty Higgins stood up.

"I think it's a marvelous plan. Our patronage has been decreasing steadily over the years. A new library will revitalize people's interest."

"If no one's interested now, then maybe we'd be better off closing the whole thing down," the chairman said.

"That's not what Mrs. Higgins is saying," Robert said. "People want a good library, we just haven't given them a good reason to visit."

Another member spoke up. "How much will this plan of yours cost?"

"I've made generous allowances for new books and incidentals. My figure runs close to five hundred thousand dollars."

Peals of laughter volleyed from one end of the table to the other and back again.

"I understand we don't have the money right now—that's why I also propose a series of fund-raisers," he added. "This is a terrific opportunity for the community to rally around a single common goal. I think if you give the people of Cedar Hole a reason to come together, they will."

The chairman of the association wiped a tear of laughter off his cheek. "The people of Cedar Hole don't have that kind of money."

"That's why we have to reach outside the community. We could have bake sales at the shopping center in Palmdale. We could sell raffle tickets in Mt. Etna. We could actually have the train come back for the Train Festival, bringing in people from all over the county!"

"Now he's talking about bringing back the train," someone muttered.

Nadine loved hearing this story over and over again up to this point, when her father seemed so idealistic and courageous. It was the next part that she hated.

"As usual, he overdid it," Bernie always added, her comment igniting a spark of resentment in Nadine. "When no one seemed interested in the plan, he pledged five thousand dollars of our savings to get the ball rolling. I learned early on that I would never have your father totally to myself. He belonged to everyone else but us."

Even in death, Robert had a strong hold on his daughter's heart. "It's not fair to say bad things about him when he's not here to defend himself."

"Since he's dead, I guess that means I can't tell the truth."

Kitty Higgins told a better story. "When your father pledged some of his own money, the association was so stunned, they actually decided to wait until the next meeting before putting it to a vote. I had never seen your father so happy as he was that month. He came to the library every single day to take measurements and go over book catalogs."

Even with all his careful planning and fund-raising ideas, the committee rejected the plan. As one might imagine, Robert was graceful in his defeat.

"Perhaps now isn't the right time for a new building, but I think you'll all agree that we should at least purchase some new books. And Mrs. Higgins could really use a new desk."

"As I understand it," the chairman said, "the best books were written a hundred years ago. What do we need new ones for?"

Kitty told Nadine that's when her father got angry. According to several sources present that evening, Robert's normally placid face turned three shades of red.

"I'll see that Mrs. Higgins gets her new books, even if I have to buy them myself."

The chairman nodded. "I'd like to make a motion that Mr. Cutler purchase the new library books with his own funds."

"I second," someone else said.

"All in favor?"

The vote was unanimous.

"Good," the chairman said, banging his gavel on the table. "Meeting adjourned. Now, did anyone bring any cookies?"

The part of the story Kitty kept for herself was after the meeting, when she and Robert went to Shorty's for a cup of coffee to discuss their defeat. Robert was heartbroken and angry, and Kitty saw no point in sharing this moment of frailty with Nadine, who had built such a strong image of her father.

"The problem is lack of vision," Robert had said to her. "Why is it so hard for people to imagine something better?"

"It's fear," Kitty had told him. "They don't know what to expect."

"That's why the plans were so detailed. I thought it would help."

"But it's still just a drawing on a piece of paper, Robert."

He brightened. "What if I built a three-dimensional model?"

Kitty remembered touching the back of his hand. "Let it go for now. Give them some time to get used to the idea of change, and next year you can try again. Maybe next time around they'll be more receptive."

"Why are we at the mercy of short-sighted people? It's total nonsense." There was a saltiness to his words that shook Kitty. Never before had she considered that Robert could be touched by cynicism. "I meant what I said about you needing more books and a new desk. If they don't have the sense to give it to you, then I'll see to it myself."

"I wouldn't ask that of you."

"I mean it, Kitty. You've worked hard. You deserve something nice. The town deserves something nice," he said. "And when you have your desk and your books, then I'm going to work on the library. I'll rebuild that place myself. It may take fifty years, but I'll do it."

"Tread lightly. Be careful of stirring up trouble."

"I couldn't care less about upsetting the association," Robert said. "Believe me, there'll be no love lost between us."

On the day he died, Robert had taken the train from Palmdale to the city in search of a new library desk. Although Nadine had no recollection of it, Bernie and Robert fought over the desk for weeks. Robert never raised his voice when they argued; instead, he presented his case with quiet persistence, until he wore her down. "She's been like a mother to me. She deserves better."

"Well, I'm sorry, but we can't afford it." At that time, little Nadine was stretching out of her baby's body into a longer, leaner form that would need a winter jacket in another few months. There was also the matter of the broken washing machine and the bald tires on the Plymouth. "We have bills. It's been two weeks since you paid Spud."

"I'll mow the lawn myself," he said. "I promised I'd do this for her."

"Wouldn't Kitty have bought her own desk by now if she really wanted one? Norm's been at the Superette a long time, I'm sure he can afford to buy his wife a new desk."

Robert looked at her then, his eyes softening out of either confusion or pity—she couldn't tell—reducing her by the enormity of his heart. "It surprises me that you don't think she deserves something nice."

"She can have the entire inventory of Nickerson's, for all I care. I'm just questioning who should be the one to give it to her."

"Kitty asks about you and Nadine all the time. She wonders why you never stop by the library," he said. "She's convinced you don't like her."

Bernie didn't, of course, and the fact that Kitty Higgins seemed to steal most of her husband's energy and resources was only part of the reason. She suspected that Robert had been smitten with the librarian for most of his life, and worse still, Kitty struck her as meek and lacking backbone. This only further supported Bernie's contention that Robert did not have a specific taste in women or anything else—meaning that, in fact, he was tasteless.

"It's not that I'm stingy," she said, brushing aside the accusation, "I'm just trying to find another way. A way that can benefit everyone. We need things, too."

Robert nodded slowly, in his infinite way of understanding. But Bernie knew it was too late. He had already made up his mind.

THE OWNER of Fairbanks Antiques, on Second Avenue, right in the heart of the city's shopping district, recalled that the last hour of Robert's life was spent sipping a complimentary cup of coffee and taking turns sitting at every desk in the shop. Robert was a thorough shopper, Mr. Fairbanks reported, examining every drawer pull and lock, resting his arms on the desktops to check for comfort. As he stood in the driveway of Bernie's house, he told her that he found Robert to be a most agreeable customer, and, if it was any comfort, he had been in high spirits.

"He said the desk was a gift." Mr. Fairbanks squeezed her hand, his eyes welling up as the delivery truck backed up to the garage. "I hope it's to your liking. Your husband certainly put a lot of thought into it."

White-gloved movers uncovered the desk with delicate precision, as though it were a time bomb on the verge of detonation. Bernie's skin prickled as she noted the antique cherry finish, the S-curve of the rolltop, the elegant spindle legs that looked as easy to snap as toothpicks. Robert had chosen well. It was a desk perfectly suited for Kitty Higgins—pretty, fragile, obsolete.

"How much did he pay?" she asked.

The dealer hesitated. "I'm not sure that's an appropriate question given the circumstances."

"Tell me."

"It was one of the most expensive pieces in the store."

She yanked her hand out of his grip. "I want a number, Fairbanks."

The antique dealer removed the starched handkerchief from the front pocket of his suit and swabbed his brow. "Well, I'd have to look it up," he said, "but it was somewhere in the vicinity of a thousand dollars."

Bernie's face went numb. When the shock began to subside, she waved her arms at the movers. "Wait a second!" The men paused on the truck's ramp. "Take it back," she said. "I want a refund."

Mr. Fairbanks's wide, flat forehead stretched tight. "I understand this is a stressful time for you, Mrs. Cutler—it's important that you don't make any hasty decisions—"

"A check would be fine, though I prefer cash."

"Please, Mrs. Cutler. Your husband put a great deal of thought into selecting this desk for you. In my opinion, a gift like this is a sign of great love."

Mr. Fairbanks's words curdled in her stomach. Bernie swallowed the nausea that was crawling up her throat in hot, bilious threads. When she had gathered herself, she signaled for the movers to continue the delivery.

"Dump it right over there."

Bernie pointed at the dying plum tree behind the house. The tree had been barren for over twenty-five years, but in one last, glorious death gasp, it was now bearing golden, palm-sized fruit.

A bank of clouds was approaching from the west, skimming the rooftops of both the Superette and the diner across the street. Mr. Fairbanks tilted his head and grunted at the sky. "We certainly wouldn't risk your beautiful desk to the elements, Mrs. Cutler. We can bring it inside the house and place it in any room you wish."

"Get right under it," Bernie called to the movers. The men eased the desk across the back lawn and rotated it beneath the plum tree until they found the angle most flattering from where Bernie stood in the driveway. As soon as they set the desk down, a saggy, overripe plum broke from its stem and splattered on the rolltop.

Fairbanks skipped across the lawn. "It certainly is a beautiful spot for writing letters," he said, using his handkerchief to sop up the puddle of plum juice. "I have a lovely little chair that would perfectly complement this desk, if you're interested. Mr. Cutler admired it when he was in. . . ." His voice trailed off with calculated reverence. "You know, he was so pleasant—I should have offered it to him for less. There was none of that dickering you have to deal with from your usual suburban shoppers. He paid full price." Fairbanks carefully folded his handkerchief and returned it to his breast pocket. "Come by the shop, I'd love for you to see the chair. I'll see that you're taken care of properly."

Bernie picked a plum off the tree and bit into it. The stone was large, but the fruit was sweet. The brightness of the acid temporarily cut through the bitterness on her tongue. "I have no interest whatsoever in chairs."

"Perhaps, then, you have some chairs you might like to get rid of?" he asked. "Or perhaps Mr. Cutler had some cufflinks? Or a pocket watch? It's been my experience that widows often feel a sense of relief when they unload. It can give you a fresh start."

Bernie slid back the rolltop. In the back there were dividers for mail and a row of small square drawers. The writing surface was smooth and polished to a dark gloss. Near the lip, there was a thin brass plate with letters etched into the surface. The brass was far too bright and untarnished to be original. Bernie leaned in to read the inscription—

There shall be no love lost

"He had us add the quote," Mr. Fairbanks said. "Ben Jonson, I believe. A contemporary of Shakespeare's. Particularly poignant, I must say, given the circumstances."

Just when Bernie thought she had become immune to shock, she felt herself tumbling again through the atmosphere with nothing familiar to cling to. A breeze kicked up and she felt her body sway. It was tempting to let go—to give in to the rising scream, to snap the thin tethers that held her together. And just when she was about to take the leap, Nadine came bounding around the corner with a handful of field grass squeezed in her droolly fist.

Fairbanks melted. "She's a darling."

Bernie picked up Nadine and carried her into the garage. The weight on her hip felt solid and steady, giving her enough of an anchor to get through the next minute, the next hour, the next day. "It's time for you to leave, Fairbanks."

"Yes, of course." He trailed her as she retrieved a flat-edged screwdriver from a toolbox in the garage. "I'll leave you my business card. Whenever you're ready to buy or sell, you let me know."

"Don't sit by the phone." Bernie set Nadine down in the driveway and handed her the screwdriver. "Go play with Daddy's new desk," she said, steering her toward the plum tree. "Go on."

A delirious giggle rose up from Nadine as she charged across the lawn toward the desk intended for Kitty Higgins, the blade of the screwdriver glinting in the fading afternoon light. The horror of the desk's impending mutilation sent Fairbanks scrambling toward the moving truck, business card still pressed between his fingers, long before Nadine made the first scratch.

When Bernie closed her eyes, she still saw Officer Comstock standing on her front step, one knee bobbing to some silent, anxious rhythm. He stared down at his shoes the entire time.

"He didn't suffer," he'd said. "Didn't even know what hit him."

The fact that Robert's death had been quick was of little consolation. While she didn't want him to suffer, it would have been nice if he'd at least had a few moments to generate a little remorse about going against her wishes. Or, even better, Bernie would have liked it if he had lingered briefly in the hospital just long enough so that she could have held his hand and felt her heart soften to him again. Instead, he was yanked at the peak of self-righteousness, full of himself and Kitty Higgins. Bernie, on the other hand, felt as though her life had been interrupted midsentence. She would be forever misunderstood and slighted. Poised on the edge of nothing.

Nadine waved the screwdriver in the air.

Bernie's vision blurred as she thought about the brass plate with its tacky declaration of love.

"That's it, honey. Right there," she said, pointing to the desk—the last word in a fight she would never win.

IT HAPPENED like this—

After Robert bought the desk from Fairbanks Antiques, he rounded the block and headed north toward the 29th Street train station to catch the rail back to Palmdale. St. Mary's Catholic Church was across the street, just one block from the station, cocooned in metal staging for the cleaning of the stone exterior that had darkened from years of engine exhaust and dust. It had been stormy and blustery all day and Robert crossed the street, walking beneath the elaborate skeleton of St. Mary's scaffolding most likely as protection from the rain. Eyewitnesses said there had been a strong gust of wind—one of those brutal lashes that gained fury tunneling through the narrow alleys between skyscrapers, inverting umbrellas and making pedestrians whimper into their collars. Robert was fully underneath the scaffolding as the wind whipped around the corner. A support bar shook loose, and with it five stories of staging platforms and iron bars collapsed. Robert was crushed instantly.

Among the personal items that were returned to Bernie and Nadine from the scene of the accident were his wedding band; a wristwatch Sissy had given him for his eighteenth birthday that had belonged to his father; and a pink plastic bottle of soap bubbles. The silver band (which Robert had chosen instead of the white gold, insisting that while they looked identical, the difference in price would be put to much better use buying library materials) had been much too soft to withstand the impact of the collapse, and came back to Bernie as a flattened oval, with dark pits where pieces of gravel had embedded in the metal. The wristwatch was permanently altered as well; the face of it had been smashed, and fell away as Bernie touched it. Time was permanently frozen at one minute before eleven-thirty and the sweep second hand, twitching and lost, vacillated between the fourth and fifth seconds on the dial. And yet, even though the watch and the ring were ruined, the soap bubbles for Nadine somehow stayed intact. The smooth, pliable bullet of a bottle remained clean, without so much as a dent or a leak. Even though Robert apparently had no time to think as the scaffolding fell, Bernie imagined that some small, fatherly impulse—an instinct even quicker than death—made him tuck Nadine's gift against his abdomen, curving his body around the bottle to keep it safe from the falling beams.

Bernie let Nadine bring the bottle to the funeral, under the condition that she did not open it until after the service was over. Nadine remembered wanting that bottle more than anything—more than eating the ice cream her mother promised for lunch, more than taking off the plastic barrettes that pulled her hair, even more than seeing her father again. In the church, and later in the cemetery, her small fingers turned the bottle around and around inside the pocket of her camel overcoat, the metal cap smooth and cool against the palm of her hand. She had never seen bubbles before, or even knew what they were, but sensed they were something grand; a special package sent down from the sky, where everyone said her father now lived.

As soon as her mother said it was all right, Nadine cracked open the bottle and kissed the wand to her lips like the pigtailed girl on the front of the bottle. But from there, the rest escaped her. She inhaled with all of her strength, coating her tongue with a sharp, viscous film that made her eyes water.

"For God's sake, Nadine," Bernie sighed. She snatched the wand from Nadine's grip. "Out . . . *out*. Like this."

Out was a revelation. From her mother's breath grew a world of translucent wonder, shimmering and expanding in a fluid whirl before snapping back into a sphere of delicate and perfect proportion. Worlds spun in pink and green, floating on the lightest of currents. Nadine reached out and touched them with her fingers, shattering them out of existence.

After a few false starts, she discovered how to push the soap out instead of taking it in, and was soon blowing satellites around her mother's large, soft bubbles. Nadine practiced her bubbles so she could show her father when he came to visit.

That night, when she was brushing her teeth, she spat in the sink.

~ Chapter Four ~

RUNNING *for* OFFICE

On the morning of Robert's accident, Francis went to the Super-ette to make a few early deliveries. The store seemed unnaturally quiet; Hinckley was nowhere to be found in the back room and even Norm was missing from the meat department. Instead of climbing the stairs to Arnie's cloister, Francis found himself drawn to the front of the store, where somber drips of conversation trickled down the aisles.

"I just can't believe it," Dixie was saying, reaching for the box of tissues she kept on a shelf underneath the counter. Norm and Hinckley were gathered around the register, along with Henny and Harvey Comstock, their eyes downcast.

"Did you hear the news?" Harvey asked, before Francis had a chance to ask what was going on. "Robert Cutler was killed this morning."

Francis's throat ran dry. He opened his mouth as though he had something to say, but clamped it shut again.

"He was in the city," Henny added. "Scaffolding collapsed on him. Killed him instantly."

"Isn't that just about the worst news you've ever heard?" Dixie cried.

"It's pretty awful," Francis answered distantly, knowing this was what he was supposed to say, but unsure how he truly felt about it.

"As soon as Kitty heard the news, she closed up the library," Norm said. "Now she's at home in our bedroom with all the shades drawn. I don't know if she'll ever come out."

Harvey shook his head. "He was a good man."

"A great man," Hinckley corrected. "Maybe the best we've ever seen around here. Remember the time at the rodeo when he cut that star into the lawn? Had you ever in your life seen anything like that?"

Francis flinched, surprised that an old wound could still feel so fresh.

"I just came from telling Bernie the news," Harvey said. "She hardly blinked. She invited me in for coffee and even set out a plate of cookies— like it was the most normal thing in the world. It was almost like she was expecting it."

Dixie stopped sniffling. "Did she cry?"

"Not a drop. Not while I was there, anyways. And I must've stayed there at least twenty minutes to just make sure she was going to be okay."

"I feel bad for that little girl," Henny said quietly.

"That doesn't sound right to me at all," Dixie said. "She always did seem cold."

"I never see her in here," Norm said. "Odd for someone who lives right across the street."

Hinckley nodded. "I hear she drives all the way to Mt. Etna for her groceries."

"It was the strangest thing. We were sitting there, drinking coffee, and I kept asking her if she was going to be all right, and she kept saying something about how she's always looked after herself and how not much was going to change." Harvey scratched the top of his head. "I didn't get that. I mean, what I was trying to get at was how broken up she was, and she kept talking about paying bills and things like that. And the whole time her eyes were dry as a bone."

"Maybe she was in shock," Francis said. "I would imagine it could take a while for something like that to sink in."

"Oh, it sunk in. I'm sure of it. If you ask me, I think she might've been relieved to be rid of him."

Dixie blew her nose. "You know, I bet that's true. I've been hearing for a long time that their marriage wasn't working out. Apparently, Bernie resented all the good things Robert was trying to do around here."

"That doesn't surprise me one bit," Harvey said.

"Don't you think we ought to take it easy on the poor woman?" Francis piped up. "After all, she just lost her husband."

Harvey snickered. "Just 'cause you're still sore about Robert winning the rodeo doesn't mean you ought to take her side."

"Cripes, Harvey, I'm not taking anyone's side, here. I'm just saying maybe you ought to lay off until Robert's body is cold."

"You're a fine one to talk about that. Since when have the Pinkhams cut anybody some slack?"

Henny stepped forward, wedging his wide girth between Harvey and Francis. "Let's keep it friendly. I know we're all feeling pretty bad right now, but I can tell you, Harvey, that Spud hasn't felt sore about the rodeo for a long time."

"Maybe he's gotten over the fact that Robert won, but you can bet he's still ticked about coming in second. Look at Hinckley over there," Harvey continued. "He came in second dozens of times, but you don't see him moping about it for years and years. Am I right, Hinckley?"

Hinckley cleared his throat. "I'd better get to work," he said, straightening a shelf of soup cans behind him. "I can feel Arnie's eyes on me."

"I know what you mean," Norm said, rushing back to the meat counter.

"There can't be a whole lot going on at the station if you've got enough time to worry about me," Francis said.

"Oh, you Pinkhams keep me plenty busy."

Dixie's eyes bounced from one man to the other with intense concentration, as though she were trying to commit the entire scene to memory. Between Robert's death and the current row, she had more than enough gossip to get her through the week.

Henny wedged himself even farther between them. "Spud, you ought to get on with your deliveries."

Francis twirled the van key around his finger. "I suppose so. Care to follow me, Harvey, in case I decide to look for some trouble?"

"You don't have to look," Harvey said with a parting shot. "You're a Pinkham. Trouble finds you."

FRANCIS SAT in the driver's seat of the Superette van for a long time without turning the ignition key. There was no one else in the back lot—no delivery trucks or kids, no pigeons or chipmunks. No cars driving up and down Thornberry. There wasn't even any rain. There was only silence, a silence so complete that slighter, less aggressive sounds usually buried beneath the din of life made themselves clearly heard. Francis noticed the shallow brush of air pushing through his nose, the cracks and snaps of the dashboard settling, the disturbing high-pitched ring that sang deep in his ear. He closed his eyes and tried to ignore the pitch but it only grew louder. Even if the dashboard finally settled and he was able to breathe soundlessly, Francis knew the high pitch would always be there. It made him wonder if there was such a thing as true silence.

He ought to have felt free—finally removed from the shadow that dogged him most of his life—but Francis wasn't the sort of man to take pleasure in another's death. It was a hollow victory, like winning a race because your opponent sprained his ankle. Or dropped out. Or mowed a five-pointed star instead of going for time like he was supposed to. Despite what Harvey thought, Francis wasn't so much taking sides against Robert, but *for* Bernie. She was the only other person in the entire town, Francis sensed, who saw Robert in the same light he did.

In the spring following Flynn's birth, the Cutlers had hired Francis to mow their lawn twice a week. Francis didn't want to take the job, but he was hardly in a position to refuse any sort of work. Most of the time Robert wasn't even home, but Bernie was, either pacing past the windows or sitting on the front steps.

"Do you like yard work?" she'd asked one time while he was clipping the front hedge.

"It's all right," he'd answered. "It's as good as anything else, I guess."

"You're never done, though. As soon as you clip that branch it's already growing out again."

"But you can't let it keep growing forever. At some point you're going to have to deal with it."

Bernadette was quiet, staring out across the street as she rubbed the firm mound of her pregnant belly. "It's kind of like my job at school. I make food, the kids eat it, digest it, and the next day I have to start all over again. Robert's lucky. At least he gets to work on projects—things with a beginning, middle, and an end. But it hardly matters to him. He'd be happy even doing what you're doing."

"You mean, even if he was just mowing lawns for a living?" Francis said with a wry grin.

Bernie withered. "If I made your work sound awful, it wasn't my intention."

"That's all right. I know it isn't much."

"It's work. Work is noble."

Francis laid the hedge clippers at his feet and drank water from the glass Bernadette left on the bottom step. She watched him drink it down. "I can get more if you'd like."

"This is plenty." Francis remembered Bernadette's eyes that day—the downturn of the outer corners, the ache just below the surface that seemed too familiar. If Harvey and Dixie and everyone else had seen it, Francis knew they wouldn't be so smug. "I'm good."

"Is it all right that I sit here and watch you? The house seems too quiet today. If I sit still long enough I can hear the blood in my ears."

"Where's your husband?"

"At some committee meeting," she sighed. "He was supposed to call an hour ago to tell me when to start dinner. We're having chops and I don't want them to dry out." She laughed lightly, touching off a brief spark in her eyes that immediately burned out. "Those meetings can go on forever. You know how it is."

"I don't, really, but I can guess." Francis picked up his clippers again. A cold meanness seized him as he thought about Bernie being pregnant and alone. His jaw took on a hard set. "You two have any plans of moving when the baby's born?"

"That's a funny question," she answered, patting her belly again.

"I've always figured that Robert would do better in the city."

"Oh no—he loves it here. He wouldn't live anywhere else."

Francis remembered a vague choking sensation taking hold at the thought of being smothered by Robert for the rest of his life.

"Seems to me that a guy like that almost has a duty to go somewhere else, instead of hanging around here and making the rest of us look bad." He attempted to soften the comment with a halting, disintegrating laugh. Now, upon remembering it, he burned with shame. A look of perfect understanding flickered behind her eyes, but then the lean, glittering loneliness she had allowed him to see was quickly ushered away and locked behind a steel barricade. She was turning cool and Francis nearly cried out as he watched the regrettable transition. Inside, his lungs turned as brittle and crisp as November leaves.

"Well, I suppose he makes us all look bad," she'd said, her lips thinning out against her front teeth. "How can you compete with self-righteousness?"

Francis roused himself out of the memory and started the van but left it in park, cranking the fan as high as it would go. He thought about Bernadette and wondered what kind of state she was really in upon hearing the news. He was sure she was just as shattered as any person would be, but strong enough to put on a cool face for the likes of Harvey Comstock. People in dire circumstances were twigs—dry or green—and either snapped in two or yielded to the event, allowing themselves to be bent and reshaped. He didn't know for sure, but he suspected that Bernadette was filled with a vital sap that allowed her to stay green. Francis felt no such vitality within himself. He felt only air in his bones. If the pressure was right, he was sure he would break in two clean pieces.

ANITA wanted to go to the funeral, but Francis wanted no part of it.

"The whole town's going to be there," Anita argued. "You worked for him. How's it going to look if you don't show up?"

"No one will even notice."

"Bernie will notice." Anita retrieved the ironing board from the linen closet and set it up in the middle of the kitchen. "You can wear your suit."

"I'll stay home and look after the boys."

"It's Friday morning. They'll be in school."

"Well, Friday morning is out. I have an appointment to get the van tuned up. Gotta keep old man Hanson happy."

Francis opened the *Gazette* and found Robert Cutler's cheery mug staring back at him. The obituary took up the entire page and ran into the next. Francis folded the paper into quarters and tossed it into the wastebasket.

"I can't imagine the garage will still be open," Anita said. "Even Shorty's is closing until three o'clock."

"The Superette isn't."

"Well, you know Arnie." She spread one leg of Francis's pants on the ironing board and smoothed it with her hands.

"All I know is that I have an appointment, and I plan to be there."

"I'd call if I were you. Maybe they've forgotten."

Anita ended up attending the funeral with the Ladies' Auxiliary while Francis leaned against the doorway of the garage bay and watched the van get tuned up. Just like Anita said, the entire garage was empty of both cars and mechanics, except for the van and one knobby-jointed kid who kept dropping his screwdriver on the floor and scratching his head as he flipped through the pages of a thick auto repair manual.

On the way back from the garage, Francis drove past St. Joseph's Church. It was after eleven o'clock, around the time he imagined the service ought to be over and done with. He pictured Anita inside, sitting among the ladies of the Auxiliary, silently stewing that he refused to make an appearance. She'd be mad at him the rest of the day, if not the entire weekend, a thought that wrenched his insides. He would not go in—that was for damn sure—but if he waited outside for her, maybe she'd soften up a little faster.

Francis did a U-turn in the middle of the road and pulled in front of the church, in the only available parking spot on the street. He turned on the radio and closed his eyes, settling in for a quick nap.

A knock on the driver's-side window startled him awake. It was Harvey Comstock, dressed in his usual uniform, with the extra touch of white gloves and a sturdy policeman's hat.

Francis groaned and rolled down the window. "What can I do for you, Harvey?"

"Looks like you're taking a nap," Harvey said, tipping back his hat.

"Is that something they taught you at the police academy? How to recognize when someone's sleeping?"

"I can't let you stand here."

"I'm just waiting for my wife to get out."

"You can park, but you can't stand."

Francis bit down hard on his molars. "You mean to tell me that I can leave the van here, as long as I'm not in it?"

Officer Comstock took the notepad off his belt and clicked his pen. "You can stay in there if you like, but it's going to cost you."

Francis unbuckled his seatbelt and stepped outside the van. "Am I a new favorite target of yours, Harvey?" he said, leaning against the door with his arms crossed in front of his chest.

"Now you're loitering," Harvey answered, writing in his book.

"Oh, for Pete's sake. You say I'm the one who can't let go and here you are, still sticking it to me because of Jackie."

Harvey ignored the comment. "I can't have you standing around doing nothing."

"What else am I supposed to do until my wife comes out?"

"Go in there and pay your respects to Mr. Cutler, like everyone else."

Francis stared at Harvey for several long seconds, then relented, walking around to the back of the van. "Knowing you, you'll probably take this as a compliment," he said, stopping short at the curb, "but among dinks, Harvey, you're the king."

THE DOORS of the church had been thrown wide open, with sprays of white and yellow lilies and gladioli spilling out onto the street. Francis dragged his feet up the steps and into the vestibule, where the bouquets stood five deep on the floor and staggered up the wall on pillars of various heights. Fancy-dressed mourners clogged the doorway leading to the nave, the warmth of their bodies opening the floral scents to a sickening sweetness. Organ music ebbed and swelled, reminding him of the old-time soap operas his mother used to listen to on the radio while she sewed.

"Feel free to move forward," one of the ushers said. "You won't see much, though. It's standing room only."

Francis noted the man's crisp suit and instantly felt ill at ease in his own dusty work clothes. He gave the usher a wan smile and hung back by the entrance, staying just enough inside the door to keep out of Harvey's line of sight.

Inside, a chorus of voices strained to the melodic demands of "Amazing Grace." To Francis's ear, there must've been hundreds of people singing along—perhaps Anita had been right in saying that everyone in town would be there. He glanced at the bulletin board, then checked his watch. The funeral had been going on for nearly two and a half hours already—how much longer could it possibly last? Pushing back against the doorjamb, Francis wriggled himself between an orchid wreath and a Styrofoam cross studded with blue carnations. He closed his eyes and tilted his head back, in a surreptitious attempt to resume his morning snooze.

"Ahem. *Ahem.*"

An indeterminate amount of time had passed before he was coaxed out of sleep by the sound of a man clearing his throat. Francis, who had temporarily forgotten where he was, yawned and slowly opened his eyes. As he gained full consciousness, he realized that the crowd in the vestibule had parted and that directly in front of him was a glossy mahogany casket and eight pallbearers trying to get through the door.

"If you could step aside, please," one of the pallbearers said. Just over his shoulder, Francis could see the entire congregation turned around, looking directly at him.

"Sure," Francis muttered, stepping over the cross and knocking over the wreath as he bounded toward the far corner of the vestibule.

The pallbearers inched past and out the door. Francis felt a woozy rush of blood filling his head. Inside that sleek box was Robert's broken body—a fact almost too amazing and terrible to fully comprehend. Bernie followed behind the casket, holding her daughter's hand. The little girl pulled a plastic bottle of bubble solution out of her coat pocket and held it up for the usher to see. Bernie took the bottle and tucked it back in her pocket.

"Not now, Nadine," she said. "I told you to wait until after lunch."

Bernie noticed Francis standing in the corner and acknowledged him with a nod. Francis lowered his head until she passed.

The congregation pressed in close behind, trapping him inside. Delia Pratt was one of the first out, wearing the same sun hat she wore to the rodeo years before, only this time her red bow was replaced with a black satin sash. Mopping her nose with a lace hankie, Delia caught sight of Francis in her peripheral vision, then appraised him from toe to head and back down again.

"Nice of you to dress up," she sniffed.

"Just came from work," he muttered.

Henny squeezed through the door and patted him on the back. "Didn't think you'd be here."

Francis smiled, happy to see a friendly face. "Came to get Anita. Is she far behind?"

"I think she was sitting up front with the Auxiliary. It might be a while," Henny said. Dixie tugged him toward the door. "You going to the burial?"

"There's more?"

Dixie frowned. "What do you think they're gonna do? Dump him in the street?"

"Actually, I was thinking they'd keep him in a glass box in front of the library."

Dixie shook her head. "Honestly, Spud."

Across the vestibule, a man was waving his arms. It was Allen. Francis groaned as he watched him wriggle his way through the flow to cut over to where he was standing. The crowd rippled and bucked to let him through.

"Hey, Spud!" he shouted, causing every head to turn in Francis's direction. "What're you doing, standing there? You running for office or something?"

"Just trying to keep my nose out of trouble."

Allen laughed, soaking Francis with the smell of bourbon. "This is quite a scene, isn't it? I had to come see. Think we'll ever have this many people at our funerals?"

"If we do, we'll never know the difference."

"I can tell you right now, you won't get a funeral like this one," Deedee Cross said. "None of us will. There'll never be another Robert."

"Oh, I don't know about that," Allen snickered. "My man Spud here came in second in the rodeo, seems to me he's next in line."

Deedee reddened. "Don't even joke about that."

"Who's joking? You're a good man, aren't you, Spud?"

Francis shrank back. "Not here, Allen. Not now."

"I'm serious. Who here votes for Spud Pinkham being the new golden boy of Cedar Hole?" Allen raised his hand. He was the only one. "Looks like you're gonna need a few more votes, Spud."

"What's he done to deserve it?" someone asked.

"Well, let's see—he got his high school sweetheart knocked up and then he married her. That makes him a pretty upstanding guy—"

"Hey, cut it out, Allen," Francis warned. "Why don't you go on home and sober up?"

"—never finished high school, but he knows a thing or two about mowing lawns. Sounds like a shoo-in, wouldn't you say?"

"This is a funeral, for God's sake," someone else said. "Show a little respect."

"Instead of crying over Cutler, you should be paying attention to Spud over here. I've got your new man."

"Just shut up, will you?" another person said.

Allen shrugged and headed outside. "Sounds like you've got your work cut out for you, Spud."

Anita suddenly appeared at the entrance to the vestibule. Judging from the look of distress on her face, he suspected that she caught part of the exchange. "What's going on?" she asked.

"You know Allen," Francis said, rushing her out the door. "He thinks he's a comedian."

~ Chapter Five ~

No One Holds *a* Grudge Like Bernie Cutler

It had been only a month after Robert's death when word got back to Kitty about the desk.

"You'd think she would've called by now," Kitty said, her hands fluttering to her throat. "No note, no call, no nothing."

Norm Higgins tossed a package of lamb chops on the kitchen counter. "Fry them this time—don't let them sit in the oven for an hour to dry out."

"Well, what do you think?"

"About what?"

"Bernie?"

Norm sighed and draped his jacket over the back of a kitchen chair. "Leave her be. She just lost her husband."

Kitty popped the top of a can of beer and handed it to him. "I understand she's going through a difficult time, but picking up the phone isn't such a big effort, is it? Plus, Shorty says it's been outside this whole time—she refuses to bring it in. I drove by the other day just to see if it was true and, sure enough, it was just sitting there in the backyard."

When she pulled into the driveway (during school hours, of course, to prevent the possibility of being caught) Kitty was stunned. The desk was delicate and literary, worthy of a quill pen. It was the kind of desk that reminded her of the decorative arts wing of the City Museum, skirted with velvet rope barriers and DO NOT TOUCH signs. It was a desk beyond her dreams, and now that it had materialized before her, it seemed to echo her deepest desire—a desire she didn't even know she'd had.

"It's her desk. I suppose she's entitled to do any damn thing she wants with it," Norm said.

"It's not her desk—it's *my* desk. Robert bought that desk for me. It's an antique, too, a fine one, and I don't appreciate it being left out in the rain."

Norm rummaged through the spice cabinet and produced a dusty jar of dried rosemary. "Rub some of this on before you fry them. And don't forget the salt."

Kitty took the rosemary from him and set it aside. "Norm—please."

He sighed. "What do you want me to do about it?"

"I don't know—say something."

Norm sighed again. "He's gone now. Let him go."

Kitty unscrewed the cap to the jar and sniffed the contents. The herbs smelled of musty pine needles. "We're not talking about Robert. We're talking about the desk."

"The only reason why you want it is because he bought it for you."

"I want it because it was meant for me. It was one of his last wishes and should be respected."

Nudging her aside, Norm grabbed a clean frying pan from the drain board near the sink. "I never said anything before, but I never liked Robert. He could make you feel guilty just for being born less of a person. I can't stand anybody who acts like they don't crap on the pot like the rest of us."

"If you think that, then you didn't know him at all."

"Didn't care to."

"You're just saying that because I liked him."

"I'm just telling it like it is." Norm heated some oil in the pan. "You have to go easy, don't put the heat too high. I frenched the bones, see? You'd pay big bucks for that in the city."

"Bernadette may not even know I'm aware of the desk—or maybe she thinks it's for her. Wouldn't that be awful? Or maybe she's going to give it to me later when she gets her strength back. The whole situation is much more complicated than you know."

"It's probably a whole lot less complicated than you're making it," he said. "Give me the phone. I'll talk to Bernie."

Kitty thumbed the pearl buttons of her sweater. "Don't you dare say anything to her. I mean it."

"Fine, then. Fret about it."

"I'm just thinking there has to be another way."

"I'll tell you what," he said, laying the chops gently into the pan, "I'll go get Hanson's van and we'll drive over there right now. We won't even ring the doorbell. I'll back up the van and we'll load it on."

She drummed her fingers against the side of her face, her eyes widening at the possibility. "No," she suddenly said, shaking her head. "I'm not going to steal it."

"What's there to steal? You said the desk is yours."

"Well—at least that's what I was told." Kitty's brain was wrestling so violently with itself that she fell into the nearest chair to gain her equilibrium. "It's just the prettiest thing—quality, you know? I can't imagine why Bernadette would leave it outside like that."

"The longer you leave it out there, the worse condition it's going to be in."

Kitty knew her husband was right; this was a situation that demanded immediate action. "I'll write her a letter first. I think that's best."

That night, Kitty composed a polite letter mentioning that she had driven by and seen the desk and if Mrs. Cutler no longer had a use for such a fine piece of furniture, the library would be happy to accept it as a donation. It took into the wee hours to get the wording just right; years of curt letter-writing had deprived Kitty of the subtle tone necessary for such delicate correspondence.

Weeks passed without a reply. Kitty followed up with two more polite letters (one could not take for granted that there hadn't been a glitch at the post office), and then there was a third, written with a slightly more assertive quality.

"I'm thinking that the woman is depressed," she told her husband after several weeks with no reply. "I bet she's been ignoring her mail." Kitty also couldn't help wondering if her closing the letter with "Robert would-have wanted it that way" might have seemed a touch heavy-handed.

"Why don't you give her a call?" Norm suggested. "Invite her over. A woman like that shouldn't be sitting home alone."

"A woman like what?"

"You know what I mean—a widow. We'll barbecue some ribs."

Kitty agreed. "Nothing too forceful—just a friendly ring," she said. "Just to see how she's doing."

Apparently, Bernadette Cutler wasn't doing very well, for when they finally spoke, her tone reminded her of the Pinkham girls—hostile and wholly distasteful. Polite conversation, in Kitty's mind, dictated that pleasantries be exchanged before addressing the marrow of one's purpose, but Bernadette had no interest in chat. She cut directly to the reason for Kitty's call.

"You can't have the desk," she said.

The flatness of her answer choked a nervous giggle in Kitty's throat. "I wasn't asking for it, directly. It just occurred to me that if you didn't have a use for it—"

"It's been working out fine as lawn furniture."

"What a shame it is to leave it out in this cold weather. Did you know the *Farmer's Almanac* is predicting snow before Thanksgiving this year? The library would be happy to store the desk for you during the winter months. We can keep it warm and dry until next summer."

Bernadette laughed. "Really, Kitty. Please."

A sudden flash of heat burned her face. "I'm trying to be civil, Bernie. What do you want me to say? Hand it over?"

"It'd be more honest."

The air in the kitchen was stifling. Kitty threw open the window. "I've always thought that you didn't like me," she whispered with her hand cupped over the receiver so Norm wouldn't hear. "What do you want me to do?"

"Nothing."

"I worked hard for that desk, Bernie. More than twenty years."

"I'm sure you did—but you're not getting it."

Kitty gently put down the receiver for a moment and leaned over the window sash to take in a deep breath of air. The clouds were heavy and blue-gray. It smelled like snow. She picked up the receiver again.

"Robert would be very disappointed—that's all I'm going to say." She slipped the receiver onto its cradle, thinking that somehow if she hung up quietly enough, she could still retain her dignity.

"Is she coming over?" Norm called from the living room. "I'll run out for some beer."

Kitty bit her lower lip. "Go get the van."

THORNBERRY LANE was the only part of Cedar Hole awake at midnight. There was a constant stream of restless movements as some businesses closed up for the night and others prepared for the day ahead. A few remaining members of Shorty's kitchen staff wiped down the floors and hauled out trash to the cans out back, metal lids slamming and snippets of radio tunes blaring every time the kitchen door swung open. The post office received mail from central processing just after one a.m.; big burlap bags of letters were tossed in through the loading dock behind the building, with errant packages crashing onto the metal bulkhead. And then there was the occasional late produce delivery to Hanson's Superette, which happened when the driver got held up in traffic or decided to stop off at the Left Hand Club for a quick beer. The boxes of lettuce were too dense and soft to make much noise, but the hiss of the rig's air brakes and the gun of its engine were enough to rouse the unfortunate residents of Thornberry from an already restless sleep.

Kitty Higgins was relieved by the activity; all the action made her feel less conspicuous as they pulled into the back lot of the Superette and hopped into Hanson's delivery van. Norm whistled as he started up the engine, backing the vehicle out into the street as nonchalantly as if they were going for a quart of milk or dropping off letters at the post office. Kitty, on the other hand, had changed her clothes three times back at the house, finally settling on a pair of midnight-blue double-knit slacks and a black wool coat—colors that would melt into the dark. She tried on one of Norm's knit caps to buffer the cold but took it off immediately. It made her feel like a cat burglar.

"I don't know if this is a good idea," she said. "One of these days, Bernie's going to come into the library and see it."

"So what if she does?"

"She might call the police."

Norm shrugged. "There are scarier things in this world than having Harvey Comstock show up at your door. If we have to, we'll give it back. No harm done."

Kitty sat a little straighter in her seat. "If she had only let me have it, then we wouldn't be going through all this. You know I don't like to think ill of anyone, but that woman seems to have an awful mean streak."

"Are you sure you want to do this?"

"Why do you say that?"

" 'Cause you're not sure of yourself. I can hear it in your voice," he said. "If we go ahead, I don't want to hear you worrying on and on about whether or not we did the right thing."

"It was your idea to get the van."

"I'm just trying to make you happy, Kitty," he sighed. "That's all I ever do."

Kitty laced her fingers in her lap. "You make me sound difficult. I'm not so difficult, am I?"

"We're here—do you want the blasted thing or not?"

Kitty opened the door and had her foot nearly on the ground before Norm rolled the van to a stop in front of the Cutlers' garage. A streetlight stood directly in front of Bernie's house, casting a beam just shy of the van's bumper.

"It's over there, in the backyard," she hushed.

Norm went first, whistling loud enough to draw attention, guided by the penlight on the end of his key chain. He was bullish, unworried. Kitty melted into his shadow, clinging close to the wide shelter of his back.

Across the street at Shorty's, a dishwasher was wheeling out a can of garbage. He gave them a wave of acknowledgment that had Kitty cringing inside her coat.

"Hey, Norm—what's up?" the dishwasher called.

"Not much," he called back. "Taking care of some business for the missus—you?"

"You know, the usual. See you tomorrow."

"Have a good one."

Kitty's fingers dug into Norm's shoulders. "Did you have to talk to him? For God's sake, Norm—we look like thieves out here!"

"What do you want me to do, ignore him? That would have been worse."

Thankfully, the windows of the Cutlers' house were dark.

Norm came to an abrupt halt. Kitty bumped her head against his back. "We've got a little hang-up," he said. "Looks like Bernie chained the desk to the tree."

Kitty might not have believed it if she hadn't taken Norm's penlight from him and shone it on the legs of the desk. A thick chain encircled each leg and was pulled too taut to be slipped off. It crisscrossed the body of the desk before being looped around the tree and secured with a padlock. The maniacal care with which the chain was rigged gave Kitty a chill.

"The chain wasn't here when I saw it last time."

"It looks like she's got that tied in there pretty good," he laughed. "I'll have to go home and get the bolt cutter."

"Oh, Norm, it's really not funny. Sick is what it is. Sick and sad."

Kitty shone the beam on the elegant curves of the desk, whose surface had been blanched by sun and rain, marred by sticky globules of fruit that had fallen off the tree and were left to decay. Her head felt light. The desk was in bad shape, but not beyond help. She pulled each drawer gently, peering into compartments perfectly suited for her paper clips and pens, imagining how regal it would look next to the circulation desk—a tribute to her dedication as a librarian and archivist. A woman who owned such a desk didn't have to chase kids between the stacks or write letters to their parents. A woman who sat at such a desk had dignity. She commanded, and deserved, respect.

At the edge of the desk, the light caught a glint of gold. She peered closer and saw a small brass plate with etched words. *There shall be no love lost*, it said. Tears sprang to her eyes. There could be no doubt in her mind that Robert had intended for her to have this very desk, for she remembered him saying these very same words the night the library rejected his proposal. At the time, the words were a promise to her that he would never give up, that he would always fight for her. Now it seemed to be saying that she had to take up the mantle and fight for herself.

"I think I saw a desk just like that one at the dump last week," Norm said. "If I had thought about it I would have picked it up for you."

"It wouldn't be the same. I earned this."

Kitty ran her hand lovingly along the writing surface. Its silky smoothness was interrupted by a series of grooves. She peered closer. "It's been scratched."

"It's been more than that."

Her fingertips sought the grooves like Braille. "It feels like letters." She shone the dim bulb of the penlight over the desktop. The markings materialized into words, carved into the wood in crude block letters:

IF IT WILL FEED NOTHING ELSE,
IT WILL FEED MY REVENGE

Kitty snatched her fingers back as though they had found a splinter. She recognized the quote from Shakespeare's *Merchant of Venice*, an obvious, pointed threat, aimed at injuring precisely and cutting her down into bewildered bits. A cold, slithering fear buried itself deep beneath her skin. She had always pegged Bernie as odd and rude, but never cruel, and certainly not psychotic. What was it about her, specifically, that Bernadette found so repulsive? Was she jealous that Kitty was happily married and had meaningful work? Even if she stretched her imagination to its outermost limits, she could not come up with anything she might have said or done that deserved such contempt. Aside from writing a few letters now and then, Kitty Higgins had always done her very best not to be offensive to anyone.

"What's wrong?" Norm asked.

"Nothing—just a few scratches." She shuddered. Norm took a step toward her and Kitty slammed the rolltop shut. "Don't bother with the bolt cutters, we're leaving it."

"Why?"

"The condition's poor. I had no idea."

"We can take it down to Pinkham's," he said. "He'll clean it up for you."

"I don't want to steal it, Norman. It's just so—degrading." She turned on her heel and stalked back to the van. "Either Bernie gives it to me or I don't want it."

Norm's mouth pinched into a familiar grimace, a look that could express either disappointment or crankiness or relief or exhaustion. They'd been married for more than twenty years and Kitty still couldn't read him.

"After all this," he said, shaking his head. "I could have gone to bed early."

"I'm sorry. I was wrong." Kitty looked back at the house. The windows were dark, but she couldn't shake the feeling that Bernie was watching from one of the upstairs windows. "Hurry up. Let's go home."

ROBERT'S FUNERAL, which should have lasted only one day, seemed to stretch on for most of Nadine's childhood. Just when Bernie and Nadine would feel themselves slipping into a groove, a comfortable space they managed to carve out without him, there would be a dedication in his honor, an anniversary service at one of the four churches he attended, a moment of silence at a meeting or football game. The Train Festival was canceled indefinitely. Mourners held a vigil outside the Cutler house on the anniversary of his death, leaving melted candles in the driveway. The Cedar Hole Ladies' Auxiliary took it upon themselves to drop in regularly for tea, bearing hot noodle casseroles and cookie platters ("Their entrance tickets"—as Bernie called them). Bernie would have ignored the doorbell altogether, but Nadine, ripe with curiosity, answered every time someone came calling.

"Look, Mom—we got flowers again," Nadine said, bringing in a bouquet of white lilies that had been left on their doorstep on the fifth anniversary of his death. A satin ribbon embossed with the words IN MEMORY was tied around the stems.

"I'm sick of my house smelling like a funeral parlor," Bernie said. "Leave them outside by the desk."

At eight, Nadine was still a few years away from questioning the desk's purpose in the backyard. It had been there beneath the dead plum tree as long as she could remember, stippled from hard spring rains and heavy snows, a permanent fixture that had ceased to be anything more than part of the landscape. She stuffed the lilies in the desk and closed the top.

Inside, her mother was planning school lunches for the coming month.

"Mom, what do those words mean?"

"What words?"

"The ones on the desk."

Bernie continued on with her work, but her eyes turned fiery. "Which ones? The ones on the brass plate, or the ones carved into the top?"

"Both."

"The ones on the plate are some nonsense your father had etched on there. The carved ones I did myself—it's a favorite quote of mine."

"What do you mean, dad's words are nonsense?"

"I mean that it's garbage, that it's not worth thinking about."

Nadine plopped down beside her mother. "But what do they say? I know it says 'love' but I don't understand all of it together." She thought carefully about the quote. "Is it about how much he loved us?"

"It means just the opposite. How much he loved someone else."

"Who?"

Bernie dropped her pen. "Really, Nadine, I don't have the energy to get into this right now."

"But how could he love anyone more than us?"

"I couldn't tell you. You'd have to ask him, but unfortunately, he's not here to answer that."

Sometimes, when Nadine was home alone, she'd pretend she was dead. She'd pull the window shades and draw the curtains on the dry, earthy shroud of her room, then she'd stretch out on top of her bedcovers and cross her palms flat on her chest, closing her eyes to the darkness. She'd try not to breathe, holding the breath still in her lungs, trying to will her heart to stop its insistent beat. Her eyes would sink back into her skull, and her mind would go slack. For a second, maybe two, she could almost feel herself withdrawing, shrinking from her body, pulling away from sensation and connection, a tiny, weightless marble rattling around inside a corpse. For that brief moment, she could almost imagine what it was like to be her father, buried underground. But then her lungs would rise again, filled with the grace of newfound breath, drawing her back to the living.

"If Dad's in the ground and he can't move, then he can't hurt you anymore, right?" Nadine leaned against her mother. "So why are you still mad at him?"

Bernie sighed and returned to her work. "Because he wasn't sorry and he never will be."

THE DAY AFTER her attempted theft of the desk, Kitty picked up a belt sander at the hardware store and, over the course of the next ten years, tried the soft sell on Bernie. She sent flowers and fruit baskets, Christmas cards and newsletters about the library's progress—not once mentioning the disputed desk. Kitty thought this approach would underscore to Bernie that she bore no ill feelings toward her and that she was a person of great kindness and unquestionable integrity. She came to the fair-minded conclusion that Bernie's hatred stemmed only from ignorance, and that once she was correctly informed that Kitty was not a self-serving, presumptuous thief, it would correctly follow that Bernie would eventually give in.

As the years wore on, Bernie did not respond to her gestures, and Kitty grew desperate. On days when the library was empty of children she locked it up for ten minutes at a time, just long enough to take a quick ride down Thornberry and back again. The desk was always there, its chains unmoved, a vile testament to pettiness. With each visit the finish had eroded just a little more, the wood warping in the rain and cracking under the summer heat. A wounded animal, it sighed and whimpered beneath her touch. The more trauma the desk withstood, the more determined Kitty was to liberate it from Bernie's ungrateful clutches. Just like Robert, it brought her life into sharp focus—the direction was clear, even if the means of getting there was not.

"Fulfilling the last wishes of the dead is an unquestionable duty," she often told Norm, who had long since ignored any comments about Robert or the desk. "I'll make sure Robert gets his last wish. I don't care how long it takes."

By the tenth anniversary of his death, Kitty's patience was beginning to wear thin. She finally decided to take her case to the Library Association.

"For the last decade, Mrs. Cutler has been holding on to library property. I think we should retain a lawyer and reclaim the desk for the town."

"And you're sure the desk belongs to the library?" the chairman asked.

"One hundred percent."

"Why, then, are you bringing this up now?"

"Believe me, this is a last resort," Kitty said. "I've been trying to settle the matter peacefully on my own for some time now."

The association abandoned their parliamentary procedure and whispered energetically among themselves. After several moments, the chairman cleared his throat and brought the room back to order. "I think we've all come to an agreement that suing for an old worn-out desk is not only impractical, but expensive."

Kitty took the news as evenly as she could, responding to the association's rejection with a pinched smile.

"However, we understand your desire to commemorate Robert Cutler's life, given that the Cedar Hole Library has never had a more generous patron and volunteer. To that end, we'd like to propose another, less expensive option. We'd like to rename the library in his honor."

"That's a wonderful idea!" Kitty felt as though she were about to burst. "We could have a dedication ceremony and invite the whole town!"

"And serve refreshments," someone added.

"And a sign," she said. "We'll need a new sign."

The chairman rubbed his brow. "We hadn't quite considered the cost of that."

Kitty sighed, but refused to let the committee's cheapness deflate her. Robert wouldn't have let it stand in the way and neither would she. "I have some money saved up. I'll take care of the sign."

"Well done," the chairman said, banging his gavel. "The library will be renamed."

As soon as a date for the dedication ceremony was confirmed, Kitty sent invitations to the entire town informing everyone, including Bernie and Nadine, of the good news.

" 'The honor of your presence is requested as the guest(s) of honor . . . ' " Nadine read aloud.

Bernie rolled her eyes. "She wrote 'honor' twice? Good Lord—and she's supposed to be an educated woman."

Nadine dug her pink fingernails into the flesh of her palm. She had recently discovered nail polish and was letting them grow. "They're re-naming the library after Dad. It's going to be the Robert J. Cutler Memorial Library. They're serving refreshments."

"For Pete's sake. . . ." Bernie snatched the letter out of Nadine's hands and looked it over. Her eyes became cold. "And what's this, printed at the bottom? Is the woman out of her mind?"

Nadine took a closer look. At the bottom of the invitation, printed in small italic letters, were the same words her father had engraved on the desk.

"Is that supposed to be some secret message for me?" Bernie shouted. "Is there anything she won't do for that blasted desk?"

For most of her childhood, Nadine had gone along with her mother's thoughts and actions, trusting that beyond her irrationality lingered a deep, balanced reason that she was too young to process. Now, at thirteen, Nadine saw Bernie as sad and foolish, a frustrating amalgam of all that was disagreeable and unfair. Everything about Bernie rubbed Nadine raw; from the outdated velour sweat suit she wore around the house, to the way she stood in the kitchen holding Kitty Higgins's invitation—hip thrust to one side, hand on the small of her back, eyes rolled up into her eyelids—as though the whole world were a dried-up ball of drivel not worthy of her.

"She can forget it. I'm not going." Bernie tossed the invitation onto a pile of junk mail containing a brochure for Shady Acres Cemetery in Mt. Etna ("Why they waste such a beautiful spot on the dead, I'll never know," she'd said) and an auction flyer from Fairbanks Antiques ("Perhaps you'd be interested in adding an elegant armoire to your outdoor setting?" Fairbanks had personally written in the margins).

"I think we should go. It's important."

"It's a vanity party for Kitty to draw attention to herself. The only people who will be there are the bored and the morbid. I wish you could see that," she said. "Why don't they name the library after someone who's alive, who can really appreciate the honor? Or better yet, leave well enough alone. Think of all the new stationery and rubber stamps they'll have to buy. What a waste."

Any excitement Nadine might have had for the event had been

sucked down into the coldest pit of her stomach. "*One* of us should be there. It'd be pretty embarrassing if we both blew it off."

"Embarrassment is a form of weakness. It means you care more about what others think than about your own integrity. Why on earth should I care what Kitty or anybody else thinks? I didn't ask to be invited."

Bernie emptied the dishwasher, absently stuffing a stack of clean plates in the refrigerator. It was another exhibit cataloged in Nadine's mind, among a growing list of evidence that her mother was criminally insane.

"If Dad bought the desk for Kitty, how come you won't just give it to her?"

"Because she's a nitwit and your father was in love with her."

Nadine laughed. "With Mrs. Higgins? She's old."

"Your father never did have good taste."

Nadine pulled the plates out of the fridge and put them away in the cupboard. "I don't believe you. You're making it up."

"Am I? Go take a look at what's engraved on that desk. Look at what Kitty put on the invitation," Bernie said. "She always had his affection and she knows it. She wants to rub my face in it."

"Do you really think that's what the quote meant? Maybe he was saying something about how much he loved Cedar Hole."

Bernie rolled her eyes again. "Don't be so naïve."

"But if it was some secret love message, why would he put it where you could see it?"

"Because he was selfish and never thought about my feelings."

"You're not making any sense."

Bernie slammed the dishwasher shut, rattling the clean silverware still inside. "Why won't you take my word for it? You barely knew your father at all, but I was married to him."

"Other people knew him pretty well and they all say great things about him."

"Of course they do," Bernie said, sounding exasperated. "He knew how to put on a good show."

Nadine opened the dishwasher and finished putting away the dishes. "I don't care what you say. I'm going to the dedication."

"Well, you're old enough to make up your own mind," Bernie said. "If you're hell bent on going, then I recommend taking a pillow. And maybe tuck a granola bar in your pocket in case you get hungry—I'm sure Kitty's going to make that god-awful apple cake of hers."

Bernie removed the invitation from the junk pile and handed it to Nadine, her fingers almost limp with what Nadine read to be surrender. She couldn't be sure if her determination had disarmed her mother completely or if Bernie was simply giving in so Nadine could find out for herself that she had been right.

"She's going to ask me about the desk, you know," Nadine said. "I'm going to have to tell her something."

"Tell her to go to hell."

"Mom."

Bernie leaned against the counter and stared out the window. The glaring sunlight gave her purple track suit an electric sheen that glowed bright and dangerous. Nadine tucked the knives deep in the utensil drawer.

"All right. Tell her she can have it."

Nadine scanned her mother's face for traces of sarcasm and irony that would betray the honesty of her tone, but there were none. "Really?"

"It's an eyesore and I'm tired of it," Bernie said. "But I'm not bringing it to her. Tell her if she still wants it she'll have to come and get it."

~ Chapter Six ~

A Bright Idea

I t was Marty who discovered the spring, or at least he was the first to recognize it for what it was. He was a senior in high school at the time, bullheaded and thick-necked, more shrewd than intelligent. Marty broke into the top ten that quarter, an honor that had Anita tripping all over herself with pride, and Francis scratching his head at how a boy who never so much as cracked a book or made honor roll managed such a feat. There were times when Marty sneaked out of his locked bedroom to make a sandwich or a phone call (both boys were blessed with a wide circle of friends and legions of adoring girls) when Francis had the urge to sidle up to his son and ask him how he did it. How he pulled off the coup. No judgment, of course, but man to man. He'd get close enough to be in the same room with him, but then Anita would walk in or Marty would shoot him a look that would make Francis bristle. *Good for you,* Francis thought as he retreated to the garage and grabbed a bag of peanuts from the secret stash of snacks he kept hidden from the boys in an empty drawer of his toolbox. *You'll never be anyone's doormat.*

Francis had seen that soggy patch of lawn dozens of times in the back corner of the yard near the pines, even stamped around it with the toe of his work boots, marveling at the deep, clear puddle that never dried up. It seemed stupid to him now that he didn't think more of it, but to be fair, a working man who scraped by on lawnmowing and grocery deliveries spent most of his time thinking about food, not water. Providing food was the ever-present strain, the unrelenting goal that, once achieved, had to be pursued all over again. Water, on the other hand, was one of the few things Francis had the luxury of taking for granted. He could open the faucets and it was always there, cold and plentiful. Reliable as air.

It was on a Tuesday, at suppertime, that Marty broke his discovery. "You know, Pop, you've got a spring in the backyard."

The first thing that came to Francis's mind was that the leaf spring on the delivery van had finally let go and that the whole suspension couldn't be too far behind. The entire thing was going to cost him a bundle. Francis groaned.

"It's right near the stand of pines at the bottom of the hill," Marty said.

Anita took a set of salt and pepper shakers in the shape of ears of corn out of the cupboard and put them in the center of the kitchen table. Collecting shakers was a new hobby of hers, a reason to get out of bed early on Saturdays and scope out the yard sales. She had sets in the shape of cows, tomatoes, teapots, cats—you name it—all of them filled to the top with salt and pepper, even when they were sitting unused in the cupboard. Francis could have bought himself a dozen leaf springs with the amount of money she wasted on salt and pepper.

"I didn't drive the van out there," Francis thought aloud. "Maybe it's the truck. I thought I noticed the rear tilting the other day."

Marty shook his head. "I'm not talking about that kind."

Francis's forehead broke into a film of sweat. He looked to Anita, who always had a better chance of deciphering the boys' code than he ever did.

"Are you saying we have water?" Anita said.

Marty nodded. "Have you seen it?"

"Sure, I've seen it," Francis cut in, thanking Anita silently as the sweat on his forehead cooled off. "You're talking about the big puddle back there that never dries up. I see it all the time."

Francis watched Marty pick up the corncobs and shake them all over his supper, even getting some on the vinyl tablecloth, as though spices were so cheap they were heaped in the backyard like sand piles. "Flynn and I had a taste. It's good, and cold."

"Flynn, you didn't!" Anita was on her feet, tilting Flynn's head back and checking his throat for ominous spots.

"I'm fine, Mom," Flynn protested. "That was days ago. My insides could've turned green by now and you would've never known the difference."

Anita smiled and kissed the top of his head. "A mother can worry about her boys, you know. There's nothing wrong with that."

"If we shoveled some sand onto it I wonder if it would dry it up," Francis said. "Or better yet, sawdust."

"Oh no—you don't want to do that," Marty said. "A spring's a good thing. You don't want to get rid of it."

After dinner, Marty insisted on bringing Francis over to the puddle, with Flynn and Anita tagging along behind. It had been a while since Francis had looked at the puddle and it seemed larger to him now, almost two feet in diameter. Marty brought a big plastic bucket with him and scooped out a half gallon of water. In a matter of minutes, the small basin of earth filled up again.

"Would you look at that?" Anita said, her voice full of wonder. She crouched down and raked the water with her fingers, then touched them to her lips. "It's so cold."

Marty and Flynn each cupped their hands and took a drink. "Go on, Pop," Marty said. "Give it a try."

"I know what water tastes like."

"Come on, old man." Anita gave his arm a tender pinch. "Don't be such a ninny."

A grumble vibrated in Francis's throat as he squatted over the puddle and cupped his hands, conscious of the boys' stares. He dipped into the pool, the water's chill stinging his skin as it filled the bowl of his hands. Pressing the heels of his palms to his lips, he tilted back his head and drank.

The sensation was strange. His tongue had long been numbed to the metallic, chlorine-heavy town water he had grown up with in Cedar Hole. In the hills, there was plenty of tax money for water treatment that produced a light, sweet product that kept contaminants down to a barely traceable parts-per-billion, but in Cedar Hole they limped along, scarcely meeting federal standards. Until Francis had taken a drink from the spring, he had never known that water didn't have to be murky and flat; that it could slip over the taste buds unnoticed, refreshing and wet and oddly intangible.

"I don't taste anything," he said, dipping again.

"That's the point, Pop," Marty said. "It's not supposed to taste like anything. That's how you know it's good."

Francis drove his hand deep into the puddle, feeling for the pulse of its secret, mystical source. "So there's water. Big deal. Show me a hole in the ground that coughs up T-bone steaks—now *that* would be worth something."

Flynn splashed water on his face and rubbed it all over his forearms, sighing with such primitive contentment that Francis had to restrain himself from reminding his son that he worked hard to provide him with indoor plumbing. Anita giggled and spritzed a little on the back of her neck.

"You're missing the point," Marty said, his voice taking on a condescending edge that made Francis clench his teeth. "There's an opportunity here. There are people who are willing to pay good money for spring water."

Francis laughed out loud, a cutting laugh that he had earned through years of living and experience. Marty was brewing some half-witted scheme and this time—this one time—Francis had the better of him.

"No one—not one person I know—would be willing to fork over good money for something they can get in their own house for free."

"I'm not talking about the boneheads who live around here—"

"Watch yourself, now—"

"—I'm talking about city people. They pay as much as seventy cents a gallon for this stuff."

"That can't be. That's almost as much as gasoline."

"Believe me, they pay it." Marty's skin started turning red just under his ears, the way it usually did when he was burning hot with an idea. "Think about it—you know how bad city water can be. It's like drinking raw sewage."

Francis eyed his son. "I wouldn't have the faintest notion what city water tastes like, and I'm wondering just how it is that you do."

Marty scooped another gallon of water out of the basin and watched it fill up again. "With all the pollution, the water's bound to be terrible. It's common sense."

"Makes sense to me," Flynn said.

"Are you saying I don't have any?"

"That's not what he's saying at all." Anita shook her head vigorously, for she was a great believer in logic and common sense, especially when it was served up so convincingly by one of her own boys. "I remember when my aunt brought us into the city when we were young. We went for tea and I remember that the tea had an off flavor. Come to think of it, it must have been the water."

"You've never mentioned before that the tea tasted funny," Francis said. "Not once, in the hundred times you've told me that story."

"So I didn't mention it—that doesn't mean it's not true."

Marty stared pointedly at Francis. "All we need is to install a pump and we can start bottling this stuff." His words were coming fast now. Francis could almost feel the heat of his breath sailing at him from the other side of the puddle. "We could sell the bottles in the city and make a fortune."

Anita bit down hard on her lower lip. Francis could see hope blossoming in her eyes, overgrowing into a wild jungle of possibilities.

"What do we know about selling water to city folks?" he looked away from her to regain his bearings. "Even if we did know what we were doing, we don't have the money to do it. How's that for common sense?"

Anita touched him lightly on the thigh. "Take it easy."

Marty scooped a handful of water and let it roll down and off his wrist. "We'll figure it out."

Flynn nodded. "It can't be that hard."

"It can't be that hard," Francis mimicked. "What do you two know about running a business?"

"It's just an idea," Anita said. "Let the boys talk. Maybe they're on to something."

Francis stood up and wiped his wet palms on the thighs of his work trousers. The remaining Pinkhams still squatted over the spring, their faces glowing with expectation.

"Go inside," he said, walking back to the house. "It's getting dark."

•   •   •

No ONE mentioned the spring again, though for the next few weeks Francis felt as if he were the object of a silent conspiracy; an outsider to the loaded silences and knowing glances exchanged between Anita and the boys. They seemed satisfied in their secret collusion, believing, it seemed, that by banding together they could break down his resolve. But Anita, Flynn, and Marty's collective cold shoulder was still not strong enough to convince him. After all, living with his sisters had made Francis used to being ignored.

One Tuesday evening, when Francis returned home after mowing lawns, he noticed that the chill that had descended upon the Pinkham household was beginning to thaw.

"Did you hear the news?" Anita said, greeting him at the door. "Allen's had an accident. He got pinned by a forklift at the factory last night."

Francis winced. "How bad is it?"

"Dixie says they're putting a rod in his leg. But at least he'll be able to walk—I suppose it could've been worse."

"I bet that rod will ache every time it rains."

Anita covered her hands with oven mitts and pulled a casserole out of the oven. "He's over at Mt. Etna General. We should go pay him a visit after supper."

Francis felt bad about Allen—the same way he'd feel about anyone who hit a bad streak—but his feelings went no deeper than common sympathy. He wished Dixie hadn't said anything, even though word was likely to get around sooner or later. Later, of course, would have been better—after the operation, when Allen was home recuperating. When Francis wouldn't be burdened with the guilt of not going to visit him in the hospital.

Francis hovered over the hot dish, trying to divine its contents. "I'm not going anywhere near there. Send him a card and call it done."

"Beef noodle casserole. Get away, it's hot," she said, carrying it over to a trivet in the middle of the table. "I'm sure he could use a friendly face."

The boys came into the kitchen, looking at Francis for the first time in weeks.

"Hi, Pop," Marty said.

"Hi, Pop," Flynn echoed.

"I'm sure Henny will go—that ought to be enough." Francis took his seat at the end of the table, between Marty and Flynn. As he looked down at his fork, he spotted a pamphlet tucked in under the edge of his empty dinner plate. It was glossy and printed on heavy card stock, with an illustrated light bulb on the front surrounded with wavy dashes to indicate rays of light. Above, in bold black print were the words: **Do You Have A Bright Idea?**

"What in the hell's this?" Francis said, tossing it in the center of the table, perilously close to the butter dish.

Anita picked up the pamphlet and laid it carefully beside his dinner plate. "Why don't you read it and find out?"

"Can I eat first?"

"The boys are going out after and we have a lot to talk about," Anita said. "It'll only take a minute."

Francis leisurely buttered a slice of bread and took two slow bites. The boys stared at him until, with a reluctant growl, he opened the pamphlet.

We Want You!

We're looking for bright individuals with marketable ideas who want to take advantage of today's fast-growing economy. Have a business idea, product, or invention but don't know how to get started? Rice Industries, LLC, America's leader in private entrepreneurial investment, has the tools you need to launch your dream. Our consultants have the knowledge and experience to take your idea all the way to the top!

You are cordially invited to a free seminar
Saturday, May 17th
At the Palmdale Arms Hotel
Ballroom A
9:00 a.m.

Francis waited until he finished eating his slice of bread before he glanced up at his family. "Where'd you get this?"

"Shorty's," Marty said. "It was pinned to the bulletin board."

"I thought we decided to leave things alone."

"*You* decided that," he said. "The rest of us still think we should do something about it."

"Go ahead. Knock yourself out."

Anita sat down next to Francis and put her hand on the inside of his wrist, the way she always did when she wanted something. "We wouldn't dream of going ahead without you," she said. "It's a free seminar. It won't hurt a bit just to listen—you could get some advice on how to start something up."

Francis shook his head. "Don't get all excited about some flashy pamphlet. This thing is for nut jobs who think they've designed a better can opener or come up with a new board game—not for a guy with a puddle in his backyard."

"A business is a business," she said. "You said we weren't going to do it because we didn't know how. Well, it says right here they're going to tell us how."

Francis gnawed on his crust of bread, then helped himself to several large spoonfuls of Anita's beef noodle casserole. "You have no idea what it takes to get something like that going—you think you can snap your fingers and it all happens, just like *that*. Look at my lawnmowing business. It took years to build it to where it is now—and it's still a struggle."

"Pop, don't think of it like a business, think of it as something we can do together," Marty said. "Like a hobby."

"A hobby, huh? Like that guitar and that pool table you begged me to buy? They're sitting in the basement right now, untouched. Why should I throw my hard-earned money out the window on something you're going to get bored with six months from now?"

"Be nice," Anita said, squeezing his wrist.

"Why are you so afraid of trying something new?" Marty raised his voice. "Is mowing lawns that great? Is delivering groceries the greatest thing in the world?"

Francis dropped his fork. "Are you listening to this, Anita? Do you hear the way your sons are talking to me?"

"They're just a little excited," she said. "Marty, be nice to your father."

"It's not my fault he won't listen to reason."

Francis picked up his fork again and shook it at Marty. "You forget who the parent is in this house."

"I'll be eighteen in three months."

"And I'll be your father forever."

Marty drank down his glass of milk and stood up. "I'm going out."

"Where?" Francis asked.

"To a friend's."

"That's no kind of answer."

Anita closed her eyes and pursed her lips. "Don't antagonize him, Francis."

Marty skipped out the door.

"Don't stay out too late, please!" Anita called after him.

Flynn drew listless circles on his plate with the tines of his fork.

"Leave your mother and I alone for a few minutes," Francis said. "We need to talk."

"But I'm not done yet—"

"Take it to your room."

Flynn filled his plate with a few more spoonfuls of casserole, then headed off to his room. Francis waited until he heard the door shut.

"I can't believe you let the boys talk like that."

Anita stacked the empty plates on top of one another and carried them to the sink. "You've got them all worked up. They can't understand how you can be so stubborn."

"Honestly, Anita, a man could get to feeling like a stranger in his own home."

"Don't be so dramatic. The boys love you," she said. "Would it be so terrible to just go and find out a little information?"

"You want me to waste my Saturday just to find out what I already know—that we can't afford it?"

"You don't know that. How can you say you know when you won't even listen?" Anita dropped her sponge in a plastic dishpan filled with soapy water and took a seat at the table. "Have you looked at our bank account lately? We don't have enough money to send Marty to school next year."

"So let's blow what little we do have on the puddle."

"Don't you want our sons to have every opportunity?"

"Now, don't go twisting things," Francis sighed. "There's no sense in gambling the little we have. Plus, there are scholarships, you know. He's done well this year."

"Why do we have to rely on that? Why should we sit back and just let things happen? What's wrong with taking a little initiative?"

"Trust me for once, will you? I'm saying no."

Anita lifted her chin and folded her arms across her chest, a posture that Francis found both draining and mildly intimidating. "You can stop acting like the king of the roost anytime now, Francis Pinkham. This house belongs to me as much as you—along with the land and that damn puddle out back. If you're not going to seize the opportunity, I'll do it myself."

"Hey, there—now, just hold on a second," he said, trying to keep the fear from seeping into his voice. "Don't get all huffy on me."

"Well, what's it gonna take?"

Francis left the table and turned on the television in the living room. A commercial for canned beans was on, showing an animated can opening his own head with a can opener. Francis sank deep into his favorite chair, taking a blurred interest. Anita followed him in, taking a seat on the ottoman in front of him, blocking his view.

"Are you going to sit there and stare at me all night?"

"If I have to." Anita rested her head on his knees.

Francis grunted.

"I want you to take Marty. He'd be so pleased."

On TV, the can turned himself upside down and spilled his canned bean guts into a saucepan.

"If I go, it still doesn't mean I'm going to do anything about the spring."

"I know, I know," Anita said, a light igniting behind her eyes. "Just promise me you'll keep an open mind."

~ Chapter Seven ~

VERTIGO

Ainsley John Smith waited for Nadine on the bench outside the abandoned train depot with a spiral notebook opened onto his lap and a pen in his hand, the same way he waited for her every morning before school. At thirteen, he was woefully thin, with long limbs, a sunken chest, and opalescent skin—his hair a baby-fine brown and prone to bouts of static electricity. Ainsley was Nadine's oldest and most reliable friend—someone who had clung to her side since the first grade, making himself useful or funny or sympathetic, depending on her mood or needs. As of late, however—eighth grade, to be exact—Nadine began to notice that Ainsley's attentions turned in a direction she didn't at all find favorable and did her best to ignore.

"You look lovely today," he said as she approached.

Nadine tucked a loose strand of hair behind her ear and coyly snatched the notebook from Ainsley's lap. "How many words you got?"

"Just a couple sentences."

Nadine scanned the notebook, but her eyes flitted over the lines without comprehension. She felt Ainsley's gaze covering her—a comforting, ever-present blanket of adoration that she clutched fiercely and refused to return. This was Ainsley, after all, someone she could never think of as more than a friend, even though he was reasonably cute, in a nondescript kind of way, and always did whatever she asked.

"Tell me what I spelled wrong," he said.

"Well, you got the 'r' and 'e' reversed here," she said, pointing out his mistake, "and the 'l' and 'y' over here."

Ainsley took back his notebook and made the necessary corrections. "What do you think of it overall? Do you think it would make a good article?"

"I don't know," she said, rereading it. "Would Mr. Holtz care that much about a few missing books of stamps at the post office? If you want to get him to hire you, you're going to have to cover something that'll really get his attention."

Ainsley chewed on his pencil eraser. "I wish we still had the Train Festival, then I could cover that, just like your dad."

"You don't have to do everything exactly like he did."

"Why not? He laid down a perfect blueprint. Everything he ever did was memorable."

Nadine could have told him that being remembered wasn't nearly as glamorous as he imagined it to be, but nevertheless Ainsley was obsessed with the idea of leaving some sort of imprint on the world. He blamed this preoccupation on a traumatic childhood incident in which his mother went into a store dressing room to try on a bra. As soon as she was done she went home, only to remember five hours later, while watching TV, that she had left her son behind in the women's lingerie department. From that moment on, Ainsley vowed never to be forgotten again.

"Afraid of being forgotten because he spent an afternoon in the panty department?" Bernie scoffed when Nadine relayed the story. "I don't buy it. All that's likely to do is turn him into a cross-dresser."

Nadine secretly wondered if Ainsley's obsession really stemmed from the fact that he was blessed with perfectly bland, unremarkable features. With a standard haircut, level eyes, a medium-length nose, and a mouth of average proportions, Ainsley was commonly handsome—unassuming and nonthreatening, forgettable and yet familiar. His presence was typical in the best sense of the word: decidedly neutral, innocuous, leaving no lasting impression. Ainsley possessed his averageness so thoroughly that on several occasions Nadine had seen people who had met him many times before introduce themselves, their eyes absent of recognition.

Ainsley was convinced he knew the best way to be remembered.

"TV and movie stars are easily forgotten as soon as their looks change. Musicians last a little longer, as long as their songs are popular. But great writers—their words stay in print forever. Even if no one reads them, they're still alive somehow."

"What about being a politician?" Nadine suggested. "People remember senators and presidents forever."

"Too much work," Ainsley said. "I'm going to be a journalist."

Nadine worried about his making such an indiscriminate decision, especially since the universe seemed dead set against Ainsley's career choice. His parents, whose lack of reproductive creativity had already produced the most average of faces, were equally uninspired when it came to naming their son. They christened him John Smith—a name so common and obvious it was destined to slip right out of the consciousness of any future newspaper-reading public. John remedied the problem by calling himself Ainsley (after a distant cousin on his mother's side), a name that was just different and quirky enough to be remembered.

Ainsley also had a difficult time with writing and reading, due to bouts with dyslexia and myopia, which went undiagnosed until the fifth grade. As far as the dyslexia was concerned, Nadine helped him with unscrambling the words, but when it came to buying eyeglasses, Ainsley's parents suspected the optometrist of milking their wallets. The Smiths, who were known throughout Cedar Hole for their thrift, found an old pair of gold-rimmed bifocals in a desk drawer and cleaned them up good with diluted vinegar and a soft rag. Ainsley wore the glasses only in the house, and spent a good deal of his time at home bumping into the corners of tables and chairs. Ainsley's road to fame via writing, Nadine thought, was likely to be a difficult one.

"What about the dedication?" Nadine said as they started walking toward school. "You could cover that for the newspaper. I'm sure that would get Mr. Holtz's attention."

"What dedication?"

"You didn't get an invitation? About the library being renamed in my father's honor?" A wounded look crossed Ainsley's face, causing Nadine to backpedal. "Maybe your mother forgot to give it to you. Or it's still in the mail. I'm sure Mrs. Higgins wants you to be there."

"That would be good—a big event like that," he said, brightening.

"I could lend you my camera. You could take a few pictures."

"Pictures, too. There's no way Mr. Holtz will be able to say no this time." Ainsley rubbed his hands together. "As soon as I start selling articles, the first thing I'm going to do is take you out to dinner. Then I'm going to buy a new pair of glasses. Then who knows? Anything is possible."

They passed beneath a broad oak, where a fat squirrel clung to the trunk. Nadine expected him to scurry up the tree as they approached, but the squirrel held still and calm, his black marble eyes following their path.

The glowing optimism on Ainsley's face frightened her a little. "Don't be disappointed if it doesn't happen right away, though," she warned. "It takes time."

"I know." He reached for her hand. "I gotta give it a try, though. Didn't your dad say, 'A man is only as great as his vision'?"

"I don't know," Nadine said, pulling her hand away. "Did he?"

FRANCIS took Webber Road. It was the longer, more roundabout way to the Palmdale Arms, but it had the advantage of being routinely familiar. The shorter, more major routes, as of late, were clogged with traffic and the landscape was increasingly disorienting; every time Francis turned his head it seemed there was a new shopping mall or fried food joint being slapped together, sometimes popping up so quickly he swore they were brought in by crane already built and plunked down whole, complete with teenage employees and paying customers.

"Why are we going this way? Route 9 is shorter," Marty said.

"Because I want to—that's why."

Just ahead was the railroad crossing. Francis knew every contour and dip so well he could navigate his way safely with a blindfold, let alone with the benefits of daylight and clear vision. Still he chose to take the tracks at a fast clip—if for no other reason than the early morning thrill of feeling his stomach drop to his boots.

"Jesus, Dad," Marty said as they became briefly airborne. Francis had failed to take his son's height into consideration, and watched with breathless fright out of the corner of his eye as Marty's head came within an inch of hitting the ceiling.

"Watch your language." The steep dropoff at the road's shoulder, which he thoughtlessly passed—even flirted with—when he was alone now seemed dangerous with Marty beside him, and he wished he had taken the quicker way instead, even if it meant getting lost.

"Mom would have a fit if she knew you were driving like that."

"It's a good thing neither one of us is going to tell her," Francis said. "You know, if you wanted to, buddy, we could go to Funtown instead and ride some roller coasters."

Marty looked down at his clipboard.

"It's your call. We don't have to do this."

"You *really* want to go home and tell Mom you flaked out after the hell she gave you the other night?"

Francis turned and stared at him. "How'd you know about that?"

"If I were you, I'd just suck it up and make her happy."

"Hey—she's making me do this because of you. Say the word, and I'll turn right around."

"I want to go."

Francis swerved gently to avoid a large pothole, which was fast becoming a small crater, just right of the center line.

"When I was your age, all I cared about was hanging out with my friends and drinking beer. I wasn't nearly so serious."

"And look at you now. You mow lawns for a living."

Francis swallowed Marty's jab, though it felt permanently lodged in his throat. "I own my own business," he corrected.

"Which is mowing lawns. Don't you ever think about bettering yourself? Doing something that matters?"

"Sure—for the longest time I prayed to high heaven that God would give me a giant puddle in my backyard so I could bottle the water and sell it to stupid rich people. And now it looks like my prayers have been answered. Boy, am I a lucky man."

Marty groaned, as if crushed by embarrassment, and stared out the window for the rest of the ride.

The Palmdale Arms was the kind of hotel that made Francis jittery even without having stepped foot in the place; a steel box that rose an impressive fourteen stories into the sky with dual tinted glass elevator shafts that you could see from the parking lot. From behind the truck's windshield, Francis watched the elevator cars zipping between floors. The sharp buzz of vertigo melted his neural circuits.

Marty jumped out of the truck. "Are you going to stare at the elevators all day, or are you going in?"

A WOMAN sitting at a card table next to the ballroom entrance gave them each name tags, a thick blue folder filled with various forms, and a sharpened pencil. "Help yourself to complimentary coffee and pastries," she said, waving them in.

Inside, rows of banquet chairs were lined up in front of an elevated platform with a projector screen behind it. Only a third of the seats were filled, mostly with middle-aged men in wire-rimmed glasses, sipping coffee from Styrofoam cups, arms draped over the empty seats next to them, their short-sleeved dress shirts snowed with flecks of dandruff and heads cocked to their one good ear. Onstage, a man in a pin-striped suit with the name JOE pinned to his lapel trotted from one end of the platform to the other. He had a microphone in one hand and a pointer in the other.

". . . my function as a scout for Rice Industries is to find hidden talent and bring it to its fullest potential," he said, turning on his heel and working back down the other side with the giddiness of a quarterhorse. "We're looking to invest in Bright Ideas. . . ."

"I'm giving it twenty minutes," Francis whispered to Marty, who, to his terror, had chosen a pair of seats in the second row, dead center. "Then I'm leaving."

"Welcome, have a seat," Joe said, pausing briefly to acknowledge them. "Before we address the *real* reason you're all here, before we get to the *real* work, let me tell you a little bit about our founder, Weldon Rice . . ."

The lights dimmed and a slide projector clicked on from somewhere in the back of the room. The screen behind the stage was illuminated with a picture of a slender, handsome man in his early forties dressed in a tailored double-breasted suit. He was standing next to the fender of a white Rolls-Royce and had one foot resting firmly on the front bumper. He leaned suavely over the bent leg, propping an elbow on his thigh, his wrist dropping loosely from the weight of the fedora in his hand. The photograph was awash in smeary light, the lean lines of Mr. Rice's body blurred as if rubbed by an electrostatic charge. His hair, dark and slick with pomade, his eyes focused on a not-so-distant dream, his teeth—winking.

"Weldon Rice was born in the city's lower south side to hardworking immigrant parents. The youngest of eight, Mr. Rice knew early on that he had a dream. . . ."

Restlessness was already rippling up through Francis's thighs. He lurched to his feet and inched along to the end of the row, bending from the waist so as not to cast a shadow on the slide screen, and worked his way to the pastry table against the wall. He poured himself a black coffee. It was strong and good. He downed the cup and then another, until he felt his mind hum.

The screen flashed to a picture of Mr. Rice as a bony, gaunt-faced teenager with protruding front teeth, carrying a wooden crate filled with glass soda bottles. ". . . by the age of fourteen he started his own business . . ."

Francis grabbed a sticky bun and shoved it tiredly in his mouth.

". . . delivering seltzer door-to-door." Joe stopped suddenly and looked at Marty. "How old are you, son?"

"Almost eighteen," Marty said.

"Would you come up onstage for a moment?"

Marty seemed pleased to oblige. He hopped over the front row of seats and bounded up onto the stage. Francis's initial instinct was to dive after him, to protect him from Joe's clutches, but he stayed by the coffee instead, chewing the dry sticky bun for fear that if he got too close he, too, would be sucked into the display.

"What's your name, son?"

"Marty Pinkham."

"Did you come alone?"

"I came with my Dad," he said into the microphone, pointing in Francis's direction. In panic, Francis whipped back toward the tray of pastries, turning his back on the stage.

Joe patted Marty's shoulder and belted a full game-show host's laugh. "Your dad dragged you here, huh?"

"No, it was my idea. I dragged *him* here."

A few members of the audience chuckled.

"*You* brought *him* here? Well . . . I take it you're a business-minded young man?"

Marty nodded.

"That's terrific, son. Remember this face," he said to the audience. "You might be looking at the next Weldon Rice!"

A smattering of applause echoed through the ballroom. Joe lightly pushed Marty toward his seat and Francis joined him, stuffing the remainder of a sweet roll in the pocket of his windbreaker for later.

Joe started rubbing his hands together so fast Francis wondered if he might set off a spark. "Before I continue with the presentation, kindly open your information packets. On the top you'll see Proposal Form A, which asks specific questions about your Bright Idea. Please take a moment to fill out the form as thoroughly and specifically as you can. Our Certified Idea Specialists will personally review your Proposals and discuss Options for you within Rice Industries."

Marty already had the form on his clipboard and was starting to fill in the blanks.

"Do we have a name for our product?" he asked.

Francis sighed. "We're supposed to know that already? I thought we came here to figure that out."

"Just give me something. I have to put down something."

"I don't know," Francis said, kneading his forehead with this thumb and forefinger. "Put Pinkham's something-or-other . . ." He trailed off. "Put Pinkham's Water."

Marty snarled. "It's kind of dull. How about Pinkham's Natural Spring Water?"

"Fine. Fine."

"How much money would we like to make in the next year?" Marty didn't wait for his father's answer—he immediately wrote down a number.

"How much?" Francis asked, peering over his son's shoulder at the clipboard.

"A million dollars."

"That's a big jump for someone who's making nothing right now."

"You have to think big, Pop, or you're going nowhere."

The pool of coffee at the bottom of Francis's stomach turned cold. Already he could see the boy's hopes being raised. Marty had stuck his foot in the door of opportunity and was determined to wedge it open. Saying no to the whole deal was already more difficult than it had been twenty minutes ago.

"I WANT TO get a job for the summer," Nadine announced over her morning cornflakes.

Bernie craned her neck in surprise, a gesture that Nadine thought made her mother look like a condemned turkey. "Where in the hell did this idea come from?"

"Ainsley's trying to write for the *Gazette*. It seems like a good idea."

"I suppose there's nothing wrong with writing articles." Bernie poured herself a cup of coffee and made her way over to the kitchen table. "It'll probably help you with your schoolwork."

"I don't want to work for the newspaper. I was thinking of maybe waiting tables at Shorty's."

Bernie rolled her eyes. "Oh! That's all I need. Do you know what would happen if you got a job there? Gums would be flapping all over town. The Ladies' Auxiliary would leave more tuna casseroles on the doorstep. Church groups would start prayer chains. People would be saying that I can't take care of my own child."

"Since when do you care what people think?"

"We'd lose our privacy, Nadine." Bernie softened, tucking a loose curl behind her daughter's ear. "It's your last summer before high school. You should enjoy it, not spend it pouring coffee for imbeciles."

For Nadine, there was no way of explaining her reasons without causing injury. It wasn't that she particularly liked the idea of work so much as she loved the idea of spending more time away from her mother. She had grown weary of the blank emptiness of a house too big for two people, and her mother's bitter rants about the shortcomings of others and the wolf-pack mentality of a small town. "One of these days I'm going to get myself a lemming and let him run right off the roof of the library," she was tired of hearing her mother say. "I'll finish off the entire population of Cedar Hole in a single afternoon."

Over Christmas, Nadine had tried to buy her mother a lemming, but the pet store at the Mt. Etna Mall didn't stock them. She had imagined how sweet it would have been just to watch her unwrap the cage, the daunting look that would shadow her smile as she realized that her snide words would finally have to be backed up with action. In lieu of the lemming, Nadine had cut out the Palmdale real estate listings from the *Gazette* and put them in a picture frame.

"What an interesting piece of art you have here, Nadine," Bernie had said, putting on her reading glasses to take a closer look. "Very conceptual."

"It's not art. It's a hint."

"You want to move?"

"No, but you do. Let's go anywhere that will make you happy."

Bernie had seemed confused by the accusation. "My job is here, the house is paid for—plus, we can't afford Palmdale." She admired the gift, nonetheless, as only a mother could, and hung the frame in the bathroom, on the wall right above the toilet.

Nadine lifted the lid of the sugar bowl and sprinkled a teaspoon over her cereal. "I'm going to need clothes and notebooks for school."

"Haven't I always given you everything you needed?"

"What about college? Shouldn't I start saving for that?"

"What if you and I took at trip? We could go somewhere for a few months, someplace where we could breathe a little."

Nadine lowered her head over her bowl, pretending not to hear the desperate pinch in her mother's voice.

"I'd love to go someplace sunny, warm," Bernie said. "Maybe down South. Wouldn't that be good?"

"I don't know."

"Think about it," Bernie said. Nadine had never heard her mother sound so hopeful. "Maybe that's all we need. A little time away."

• • •

"WAKE UP. They want to see us."

Onstage, Joe was trotting back and forth, droning about the wonders of direct marketing. In a lethargic fog, Francis felt himself being brought to his feet and pushed to the end of the row, where a smiley man in a suit and a long-legged woman in a skirt absorbed Francis and Marty into their fold.

"We've been reviewing your Form A," the woman said, taking a firm hold of Francis's upper arm. The name tag above her ample breast read, JANET. "We'd like to have a Product Conference with you." Briskly, Francis and Marty were ushered out of the ballroom and down a long corridor into a windowless conference room. Inside, there was a round table with four chairs and a platter piled with pastries.

"We're very excited about your product," the man said, closing the door. His name was Terry, and he began speaking even before everyone had taken a seat. "It appears to have everything Rice Industries is looking for."

Marty squirmed, leaning far forward on his folded hands. Francis blinked back the sleep in his eyes and reached for a cheese Danish.

Terry took a fancy black and gold pen from his jacket pocket and scribbled notes in the margins of the form. "What do you know about the spring water business?"

"It's mainly an urban product," Marty said, in a strong, self-assured voice that made Francis do a double-take. "We want to target city folks with disposable income who don't have access to good-tasting—"

"Nothing," Francis interrupted. "We know nothing."

"I imagine that's why you're here," Janet said with a laugh. "To learn everything you can."

Terry tapped the end of his pen against the tabletop. "How far along are you in your business plan?"

Marty opened his mouth but Francis cut him off. "We haven't done a thing. The spring's just bubbling out of the ground. I might not even do anything with it—just let it puddle up," he said with a nervous laugh.

"It's good that you haven't done anything—it's best, really," Terry said. "Mr. Rice will be very pleased."

"You're in a prime position," Janet said, nodding.

"And what does that mean?" Francis took a bite of his Danish.

"She's referring to your status as a possible investment for Rice Industries," Terry said. "We only work with the best three ideas from each regional conference."

Janet leaned in toward Francis. She smelled like talcum powder. "If Mr. Rice chooses Pinkham's Natural Spring Water, he will build your business from the ground up—so to speak," she said with a giggle.

"What's this all going to cost me? Twenty-five thousand and a kidney?"

Terry sniffed politely. "There are no start-up fees, Mr. Pinkham. Rice Industries takes care of everything from equipment to advertising and distribution. All that is required of you is fulfillment of the orders."

Janet laid her hand lightly on Francis's wrist. "It's like any business relationship, Francis. All that Mr. Rice asks for is a fair percentage of sales."

"And how much is that?" Francis asked, hoping Janet wouldn't take her hand away anytime soon.

"That will be negotiated between you and Mr. Rice at the appropriate time," Terry said.

"It's fair, though," Janet added. "He's a fair man. He doesn't need the business, really—he does this because he likes to help others get started. He will make you rich."

Marty sucked in a breath of air and nudged Francis.

Terry cleared his throat. "Let's not start making promises like that just yet, Janet. They still have to be selected."

Janet frowned sheepishly and pulled her hand away. "Sorry—I can get carried away sometimes. It's just very exciting."

Marty, who was twitching to the point of bursting, finally spoke. "What can we do to increase our chances of getting selected?"

"Marty—" Francis warned.

"No, no, it's fine," Terry said. "Enthusiasm is definitely encouraged. We also require a certain level of commitment from our business partners. We want to know you're serious, just as, I'm sure, you want to know that we are."

"We're very serious," Marty said. "My father owns his own landscaping business."

"I mow lawns, basically," Francis corrected. "And I'm pretty happy doing that. To be honest, I'm not interested at all in starting a water business. It seems more trouble than it's worth."

"Being a businessman already, you know what it takes," Terry said. "It's hard work."

"You're right about that." Francis leaned back in his chair and glared at his son, happy to hear his opinion corroborated by someone else. "We get by fine right now. I don't see much reason for making my life harder."

Janet's eyes took on a dreamy haze and suddenly her hand was back on his, caressing his veins with the tips of her fingernails. "Francis, I want you to imagine something for a minute. Imagine what your life would be like if it was *easier*. Imagine having more money than you ever thought possible. Imagine having the admiration of your family and friends." Her voice dissolved into a whisper. "Go ahead and close your eyes. Imagine."

Francis was both embarrassed and pacified by the rhythmic stroke of Janet's fingernails, and laughter rose up from his belly as he closed his eyes, but quickly died in his throat.

"Can you see it?"

"Oh yeah, I see it," Francis lied. All he saw was the backs of his eyelids.

"What do you see?"

Francis sighed. He waited several long moments, hoping some sort of vision would suddenly appear, but nothing came to him. "Nothing. I don't see anything."

"Try," Janet said, wrapping her fingers around his.

Francis breathed in deeply, hoping to give the appearance of imagination, but his mind was focused solely on Janet's fingers and her name tag, which was at that very minute only inches away from him, hovering above that very well-shaped breast.

He opened his eyes. "What am I supposed to see?"

Marty dropped his chin to his chest and hammered the top of his head with his fists. "You're supposed to pretend—can't you *pretend?*"

"It's all right," Janet said. "Sometimes it takes a while to get used to new possibilities."

"We shouldn't keep you any longer than we have already—there are many more interviews to do." Terry stood up and offered Francis his hand to shake. "It was a pleasure meeting both you and your son."

Janet smiled. "We'll contact you by phone sometime within the next few weeks if Mr. Rice decides to go with your company." She shook his hand warmly. "We do hope that you'll stay through the afternoon—Joe has some wonderful marketing presentations planned that I think would be very helpful to you."

"And be sure to fill out Form B in your folder before you go. It's a personality profile that Mr. Rice needs as part of the evaluation process," Terry added. He gave Marty a firm pat on the shoulder. "No cheating, now, Marty. Your father needs to fill this one out on his own."

Janet opened the door. "Do you have any quick questions before you go, Francis?"

"Yes," he said, smoothing down his hair. "You people serving lunch?"

When Kitty Higgins heard that Ainsley wanted to cover the dedication ceremony for the *Gazette*, she couldn't have been more pleased. She retrieved the old metal box she kept high in the library's kitchen cupboard and presented it to him. "Every good thing that ever happened here in Cedar Hole is in this box. Maybe it will inspire you the same way it inspired Robert."

The box was filled to bursting, the hinged lid unable to close completely. Ainsley carried it over to the reading table, his stiff hands pressing and pious. Nadine trailed close behind.

"It's heavy," he said.

"I should get a bigger box," Kitty said.

Nadine lifted the lid. Inside were hundreds of clippings from the *Gazette*—every single article that Robert ever wrote about Cedar Hole. Interspersed between the articles were index cards written in Kitty's own hand, detailing Robert's own acts of creativity and kindness.

Ainsley scribbled furiously in his notebook. "This is fantastic. Do you think I could take it home?"

"I'd rather you kept it here," Kitty said. "But you can look at it whenever you want."

Nadine closed her eyes and let her fingers run through the thick pile of clippings. It was like holding her father's heart in her hands. "You loved him, didn't you, Kitty?"

"Norm and I never had children of our own. I always thought of him like a son."

Of course there had been love between them, Nadine thought, but leave it to her mother to turn an innocent relationship into something illicit. "He loved you, too."

"Oh, I don't know," Kitty said, biting her lip. "I'd just like to think that I made his life a little better."

Ainsley pulled an index card from the box. " 'Robert vows to raise enough money to renovate the library himself,' " he read aloud. "How much did he raise?"

"We never got that far. But I have no doubt that he would have done it. He was just that type of person."

"Mom's giving you the desk, you know," Nadine remembered. "She said you can pick it up after the dedication ceremony."

Beneath her composed librarian exterior, Kitty Higgins seemed to be breaking apart in three distinct phases. First, Nadine noted a look of shock flitting in her eyes, followed by the surrender of exhausted relief, and finally—and even more understandably—the immediate tightening of suspicion. It was a circle of emotion Nadine had ridden herself time and time again.

"Is this a joke?" Her hands were lost hummingbirds flickering at the collar of her starched blouse. "Or is she just trying to work me over?"

"She seemed serious at the time. But she could've changed her mind already."

Kitty pressed her lips together. "Wouldn't that be something? If she really means it?"

"Don't get too excited," Nadine cautioned, slightly panicked at the very real possibility of her mother retracting her promise. "It's not in the best condition."

"Your father wanted me to have it. I'll take it no matter what condition it's in."

~ Chapter Eight ~

SPUD TAKES a MEETING

The phone call came early on Sunday morning, before Francis even had a chance to finish his first cup of coffee.

"*Francis?* It's *Janet* from the Bright Ideas Seminar," she chirped. "How are *you* this morning?"

Francis was suddenly awash in warm memories of cheese Danishes and Janet's generous bosom. "I'm doing all right."

"I have terrific news! Mr. Rice wants to meet with you in person! Isn't that wonderful?"

Francis swallowed a quick swig of coffee. "Hold on a second—I thought you said it would take weeks to hear back."

"Normally it does, but your proposal is so strong that he wants to see you right away. This is *very* good news for you, Francis. I've never seen him this interested before—how does eleven-thirty sound?"

"This morning?"

Janet giggled. "Do you have better plans?"

Francis thought about his weekly date with the television and a six-pack of beer. "It's my day off."

"I understand—and believe me, normally Mr. Rice wouldn't expect to meet someone on such short notice, *especially* on a Sunday, but he feels strongly that we move on this opportunity right away. The market is right and we don't want to waste precious time."

Francis scratched his unshaven jaw. "I don't even know where he is—"

"He'll come to you. He's on his way now," she said. "He'd like to take your family out for brunch."

"Brunch, huh?" Francis laughed. "Sounds fancy."

"Nothing is required of you—there's no commitment at this time. Just enjoy your free meal and listen to what he has to say," Janet breathed in his ear. "I'm *so* excited for you, Francis. This is a tremendous opportunity. I'm sure your son Marty will be thrilled to hear the good news."

Francis stared out the kitchen widow at the stand of pines in his backyard. The puddle glistened slick and still in the morning light. "This doesn't mean I'm going to do business with him, understand? I'm just going to hear him out."

"Understood. So eleven-thirty, then!" Janet hummed. "It's been nice talking to you again. Mr. Rice looks forward to meeting you."

He hung up the phone and sat down at the kitchen table, quietly drinking the rest of his coffee before making the announcement that would unleash chaos on the household. The whole business felt cold and slippery, already in motion and wriggling away from him before he even had a chance to decide whether or not he wanted to be part of it.

Before he had a chance to see the bottom of his cup, Anita padded into the kitchen in her quilted bathrobe and terry-cloth slippers. Francis groaned inwardly. A fancy brunch was just the sort of thing she lived for. Just the sort of thing he didn't want her to get accustomed to.

"Who was that on the phone?"

"Janet—from Rice Industries."

Anita froze with her hand on the refrigerator door. "It's early," she said tentatively.

"Mr. Rice wants to see us. This morning."

"This morning?" She gathered the robe around her and opened the refrigerator. "I'd better get to the store—I'm all out of eggs."

"You don't have to do anything," Francis said, unfolding the paper. "He's taking us out for brunch."

"Brunch? How elegant! Where are we going?"

"Hell if I know."

"He's interested? He likes us?"

"I suppose so, if he's coming all this way," Francis said. "Don't get all excited just yet. We have to hear him out first."

She closed the refrigerator door and chewed the corner of her mouth. "I'm supposed to go to the dedication ceremony today with the Ladies' Auxiliary. I'll have to call Dixie and tell her I won't be there."

"Don't tell her why."

"What am I supposed to say?"

"Make something up. Tell her you're sick."

"Oh, come on. Don't be foolish."

"I'm not kidding," Francis said. "You haven't said anything to anyone, have you?"

"No. Not yet. There hasn't been time."

Francis nodded. "Good. Keep it to yourself for now."

Anita popped two slices of bread into the toaster. "For goodness' sake, Francis. You're acting like you've committed a crime. You should be proud. This is a good thing."

"We'll see about that," he said.

"I hope you'll seem more enthusiastic when he comes."

"I don't promise anything."

"I'll press your suit."

"I haven't worn that since we got married. I couldn't wish myself into that thing."

"Then I'll press a dress shirt and a pair of slacks," she said. Her voice was wavery and thin and her words were coming at a fast clip. "You're wearing a tie."

Francis tried to swallow the last of his coffee, but it didn't seem to want to go down without a struggle. "I haven't said yes to anything, Anita. Don't get your hopes up."

"It's brunch. We need to look nice."

"I mean it, Anita. This will probably turn out to be a big nothing."

She set the iron on the counter and cranked it to its hottest setting. "Do we have any shoe polish?"

By ELEVEN O'CLOCK, everyone was sitting in the living room—Francis and the boys in dress shirts and ties, hair combed wet off their faces, Anita in a belted knee-length dress and dangly earrings.

"What's the purpose of these godforsaken things?" Francis said, tugging at the knot at his throat to give himself an extra inch of breathing room.

"To keep your collar together," Anita said.

"Isn't that what buttons are for?"

She beamed at the boys. "We all look so nice. We should take a picture."

Francis grumbled as he went to the back closet. He set up the tripod and focused the camera. "Flynn, sit beside your mother on the couch," he directed. "Marty, stand next to the couch with your hand on her shoulder."

"Wait!" Anita said, waving wildly at him through the lens. "Let's do this in front of the fireplace. It'll be cozier. Maybe we'll even put it on our Christmas cards this year."

Francis waited as the boys moved a rocking chair in front of the fireplace. Anita took a seat in the chair and Marty resumed his pose with his hand on her shoulder. Francis instructed Flynn to kneel at his mother's feet.

"Is everybody ready? I'm setting the timer." He dashed across the living room and ran behind the rocking chair, grimacing for the camera just as it clicked.

"Let's do another, just in case that one didn't take," Anita said.

As Francis adjusted the camera again, there was a solid knock at the door. Everyone froze, their eyes darting from one person to the next, stunned that someone had pulled up in the driveway and walked all the way to the front door unnoticed. Marty lunged for the door.

"You hang on, there, Mr. Martin," Anita called after him. "Let your father answer the door."

Marty retreated. "Please be nice," he murmured.

"I'll be as nice as I'd be to any guest," Francis said. "But don't count on me falling to the floor and licking his boots."

Francis nudged Marty out of the way and opened the door. Mr. Rice was standing on the front step, dressed in a beige linen suit with a brown silk tie and matching fedora—an older, plumper, less moony version of the picture Francis had seen at the presentation. His skin was buffed and smooth, his cheeks accented by two deep, welcoming dimples. His nostrils flared pleasantly as Francis examined Mr. Rice's clean fingernails and gold knuckle ring topped with a flat, square onyx. He smelled, pungently, of aftershave.

"Good morning, is this the Pinkham residence?"

"If it isn't, our real estate guy's got some explaining to do," Francis said.

Mr. Rice let out a hearty laugh. "You must be Francis. I'm Weldon Rice."

At the end of the driveway was the same white Rolls-Royce Francis had see in the picture. In person the car gleamed crisply in the sun, instead of fuzzy edges filtered through a greased camera lens. In the back of his mind, Francis had thought the Rolls as nothing more than a fancy prop, that the picture was snapped surreptitiously at a dealership—he never once imagined that Mr. Rice actually owned it.

Francis numbly shook Mr. Rice's hand, absorbing the gorgeous creampuff at the end of his driveway, when Anita wedged herself in the doorway and offered Mr. Rice a gracious smile.

"Anita Reynolds Pinkham," she said, gently pushing her husband aside. "Won't you please come in?"

Marty and Flynn had seen the car, too, and both looked pale and stricken as Mr. Rice entered. "Hello, boys," he said.

Flynn nodded silently, fingers laced behind his back. Marty's white cheeks suddenly flushed scarlet as he shyly held out his hand. "It's great to meet you," he said. "I'm Marty."

Mr. Rice gave Marty a friendly chuck on the shoulder and glanced up at the tripod set up in the middle of the living room. "Looks like I've interrupted a family portrait."

"We're almost done." Anita looped her arm through his and led him into the living room. Francis couldn't help noticing how vibrant Anita looked on the arm of a rich man, as though she were right where she belonged. "Perhaps you'd be so kind as to take one with us? It would be an honor."

"The honor would be mine," Mr. Rice said, removing his hat and placing it over his heart.

• • •

"IT IS PRETTY," Francis said, tracing his finger around the perimeter of the door handle, the only part of the car he dared to touch. The boys slipped eagerly across the leather upholstery of the backseat. "Don't touch anything!" he hissed in their wake.

Anita, who had begged for a moment to freshen up before they left, hurried out of the house with an old navy sport coat draped across her arm, some long-forgotten article of clothing Francis vaguely remembered wearing to a funeral many years ago.

"You forgot your jacket." Anita winked, panting gently beneath her dress. The jacket smelled of damp air and cedar chips. They locked eyes for a moment as she tightened Francis's tie against the knot in his throat and brushed his shoulders with the flat of her hand. "Don't tug on it," she whispered.

"Bought her in England," Mr. Rice was saying, holding the rear door open for Anita like a chauffeur. She gracefully slid in the back next to the boys. "Off some earl who was going bankrupt trying to repair the crumbling stones of his old castle. It was quite a steal, but the shipping and taxes were a big hassle. I don't think I'd do it again, given the chance."

Mr. Rice closed the door firmly behind Anita, then opened the door for Francis. "Hop in."

Francis did not enjoy the sensation of having another man open the door for him, but under Anita's watchful eye he slid passively into the passenger's seat. He was startled by the unexpected presence of a steering wheel where there should have only been a glove box.

"They drive right-handed over there," Mr. Rice laughed, reading the look of surprise off Francis's face. He tossed the key at him. "Start her up."

"I don't think so." Francis kept his hands rigid against his sides.

"No, no—go ahead. Please."

Anita touched the back of his head. "The man's insisting."

Francis's scalp tightened beneath Anita's fingers. He stared at the glossy wood trim and breathed in deeply the scent of leather, becoming suddenly and irretrievably aware that there was another level of things in this world that he had only guessed about. He put the key into the ignition and started the engine. It purred.

"She's a kitten," Mr. Rice growled, sliding into the passenger's seat. "Be careful with the shifter—sometimes it sticks."

"You can drive here with the steering wheel on the wrong side?" Francis asked.

Mr. Rice shrugged. "Haven't been stopped yet. Do you know how to get to the Boathouse Café in Palmdale?"

A light, almost inaudible gasp of pleasure came from the backseat. "You know where that is." Anita slid forward and grabbed the headrest, exhaling into Francis's ear. "It's just over the town line. You take a right at the four corners and keep going for about a mile." She turned to Mr. Rice. "This is such a treat. I haven't been there in years. We went once when my cousin Tish got married. If I remember right, they had the most wonderful seafood Newburg."

"I've never been there myself, but one of my clients says it's good." He leaned over and gave Francis a lighthearted elbow poke. "Or if you'd like, we can just sit here in the driveway instead."

Francis reached for the door handle.

"No, no," Mr. Rice said, holding him back. "You're going to drive. Don't worry—I'm insured," he said with a round, full-bellied laugh.

"Come on, Pop," Marty said. "I'm getting hungry."

Francis stiffened. "You don't understand, the steering wheel's *on the wrong side.*"

Mr. Rice settled back into the passenger's seat, his knees comfortably splayed. "We're not going far. Let's get the show on the road before they give our table away."

Francis finally eased the car onto the street and turned down Webber Road, just as he had done the day before. It was strange enough to be sitting on the right side of the car—he was rarely a passenger—but the graceful arch of the hood ornament and the solid grip of the steering wheel made his head feel queasy and light. He responded to every familiar rut and curve with startled exaggeration and caution. When they came upon the rise at the railroad crossing, he slowed the car down to a near crawl.

"That's a good man," Mr. Rice said. "You look like you've driven one of these before."

The Boathouse Café sat on the edge of Crescent Pond, a clear, three-quarter-moon-shaped body of water that technically straddled the Cedar Hole/Palmdale town line. An impartial cartographer would have drawn the border straight through the pond, declaring it for both towns, but Palmdale greedily claimed it as its own. The Palmdale line ran straight until it hit the water, then slyly curved, following the outer edge of the pond until halfway down the opposite side, where it suddenly shot off straight again.

The restaurant was not really a café, but an all-American chop house that served up the plain, straightforward food that the residents of Gilford County craved. While the chewy steaks and red apple ring garnishes were uninspiring, the Boathouse Café did have two jewels: the Sunday brunch buffet and a beautiful view.

The entire wall facing the pond was made up of windows. The best tables were lined up against the glass, lending a clear view of the pond. When it wasn't raining and the wind was calm, the water was still, reflecting the white birches that fawned over the far bank. The pond was too small for life-sized boats, but there was an entire fleet of radio-controlled models for rent at a kiosk on the edge of the parking lot. For a quarter, a youngster could set sail across the length of the pond, while Mom and Dad watched from their table, drinking coffee.

When Mr. Rice confirmed his reservation with the hostess, Francis nudged Anita. "They're charging fifteen dollars a pop for *breakfast*," he whispered, pointing to a wipe board above their heads listing the day's specials. "I can't eat fifteen dollars' worth of breakfast."

"And don't try," she warned.

The hostess led them to a choice window table, set with water goblets and maroon linen napkins artfully folded to look like sailboats. "Help yourself to the buffet whenever you're ready," she said. "Your server will be right back with the champagne."

"*Champagne?*" Anita pressed her fingertips into the hollow of her throat. "How continental!"

"What would brunch be without a little champagne?" Mr. Rice said with a wink.

"Probably five ninety-five," Francis muttered.

Marty tapped a staccato rhythm with his foot against the base of the table, making the crystal salt and pepper shakers dance. "So what's your spiel, Mr. Rice? How are you gonna make us millionaires?"

"Marty!" Francis snapped.

"Stop that, now." Anita touched his knee to make him stop tapping, then returned the shakers to their proper place, lovingly turning them in the light.

Mr. Rice laughed. "It's all right. I suppose he's never taken a meeting before," he said. "It's not proper form to talk business right away, son. First we start with the pleasantries. Why don't we help ourselves to the buffet?"

Flynn was the first one to grab a plate, piling it high with omelets and hash browns. He pinched a fat sausage link from a silver chafing dish with a pair of tongs and warmed it over the Sterno flame below. The sausage started to crackle and flame as Anita passed by. She slapped the link away from him and it rolled onto the white buffet tablecloth, leaving a trail of grease. "What are you doing?"

"It looked cold," he said.

Francis passed over the tureen of cream of cauliflower soup and the baskets of muffins and fresh fruit and headed straight for the toque-wearing teenage boy at the end of the table, who sawed at the flank of a steamship round of beef as though he were in shop class. The boy draped two pink-tongue slivers across his plate. Francis nodded. "Keep going."

"The crêpes suzette is marvelous!" Anita cried when they returned to the table. "The chef flambéed it right in front of me."

"I'm glad you're enjoying yourself," Mr. Rice said. "I have to say, Mrs. Pinkham, when my associate, Janet, told me you had two teenage boys I didn't expect you would be so young."

"I was a young mother." Anita spoke as though it were a point of pride rather than embarrassment; something Francis had never been able to do. She smiled. "The boys are my greatest joy."

Flynn grinned as he steadily plowed his way through his food. Marty poked distractedly at his Belgium waffle covered in whipped cream. "Do you have any children?" he asked.

"I have not had that pleasure—yet," Mr. Rice answered. "I was married briefly in my twenties. My wife miscarried twice."

Anita pressed her napkin to her lips. "You poor thing. That must've been terrible for you."

"A big disappointment, no doubt about that."

Francis tugged at his collar. Anita had tied his tie so tight it hardly budged. "Did anyone try the beef? It's delicious. The horseradish sauce is really good."

A waiter placed three champagne flutes on the table, each containing a half strawberry, and poured champagne into each. The boys, to their dismay, each got a Shirley Temple.

"What do you think, Spud?" Anita stared in wonder at her floating strawberry half. "Should we let the boys have a sip? It's a special occasion."

"I suppose they can have a little."

Mr. Rice raised his glass. "To new opportunities!"

Marty stole his father's champagne flute, leaving Francis to toast with his water goblet. "To new opportunities!" they all repeated, clinking glasses.

Outside, a blue and red schooner was gliding across the surface of the pond, altering its course sharply to startle an unsuspecting duck.

"I might have missed something yesterday," Francis began, clearing his throat, "but what exactly is it that you do?"

"He buys companies, Pop." Marty leaned toward Mr. Rice. "Don't mind my dad—he slept through the whole seminar."

Francis glared at his son. "After you finish eating, you two boys should head out there and try your hand at the boats."

Marty rolled his eyes. "Those are baby boats."

"I don't know about that. They look like a good time to me," Mr. Rice said, digging two quarters out of his pocket and handing them to the boys. "Marty's partly right—I do involve myself with various companies, but I don't buy them, I *grow* them."

Anita arched her eyebrows and took a sip of champagne. "That sounds exciting."

Francis worked a piece of steamship roast between his teeth and tried to swallow. "I'm not sure I understand what that means."

"It means he's an investor," Marty sighed.

"That's enough, now," Anita said. "Go outside. Marty, make sure Flynn doesn't fall in."

Marty threw down his napkin and left. Flynn snatched a slice of cherry cheesecake from the dessert table and followed his brother out the door.

"I find good men like yourself who want to start a business but don't know how," Mr. Rice said. "I give them the capital and the contacts necessary to get their businesses off the ground."

Francis retrieved his champagne flute, only to find it empty. "It seems to me that someone who's rolling in money has better things to do with his time."

Anita paled. "Francis—"

"Well, let's be honest here—I mean, look at the car. If you've got a car like that, why bother yourself with a bunch of half-wits who don't know what they're doing?"

Anita's lips pinched. "Mr. Rice, I apologize."

Mr. Rice shook his head graciously. "There's no need. This is a serious undertaking and you have every right to ask questions. No, I don't need the money, but let me ask you this, Francis—what would you do if you had a million dollars?"

"I'd never work another day in my life."

Mr. Rice nodded. "I said the very same thing—but as soon as I earned my first million, I felt differently. Life can suddenly get strange when you have money. Don't get me wrong—it's wonderful to provide for the people you love and to buy whatever you want—but I had been struggling so long that I felt lost the moment the struggle was over. I was miserable sitting home all day, buffing my fancy cars. Imagine!"

"I can't, really."

"I told myself, I said, 'Weldon, you need a challenge. Why not help others who are less fortunate make their dreams come true?' And that's when I discovered my life's purpose."

Anita folded her hands primly in her lap. "You seem very self-aware."

"When the truth's staring you straight in the face, it's hard not to look. I met a guy just outside of Albuquerque, New Mexico, who had a design for a yo-yo—I can't remember what was so special about it, probably nothing, to be honest. But I liked the fellow, and I liked his spirit. I decided to take him on as my first client. I gave his product a catchy name and sent it off to a manufacturing friend of mine. Then I put it in a catalog and we moved two hundred thousand units the first year alone."

"Wow!" Anita said.

"It's not tough, really. It's just a matter of recognizing a good idea, knowing the right industry people, and having a knack for getting a product into the hands of the public."

"Yo-yos, huh?" Francis said.

"Not a very exciting idea, I know," Mr. Rice laughed. "But it's all in knowing what to do with it. Creative marketing. For instance, what kind of catalog do you suppose I sold the yo-yos in?"

Francis jammed two fingers down into the gap between his necktie and collar and tugged at the knot. "Oh, I don't know," he said. "I don't know much about those sorts of things."

"Take a guess."

"A toy catalog?" Anita ventured.

"Aha!" Mr. Rice raised an index finger in the air with an expectant delight. "That's what my friend in Albuquerque thought, too." His smile faded and he glanced over his shoulder at the table behind him, then leaned in close, dropping his voice to a conspiratorial hush. "Geriatric medical supplies!"

Francis leaned in. "Excuse me?"

Anita's eyes widened. "You didn't!"

Mr. Rice nodded, looking pleased with himself. "When people hear the word 'yo-yo,' they think toy—but sell it alongside bedpans and walkers and it suddenly becomes a 'therapeutic device for arthritis.' "

Francis forked a piece of gristle on his plate. "Sounds like lying to me."

"Not at all—I did the research. Yo-yos are frequently used in nursing homes to help the elderly relieve the pain of arthritis and maintain good eye-hand coordination. Did our customers know they were buying yo-yos? Of course they did, they'd seen them their whole lives and even played with them as children. Had they ever thought of using a yo-yo to help them with arthritis? Never. It's all a matter of taking a familiar product and giving it a new twist."

Francis looked out the window and saw the boys by the edge of the pond. Flynn had pushed a green and yellow boat with the number "49" on its sail away from the bank and guided it across the water with the remote control. Marty chatted with a slender blond girl who seemed to be watching over her baby brother.

"I'm only sharing this story with you to show you what I can do with a simple product—I want you to have confidence in me. I could do very well for you."

Anita finished the last of her champagne. "You certainly are a creative businessman."

"Thank you, Mrs. Pinkham."

"But what can you do for water?" Francis said. "It seems to me that only a fool would pay for something they could get for free."

Mr. Rice motioned to a nearby waitress and beckoned her to get him a slice of cake from the buffet and another round of champagne. "I understand that Cedar Hole is a provincial town with provincial sensibilities—but are you aware of the health revolution that is taking place in urban centers of our country?"

Anita nodded vigorously. "I remember reading something about that in one of my women's magazines."

"There's a wealth of good information to be had in those publications," Mr. Rice said with a nod. "More and more people are working at desk jobs, where they are sitting eight, ten hours a day. All that non-movement tends to make the humors sluggish—if you'll pardon my old-time vernacular. In order to maintain proper health, a person has to actively seek physical recreation."

"They ought to be mowing lawns for a living. They'd get plenty of exercise." Francis stared at the waitress as she set down a thick slab of chocolate cake in front of Mr. Rice. "I think I'll have one of those, too, if you don't mind," he said, pointing to the cake.

The waitress's mouth puckered. "The dessert table's right over there, you can help yourself anytime."

Mr. Rice took a bite of cake and then a sip of champagne. "People are spending crazy money on memberships to health clubs."

"Oh yes! And exercise clothes," Anita added. "And from what I understand it's very expensive. Those leg warmers go for ten dollars a pair."

Francis nodded knowingly, though his head bubbled over with useless bits that were making no firm connection in his mind.

"It used to be in the 1800s that leisure was a sign of wealth and status. Now it's turned the other way," Mr. Rice said. "Exercise is."

"But what does this have to do with my water?"

"When you exercise, you sweat. You get thirsty. But you can't very well take a sink tap out with you jogging, can you? You need a bottle of water."

Slowly, Mr. Rice's disparate statements were beginning to fuse together.

"Water is the new wine," Mr. Rice said. "Yuppies are developing an allegiance to certain brands—they even argue about the taste! Can you imagine?"

"That's what we've been trying to tell him," Anita said. "People will pay big money for this in the cities."

"There's no question." Mr. Rice rapped his onyx-ringed knuckle on the table to fortify his point. "I haven't tasted your source, Pinkham, but I'm assuming it's quite fine or you wouldn't be pursuing a business."

"It doesn't taste like anything to me," Francis said. "It tastes like air."

Mr. Rice closed his eyes and smiled. "Perfect. Provided the quality tests come back fine, we should be in good shape."

Anita dabbed the corners of her mouth with a napkin. "This is *so* exciting!" she said, squeezing Francis's arm. "Aren't you excited?"

"Let's hold on a minute—we're not there just yet," he pleaded.

"Tell me, Francis, have you had the privilege of traveling this great country of ours?"

"I've seen my fair share," he lied.

"How about the West? Arizona? Nevada? Good old Cali?" Mr. Rice cut his fork into the cake and fed himself a greedy bite.

"Haven't quite made it there as of yet."

"But we'd like to," Anita added. "I've heard it's beautiful out there."

"Yes, ma'am, it certainly is. There's nothing like the desert. When the light hits the sand just so, it reflects right up into the sky turning the clouds pink. That sure is a sight." Mr. Rice tamped his mouth with his napkin and rubbed his soft fingers together as though he were working himself up to a significant point. "There's a saying in the desert—water equals life."

Anita's throat hummed.

"You see it on signs in gas station windows. It's to remind travelers not to go on a long trip without at least a few gallons of bottled water stashed in the trunks of their cars."

"Is that a selling tactic?" Francis smirked.

"Not at all. This is dead serious," Mr. Rice said. "The roads are quiet out there, and if your car breaks down it could be a long time before you see any help. You can go a fair amount of time without food, but without water, you've got only a couple days at most."

Anita hummed again and took a sip of champagne. "It's all so—*dramatic.*"

Mr. Rice nodded slowly. "I think it puts our situation in perspective. Don't you?"

~ Chapter Nine ~

HEIR APPARENT

On the morning of the dedication ceremony, Nadine wrestled into her first pair of nylons and stole a pair of low-heeled pumps from her mother's closet. She clipped her soft curls back into a silver barrette, then tinted her lips with a tube of pale pink lip gloss which she had bought at the Superette. The years had curdled Bernie's opinion of totems of feminine beauty, but Nadine didn't care what her mother thought. Today was for her father, a day in which her mother didn't factor at all. Nothing Bernie said could touch her.

"Courting trouble today, are we?" Bernie pinched at the pleats of nylon that bunched at Nadine's skinny knees. She reached into her purse and pulled out a twenty-dollar bill. "Here's some bail money in case you need it."

Nadine folded the bill in fourths and tucked it into her vinyl clutch purse, next to the pocket camera she was bringing for Ainsley. "What are you going to do all day?"

"I don't know. I thought I might trim my toenails. Or bake tea cakes in breathless anticipation of Kitty's arrival." Bernie reached for the garment tag sticking out of the collar of Nadine's dress and tucked it back in. "Actually, I got some travel books for our trip. What do you think about New Orleans?"

"It's kind of far, isn't it?"

"I thought that was the point—to get away." Bernie then began to fuss with the barrette in her daughter's hair, until Nadine shook her off. "Are you walking over by yourself?"

"Ainsley's going with me."

"Oh?"

"Don't look at me like that," Nadine said.

"Like what?"

"We're just friends."

Bernie smirked and shook her head. "Poor Ainsley. He doesn't know what he's up against."

Nadine didn't know whether to lash out at her or burst into tears. Instead, she rolled her eyes. "And you wonder why I never bring him over here."

"He's a sweet boy, Nadine. Be gentle with his heart."

Ainsley met her at the depot. "Boy, you look nice," he said, his eyes grazing the hemline of her skirt.

"Thanks." Nadine soaked up his admiration and simultaneously disregarded it. "Here's the camera. It's already got half a roll of film in it."

He tucked the camera into the pocket of his baggy-shouldered blazer. "We should probably get you over there. I want to get a good vantage point."

At most, Nadine expected to see Kitty and the members of the association, maybe even a few nosy neighbors with nothing better to do on a Sunday afternoon, but when they rounded the corner in front of the Superette, a crowd of nearly a hundred people had gathered on the front lawn of the library. Wooden folding chairs were set up in rows outside the library steps, facing a sheet-covered rectangle hanging above the front door. People scrambled to find a place to sit while the association members brought out more chairs. Nadine's feet wobbled in her pumps as she walked toward the podium at the entrance, her fingers digging into Ainsley's arm for balance. "I hate her for missing this," she muttered.

Kitty Higgins buzzed around the podium, shuffling her stack of index cards, smoothing down the front of her prim twill suit, tapping on the microphone. She smiled warmly at Nadine for a brief moment, then looked past her shoulder into the crowd beyond.

"Where's Bernie?" Kitty asked.

"My mother's not well," Nadine said, satisfied that her answer spoke the truth, no matter how indirectly. Kitty suddenly looked crestfallen, and Nadine was certain this had nothing to do with her mother's absence. "Don't worry. You can still come by after and get the desk. She said so."

The light behind Kitty's eyes burned brightly again, and she clapped her hands together with joy. "Wonderful. Simply wonderful—" She caught herself, and became visibly sober. "Not to say that your mother's not feeling well is a *good* thing."

"It's okay. I know what you mean."

Ainsley took a folding chair from one of the association members and plopped it in front of the first row, off to one side so that he could get a clear, fixed view of the podium. He snapped a few test pictures of Nadine.

"Don't spend all your time on pictures," Kitty said. "Make sure you take plenty of notes, too." She took her place behind the podium and smiled at Nadine. "Come on up here, honey. I think it's about time we got started, don't you?"

Nadine climbed the steps. She became acutely aware that the eyes of the entire crowd were upon her, sizing up her resemblance to either her father or her mother and no doubt passing judgment accordingly. The sudden attention was almost crushing. Nadine tucked back from the podium. She distracted herself by concentrating on the roughness of the cheap nylons against her legs, the cold damp of her armpits, and the way her new barrette pulled at her scalp.

"Thank you all for coming," Kitty said into the microphone, "on what is truly a special occasion."

She then launched into a gushing overview of Robert J. Cutler's life, her affection for him tossed out so nakedly that Nadine found herself shrinking back even farther from view of the audience, until her entire person was obscured by Kitty. She looked out past the crowd and saw clusters of people gathering on the sidewalk, cars slowing down as they moved past. At the other end of Main Street, the firehouse siren churned a mournful wail, giving Nadine respite from embarrassment as Kitty's voice was drowned out. Her eyes darted across the windows of the buildings on Main Street, searching for fire or even a plume of smoke coming out of them, but there was none to be seen.

"To help us today with the unveiling, I'd like to introduce to you Robert Cutler's daughter, Nadine. . . ." Kitty hustled Nadine to the forefront and planted her in plain view of everyone. The crowd broke into applause. Ainsley jumped to his feet and snapped pictures. Nadine's shoulders curved forward a little. Unsure of what to do with her hands, she waved.

Kitty handed Nadine a dangling rope that was attached to the sheet covering the sign. "I now present to you, the Robert J. Cutler Memorial Library!"

Nadine gave the rope a tug, and the sheet floated to earth. Bulbs flashed. The sign, which had been carved by Jackie Pinkham, was black with elegant gold letters.

Afterward, a throng gathered around Nadine, offering compliments and stories about her father, sometimes speaking of him in hushed, reverential tones; other times bursting with a fondness so fresh it was as if they had just spotted him walking down Main Street. She recognized people from the town planning board, Shorty's, the Superette, plus members from the three local churches and the staff of Cedar Hole Elementary. Nadine expected people to ask after her mother and her whereabouts, but no one did.

"You look just lovely, sweetie," Deedee Cross said. "Your father would be so proud."

Louise Riley slid her sunglasses down her nose and stared up at the sky. "Would you look at that blue? It's like he's smiling down on us."

Miss Delia Pratt pushed through the circle and latched on to Nadine like a drowning woman, the neckline of her blouse cut to an embarrassing depth.

"Your father was perfect," she barked in Nadine's ear, her breath smelling of alcohol. "If I had only been a little younger, things might have been different."

"He wouldn't have wanted you, Delia," Louise said. "He wasn't the type to go after hussies."

Delia steadied herself against Nadine's shoulder. "You ought to know, you dried-up old bitch."

Nadine helped her former teacher regain her balance. "Miss Pratt, maybe you should go get something to eat and sit down."

"He liked me," Delia murmured. "He *did*."

"Would you listen to this?" Deedee scoffed. "Go home, Delia, before you embarrass yourself."

"Too late for late," Principal Nelson said.

"Come on, Dickie," Delia slurred. "Play nice."

Ainsley interrupted his interview of a group of association members to bring over a folding chair. Nadine eased Delia down. "Ainsley will stay with you and I'll go get you a piece of cake."

Delia looked up at Ainsley, confused. "Who are *you*?"

"Ainsley Smith, Miss Pratt. Actually, my real name is John Smith. I was in your class five years ago."

She gave him a hard stare. "I don't remember you."

"I've changed a lot since fourth grade."

"Are you the kid that used to shoot spitballs at the chalkboard? You could really shoot far."

Ainsley shook his head. "You're thinking of someone else."

"Hey, Delia," Louise called, "seen any good sights at the landfill lately?"

A snicker undulated through the crowd.

"Just your old boyfriends, Louise," Delia crowed.

"It's such a shame," Deedee finally said when everyone fell silent. "The good Lord always takes the best ones early. The lousy ones seem to stick around forever."

Mr. Rice drove back, taking the long way home. He meandered through Palmdale neighborhoods, with their brick houses and neatly groomed hedges that Francis knew must have taken hours of sculpting. Every white-columned portico elicited a deep sigh from Anita.

"The house I grew up in was like that," she'd say periodically, coupled with, "We had a fireplace" or "You should have seen how it looked all decorated for the holidays."

"Where's your old place?" Mr. Rice asked, glancing back at her in the rearview mirror. "Should we drive by it?"

"Oh! Could we? I haven't been by there in years."

"Just tell me where to go."

There was a weight in Francis's gut that he knew was more than just from the pounds of steamship roast beef he ate. "I can drive us by it this week," he said. "Let's not waste any more of Mr. Rice's time."

"It's no trouble. My whole day is open for you."

"No sense in turning around now, anyway," Anita argued. "We're almost there."

Anita's childhood home stood on a graceful corner lot surrounded by an old stone wall and a thicket of mature walnut trees. The house was an antique Colonial painted the color of maple syrup and trimmed in buttercream. The screened porch off to one side of the house had a swing. A wrought-iron gate near the back sheltered a rose garden.

"They repainted it," Anita said, her voice almost a whisper. "It used to be white. And the shutters were black. My sister and I played on the porch year-round. Even in the snow."

"It's a beautiful home," Mr. Rice said.

"We were only here until I was eight—but I have very clear memories of it. When I close my eyes, I can see my mother polishing the fireplace mantel for Christmas and my father stringing lights on the tree. It was cozy."

"I thought you said the place was drafty—you were cold all the time," Francis said.

"Well, that's true," Anita conceded. "It *was* an old house, after all. But it was still a lovely place to live." She leaned forward and squinted at the window. "No, I don't think I like that color at all. It looks—I don't know . . . *sticky*."

"If it was still yours, what color would you paint it?" Mr. Rice asked.

"Maybe the original white—or a soft yellow. I just love yellow."

"Yellow is a nice color," he agreed. "As long as it's not too bright."

Anita nodded. "It has to be warm—like a pale gold. Those greeny yellows are chilly. They hurt the eyes—"

"I just saw someone looking out the window upstairs," Francis interrupted. "We should get a move on. I'm sure they don't like us staring at their house."

"Maybe they'd let us in. Do you think they'd let us take a look around?"

"It's Sunday, Anita," Francis said. "They're probably still eating dinner."

"If they're still eating, then why would someone be upstairs?"

"You can't just knock on someone's door and barge in unexpected. Especially when you're a stranger."

"I'm not a stranger. I used to live here."

Francis worked at the top button of his shirt until it finally let go. "For God's sakes, Anita, you're a stranger to *them*."

"Francis has a good point," Mr. Rice said. "Perhaps you could come visit another time."

Anita settled back in her seat. "It would have been nice to show the boys."

Francis didn't think Anita would give in so easily, but he was glad she did.

"Who knows," Mr. Rice said as they drove away, "if this business takes off, you might be able to afford a house just like that one."

"Oh, I don't know about that," Anita said with a nervous laugh. "We'll just have to see. It would be fun though, wouldn't it, boys?"

Both Flynn and Marty nodded, dumbstruck.

For someone who needed directions to the Boathouse Café, it seemed to Francis that Mr. Rice knew his way around the area very well. He navigated his way back to the Cedar Hole town line with little trouble.

"Take a left over here," Francis guided, trying to steer him toward less-inhabited roads.

Mr. Rice ignored his suggestion and instead went straight—directly toward the heart of town.

Francis panicked. "You don't want Main Street—it's out of the way."

"Like I said, I have all day. If it's all right, I'd like to get a good look at this beautiful community of yours."

"Let the man drive where he wants," Anita said.

As soon as Mr. Rice turned the car down Main Street, he slowed it to a near crawl. Francis cringed when he saw the enormous crowd lingering on the front lawn of the library.

"What's going on here?" Mr. Rice asked.

"They're having a dedication ceremony—I didn't think it would still be going on." Anita leaned across Flynn's lap to get a better look out the opposite window. "I bet Kitty's in her glory. Oh look, boys—the sign's up. 'The Robert J. Cutler Memorial Library.' It's beautiful. Jackie did a beautiful job."

"Who's Robert Cutler?"

"He was an honest, good-hearted man," Anita said. "Our finest, really."

"I bet our man Francis here could give him a good run." Mr. Rice rolled down the window and waved at the crowd. It no longer seemed to Francis that he was riding in a fancy car so much as he was the conspicuous passenger of a parade float decorated entirely with hundred-dollar bills.

"How are you doing today? Fine weather we're having," Mr. Rice said to everyone and no one in particular. People turned away from their conversations to stare. Children ran alongside the car, watching their warped reflections in the chrome. Francis pressed his chin to his chest and sank down into his seat.

"Are you famous?" someone yelled from the sidewalk.

"No, no," Mr. Rice said with a laugh. "Just a friend of the Pinkhams, out for a Sunday drive."

"There's Dixie!" Anita rolled down her window. Mr. Rice stopped the car right in front of the Superette. "Dixie!"

"Anita?" She squinted, sidling up to the car. What on earth are you doing in there? I thought you weren't feeling well."

"A lot has happened. I'll have to call you later."

"You'd better," Dixie said, sticking her head through Anita's open window. "Nice-looking car, Spud. What'd you do, steal it?"

Francis straightened up a little. "I thought I'd do a little bodywork on the truck. Came out good, didn't it?"

Dixie tilted her head to the side and stared at him, as though she weren't sure if he was kidding or not. "You free to do some deliveries later?"

"It's Sunday, Dixie."

"I know, but there's some spring cold going around. Everyone and their mother wants chicken soup and aspirin. How about four o'clock?"

Tension crawled up the back of Francis's neck and over the top of his head, coming to rest just above his brow. "I'll see what I can do."

Dixie waved good-bye to Anita. "Call me," she mouthed to her.

"There's a table over there with cake," Flynn said. "They have red punch, too."

Anita sighed. "You can't *possibly* be hungry after that lovely brunch we just ate."

"Growing boys," Mr. Rice laughed. "They sure do eat a lot, don't they?"

"Sometimes I think it would be cheaper to have a pair of black Labs," Francis said.

The sun beat down on the windshield, cooking the interior. The scent of leather bloomed in the heat. Francis cracked his window just enough to let in a wisp of air, but not enough to invite conversation with a man who was staring at the car's front fender.

Flynn nudged Marty to open the door. "Let's go see what they've got."

"Boys—" Francis started, but it was too late. They were already out of the car and crossing the street.

Mr. Rice drummed his fingers against the steering wheel to a silent beat and frowned at Francis. "You're in the grocery business, too?"

"Just part-time—full-time during the winter when I'm not cutting grass."

"Landscaping's hard work."

"Especially around here. We have what you'd call 'fast grass.' It grows so quick it's hard to keep up. But I like it."

"Would you do it even if you didn't have to?"

"I don't know," Francis said. "It's not something I think about."

NADINE wandered over to the refreshment table, where Flynn Pinkham was shoving cookies into the pockets of his baggy dress pants.

"I didn't know your father had so many fans," he said to her. He piggy-backed one cookie on top of another until a stack of six was caged within his fingers, then deftly released them at his hip, where they slid like parking meter coins into his pocket.

Nadine ran a resistant knife through Kitty's untouched apple cake, cutting it first into quarters, and then into eighths. "He helped a lot of people."

"You'd think he'd cured a disease or something."

On the rare occasion when she saw Flynn Pinkham, Nadine couldn't help thinking back to elementary school, when he licked a frost patch on the monkey bars and froze his tongue to it. Miss Pratt, who lacked the common sense to free him with a cup of warm water, yanked him loose, leaving behind a tiny piece of his tongue still stuck to the pole. Nadine remembered clambering around with the other kids to get a good look at the morsel of tissue. It was pale and moist and reminded her of the chewy, offending bits in her mother's holiday clam dip.

Marty downed a cup of punch. "What did he do besides write newspaper articles?"

"I don't know." Nadine shrugged, slightly taken aback. She was not used to defending her father to anyone besides Bernie. "He was a champion for the library. He wanted to do great things with it."

"I never go in there," Marty said, shoving a brownie in his mouth. "The place depresses me."

Threads of people started pulling away from the library and began circling around the fancy car parked across the street. A woman in the backseat was waving in her direction. Nadine had never seen a car like that in Cedar Hole or anywhere else—it was the kind of car she imagined existed only in the movies.

"Hurry up," Flynn said. "Mom's waiting for us."

"Let her wait," Marty said, filling a paper plate.

Nadine scratched at her barrette. "That's your car?"

Marty nodded. "We just bought it," he said. "I wanted black, but Pop just had to have white. Looks cleaner longer."

"Bet you didn't know mowing lawns could buy something like that." Flynn started to snicker, but Marty gave him a playful slap on the back of the head.

"No way," Nadine said.

"I swear." Marty put his hand over his heart.

Flynn took a bite of apple cake, made a face, then put it back on the tray. "Our dad has this business idea that's going to make us rich."

"We're going to be millionaires."

Nadine's eyes narrowed. "You're messing with me."

"I'm not," Marty insisted. "See that guy in the car with the hat? We just had a business meeting with him to iron out the details."

She looked over at the car and the smooth way it gleamed in the light. Mr. Pinkham was sitting in the front wearing a suit and tie. She had never seen him dressed up before. "So what's this idea?"

"We can't talk about it," Flynn said.

"Not yet, anyhow," Marty corrected. "Not until we're established. But let's just say that when things get rolling, Pop's going to have more than just a lousy library with his name on it. They'll probably name the whole town after him."

"WHAT ARE those boys doing?" Anita sighed. "I know Flynn saw me. He looked right at me. Francis, go get them."

"Me? I don't want to go out there."

"They'll listen to you. Hurry, before they inhale everything on that table."

Francis slid out of the car and was immediately absorbed into the mob. Head down, he pushed through and across Main Street, with the crowd trailing close behind.

"That man is a born leader," Mr. Rice said.

Anita's throat ran dry. She scoured the inside of her purse for a peppermint. "You really think so?"

"Look at how people are following him."

"That's not normal, though," she said. "Everything in his life's been a struggle."

"That's all about to end."

"I'd like to believe that."

"You have to. He needs you to." Mr. Rice swiveled in his seat and looked at her. "I've seen men like Francis before. They're like battered-up furniture. All it takes is a little ambition, a little elbow grease, and they can take on a whole new life."

Anita watched her husband's back disappear into the crowd. She slid forward and gripped the headrest of the seat in front of her. "Just between us, Mr. Rice—do you really think this business venture could work?"

"I feel very strongly about it." His genial tone turned sober. "You have a tremendously important job here, Anita. Francis can't quite see his potential. It's up to you to have that sight for him."

Chapter Ten

BERNIE GETS
the LAST WORD

Francis felt as though he were drowning in voices.

"What in the hell is going on here, Spud? Did you rent a Rolls just for the dedication?"

"I always thought he was overcharging me for my lawn. Now I know."

"I never seen you dressed up before. Did someone die?"

"You know they didn't—he wore work clothes to Robert's funeral."

"Maybe it's a wedding, then. Is one of your boys having a shotgun wedding?"

His fast walk turned into a light run as he hit the library walkway and made a straight line for the refreshment table. The boys were still laughing and stuffing their faces. Francis seethed. He clamped his hand under Flynn's arm and peeled him away from the table.

"Ow, Pop—watch it!"

"Your mother's been waving at you like a maniac for five minutes. Now come on, let's go."

"Don't get mad at me. I saw her. Marty's the one who's been taking his sweet old time."

Marty coolly refilled his cup with punch.

"You heard me, Marty."

"What's the big emergency?"

The group that had been trailing Francis since the car finally caught up. Principal Nelson stepped forward and nodded at Marty. "Maybe you boys can tell us what's going on here—your father's not talking. Is this some kind of stunt to upstage the dedication?"

Francis glared at Marty. "Come on, let's go."

"Not at all," Marty said, feet planted firmly in place. "We just happened to be driving by and we stopped to see what was going on."

"In a Rolls-Royce?"

"Hey, if you're gonna drive, you might as well do it in style." Marty grinned. A few people chuckled. The dress shirt clung wetly to Francis's back.

"Who's that man in the car with you?" Louise Riley asked.

"He's—"

"No one," Francis interrupted.

"—my father's business partner," Marty finished.

The revelation barreled over the crowd and to the far reaches of the lawn, repeating in a chain of murmurs that drew nearly everyone present into an ever-growing circle around Francis.

"What's he talking about, Spud?" someone yelled. "Tell us what's going on."

"He's just fooling with you," Francis said. He had both boys by the elbows now and was pushing them out of the circle. "Never trust the rantings of a teenage boy."

"Come on, Pop. Tell them."

"Now is not the time."

"What? You can't keep it quiet forever. How are you going drum up any business?"

Hinckley Hanson pushed in from the side. "What kind of business are we talking about here, Spud? I hope you're not thinking about groceries."

"Oh, it's bigger than groceries."

Francis gritted his teeth. "I'm warning you, Marty."

"Now you got us all wondering," Hinckley said. "You can't just keep it to yourself."

The sides of Marty's mouth twitched. Short of gagging the boy with his necktie, Francis had the helpless feeling that nothing would keep him quiet.

"What we've got planned," Marty said, "is bigger than any of you can imagine."

NADINE handed a slice of apple cake and a cup of black coffee to Delia, who was watching the scene nearby.

"Who's that all dressed up?" Delia said, wagging a finger at the crowd.

"The older one? That's Spud Pinkham."

"Spud?" Delia squinted hard. "He cleans up real nice. Like a TV weatherman."

Nadine edged away from Miss Pratt and near the outer ring of the crowd. She busied herself folding chairs, but kept an eye and an ear toward the unfolding spectacle.

"That's enough," Francis was saying. "We're going home."

"Are you selling cars, Spud?" someone asked.

"I'm mowing lawns and delivering groceries, that's what I'm doing. Nothing else is going on right now."

"Then how'd you go about getting that Rolls over there?"

"We're just taking a little ride, that's all," Francis said.

"It's a test drive," Marty said. "For when we buy our own."

Francis shook his head. "Don't listen to him, we're not buying anything."

But the more Francis seemed to protest, the more the crowd didn't believe him. Ainsley came trotting up to Nadine with his notebook open and his pen in hand. "I can't believe this," he whispered to her. "Two stories in one day." He stepped into the middle of the circle and raised his hand. "Mr. Pinkham—can you tell us when you'll be making your announcement?"

"Please, just drop it. There's nothing to tell."

Marty, on the other hand, who seemed to be enjoying the attention, opened his mouth as though he were about to spill some great secret. The crowd leaned in with expectation. As soon as he recognized that he had them, he closed his mouth, as though he'd suddenly thought better of it. "Soon," he said. "My father's right. Now's not the time."

"Aw, he's got nothin'," Louise Riley said. "This is just some big stunt to take away from Robert. Shame on you, Spud. After all these years."

As the crowd's curiosity began to shift toward suspicion, they began to disperse into smaller, tittering clusters.

"Imagine," Nadine overheard, "putting on a scene like that."

"I'm not surprised. You'll never know what level those Pinkhams will stoop to."

Nadine watched Francis usher Flynn and Marty all the way down the front steps of the library and across the street. The boys, she noticed, stood tall and proud, but Francis kept his head low the entire time, his eyes never leaving the pavement.

"I'VE JUST ABOUT had it with you two," Francis said as he pushed them toward the Rolls. "You can forget about this whole thing. I'm telling Mr. Rice it's off."

"You can't do that, not now," Marty protested. "Everyone's wondering what's going on. If you quit now, they'll really think you were putting on a show."

"If you'd kept your mouth shut, they wouldn't be thinking anything."

"Didn't it feel good, though, to have all those people paying attention to us? We had 'em, Pop."

"Just get in the car."

The boys climbed into the backseat. As Francis was reaching for the door handle, a truck pulled up alongside the car. "What in the hell is going on here?" a voice yelled out the window.

Francis's joints stiffened automatically, the way they always did when he was in the presence of his sisters. "Not much."

Jackie slid across the bench seat and hung out the open window, giving Francis's outfit the once-over. "You get a job as a chauffer or something?"

"Nice job on the library sign. Looks great."

"Yeah, I was just driving by to see how it came out. I wanted to make it bigger, but Kitty couldn't afford it." Jackie gazed at the sign through the windshield, then suddenly snapped to attention. "So really, what's going on here?"

Francis leaned into the truck and dropped his voice low. "We're having brunch with an old friend. He came to show off his new car."

Jackie squinted. "Who?"

"Weldon Rice."

"Never heard of him."

"He's from Palmdale. Went to elementary school with Anita." He backed away from the truck and grabbed the door handle of the car. The lie rolled so smoothly off his tongue it made Francis shiver.

"Old friend of Anita's, huh?" Jackie's eyebrows arched. "You'd better keep an eye on him or else she's likely to run off."

"I'll keep that in mind," he said, getting into the car before she could ask him anything else.

AFTER THE dedication ceremony, Delia Pratt drove to the Cedar Hole Police station under her own impaired power to have it out with Harvey Comstock. The cup of black coffee and piece of cake Nadine had given her helped sharpen her reflexes somewhat, though her impulses and thirst for war remained woefully intact.

As Delia was tearing into the parking lot, Harvey was just dozing to the crackle of the scanner, slumped over the remnants of a meatloaf TV dinner. Each compartment was licked clean save for the brownie, which Harvey forgot to remove the plastic from before microwaving and was now a gluey mess. The dispatcher was alerting the Burnsville police to a reckless driver on the outskirts of Palmdale, and in Harvey's drowsy, predigestive state, he imagined himself behind the wheel of his squad car in hot pursuit. The squeal of Delia's tires chafing the dirt of the station lot did nothing to rouse him; rather, his mind incorporated the sound into the dream. It wasn't until Delia trounced into the station and slammed the door behind her that Harvey snapped to consciousness, with three errant kernels of corn pressed firmly to his cheek.

Delia's lungs burned hot from the cigarette she sucked down on the way over. "It's *Delia,*" she snapped at his blank look. "Or maybe you don't recognize me because I'm not flat on my back with my knees up to my ears."

Harvey pushed the TV dinner tray aside, the corn kernels dropping off his face one by one. "You're not supposed to be here. The sheriff might stop by."

"And what if he does? Are you going to arrest me?"

"I could—you've been drinking." He said this in the familiar police-man's cadence, as though he were informing her of something she didn't already know. "Why don't I drive us somewhere? I could leave for a half hour or so. I'll put a sign on the door."

"I'm not going to that stinking landfill again."

Harvey tugged at her elbow, and without any further persuasion, Delia sank into the chair beside his desk. "Have some coffee," he said.

She watched him fill two Styrofoam cups with teaspoons of sugar and nondairy creamer. The sickly sweet smell calmed her mood. "You'll never guess who showed up at the dedication in a Rolls-Royce."

Harvey splashed a little coffee on his desk. "A Rolls? Who?"

"Spud Pinkham."

"No shit."

"He was all dressed up, too. In a tie."

He handed her a cup. "What was that all about?"

"He wouldn't say, but Marty was going on about some business deal they were working on."

"Hunh." Harvey scratched his head. "That sounds funny. I wonder what he's up to."

"Something big, apparently." Delia kicked back in her chair and propped her feet on top of Harvey's desk, nearly tipping over. "It got me thinking, though. If Spud can get his act together, why can't I? I'm almost fifty, Harvey."

"Jeesh, Delia, so am I."

"It's not the same for you." In Delia's mind, men didn't succumb to age as quickly as women did. It had an odd way of working for them. The few pounds he'd gained over the years had been distributed evenly throughout, filling his face just enough to smooth out the wrinkles. The lines that radiated from the corners of his eyes were finer than hers. In-stead of making him look weary, they gave Harvey a soft kindness.

Delia stared into her cup. Her head buzzed. "How come you never married me?"

Harvey drank down half of his coffee in two gulps. "I didn't know you wanted to."

"How could you? You never asked."

"I didn't think you were interested. You always seemed fine enough on your own," he said. "Truth be told, Delia, I never thought you liked me much."

Delia kicked the pointed toe of her pump into the side of Harvey's metal desk, making a thunderous boom. "I wasted all my time on you when I should've been going after Robert Cutler. *He* would have married me."

"State law says you have to be at least eighteen years of age to marry. Plus it's illegal to have relations with a minor."

"Not when he was a kid, nitwit—later, when he was a man." Delia sank her teeth into the soft edge of the Styrofoam cup. "There was only fifteen years between us. When he came to school that day I tried to get his attention but his eyes were all over Bernie."

Harvey hooked his thumbs into the front of his belt. "You never told me you liked him."

"Of course I liked him. He was the only decent man in Cedar Hole."

The indirect insult grazed the top of Harvey's crew cut and brushed right past him. "You never told me you liked him in *that* way."

Tears clotted Delia's lashes. "You know, you're not the only person who ever showed interest in me, Harvey. I've had plenty of offers."

"From who?"

"I'm not telling. That's personal."

"What kind of offers?"

"Good offers. I'll say that."

Harvey's face paled. He leaned over her chair, his hands braced on the armrests. "Has anyone ever offered, you know, to take you to the landfill?"

"Harvey—"

"Please answer the question."

Delia was taken aback by Harvey's sudden show of jealousy. With his bulky frame and pudgy cheeks she began to think he was a visually pass-able, if not mentally stunted Cabot. "No. *Officer*."

"Good." Harvey backed away from the chair and nodded, as though he had just proven an important point. "If anyone ever does, you tell me, 'cause I would like to have a word with them."

"I will. I promise."

"All right, then." Harvey plopped down into his chair. He swiveled back and forth a few times, and soon his face melted from a look of ten-sion back into its former undisturbed self. His jealousy was a slippery snake that eluded Delia as quickly as she had captured it. She crossed her legs and attempted another desperate grasp.

"Norm Higgins flirts with me at the meat counter sometimes."

Harvey paused midswivel. "That doesn't make sense, Delia. Norm's a married man."

"Like that makes any difference," she scoffed. "I'm telling you, he's *quite* interested."

Harvey slowly turned himself forward and leaned over the desk. Prop-ping his face with his hands, he secretly wished he had never woken up from the high-speed chase. "I'm going to have to say something to him."

Delia grabbed his arm in panic. "No, you don't. Don't start any trou-ble."

"I have to. It's only right."

"Let it rest." Delia gripped harder.

"I don't like this," he fumed, pacing the length of the station. "I don't like this at all."

"I'm a single woman, Harvey. That's what happens."

"Would a ring on your finger make a difference?"

"I don't know. Probably."

He continued to pace the floor, from his desk to the holding cell and back again. "All right, then," he said after several long beats. "I'll marry you. You'll be my girl."

"You're stuck in the fifties, Harvey. They say fiancée now."

"You can be that, too, if you want."

Delia's afternoon of defeat in front of Deedee Cross and Louise Riley was quickly beginning to fade. "I'll need a ring. A diamond."

"Okay."

"And no more trips to the landfill. From now on, you take me to your house."

"If you get a ring, what do I get?"

She stood up. "I don't know. I'll have to think about it."

Delia blew Harvey a kiss from across the room and strode out of the Cedar Hole Police Station a hussy no more.

"You think you know people," Ainsley said as they folded and stacked chairs. "Who would have thought that all this time Mr. Pinkham was a millionaire?"

"I don't know that he is," Nadine said.

"Well, you don't go riding around in a Rolls-Royce unless you have something going. I wonder what he's up to. I mean, how can you keep something like that a secret?"

Of anyone in Cedar Hole, Nadine thought Francis Pinkham might have the easiest time keeping a secret. Even though he had been mowing their lawn and delivering groceries to the house since she was young, she hardly knew anything about him other than that he was quiet and forgetful. She knew he was quiet because he rarely spoke, except maybe a brief conversation with Bernie every now and then, and also that he was forgetful because he always put extra groceries in their bag and gave back too much change. Nadine also knew that many years ago, when he was a teenager, Mr. Pinkham had competed against her father in the rodeo and lost. Growing up, she'd heard that he never quite got over the loss, that he was a bitter and jealous man. As a result, she had always been a little afraid of Francis Pinkham, thinking that maybe the animosity he felt toward her father would one day be transferred to her.

"You don't suppose it was all a hoax, like Mrs. Riley said, to ruin the dedication?" she wondered aloud.

"I don't know, maybe," Ainsley said. "But you'd have to be a crazy person to take something that far."

Kitty wrapped up the remainders of the refreshment table. "Who would take a bite out of a piece of cake and put it back?" she said, tossing a half-eaten slice of apple cake in the trash. "Is someone trying to tell me something?"

"I thought it was good," Ainsley said.

"I'll let you take the rest home, then. Norm never touches it. He doesn't have much of a sweet tooth." Kitty stacked plates of cookies and brownies and gave them to Nadine. "I called him, by the way. He's getting the van. I'll scoot you home and we'll meet him there."

"Don't get too excited," Nadine warned. "Remember, the desk is in pretty rough shape."

"I don't care. Let's just get this over with."

When they turned into the driveway, Bernie was sitting on the side stoop in a pair of demin cutoffs and a T-shirt, a garbage bag at her feet. Both Kitty and Nadine looked over at the plum tree, whose gnarled, sickly limbs had long since surrendered to rot. Bernie had never bothered to cut the tree down, needing it to tether the desk. But now the desk was gone, and the thick chain that had been holding it in place slumped at the base of the tree trunk in relief.

Kitty seemed to take the desk's absence as a sign of Bernie's good faith. "Looks like she hasn't changed her mind." She got out of the car and slowly approached her, staying several tentative lengths away, as though she were greeting a leashed Doberman. "Your daughter did very well today. You would have been very proud."

Bernie was quiet, looking relaxed and content, her skin bronzed by a day out in the sun. The paved driveway was slick with water, making Nadine guess that her mother had foregone clipping her toenails for washing the car instead. On the surface, everything seemed fine, but Nadine couldn't shake the creeping fear that was inching along her back. She strategically placed herself between the librarian and the stoop, just in case her mother's good mood took an aggressive turn.

"I have some leftovers from the reception," Nadine said, handing Bernie the plate of sweets. The air around her smelled slightly acrid, like a scorched pot. Bernie took a peek under the plastic wrap and sniffed.

"Any of your famous apple cake, Kitty?"

"Unfortunately, no. I gave it to Ainsley."

"Well, that *is* unfortunate—for Ainsley." Bernie handed the plate to

Nadine. "Honey, why don't you take the food inside and put it in the fridge? We don't want it to spoil out in the heat."

Nadine took the plate from her mother, but she didn't move.

Kitty ventured a step closer. "Nadine said you weren't feeling well."

"She did? Actually, I feel just fine, thank you." Bernie turned toward her daughter. "I didn't realize my child had suddenly taken up lying."

Nadine gritted her teeth. "I never used the word 'feel.' I said you weren't well."

Bernie nodded. "Right, I see your difference. You've always shared your father's love of wishful thinking."

Kitty looked over her shoulder at the back lot of the Superette. The van was just sitting there. "I won't keep you long. As soon as Norm brings the van over, we'll be on our way."

"I'm sorry you bothered him at work," Bernie said. "He must be pretty busy."

"People always need their meat."

"Well, maybe there's still time to catch him before he leaves." Bernie got up from the stoop and picked up the garbage bag next to her. There was an oppressive thickness in the air that saturated Nadine's lungs. "Here's your desk."

Kitty received the bag with trembling fingers, lips pulled taut against her teeth.

"No, Mom . . ." Nadine begged.

Kitty let the bag fall open at her feet, exposing the white-black chunks of burned wood mixed in with the jangle of door pulls, all soaked damp and smelling of ash.

"The brass plate didn't burn. I guess there *is* no love lost, is there, Kitty?"

"What have I done?" Kitty choked. "Would you please tell me?"

Bernie went back into the house, the screen door slapping behind her.

PART FOUR

~ Chapter One ~

RICE MAKES HIS PITCH

This is the puddle," Francis said.

Everyone returned from the restaurant in good spirits; Anita still flushed from the glamour of champagne; the boys sedated by their full bellies and a ride in a fancy car; Mr. Rice buoyed from good conversation and pretty waitresses. Even Francis managed to relax a little—away from the crowd and the questions, he was back in his element, finally able to loosen his tie enough to breathe freely.

"I noticed it first," Marty said, poking the spongy border of the puddle with a stick. "It never seemed to go away."

"You're a bright young man," Mr. Rice said, squatting down on his hams to take a closer look. "I'm not sure I would have noticed this myself." He put his hand in the pool and made swirling motions, spiraling down deeper.

"You can taste it if you want."

"Marty." Francis squeezed his son's shoulder. "We've heard enough from you today. Let him be."

Anita gnawed delicately on a knuckle as Mr. Rice scooped a handful and took a genteel sip. "Very nice," he said, standing up. "What we're going to need to do here is install a pump. We'll build a shed big enough to house the whole operation—I'm thinking four spigots with room to cap, box, and store. If we get going by next week, I think we could be in operation by the end of the month."

Francis dipped into the pool and dabbed his damp fingers across his forehead. "That's awful quick."

"No sense sitting on an opportunity. What do you think, Anita? Does that sound good to you?"

"Lovely. The sooner, the better."

"Boys, do you think you'll be able to put in time to help your father become a millionaire?"

Marty nodded vigorously; Flynn shrugged.

"Let's not get carried away, here—there's still a lot we need to talk about," Francis said.

Anita smiled placidly, as though lost in some long, faraway dream. Suddenly she snapped back to reality with a quick jerk, laughing in spite of herself. "I'll go make some coffee," she said. "Boys, let's leave the men alone to talk business."

When the rest of the Pinkhams were out of earshot, Mr. Rice turned to Francis. "I can tell you're apprehensive, and that's not such a bad thing. If I were you, I'd probably be feeling the same way myself. I'd be thinking, *Who's this jackass to come here and tell me what to do with my land and my company?* Am I right?"

"I don't think you understand how much I have to lose here."

Mr. Rice scanned the landscape and squinted at Francis's house, as though he were trying to see it through Francis's eyes but was having a good deal of trouble. "I'm not asking for anything up front—you don't have to give me a nickel."

"It's a wild idea. People don't do things like that around here."

"If it goes belly up, you won't owe me a thing."

Francis pressed the toe of his loafer into the ground. "What kind of guarantee can you give me that it's going to work?"

"This is business, Pinkham. I'm not going to promise you anything. But I can tell you, deep in my gut, I think you're sitting on a gold mine." Mr. Rice shoved his hands into the pockets of his trousers and began to walk around the puddle in hypnotic circles. "You know what you have here? It's a gift. Pardon me for getting religious on you, but it's like God decided one day that Francis Pinkham was going to catch a break—and so He plopped this strange puddle in the middle of your backyard. It would be a sin to thumb your nose at it."

"I don't know if I believe in that sort of thing."

"Well, all right. You're entitled," Mr. Rice said. "Forget the reason why it's here—what matters is that you have an *opportunity*. Why do you think I've gotten to where I am in life? It's because when I see an opportunity, I jump on it."

"How much do you want?"

"Sixty percent is my standard cut."

Francis laughed, despite the chill that shot through his spine.

"Now, hold on a minute—you've got to consider what that sixty percent buys you." He counted out the reasons on his fingers. "We're talking marketing, promotion, distribution, bookkeeping, plus all the equipment and supplies to get you up and running in the first place. And don't forget—I don't want anything from you up front except your time and energy."

"Still, it's awful steep."

"Again—you've got to consider what it takes to run a business. I'm taking care of all of that."

Francis took a seat on an old tree stump and said nothing for several minutes.

"You've got two bright sons, Pinkham—especially that Marty. Janet told me all about him. I understand he won't be attending college next year."

"Not unless he gets a scholarship. We don't have the money for that sort of thing," he said. "He'll be all right. I did fine without it."

"I never went, either," Mr. Rice said. "The way costs are, it's a wonder anyone can afford it. If you had the means, I'm sure you'd want him to go, though."

"Sure, if we could afford it."

"What if I told you that by this time next year, you could have enough to send *both* Marty and Flynn to college? What would you say to that?"

"You think this puddle is as good as all that?"

"Even better." Mr. Rice squatted down again and dipped his hand in the pool, the water line coming up to his onyx ring. He had to be in his late forties, maybe even early fifties, Francis guessed, and every hair on his head was as black as shoe polish. "Think about what this could do for the boys. Not only could it buy them an education and a better life, it would give them good, practical experience at running a business. It would teach them fiscal responsibility."

"Come again?"

"It would make them good at handling money. And think about Anita. We had a little talk when you went to get the boys. She's a fine woman, and she's very proud of you, but I get the sense that she's ready to take the next step. If you had more money, you'd be able to take her to fancy restaurants and buy her a nice, comfortable house. You'd be able to give her the life she deserves. Think about *that.*"

Francis's forehead ached. He was tired of thinking. "I could do this on my own, you know. I don't need a partner."

"Sure you could—but it'll cost you. And distribution could be tough. You don't have the same contacts I have. You don't have the same marketing strategies under your belt. Let me show you something." Mr. Rice reached into his suit jacket and pulled out a small glass bottle with a dropper built into the screw-top. "This here is what's going to turn Pinkham's Natural into gold."

Mr. Rice held the bottle up to the sunlight. The liquid inside was a murky brown, with a reddish tinge across the top. It looked like blood.

"That right there is going to be your key to success," Mr. Rice said. "It's a food-safe dye—one drop per bottle and that water of yours will turn a gorgeous pink. It's a play on your name. Came up with the idea myself."

"Won't it taste funny?"

Mr. Rice shook his head. "Tasteless, odorless, but completely pleasing to the eye. It's the eye that buys, Pinkham. Tuck that away in that head of yours. In marketing, we call this technique a *gimmick*—it's that little something special that distinguishes your product from all the others."

"I know what a gimmick is." Francis's mind was reeling. He wished Anita were there to help him sort things out.

"Do you know how many brands of water are out there? Dozens! All of them clear—no, *invisible*—on the shelf. But Pinkham's Natural will be a rosy, healthful pink—the kind of pink the complexion one gets after a brisk autumn walk." Mr. Rice reached into his suit coat a second time for a pen and a scrap of paper. "I like the sound of that—I'd better write it down."

"It sure is a lot to think about."

"Would you have come up with an idea like that on your own?"

"Probably not."

"Off the top of your head, can you name three plastic bottle suppliers? Quick, now—you need to know this sort of thing."

Francis shook his head.

"Honestly, it's no sweat off my nose if you don't go into partnership with me, Francis. Can I call you that? Tell me you'd rather do the whole thing on your own—that includes scraping together the capital—and I'll give you this little bottle of dye." Mr. Rice handed the bottle to Francis. "Go on, take my idea. I'll let you have it for nothing. We'll just shake hands and part friends right now."

Francis turned the bottle over in his sweaty hands. "It's just that if it doesn't turn out—"

"No need to explain—I understand. Hey, you're not the adventurous type and that's okay. We can't all be. It's not a problem. I can find another partner like *that*," he said, snapping his fingers. "It's just as well, really. I'm looking for someone with guts. Someone who's willing to stick his neck out and make something happen."

Francis rubbed his chin until he thought it would turn raw. "Well, I can't do sixty."

Mr. Rice parted his lips, exposing his white, winking teeth. "Is that what you're doing, Pinkham? Are you sitting there, trying to break me? I never would have guessed. You've got the best poker face I've seen—we ought to go to Vegas. We'd clean up, you and me." He put his foot on the edge of the stump and leaned over his knee, just like in the picture Francis had seen at the seminar. "I like playing the game as much as the next guy, but I'm going to need an answer today. The water market's *exploding*—we're in a prime position to turn this into something *big*. Let's do this, Pinkham. Tell me you'll do it right now."

Francis felt as though something were quickly slipping away from him. *It's for the boys,* he kept telling himself. *It's for Anita.*

"I'll let you have fifty."

Mr. Rice slapped his knee. "I knew I picked the right man."

• • •

THE NEXT morning at the diner Francis decided to have a donut with his coffee, though he kept it to the modest plastic-wrapped kind Shorty bought from the Superette, instead of the fancy cream-and-jelly-filled numbers delivered every day from the Mt. Etna Bakery. They were only fifty cents more, but the dark pocket of jelly that puffed just below the surface and the swirls of cream suggested an extravagance he wasn't yet ready for. *Maybe someday soon,* he thought as he liberated his plain, dry donut from its cellophane pouch.

Henny joined Francis at the counter with a newspaper. "What's this I hear about you driving all over town in a Rolls-Royce yesterday?"

"I wasn't driving. I was just riding, mostly."

Shorty poured Henny a cup of coffee and hovered nearby, refilling an already half-full napkin dispenser.

"Dixie's all worked up about it—everybody is. She said she talked to Anita and you guys are going into business or something?"

"It looks like it. Though things haven't started rolling just yet."

"Well, this is the first I've heard of it."

Francis swallowed a bite of dry donut. "Now, don't get too worked up—it all happened pretty quick. I've hardly had a chance to catch my breath."

"A Rolls-Royce. Jesus, Spud."

Shorty put down his stack of napkins. "I saw it. It looked like a pearl."

"Now, just hold on a second," Francis said. "It's not like I bought the damn thing. It belongs to someone I know."

Henny scratched at his thick brown beard. "I don't know anyone like that. And neither do you."

"He was cruising down the street real slow," Shorty continued, his stubby hand slicing through the air. "You woulda thought there was a movie star in the backseat."

Francis shook his head. "I didn't want none of that. It was his idea."

"Dixie said he looked like a real fancy fella."

"He had one of those old-fashioned hats," Shorty said, "and a shiny white suit. I think they call that a shark suit."

Francis spread the paper across the counter. "What do you want first—front page or sports? Look at that—the Wildcats shut out the Mules nine to zip. Not much new there."

Henny ignored the paper. "So where'd you pick up this new 'friend' of yours? Down at the Left Hand Club?"

Francis slowly chewed his donut, taking sips of coffee in between bites to help it go down. "If it's all the same, I'd rather not say just yet. Not until I'm sure how things are going to work out."

There was a long, dull silence between them, punctuated with the plodding thunk of Henny's knuckles hitting the counter. Shorty closed the napkin dispenser and shuffled off to the end of the bar but kept an ear trained in their direction.

"I kinda wish you had said something to me, Spud. If you're sitting on something good it woulda been nice for us to go in together, instead of bringing in someone from the outside."

"It's not like that. This whole thing is spinning so fast I haven't had time to think about anything. And right now I'm not sure I haven't made some awful mistake—you might just be thanking me down the road for not roping you in."

Henny lowered his head. "Is it illegal?"

"Course not," Francis scoffed. "What did Anita tell Dixie?"

"Not much. I guess Anita was excited, but she wouldn't tell what it was you got yourself into."

Francis watched Shorty out of the corner of his eye, then swiveled his stool so that his back was to him. "It sounds so crazy, I hate to even say it."

Shorty seemed to sense that something big was afoot. He pulled a white towel out of his back pocket and wiped down the far end of the counter, slowly making his way down toward them.

"I'm feeling hungry this morning, Shorty," Henny said loudly. "Why don't you make me a short stack with a side of ham?"

Shortly nodded grimly and disappeared behind the swinging kitchen doors. Henny waited until he was safely out of earshot before he continued. "Well, if you know someone with a Rolls-Royce, I imagine it can't be all that crazy."

"You've got to keep this to yourself, Hen. I mean, you can't even tell Dixie—at least not until I say the word."

"You know you can trust me."

Francis crinkled the cellophane in his fist and held it up to his mouth.

"We've got a water spring in our backyard. This man named Mr. Rice wants us to bottle it and sell it."

Henny looked up from his paper. His eyes were smiling. "You're shitting me."

"Apparently, people pay good money for the stuff in the city."

"I bet they do."

Francis released the ball and the plastic unraveled itself onto the counter. "He says the market's real good for that sort of thing."

"I bet it is," Henny said. "So what are you going to do?"

"I told him yes, but I don't know."

"He's not sticking it to you, is he?"

"Oh no, we've worked out a fair deal."

"If everything seems square, Spud, then you have to do it."

"I just don't see it, though." Francis tapped his fingers against the edge of his cup. "It's only a puddle. It's hard to trust it, you know?"

"Don't think too hard," Henny said. "It's time you had something good for yourself, after what you've put up with. It's just your turn, that's all. Everyone has their turn."

Shorty plowed through the kitchen door a few minutes later, with a plate of pancakes in one hand and a plastic squeeze bottle of syrup in the other. Henny squeezed half the bottle on the stack.

"Easy," Shorty said. "That's got to last me all day."

"Just water it down like you usually do," Henny said with a wink.

Shorty refilled their coffee cups and stood by expectantly, as though he were hoping they'd forget themselves and continue their conversation in his presence. Francis stirred in a spoonful of sugar, his lips sealed tight.

"You forgot my ham," Henny said.

Shorty sighed and returned to the kitchen.

He waited until the swinging door came to a stop. "So what's supposed to happen next?"

"Tomorrow, someone's coming to test the water," Francis said. "I'd appreciate it if you kept this whole thing to yourself. At least for a little while."

"I won't say a word."

As Francis stood and put on his jacket, Allen knocked on the front window, his body propped up by a pair of crutches. Through the glass door Francis could see that Anita's report had not been an exaggeration—Allen's knee appeared to be suspended within an intricate cage of pins and wires, and the left side of his face was traced by an oval of yellow-gray—an obvious remnant of what must have been a hard impact with the cement floor.

"Hold on to your wallet," Henny muttered, tucking into his pancakes.

Francis forced the corners of his mouth toward a smile as he held open the door for his old friend. "Hi, Allen."

"Hey, Spud. Good to see you." Instead of going through the door, Allen propped it open with his crutch and stood right in the middle of the entrance, blocking a smooth escape. "I kept an eye out for you at the hospital. Thought you might drop by."

"It's been real busy—I just heard about the accident yesterday," he lied. "How you holding up?"

"As good as can be expected, I suppose. It looks like I won't be able to go back to Wear-Tex for at least three months, though. Maybe even six if it doesn't heal right," he said. "Got a steel rod in me now."

"That's what I heard." Francis made an attempt to slip through the narrow opening between Allen's body and the doorframe, but the mechanical knee jutted at an angle that made it impossible for him to get by without making contact.

"Got a concussion, too," he said, pointing to the bruise on his cheekbone. "Good thing the guys at work kept me awake. I coulda gone into a coma."

"Well, that's a consolation."

"So how are things with you? It seems like forever."

"Pretty good." He shrugged. "You know how it is."

Allen stepped aside to let Francis through the entrance, then let the door swing closed behind him. He shuffled and jockeyed his way onto the outside step, spreading his crutches like wings on either side, trapping Francis in the alcove.

"I hear you're doing pretty good, though," Allen said. "I heard you were driving around town in a Rolls the other day."

"It wasn't mine."

"I heard you might be starting up some sort of business."

"Nothing's settled yet," Francis said.

"You wouldn't even tell an old friend?" Allen frowned, gazing through the restaurant window. "Does Henny know?"

Francis shrank back. "It's kind of an experiment. It's too soon to get into it."

"I heard it was something big."

"There's a lot of talk. You can't always believe it."

Allen tapped the end of one of his crutches against the pavement. "I wish I had that kind of money to play with. The factory will give me a decent settlement, but the medical bills are unbelievable. And who knows if I'll ever be able to work again after this."

"That's rough."

"Oh, you don't even know."

Francis took the pause in the conversation as an opportunity to make a break. He fumbled for the truck keys in his jacket pocket and made a tentative edge toward a narrow opening between Allen's good leg and the side of the building. "Well, I've got to run. You take care, now."

Allen didn't move. "I don't suppose you could use some help, could you?"

"Help?"

"With the business. You need workers, don't you?"

"Oh. Like I said, it's early yet. For now I've got the boys."

Allen nodded. "My arms are just fine, you know. In fact, they've gotten real strong."

Francis didn't look him in the face. Instead, he focused on the laminated menu posted in the front window. "I'll tell you what—if things get going real good and I need more help, I'll give you a call."

Out of the corner of his eye, Francis saw that Allen was grinning. "You and me working together—that would be something, wouldn't it?"

"Let's not get excited just yet," Francis said. "It's got to depend on a lot of things."

"That's good enough for me. Hope is hope, isn't it?" Allen laughed and moved aside, letting him through. "You just made a crippled man's day—did you know that?"

"All right, then," Francis said, backing down the sidewalk. "I'll see you around."

~ Chapter Two ~

NEW ENDEAVORS

In the long aisle between the stacks, in the slick section of wood floor dubbed Sock Alley, Kitty felt a tender giving underfoot. She stopped, pushing against the floorboard with the toe of her low-heeled pump, then tapped four times. The surface remained intact but just beneath there was a faint hollowness, a troubling change in density. Kitty took at quick look around the library to make sure she was alone, then dropped to her knees.

She sniffed along the gap between the boards and rapped her knuckles against the wood. With a fingernail, she flaked the edge of the plank. *Decay.* It was just as she thought—years of wet boots and melting snow had seeped down into the wood and rotted the board from the inside out. There was no telling how widespread or deep it was. "If I hadn't found it," Kitty mumbled to herself, "no one would have ever noticed."

She returned to her two desks (the first being the old pine table, and the second a mottled lump of carbon she kept in a mayonnaise jar on top of the first) and buried her head in the nearest book, which happened to be a picture book of trains lying in the return bin. She scolded herself against crying, her recent hair-trigger response to everything from loud noises to a rubber stamp pad that ran out of ink.

"Mrs. Higgins?"

Kitty looked up from her book. Nadine and Ainsley were standing by the door.

"Are you all right?" Nadine was saying.

Kitty swallowed despite her swelling throat. "Just reading about trains." She flipped the book around to show them the picture of a sleek steel bullet. "The one that used to come through here looked like this. Have you ever gone to Palmdale to see it? We should go sometime—just the three of us." She cleared her throat. "Ainsley—you could even write a newspaper article about it."

"I don't know," he said. "I still haven't heard back from Mr. Holtz."

"It's only been a few days. You can't give up hope yet."

Kitty closed the train book and dropped it back in the return bin. She sensed a quiet mood descending on Nadine, who was standing beside her desk, turning the mayonnaise jar over in her hands.

"I couldn't bring myself to throw it out," Kitty explained.

"Doesn't it make you sick?"

"I just think about your father's intent, that's all." Kitty wondered if Nadine could tell she was lying. In truth, the lump of ash seemed covered in tiny, invisible thistles that pricked her every time she looked at it. Yet, a stubborn impulse compelled her to display it as some sort of damp victory.

Nadine replaced the jar on the desk, her shoulders withering. "I'm so sorry she did that to you. If I had known, I wouldn't have brought you over."

"It's not your fault. Your mother's a sick woman. If I were you, I'd start to distance myself from her."

"I don't know how I'm going to do that," Nadine said. "She wants us to go on a trip to New Orleans this summer."

Ainsley looked stricken. "For the whole summer?"

Kitty shook her head. "This isn't good. You can't spend that much time with her. She'll poison you."

"I wanted to get a job instead, but she was dead set against it."

"You could work with me on the *Gazette*," Ainsley said.

"She's worried people will think she can't take care of me."

"People *already* think that," Kitty said. "Believe me, Nadine, that has nothing to do with it. Your mother loves control and she's terrified of losing control over you. If your father was here, what do you think he'd say?"

"He'd let me do it."

"Of course he would, because he was a reasonable man. You're getting old enough, dear, to start thinking for yourself."

Nadine leaned over the circulation desk, her eyes wild with thought. "I really don't want to spend weeks alone with her. I'd rather work."

"Wise girl. I think I can help you with that." Kitty picked up the phone and gazed at the mayonnaise jar on her desk, the blackened brass plate rising victoriously from the ash.

MR. RICE sent over a man to survey the puddle. He collected samples of water in small plastic vials and took measurements of the yard, working with wordless efficiency as he staked out a twelve-by-twelve-foot rectangle. Shortly after, a team came with a large drill. Anita spent hours by the window, keeping Flynn by her side and out of harm's way, talking to him in excited whispers as they watched the progress. Marty sat on the gentle rise just above the spring, knees pressed expectantly to his lips, silent but poised for action. When someone asked him for a hand or a glass of water he jumped to life and retreated sullenly to his perch the moment he was dismissed. Francis could not bring himself to be so close. He holed himself up in his den, stealing glances out the window every few minutes, his stomach kneading worries as the drill tore deep into the lawn.

Mr. Rice called to report on the progress being made. "The tests came back—the water's pure. Even better than I'd hoped," he said. "The sooner we get the shed built and the spigots running, the sooner we'll have a positive cash flow. Unfortunately, my construction team is overextended right now. They've got a project in Canada that's running way behind schedule. I don't think I can get them over to you for another month or so."

"My sisters are builders, you know," Francis said. "One of them's even a plumber. They could get the shed up and running no problem."

"You're kidding me. How soon do you think they could get it going?"

"I don't know—I'll have to ask. Maybe a week or two."

"Well, that's what we're going to have to do. It's good to get family involved—I try to do that whenever I can." Rice laughed. "Here I was, all worried about having to wait, and you had the solution all along. I'm not a superstitious man, Pinkham, but I am a believer in signs. When things roll smoothly, that's a sign that you're doing the right thing."

Once Francis confessed to Jackie the real reason for his ride in the Rolls-Royce, Jackie was more interested in the project than Francis thought she would ever be. She stopped by the following morning to draw up the plans. "Breakfast," she said with a smirk as she pulled a long-necked beer from a small cooler she had stashed behind the seat of her truck. "Want one?"

The sun was a beating hammer and it wasn't even noon. Francis shook his head, though just looking at the condensation beading up on the outside of the bottle made his thirsty tongue feel like a cotton rag.

"It was good of you to come."

"And miss the train wreck? Hell, I want a front-row seat." She flicked the bottle cap into the hedge. "Besides, I need a break from those two nuts we're working for in Palmdale. The wife paces the floor all day making sure we don't leave grease marks on her white walls. She's one of those demented city transplants. They buy an overpriced house on no land and think they have a palace—the same kind of idiot," she said, giving Francis a sharp dig in the arm, "who will buy your water."

"As I understand it, city water tastes pretty bad," he said, trying to muster some authority on his subject. "Plus there's the whole exercise craze to consider."

"Right," Jackie said with a snort, "I almost forgot about that exercise craze."

"Mr. Rice has done his research." Francis found himself gushing, revealing far too much, but it seemed as though she were silently pushing him, goading him into proving himself. "We stand to make quite a bundle."

"How big you want it?'

"We're shooting for four spigots. And room for boxes."

She examined the hole the drillers left and measured a box around it by walking one foot in front of the other. "I can pour you a cement floor, if you want."

"I'd appreciate it."

"I want to be paid up front."

"Not a problem. Mr. Rice said he'd reimburse me."

"Insulation? Windows?"

"Better keep it simple," he said.

"I don't know what Rae's going to want to charge—you'll have to sort that out with her."

"I understand."

Jackie took a long pull from her bottle, one eye staring right into his heart. "You don't look so sure about all of this."

"Oh, I'm sure. Sure enough, anyway. I figure it's gotta beat mowing lawns."

"Maybe." Jackie laughed. "Unless the whole thing flops. Then you'll just look like an idiot."

Francis crossed his arms in front of his chest and leaned back on his heels. "So when do you think you'll get this all done?"

"Soon as possible," Jackie said, taking another pull on her beer. "This horror show's going to be the highlight of my summer."

NADINE sneaked out of the house with a skirt and blouse borrowed from her mother's closet, arriving at the store fifteen minutes early for her interview. Mr. Higgins was waiting for her at the meat counter, stacking cellophane-wrapped packs of ground chuck and pork ribs. He wiped his hands on the front of his apron and seemed to smile not exactly at her, but at the air around her. "I wish it was up to me, but you have to impress the big boss," he said, pointing to the mirrored window above the deli. "Just go through the swinging doors and up the stairs. Good luck, and don't let him get the best of you."

Upstairs, Arnie Hanson pushed aside his TV tray and patted the faded plaid couch beside him. The fabric was split along the seams, revealing tufts of foam stuffing. "So you're Cutler's girl," he said, touching the binoculars that hung from a cord around his neck. "How old are you, dear?"

"Thirteen."

"A little young to start work, don't you think?"

"I can work a few hours after school and on weekends." Nadine folded her hands on her lap. "And I can work all day during the summer."

"That's mighty ambitious."

"I need to get out of the house."

"So go outside and mow the lawn."

Nadine pinched her lips. "I'd like to have a place to go and to earn a little money."

Arnie grunted. "I know what you mean. What's so great about the outdoors, anyway? It rains all the damn time." He picked up his binoculars and scanned the aisles. "Your mother's fine with it?"

"She doesn't know yet."

He laughed. "I don't need Bernie getting mad at me for hiring you. We all know what happens to people who get on her bad side."

Nadine shrank inside her mother's blouse. "She won't mind. I promise."

"You'd better have her call me, just to be sure."

"No, please," she said. "I can handle my mother. And I'm not anything like her, in case you were wondering."

Arnie swiveled in his chair and stared at her through his binoculars. "You don't look like you have a big appetite. You're a bit on the skinny side."

"I burn it up fast, I guess. I like to eat, but I wouldn't take anything without paying for it first, Mr. Hanson."

He dropped the binoculars and studied her. "Anyone with Robert Cutler's blood in her veins can't be all bad. I need someone to cover the deli—think you can start tomorrow?"

"I can start today if you want."

"That's a girl," he said. "I can't pay you much, you know."

"That's okay. Thank you, Mr. Hanson." Nadine held out her hand and he shook it. He smelled like rancid potato chips.

"You go on now. Norm will show you around," he said. "Make your father proud."

"WHERE HAVE you been?" Bernie asked the moment Nadine walked through the door. "In my clothes, no less."

Nadine looked down at her mother, who was sitting cross-legged on the living room rug, surrounded by piles of travel books, each bearing the smeary stamp of the Palmdale library. "I was at the Superette."

"Dressed like that?"

"I got a job. I'm working there now."

Bernie slammed her book shut. "Honestly, Nadine, does nothing I say penetrate? I thought we decided you weren't going to get a job, that we were going on a trip instead."

"I don't want to go now."

"Why not?" Bernie rolled up onto her knees and took her daughter's hands in hers. "Is it New Orleans you don't like? I've been thinking it'll be too muggy there. Dry would be best—somewhere it hardly rains. Like the desert." She picked up a glossy book showing the colorful strata of the Grand Canyon. "How about Arizona? We could get on one of those mule tours—it might be a little late for reservations, but who knows, maybe someone will cancel."

Nadine looked down at her mother, feeling strong and spiteful as she towered over her. "I don't want to be in the car with you that long."

"I know road trips can be boring. We'll fly instead. We'll just have to cut back on our hotel budget."

"I don't want to go anywhere with you. Not after what you did to Kitty."

Bernie's smile froze. "You've been talking to her. What's she saying to you?"

"I'm old enough to see it for myself," Nadine said evenly. "You're mean and cold and I don't want to end up like you."

The remark hit its target, not glancing off Bernie's scaly exterior but sinking deeply in her vulnerable underbelly, hitting more cleanly than she intended. Nadine flinched, both panicked and satisfied that she could inflict injury as cruelly as her mother.

"She keeps the ashes in a jar on her desk. You didn't even want the thing, and then you had to go and burn it. That's sick, Mom."

"If you don't want the trip, that's fine. If you want a job, that's fine, too. But I won't have you taking Kitty's side."

"Well, I'm not going to take your side."

"Then don't take any side. This is between me and her—it doesn't involve you."

"Sure it does, because I have to live in this town and listen to all the things people say about you." Nadine swallowed to keep her voice from breaking. "I have to clean up your messes."

"Then I guess you can take care of this one, too," Bernie said, standing up from the pile of books. "And when you're done, there are some dishes in the sink. I'm going up to bed."

~ Chapter Three ~

TAKING *the* PLUNGE

In the world of fine jewelry, Delia Pratt's engagement ring would have hardly been described as exquisite, but in her eyes it was a small wonder. Purchased at the Service Merchandise jewelry counter during Harvey's lunch break, the diamond was only a fraction of a carat: a round gem crafted by the hands of an apprentice diamond cutter, who cut the stone so shallow that it captured light dispersed in fizzy, obtuse angles, giving the diamond more of a hazy shine than a sparkle. The setting, forged in white gold, was that of a rose, with the diamond nestled in the center of the bud, pinned by four prongs. The petals were polished to nearly the same brightness as the diamond, and from several yards away it gave the illusion of a much larger stone. Delia, who had not expected to feel anything close to excitement, was moved to tears.

"Oh damn," she said, lighting a cigarette.

Harvey wobbled on one knee, the damp earth soaking through his uniform. "So you like it?"

"Crap, Harvey. It's beautiful—you did good."

Harvey thought of giving her the ring while she was on the swing set behind the elementary school (it was the pink-tint soft-focus poster of a man pushing a woman on a rope swing that he had seen behind the jewelry counter that had given him the idea), but Delia didn't want such a monumental event taking place so close to work. Instead, she made him take her to the front lawn of the library, where the entire town could bear witness.

"Let me put it on your finger," Harvey said.

"I want to sit down first." She crossed the lawn and headed toward Robert's memory bench.

Harvey eyed the gold plaque on the back of the bench bearing Robert's name. "Does it have to be right here?"

"What's wrong with it?"

"Nothing."

"He was a good man, Harvey. It's like he's giving us his blessing." Delia crossed her legs and arranged herself in a fetching pose. "Go ahead."

Harvey kneeled again, and slipped the ring on Delia's finger.

"Not the middle one—the ring finger," she corrected.

"Delia . . . what's your middle name?"

"Imogene."

"Really?"

"You think I'd make that up?"

"Delia Imogene Pratt, will you be my wife?"

Delia waited until he slid the ring all the way down to the base of her finger. She tilted her hand in an attempt to catch the last spark of fading light, but the ring, despite its best efforts, failed to comply.

Harvey cleared his throat. "Aren't you going to say something?"

"Give me a minute, please. I'm thinking."

"Didn't you think about this before?" he asked, wobbling on one knee.

"Sure, but I don't want to look desperate." She waited a beat or two, then smiled. "Yes, Harvey Comstock. I'll marry you."

"Good," he said, giving her a quick, dry kiss on the lips before standing up again. "I'm hungry. Let's go to Shorty's."

"Cripes, Harvey, it's a nice evening out here. Can't you enjoy it for a minute?" Delia patted the empty space beside her on the bench and he sat down. "I feel like we should tell someone first. Let's go back to your house and call your mother."

"I already told her."

"What did she say?"

"Not much. She seemed happy enough."

"She didn't cry or nothing?"

"I don't think so," he said.

Delia frowned.

"We could go to the diner and make the big announcement in front of everyone, if it would make you feel better. We'll celebrate with hot pastrami sandwiches."

Delia rose from the bench and smoothed the hair back from her eyes. "I could stand a little something to eat," she said. "Now that I'm your fiancée, you have to buy me dinner."

"After the ring, I don't have much left. I only have enough in my pocket for one."

Delia snaked her arm around his. "Figure it out, Harvey. Put it on your tab or something," she said. "Just don't embarrass me."

FRANCIS called Mr. Rice as soon as the shed was finished. "It's very fine. You should see it."

"I won't be able to get down there for a while yet," Mr. Rice said. "You'll be getting a shipment of plastic jugs and caps, plus some cardboard boxes any day now. The way that works is you'll be paying for the delivery when it arrives, and then I'll send along a check."

"I thought you said I wouldn't have to pay for anything—I'm already out for the shed."

"That's the way these things work. I can't be there to write out a check every time you need something—you're going to have to front it the best you can until I can reimburse you," he said. "I know I explained this to you."

Francis cleared his throat. "It's not easy right now."

"Janet's cutting you a check right now for part of the shed. From that, you'll definitely have enough to cover the bottles and boxes. That's how you'll be covered. It might seem tight now, but as soon as we start selling, it will be very smooth."

"All right," Francis exhaled.

"So once the bottles arrive you can get to work. I've got two cappers on order that should be coming your way. You just fill, cap, and box. Another truck will come by at the end of the week to pick up the filled bottles. That's it."

"What about labels?"

"We're not quite set on that yet. I'm not happy with the logos that my graphic designer has come up with so far."

"My son Flynn's real good at drawing, you know. He has some ideas."

"Now, there's a thought. I'll keep it in mind," Mr. Rice said. "We're going to need a hundred cases from you to start. Do you think you can manage?"

"Between the four of us, I think we can do it."

"Good man. We'll talk soon."

EVEN THOUGH Mr. Rice provided the building and the equipment, making the spring shed into a comfortable place to work was up to Francis. Two spigots were three feet off the floor, spaced four feet apart against the eastern wall, with the other two against an adjacent wall. Francis wasn't even halfway through filling the first plastic jug when he realized how uncomfortable it was to stand up holding the jug in midair, so with some plywood and scrap two-by-fours, he slapped together two long, crude tables to run beneath the spigots. Measuring had always been Francis's point of failure when it came to furniture-making and this project was no different; he had to saw the legs down until the tables were the right height to allow the jugs to slide beneath the spigots. After several attempts at correcting the problem, the legs were still uneven, creating a serious wobble. It was only a minor nuisance when a jug was empty, but once filled, the weight of the water shifted the table from one side to the other, tilting the mouth of the jug just enough to trap it beneath the spigot. Extricating the bottle of water required a delicate touch: either bringing the table into perfect balance so that the container could slide out from underneath the spout, or lifting the jug by the handle (his preferred method) and pulling it out at an angle, careful not to spill the contents. Both approaches were time-consuming and cumbersome, but Francis would have rather ignored the wobble than admit his defeat as a carpenter. Finally, when his wrist began throbbing in rebellion, he ripped two flaps off a cardboard box and jammed them beneath the two short legs.

Francis had asked Jackie not to build windows to save money, but now he wished he had sprung for them. Spending several hours a day in a small room lit by a single hanging lightbulb had the same disorienting effect on him as if he were swimming deep in the ocean and couldn't remember which way was up. His watch ticked away the mornings and afternoons but he didn't trust it—it had to be later, somehow, than it already was. He brought in a floor lamp from the house to brighten the shed and soften the shadows, and on dry, temperate days he left the door open, turning periodically in his folding chair padded with egg crate foam to look at the grass. An oscillating fan kept the air from being stale, though wafts of warmth and cold whistled through the gaps in the crude wallboards.

The system Francis had worked out for himself was to line up a case of empty sterilized jugs to his left, fill them one by one, and pass the filled jugs off to the right. Then he put one drop of red dye into each bottle, a plume of liquid smoke that thinned and curled in the water, stretching out into a web of dark pink threads. He sealed the bottles with one of the two cappers Mr. Rice had given him, a simple, hand-operated lever that placed a plastic cap and safety ring over each jug and sealed it tight. The caps were dark pink, another of Rice's marketing choices, which he felt would have a strong appeal for women, who made up, according to his calculations, eighty percent of the water-buying public. Once the bottles were capped, Francis gave them a sturdy shake, so the dye would mix properly, until it began to meld into the color of rose quartz. The pink-on-pink color scheme was hard on the eyes after a long shift, but Francis kept his opinions to himself.

The water jugs were then loaded into cardboard shipping boxes, six to a case, without labels, and the boxes were stacked along the two empty walls, with plywood pallets laid in between for strength. Once a week, a white delivery truck arrived from the city and two men loaded the boxes into the back. They worked quickly, speaking to neither Francis nor each other. As Francis understood it, once the water reached Mr. Rice's offices inventory was taken, the labels were slapped on, and the cases were divided up for distribution.

Marty did the majority of the work, with Flynn putting in a few hours and Anita helping out when she felt like it. Francis put in a solid six hours every day, between lawns and deliveries. Together, they barely

met Mr. Rice's quota, which discouraged Francis, though Marty was optimistic.

"We haven't found our rhythm yet—that's all," he said. "Once we find
that, we'll be churning out cases in no time."

Francis tried running two spigots at a time, but he was never fast
enough, or he'd concentrate on one and forget about the other, and suddenly there would be an overflow. Spills had a way of unnerving him, and
he'd carefully sop up the spill as though it were something flammable or
unspeakably precious. Marty would watch him, with his sponge mop,
disapproval radiating from every pore.

"It's just water," he'd say. "There's always more."

"You don't know." As quickly as the puddle appeared, it seemed to
Francis that it could just as easily be sucked back into the earth. Or there
was always the threat of sabotage, that Jackie might sneak into the shed
in the middle of the night and turn the spigots on full blast, until all the
water would drain from the spring. He had dreamed of this; of stepping
into the shed one morning and turning on the spigot only to have a puff
of dry sand spill out. He was convinced that good fortune was not a permanent condition (Robert Cutler being a prime example), but he'd hold
on tightly as long as fate would allow.

Anita kept a plastic cup near her spigot and every six jugs or so she'd
stop for a break, filling her cup with water and taking a deep drink.

"Don't drink up all our profits, now," he teased, only half joking.

Once school let out for the summer, Flynn usually strolled in after
lunch, thumbs hooked into the belt loops of his jeans, shoulders loose
and unburdened from the cares of the world.

"Took you long enough," Marty said. "It's almost one o'clock."

"I had stuff to do."

"Like I don't? Put some boxes together."

"Put 'em together yourself."

"Everybody calm down," Francis cut in. "It's Flynn's summer vaca-
tion—he's entitled to have a little time to himself." He turned to Flynn.
"Go get the boxes like your brother asked. We've got a lot of work ahead
of us yet."

Flynn grabbed a few flats of cardboard from the stack in the back of
the shed and began the process of folding and taping them into three-

dimensional boxes. Francis looked away from the slow piddle of his spigot to watch his son work. Flynn had a knack for assembling boxes lightning-quick, yet his arms moved with an unhurried grace. He studied Flynn as though he were a magician, looking for the sleight of hand, waiting for the misdirection, and still he could never nail down exactly how the boy did it. Poof! There was one box. Poof! There was another. One by one they appeared, as easily as if he had pulled them out of his shirtsleeves. The secret to Flynn's speed (a mystery Francis would never solve) was in the confidence and economy of his movements. Not a single rotation of the wrist, not a flex of the fingers was wasted—every flap was bent with complete surety and force.

The air inside the shed was thick with the smell of sweat. Marty pushed a jug aside and stuck his head under the tap, letting the water roll down the back of his neck. It pooled on the table beneath, dripping onto the floor.

"That's better," he sighed, working it through his hair. "This place is going to be hell come winter."

"If there's money, we'll put up some insulation and drywall," Francis said.

"I'm thinking about the pipes, though. Won't they freeze up on us?"

Francis shook his head. "We'll bring in a propane heater to keep it warm."

"When's the money supposed to come?" Marty asked. "It's been a while."

Francis capped a jug and slid it down to the end of the table. "Soon, I suppose."

"Don't forget my cut."

"Everyone'll get their share. We've operating expenses, you know."

"What's Flynn's share? It better not be the same as mine, because I do ten times as much work—plus, I'm older."

"Ask your mother. She has it all worked out." Francis labeled the finished water jugs and loaded them into one of Flynn's boxes, turning the bottles so that the handles all pointed toward the northeast corner of their individual compartments, as per Marty's instructions. It was a fussy detail Francis never would have thought of, but he had to admit it gave the case a professional, manufactured look.

"Take it all—I don't care," Flynn said.

"Liar," Marty said. "What about the stereo you told me you wanted?"

"I saw an old one when I went to the landfill with Pop yesterday—I could take it home and fix it up."

Francis smiled to himself. No matter what happened, he thought, Flynn was resourceful and resilient enough to make it through. With Marty, though, he had some doubts.

"We're businessmen now." Marty finished filling the last of his jugs and started capping. "You can't go around picking trash."

Flynn frowned and helped Francis load boxes.

"We have an image to present. You need to think about what other people see."

"Why? No one in Cedar Hole buys our water."

"Pop—tell him."

Francis sank deep into the egg crate. "What Marty means is that in order for us to do well, it's important that people take us seriously. If they see you scrounging around for things, they're going to think we aren't making any money."

"But we're not," Flynn said.

"Not yet. But we will."

"I still don't get it."

"You don't have to," Marty said. "Just do what we say. When I get my cut, I'm going to buy a nice suit."

Flynn rolled his eyes. "Well, whoop-de-doo. What are you going to buy, Pop?"

"I haven't thought that far ahead. Maybe a riding mower."

Marty's eyes glittered in a way that numbed Francis. "You should hire someone to mow the lawn for you. That would get the neighbors all worked up."

"I can take care of my own yard. I don't need anyone else to do it for me."

"It's just an idea."

"We've had enough of those, haven't we?"

•   •   •

"IF YOU SLICE a hard-boiled egg and put it on top, that potato salad would look real pretty," Bernie said, her breath fogging up the glass of the deli case. "Or even a little paprika to give it some color."

"Mr. Hanson doesn't want me to do anything extra," Nadine said. "It's fine the way it is."

"I think you put too much mayonnaise. A touch of mustard is always nice. Gives it a nice zing."

"I didn't make it," Nadine said. "It comes delivered in a bucket."

Bernie wrinkled her nose. "Well, in that case, I'll just have a half pound of that boiled ham on the end. Is that low-salt or regular?"

"Low-sodium."

"That's my girl."

Nadine leaned over the counter. "What are you doing here?" she hissed, her skin burning with embarrassment as Norm Higgins shuffled nearby in the meat department. "Why don't you go home?"

"There's nothing wrong with a mother visiting her daughter at work, especially if she's a paying customer," Bernie said. "Slice it thin, now."

Nadine turned the dial on the meat slicer to the finest setting, shaving the ham into ribbons thin enough to see through and delicate enough to disintegrate to the touch.

"You look so sweet in that apron of yours," Bernie said. "Like a doll."

"Mom, *please*."

"Just like her mother," a voice called from across the meat counter.

A tight-lipped smile spread across Bernie's face, but Nadine could tell that beneath the smile her mother was gritting her teeth. "And how are you today, Norm?"

"Fine now that you're here. How come we never see you anymore?"

"Keeping busy, that's all."

Norm wiped his hands on his apron and leaned against the meat counter. "I was telling Nadine that I thought you were sneaking out on me to that big supermarket over in Mt. Etna."

Out of the corner of her eye, Nadine watched Norm Higgins. Given that her mother had just torched his wife's desk, she expected to see animosity on his face. Instead, his eyes were two big sponges, soaking in the view just below the neckline of her mother's blouse. Nadine felt sick to her stomach.

"You caught me," Bernie said, the corners of her mouth digging deeper into her cheeks. "Nothing personal. Just convenience."

Norm licked his lips. "I can get you a real nice deal on some chicken thighs, if you're interested. You can barbecue 'em."

"We all know I *am* a fan of fire," Bernie said, sending Norm into a convulsive fit of laughter. "But my little girl's going to fix me up right here."

Nadine shoved the ham shreds into a plastic bag and slapped it closed with a sticker.

"Thank you, miss," Bernie said with a wink. "How about some of that roast turkey?"

"It's old. I cut some mold off the end this morning."

Bernie puckered her lips. "How about some pickles?"

"They're dill. You hate dill."

She sighed. "Then I guess that's it. You having dinner at home?"

"I don't know."

"Okay, then," Bernie said heavily. "I guess I'll see you *whenever*."

Nadine grabbed the spray bottle of bleach and began wiping down the counters, saying nothing as her mother turned to leave.

" 'Bye, now," Norm called, his eyes following Bernie down the aisle. "Don't be a stranger."

GETTING OLDER, to Bernadette's surprise, did have something to recommend it. There was a certain lightening of responsibilities to both oneself and others that made that inevitable downward slope toward death almost tolerable. Nadine, who had rendered Bernie irrelevant from the moment she learned how to boil spaghetti, demanded virtually nothing from her now that she wouldn't have expected from the concierge of a fine hotel—as long as there were fresh towels and toilet paper, a fully stocked pantry and cable TV, there were no complaints. When it came to the Ladies' Auxiliary and the other members of the Cedar Hole community who had expected her to carry the torch for Robert, one too many unreturned invitations and casserole dishes finally got the message across. No one bothered her anymore.

Bernie took a shower and lingered in the bathroom mirror, watching her gourdlike breasts on their incremental journey downward, a vision that was both fascinating and horrifying. They were no longer beautiful, nor were they expected to be—and now, having outlasted their service, both sexual and maternal, they were released from all obligations. This certainty did not bear heavily on her, but did quite the opposite; it sustained her gently in its promise. She would no longer be troubled by the mind-spinning adrenaline burst of youth, with its tremulous blank pages to be filled. Aside from Nadine's adolescent fits, Bernie could live the rest of her days in the steady, even lull of predictable peace.

Or at least that's what she had thought until that day at the Superette, when Norm Higgins had looked at her the way he did. She didn't recognize it at first—that glint in the eye, that wolflike hunger—no one dared look at Robert Cutler's widow that way, and so she had mistaken his leering for something that had to do with the desk. Anger, gratitude, peevishness—on Norm it all looked the same. But then his eyes traveled that long brazen road from her face to her breasts and suddenly Bernie knew. It was lust.

Her first reaction was panic, then offense. He had no right to think of her in that way . . . or did he? In truth, Norm could think of her in any way that pleased him and there was absolutely nothing she could do about it. For a moment, she had considered calling him on it, exposing his lurid stare for what it was, but Nadine was there, and Bernie didn't want to give voice to Norm's thoughts. What went on in a person's mind was pure imagination, but when someone else acknowledged it, it suddenly became real. And so she had left.

But she'd been thinking of him ever since.

It was no great compliment to be ogled by Norm Higgins, and Bernie knew that. His taste in women was broad and democratic—he reminded her of Robert in that way—and his choice of wife was a testament to poor judgment. She knew better than to be flattered by his attention, yet she found herself clinging to it. Or rather, it clung to her. It was there when she undressed at night and picked out her clothes for the day. It was in solitary moments—reading the paper or making dinner—when she became self-conscious, as though Norm were in the room with her, watching her. It was there when she studied herself in the mirror, trying to see what she had so long ignored. To see what it was that he found attractive.

Bernie couldn't help but wonder what Robert would have thought of her girlish obsession. She imagined him laughing at her—not meanly, but a lighthearted, generous laugh. He'd think she was being foolish, but he'd be glad for her just the same for having something for herself. Never mind that Norm was a married man. Never mind that he was married to Kitty. The Robert in her mind glossed over such details.

The lapse of time made him softer to her now, a burnished gold instead of the showy brass she always took him for. She wondered how he would have weathered middle age, if his hair would have thinned at the crown or the forehead, if his gray would have started at the temples or salt-and-peppered his head. Would he have thickened in the middle, or held on to his lean waist? Would they have stayed together? Would he, in spite of the person she had become, still have loved her?

It was easy to imagine Robert unchanging and loyal, his vast capacity for love and forgiveness never diminishing, but Bernie's darker impulses led her to believe that had he lived long enough, she would have seen the end of his limits. It became plain to her the moment she lit the fire under Kitty's desk that Robert would have eventually given up on everyone. He would have let Kitty Higgins, the Library Association, the *Gazette,* and every committee in town pull at him until he snapped. It might have hit him all at once—a bolting cold sweat in the middle of the night—or it might have been a slow seduction, the urge to hit the gas pedal and never let up. When the flames finally caught and the damp wood sizzled in the fire, Bernie decided that if Robert had lived he would have left her, and maybe even Cedar Hole, too. And she would be standing in the exact same spot she was in now, alone, thinking of Norm Higgins.

From the bathroom, Bernie heard the screen door shut. She tied the sash of her bathrobe and went downstairs.

"You're getting ready for bed already? It's only six," Nadine said.

"I felt like taking a shower." Bernie ran her fingers through the end of her daughter's braid and opened the refrigerator door. The cool air prickled her skin. "There isn't much. I could make you an omelet. I'll put some salsa in it—how does that sound?"

Nadine shrugged. It was the closest thing to a signal of approval that she was likely to get.

"Where's Ainsley?"

"Home. I'm going over there after dinner."

"Why don't you bring him here? We could play Scrabble."

"We're going to watch a movie. Besides, Ainsley can't spell."

"That's funny for a writer."

Nadine sneered as she watched Bernie wiping her fork on her robe. "There's a dish towel by the stove."

"I like terry cloth better."

"Not everyone can spell, you know. It doesn't mean he's dumb."

"I know. I never said he was."

"You said it was funny."

"I meant *unusual*."

"What do you mean by that?"

"I didn't mean anything. Nothing at all." Bernie cracked some eggs into a bowl, then poured the eggs into the frying pan. The bowl was small and plastic but it suddenly felt heavy in her hands. Everything felt heavy—the fork, the handle of the pan, the robe hanging from her shoulders. More than anything, she had an oppressive desire to lie down on the couch and drift off to sleep.

"So tell me about work."

Nadine sifted through the silverware drawer in search of a fork that met her specifications. Coming up short, she sighed and rewashed one in the sink. "There's nothing to tell."

"Any interesting customers?"

"No. Not really."

"How's Mr. Hanson?"

Nadine shrugged. "I wouldn't know. He doesn't talk to me much."

Bernie cracked a few more eggs into the bowl and beat them with a fork, her heart thumping wildly in her chest. "What about Mr. Higgins?"

"I don't know. He's okay, I guess—he's never said anything about what you did, if that's what you're wondering."

"He doesn't seem mad, then."

"I don't know. He always seems the same."

A pat of butter melted in the hot pan and Bernie felt vaguely embarrassed. Still, she was compelled to press on. "Does he ever talk to you?"

"A little. Why?"

"Just wondering. What sorts of things does he talk to you about?"

Bernie pretended to concentrate on her omelet while she listened to
Nadine's lazy chewing and her slow, dramatic gulps of juice. "Meat," she
said finally. "Stuff about the store."

"Does he ever say anything inappropriate?"

"Like what?"

"I don't know." The eggs began to stick to the sides of the pan, and
Bernie minced them with the edge of her spatula, forgoing the omelet
for a mess of scrambled eggs. "Does he ever flirt with you?"

"Ugh. That's gross."

"Well, does he?"

"No."

"That's good," Bernie said. "You're getting to that age now when men
are going to start noticing you. You have to be careful."

"I saw him looking at you the other day."

Bernie's pulse quickened. "Who?"

"Norm."

"When?"

"When you were in the store. His eyes were all over you."

"Huh," Bernie said. She stirred and stirred and stirred with her head
down, until the soft curds broke into gray bits of gravel. "I didn't notice."

"Sure you did," she said in her smug, all-knowing way. "You loved it."

"Don't talk to me like that."

"It's true isn't it?"

"I don't like this change in you, Nadine. I'm your mother and I deserve respect."

"You should have thought about that before you torched Kitty's
desk."

"Are we going to keep rehashing this?"

Nadine dropped her fork onto her empty plate with a clang. "I'm
leaving."

The kitchen door slammed. Bernie looked at the pan full of mealy eggs on the stove and wondered if she should go over to the Superette and pick up another dozen.

FOR SEVERAL weeks they worked in a vacuum, having no contact with Mr. Rice outside of the deliverymen and their silent pickups. Then, one day, they got a call.

"Things are going well, Pinkham, better than I could have imagined. Janet's sending you a nice check, pronto. I threw in a little bonus because you've been patient. Things are good, they are very, very good."

Francis dared not to speculate as to what "very good" meant to Mr. Rice. He tried not to think about numbers or money or any of the other things that gave rise to the electric hope that was now crackling in his ears. Instead, he tried to think of practicalities. "The label. How did that turn out?"

"Fine, very fine. Forceful, I think. Commanding. We have your name in bold letters—takes the edge off all that pink. I bet you were worried about that, weren't you?"

Francis allowed himself a small, breathy laugh. "It's a little girly."

"Not with the label, though. I assure you."

"Are you going to send them down here so we can put them on ourselves?"

"I've been mulling that one over," Mr. Rice said. "I've decided we'll just keep things the way the are. We'll save you that extra step so you can keep up with the output." He paused. "I'm going to need two hundred cases from you this week."

Francis's heart jumped. "We're just barely getting by as it is—"

"If we're going to keep this thing running, I need your full commitment. You're the most important piece of the puzzle."

"I'm doing everything I can—it's hard with two other jobs going."

"Groceries? What does that pay you?"

"Not much, but it's steady."

Mr. Rice sighed. "Listen to me, Pinkham. Now, I don't know a whole lot about what you've got going at the grocery store, but it doesn't take a genius to figure out that you're being taken advantage of over there. I wasn't going to say anything that Sunday we went out for brunch—we were having such a good time, I wasn't about to spoil it—but I bet you spend just as much on gas as you get in tips."

"I do get ahead—a little. I wouldn't do it if I didn't."

"It's not my place to tell you what to do—I'm just saying that if I were in your position, I'd start thinking a little more about myself."

"I've been there a long time."

"That's reason enough to cut it loose, don't you think?"

Francis gripped the receiver hard in his hand. "I don't know that I'm ready for that just yet. Maybe Flynn and Anita could chip in a few more hours. I could work after dinner to make the quota—"

"Hey, work it out any way you need to—as long as I get my two hundred cases. I'm just pointing out what looks like the easiest, most obvious thing. Hell, while you're at it, I'd cut out the lawnmowing thing, too. But it's not my business," he said. "You can't move ahead in this world if you let yourself stay tied down to things. And that's all I'm going to say."

"I appreciate your advice."

"Look, I've got to scoot. You keep an eye out for that check."

"Will do."

"Just remember, the more you pour, the more you'll make."

~ Chapter Four ~

MEDIUM WELL DONE

How's Nadine doing at the store?"

Norm Higgins tossed over onto his side. The old mattress usually dipped beneath his weight, perfectly compressed to the contours of his body, but Kitty recently got it into her head that it suddenly needed to be flipped after twenty years of use. He bobbed up high now, the springs digging tight into his back. Struggling to stay far from the middle, he shimmied away from where the mattress took a drastic slope straight down into the beloved depression now cradling Kitty's rigid torso, and clung to the edge of the mattress to keep away from her two spindly legs and the icy flippers at their terminus.

"Fine," he mumbled in the dark.

"That's good." Kitty's voice was far too loud and bright, nicking the edges of his sleep. "I knew she'd do well. Smart girl. She's got a lot of Robert in her."

"Hmmph."

"Does Bernie ever go to the store to see her?"

Norm could almost hear the thoughts circling in that head of hers. He pushed deep into the pillow, letting the fiberfill puff up around his ears. "I've seen her a few times."

"Does she talk to you?"

His eyes snapped open to the black wall. "Sure."

"Is she chilly? Or does she bother to make small talk?"

"Does it matter?"

"I'm curious—considering what happened."

He was fully awake now. "She seems fine. Perfectly normal."

"That's odd." Kitty fell quiet for a long time—so long that Norm started to relax again, thinking she had drifted off. "Does she ever ask about me?"

"No."

"No?"

"Kitty—"

She kicked her leg out and grazed him with the cold sole of her foot. "I just don't understand it, Norm—I really don't. I never did anything to hurt that woman, *ever*. I go out of my way to be kind and pleasant."

"You could stand on your head twenty-four hours a day and that still won't make people like you."

She sat up. "People? What's this *people*?"

Norm pulled the covers tight to his chin. "People like Bernie. People in general. You can't make everyone like you, Kitty. And you shouldn't care."

"I don't know that I *care*. It's just curious. I wonder sometimes if there's something I don't know: Do I smell bad? Does my face look angry when I'm not smiling?"

"You don't smell bad."

"Then what is it? Tell me."

"Are you really asking?"

"What do you mean?"

Norm kicked his legs and wiggled up toward the high edge, hooking his leg over the side of the mattress to keep from sliding down again. "You care too much about things, Kitty. It wears people out."

He felt her roll over toward him and draw her knees up to her chest. "Do I wear you out?"

"We're not talking about me."

"Well, do I?"

"No," he said, in spite of his compulsion to tell the truth.

"I don't understand," she said, putting a trembling finger on the small of his back. "How can someone care too much?"

"When they can't leave something alone."

For once she listened, and soon her breathing became even and steady. Finally, she cleared her throat and said in a quiet, thin voice, "That's the worst thing I've ever heard."

Norm rocked fitfully against the stiff springs, knowing that Kitty would spend the rest of the night staring up at the ceiling.

BERNIE had a craving for meat.

Specifically, a thick porterhouse cooked on an outdoor grill. While Nadine was at work, she drove down to the Mt. Etna Mall and purchased a small charcoal barbecue, along with a bag of briquettes, a can of lighter fluid, and a tube of Cinnamon Sugar lipstick. She put on a red skirt, a pair of flip-flop sandals—no point in looking *too* obvious, she decided—and a white blouse, leaving the top two buttons undone. She pinned her hair off the back of her neck and smeared her lips in Cinnamon Sugar.

At the Superette, Nadine gawked at her. "Why are you dressed like *that*?"

Bernie smiled lightly, rubbing the slick between her pursed lips. "It's a lovely day outside. I felt like looking nice." Out of the corner of her eye she watched for movement in the meat department, but from what she could tell no one was there. "I went to the mall and bought a barbecue! I thought it would be good for us to eat a nice barbecued steak for once—"

"Given your love of fire."

"You could even invite Ainsley over if you wanted," she said, ignoring the comment.

"Whatever." Nadine drummed her fingers on the deli counter. "Are you gonna order something? I can't stand here talking or Mr. Hanson will get mad."

"I'm your mother—I can talk to you anytime I please."

"Okay. Just order something so I look busy."

Bernie sighed. "Give me a pound each of potato salad, macaroni salad, and coleslaw. Do you think Ainsley would like some pickles on the side?"

"You don't like any of this stuff. It has too much mayonnaise."

"It's good in a pinch. I'm going to be spending all of my time figuring out the barbecue." She rubbed her lips together again, and this time she openly glanced at the meat counter. "Is Mr. Higgins around? I need a good steak."

"There's about twenty of them wrapped in the case."

"But I need a good one. I don't know much about picking out a good steak."

Nadine pressed a buzzer with her thumb and began scooping the salads into separate plastic containers. "I'm surprised you didn't buy one at the supermarket when you were in Mt. Etna. I'm sure they have better stuff."

"I figured it would be nice to give your employer a little business."

Nadine pressed the buzzer again, more urgently this time, until Norm finally emerged from the meat cooler. He had a dark, crusty look about him that made Bernie's stomach heave, but when he smiled, her head swam with light.

"Sorry to keep you waiting, Bernie. I was just going over the week's orders."

"No rush—I'm visiting with my daughter."

"You look lovely, as always," he said, staring nakedly at her rear end. "What can I do you for?"

Bernie felt her face burn hot. Embarrassed by her sudden flush, she felt it burn hotter still. She walked over to the meat counter, running the tip of her tongue over her teeth. "I need a nice, good steak to barbecue."

"Let's see," he said, examining a few packages. "What do you like, tenderness or flavor?"

"Can't I have both?"

Norm smirked at her. His wandering eyes looked hooded, sleepy. "You want it all, don't you?"

"A girl can try."

"I bet you'd like a couple a nice rib eyes. I got some good ones in the back that I haven't put out yet," he said. "Can you wait a minute or two?"

"As long as it takes."

A thrilling, adolescent tingle fanned itself against her belly. As Norm pushed through the swinging doors to the back room, Bernie absently smoothed her lips with the tip of her finger. "So what do you think? Should we get some pickles?"

"I don't care," Nadine said. "Do what you want."

"Maybe not, then. What about a nice cake for dessert? It's so beautiful out—I kind of feel like celebrating."

"Whatever."

"Don't look so glum, honey. It's just dinner, not a life-or-death situation."

Nadine slapped the salad containers onto the counter.

"I'm thinking strawberry cream cake. Wouldn't that be good?"

Norm returned with the steaks wrapped in white butcher's paper. He wrote the price in black grease pencil, and underneath it, he wrote a phone number.

"If you have any questions about how to cook it, just give me a ring."

FOR THE FIRST TIME since the whole operation began, Francis was feeling optimistic. He canceled all of his lawn appointments for the week so he could free up enough time to make Mr. Rice's quota. His clients were understanding, if a little curious. Then, on Tuesday afternoon, the brakes on the Superette's van started to grind and Francis knew it was time to take Mr. Rice's advice. It was time to cut himself loose.

Arnie was ready for him by the time he reached the stairs.

"I haven't had any calls this morning. You'd better not be driving around on my dime."

"I'm not delivering today," Francis said. "I came to tell you that I'm quitting."

A nearby TV tray held a plate piled with chicken bones. Hanson peered through his binoculars and made a note on a greasy paper napkin. "THEY'RE ALMOST OUT OF QUARTERS ON REGISTER TWO," he yelled.

Hinckley emerged from the kitchen, wiping his hands on a towel. "What's this about you leaving?"

Arnie set down his binoculars and proceeded to suck on a chicken bone. "Don't worry yourself about it—I'll just jump up, click my heels together three times, and skip down the stairs."

"I'll get to it when I can, Dad."

Francis cleared his throat. "I don't want to leave you in the lurch," he said. "If you need me to stay an extra week or so, I will."

"They're going to need some ones pretty soon, too," Arnie added.

"Give me a second, Dad. Francis is here."

"For God's sake, do I have to do everything? Why don't you just shove a broom up my ass so I can sweep as I go along?"

"Hold on a minute and I'll get you one," Hinckley said, shaking his head. He looked at Francis. "We're awful sorry to see you go, Spud. Does this have to do with the water?"

Francis cringed. "How'd you hear about that?"

"I'm not sure," he said, scratching his chin. "You know how word gets around. Things going all right?"

"Seem to be."

"Don't get too worked up," Arnie said. "I've been in business a long time and I don't think you've got much of a chance."

"Dad—"

"It's worth a try," Francis said.

Arnie wagged a chicken bone at him. "Keep your nose out of trouble and maybe you'll be all right. The minute people sniff scandal, they'll turn right the other way."

"Never mind him," Hinckley said. "I'm happy for you, Spud." He grabbed a money envelope and went downstairs.

Arnie smacked his lips. "How's the van running?"

"Fine." This, in fact, was the truth—the van had no trouble running at all. It was stopping that was becoming a problem.

"How's the oil?"

"You've got about fifteen hundred miles left on it."

"Gas?"

"About half a tank."

"You should have filled it."

"Sorry about that."

"Not a problem, I'll just put it on your tab."

Francis tried to hand him the keys but Arnie didn't take them. Instead, he set them down on the TV tray. Francis stepped back and reached for the doorknob. "All right, then, take care. If I hear of someone who might be interested in the job, I'll let you know."

"Don't bother," Hanson said. "I'll find someone. Any schmuck can deliver groceries."

For a brief instant, Francis thought about shaking Hanson's hand, but almost as soon as the thought occurred to him, Hanson picked up his binoculars again.

As soon as her mother left, Nadine wiped down the sink and the sides of the deli case, nested the empty plastic cartons, double-wrapped the cut ends of cheeses to keep them from drying out, and stirred the pickle barrel, floating fresh ones to the top. Not once, during all of this, did she allow herself to think of her mother, or Mr. Higgins, or the greasy stares that had passed between them.

When she looked up from the barrel, Mr. Pinkham was standing at the counter, pulling a square of folded paper from his shirt pocket. "Let's see, now. I'm supposed to be getting a pound of American cheese. . . ."

"Hi, Mr. Pinkham."

He looked up from his paper, startled, then squinted hard at her. Nadine suddenly felt embarrassed, as though she had caught him at a personal moment, like zipping up his fly.

"When did you start working here?" he asked.

"Not too long ago," she said, looking down. "You said American, right? Yellow or white?"

"Oh, I don't know what she wants. Whatever you got."

Yellow was by far the most popular, and the current block had been sliced down to the heel. Even though there was plenty of white, she unwrapped a new block of yellow, because it would be the freshest.

Mr. Pinkham paced in a circle with his hands in his pockets while she sliced, an aimless whistle curling between his teeth. For all his surface casualness, Nadine thought he seemed deeply consumed by something, his lips occasionally breaking from their tune to form silent word fragments of either past or future conversations that appeared to be playing out in his head.

She double-wrapped the cheese in paper and slid it across the counter. He didn't notice.

"You're all set. Can I get you anything else?" She waited. "Mr. Pinkham?"

Francis snapped to attention. "No, that's it." He put his hand on the package and paused a long moment. "Say, is everything okay at home?"

Nadine gave him a sidelong glance. "Yeah."

"It's just because of the job—you and your mom aren't in any kind of trouble, are you?"

"We're fine. I just wanted to get out of the house."

Mr. Pinkham scratched his chin. He looked up at the mirror on the wall and leaned in toward the counter. "This is none of my business, but you ought to be careful of Arnie. He'll rob you blind if you give him half a chance."

She bristled. "He's been good to me so far."

"Maybe it'll be different with you than it was with me. Just keep your eyes open." He took the package of cheese and stepped away, then pivoted on his heel and came back to the counter. "And another thing— don't get too comfortable here, in Cedar Hole, I mean. I'm starting to realize there's a price to be paid for letting things go on too long."

Nadine wanted to press him further, to understand exactly what he meant, but by the time the words came to her, he was already gone.

AFTER DINNER, while Bernie hummed ballads and scraped the leftover salads back into their respective containers, Nadine and Ainsley stretched out in the backyard, beneath the arthritic plum tree. New grass sprouted where the cherry desk had been, pushing its way through the dry yellow patch. There were no leaves on the plum tree, of course, since it had been dead for a number of years, but Ainsley thought it would be poetic to stare up at the brittle branches and watch them scratch at the sky.

"You don't think it's going to fall on us, do you?" she said, letting Ainsley take the side closest to the tree trunk. "It *is* rotting."

Ainsley stamped his foot against the base. "It seems solid to me. Even if it did, it's too small to do any major damage. It would probably poke an eye out at the most."

"That's comforting," she said, starting to sit up. "I think I'll go sit on the porch instead."

"No," he said, tugging at the shoulder of her T-shirt. "Stay here. You'll be fine—I promise."

Nadine nestled against the grass, taking solace in the solid ground beneath her, trying to convince herself that the earth was holding her up instead of pulling her down.

"Ainsley, do you ever think about leaving?"

"Cedar Hole? No."

"Not ever?"

"Where else is there to go?"

"A million places." Nadine tilted her head toward the open kitchen window, where Bernie was washing the dishes. The hiss of the water faucet was punctuated with the frequent clash of plates.

"I doubt any place is better than this. I think, when you come down to it, most places are the same," Ainsley said.

"Palmdale's better. I think if Mom and I moved to Palmdale, things would be a lot better. We'd be able to melt in. We wouldn't have the pressure of everyone watching everything we do. We could start fresh."

"Aw, things wouldn't be all that different. You don't suddenly become somebody different just because you live in a new place."

"Well, if she's not going to be any different, then maybe I need to get away from her." Nadine plucked a blade of grass and sucked it between her teeth. "She can just look at me and I cringe. And when she talks, her voice hits me like tiny pinpricks. That's hate, Ainsley. That's the start of hate."

Ainsley lay quietly beside her. Nadine continued to chew on the blade of grass, watching his chest rise and fall out of the corner of her eye. "I don't want you to leave," he finally said. "I'd miss you too much."

"I was thinking you might go with me. I couldn't do it alone." She spat out the last of the chewed blade. "Would you go?"

Ainsley looked up at the kitchen window, then flopped over onto his side. "Where? Palmdale?"

"No—she'd find us there. We need to go someplace where we can get lost—like the city."

A light breeze blew across the backyard and the branches of the plum tree creaked. She could feel his eyes chasing the contours of her cheek. "I don't see how that's going to fix anything," he said.

"She's poisoning me."

"Come on, Nadine. It's not as bad as all that."

Nadine snapped another blade of grass and worked it between her front teeth. The taste was tart and deeply green—almost bitter. "Mr. Pinkham came into the Superette today. He said something about not getting too comfortable here and letting things go on too long. I've been thinking about that all afternoon, trying to figure out what he meant, and I think I know. You can't sit back and let things just happen to you. Sometimes you have to step up and push them in the direction you want them to go."

Ainsley rolled onto his back. "I wouldn't put too much stock into what Spud Pinkham says. I've been doing some investigative journalism on that business of his so when Mr. Holtz calls me I'll have another story ready. Anyway, it turns out that the big business idea he has is bottling water from a spring in his backyard and selling it."

"What's wrong with that?"

"According to what I've been hearing at Shorty's, it's a harebrained scheme. Nobody's going to become a millionaire selling water."

"Maybe he's got plans you don't know about."

"I suppose," Ainsley said, "but look what the guy's done so far. That ought to tell you where he's going."

She rolled onto her side. "So you don't think he's right."

"Well, sure, you could force things to go the way you want, but what if what you want isn't the best thing? Your father had a better way—make the best of whatever happens," Ainsley said. "I'd trust his way over anything else."

Nadine flopped onto her back and stared up at the clouds. The edges were charcoal tinged with coral light from a hidden, setting sun.

~ Chapter Five ~

FRANCIS KEEPS HIS PROMISE

The check arrived in a plain, hand-addressed envelope. As of late, Anita had been making herself present every time Francis returned to the house with the mail; eyeing him as he sorted through the bills, holding her tongue until she could no longer stand it, then asking the question that made him wince. He knew she wanted to turn it into some hokey production, into a family moment with the boys hovering over his shoulder to get a glimpse, with pictures taken and a round of water in wine goblets for an imaginary toast. But he wanted it quiet; to be able to take it all in peacefully, a humble, grateful hush that wouldn't scare the good luck away. He teased her, steeling his face as he flipped through the mail—the bills, the weekly Superette circular, the gold credit card offers that still came addressed to the home's previous occupant.

And then one day, while Anita was out running errands, there it was. It was written in an efficient, slanted script, as compact and elegant as Janet herself. With the blade of his pocketknife, he sliced through the end of the envelope. His heart throbbed wildly in his chest—taking him by surprise. He had been careful not to let himself get in too deep just yet. He tried to have no expectations whatsoever until he was assured some success, but a vague, uninvited hope had bored its way in. It was too late to harden himself to the possibility of disappointment. He wanted to succeed.

Anita blew into the kitchen with a bag of groceries. "I stopped by the bank to see what was happening with our credit card application. Would you believe they turned us down? I talked to the branch manager and explained our situation—he still thinks we're too much of a risk. What's it going to take?" She put away a gallon of milk and then turned to him, looking at the stack of mail in his hand. "Anything?"

"This," he said, handing her the check.

Anita covered her mouth with her fingertips, her eyes softening in a way that stirred within him feelings of pride. "A thousand dollars? Is this right?"

"Most of it's going to Jackie to pay for the shed, but Rice threw in a little as a bonus for our patience," he said, clearing his throat. "He's doubled the order for next week." He carefully laid it on the kitchen table next to Anita's ceramic corncob shakers. "He says this is just the beginning."

Anita threw her arms around Francis's neck, her lips pressing against his earlobe, her breath peppered with tiny sobs. "Thank you for doing this," she whispered. "Thank you."

CHECKS CAME regularly, in increasing amounts that continually shocked and pleased the Pinkhams. Francis stopped opening the checks in private and just handed them over to Anita. She had a careful, breathless way of opening the envelopes, sawing through the short end with a steak knife, then blowing into it and plucking it out with her thumb and forefinger. Francis never stared over her shoulder to look at the amount; just watching her sigh, with one palm pressed to her chest, told him all he needed to know.

"It hardly seems possible that we bottled that much," she said, her brow furrowed over the check. "He must be overpaying us—it seems like we're getting almost five dollars a gallon."

"There's no way we're getting that much," Francis said. "You can't count the reimbursements or the bonuses. He tosses those in for good faith."

"It's just so . . . so *much*."

"Why don't you give him a call, then? Tell him we don't want his money and we're sending it back."

Anita laughed a soft, girlish laugh that made Francis slip his arm around her waist. "Don't be foolish."

The first thing Marty did with his share was buy himself a new suit. He modeled it with a pair of brown loafers and a vinyl briefcase stuffed with so many papers that Francis was convinced half of it had to be his old tests from school. Francis's throat thickened a bit when he saw the boy dressed up. He couldn't help it.

"I still can't figure out what you need that getup for," Francis said, clearing his throat.

"We're going to be taking meetings someday. I need to look professional."

"Well, you be sure to keep it for best, then. Don't go running all over town looking like some bigwig."

Marty stood in the middle of the kitchen while Francis and Anita finished up their lunch, and tried to coax his necktie into a half Windsor. "There's nothing wrong with looking successful, Pop."

"Oh yes there is. You start acting like you're better than everyone else, you're asking for trouble."

Marty shrugged. "Maybe we are better than everyone else. Or at least we're going to be."

Anita brushed a few flakes of dandruff off Marty's shoulders. "Dad, doesn't our boy look smart?"

"More like a smart-ass."

"Cut it out." Anita frowned. "Marty deserves his share and he's entitled to spend it any way he pleases."

Francis brought his water glass over to the kitchen tap and refilled it. After tasting the spring, he thought Cedar Hole's water had a bitter edge that tarted up the tongue like cheap gin.

"I can't believe you still drink that stuff," Marty laughed. "Go grab a gallon from the shed. Live a little."

The back of Francis's neck bristled at the sound of the boy's laugh—when did it become so smooth and controlled? It was more of a punctuation mark, a courtesy, than a true expression of humor. Francis remembered when the boys were younger and used to run around the house shrieking at a pitch sharp enough to puncture an eardrum. Both he and Anita used to cover their ears with their hands, though sometimes, when the kids were particularly rambunctious, Anita would put on a pair of furry earmuffs. Even though it often left him with a headache, Francis thought he favored the shrieking to the oiliness of Marty's adult voice.

"I'm not about to drink up the profits," Francis said. "As far as that suit goes, it seems to me that if you're an honest man with a good business, it doesn't matter what you wear as long as you look clean and have a good handshake."

"Think about Mr. Rice. I'm sure he didn't get to where he is today by going to meetings wearing work pants and plaid shirts," Marty said. "Successful people don't usually look so—provincial."

Francis cocked an eyebrow, unsure if he had just been insulted. "Did you hear that, Anita? Our boy's been reading the dictionary again."

Marty pulled his wrist out of his jacket sleeve and looked at his watch. It was some fake-leather number Anita had picked up at the drugstore for his birthday a few years back. The wristband was peeling apart in layers like cardboard, and the once-yellow-gold bezel had rubbed silver on all the edges. Marty checked the time, then tucked the watch carefully back into his sleeve. It was out of sight, but Francis knew the watch was still there and for some reason he couldn't quite identify, the thought of it brought him a deep sense of satisfaction.

"We should buy something, too," Anita said. "To celebrate. We could hire Jackie and the girls to redo the bathroom. I'd love to finally get rid of that green tile."

"Let's put it away and think about it for a while," Francis said.

Anita put her arms around his neck and kissed him on the cheek. "Or how about a new couch, then. Leather?"

"We'll see."

JANET continued to call with the weekly order. Mr. Rice wanted an extra two hundred cases.

"That's a bit more than we can handle right now," Francis said, feeling a line of sweat breaking along his hairline. "Put Rice on the phone for me."

"Can't," Janet said. "He's traveling through Southeast Asia right now in search of new markets. Actually, if you could do an extra three hundred, that would be great."

Francis's eyeballs rolled dryly in his skull, burning from long hours at the spigot. Pushing a mower had always been strenuous work, but it hardly compared to lifting and boxing gallon jugs of water. His back muscles seized against such unreasonable demands. He began to hate any kind of wetness, going so far as to carry one of Anita's froofy umbrellas between the shed and the house when it sprinkled. Taking a shower made him queasy. When he collapsed in his recliner at the end of the day, all he saw were gallon jugs and pink caps scratching at the backs of his eyelids.

He woke to the cyclic laughter of *The Tonight Show*. Anita and the boys were silent in their rooms. Bathed in the blue twilight of the television, Francis began to doubt the existence of all that had come to pass in the last few weeks, wondering if, at worst, it had all been an extravagant hallucination, or, at best, an overly optimistic exaggeration. Even his sore forearms did nothing to convince him of the spring's reality; in a groggy stupor he rose from the depths of his recliner and shuffled over to the kitchen window. To his relief, the shed was standing lean and crisp in the exact spot he'd hoped it would be. He stood at the kitchen sink for several minutes, soaking in the fruit of his accomplishment.

Just as the tug of sleep was about to lure him to bed, Francis was shaken awake by a curious sight. The previously dark shed was suddenly lined in thin yellow horizontal stripes. He rubbed his eyes and looked again, leaning close to the window as his mind tried to construct an adequate explanation for the change. As the drowsiness began to lift, Francis realized he wasn't seeing external stripes at all, but the cracks between the boards and a light shining from within. Someone was in the shed.

Francis jammed his feet into his work boots and tripped out the back door. His first thought was that it was Marty, working late into the night to meet the quota, in which case he was primed to tell him to get some sleep, and, after some verbal acrobatics on Marty's part, eventually giving up and leaving the boy to his own devices. But then as he crossed the wet lawn, it occurred to him that it was probably Flynn sneaking around with some girl.

The door was cracked open. He approached slowly, rapping his knuckles on the door. He paused to give Flynn and the girl a moment to compose themselves then pushed open the door.

But it wasn't Flynn.

"Allen? What in the hell are you doing in here?" Francis tried to keep his voice steady, despite his wide-eyed confusion.

Allen had one finger frozen on an open spigot, letting water splash onto the table. "Didn't think I was gonna ever get an invitation, so I thought I'd come and see what the fuss is about on my own." He cupped his hand under the stream and took a taste. "Mmmm—like champagne."

"We've been so busy—"

"I can see that." Allen let go of the spigot and hobbled on his crutches into the corners where the filled cases were stacked. He opened the flaps and sniffed inside the box. "How come it's pink?"

"We add a dye. To make it more interesting."

He pushed aside an empty box with his crutch and surveyed the deepest corners of the shed. "What's that over there?" he asked, turning back toward the spigots.

"That's the capper." Francis chewed the inside of his cheek. "Look, it's late, Allen. Why don't you head on home and I can show you how all this works tomorrow?"

"You know, I went over to that wholesale place near the mall, looking for Pinkham's Natural, and the manager said he'd never heard of it. I was kinda disappointed. I wanted to stop somebody in the aisles and say, 'Hey, see that? I know that guy.'"

"We're not distributing around here."

"Why not?"

"My business partner has other ideas."

"Business partner, huh?" Allen looked him up and down. "You a millionaire yet?"

Francis forced a laugh. "Hardly."

"But you will be, right?"

"You're getting ahead of yourself."

Allen pulled up one of the folding chairs and fell into it. "My leg's not healing good, Spud."

"Sorry to hear it." Francis rubbed his chin, trying to find a graceful exit. "You should be home getting some rest."

"But like I said, the rest of me still works good. The crutches have made my arms real strong."

"I'm sure that's true."

Allen stared at the floor a long while. "I'm trying not to beg, here."

Francis shook his head. "I've got nothin' for you, Allen."

"Then how come I'm hearing all over town you've got more work than you can handle?"

"Who said that?"

"It's what I've been hearing. You're not getting help on the outside, are you?" Allen asked. "You wouldn't go behind my back and get someone from out of town, now, would you?"

"It's just me, Anita, and the boys, I swear. I don't have a place for you here, but if I did, I'd hire you, I promise."

"I don't know that you would."

Francis sighed. "Just what are you driving at?"

"It's all well and good that you've got something, but don't go hoarding it all." Allen struggled to his feet and tucked his crutches under his arms. "There are plenty of people around you who deserve a piece of happiness. Don't you forget it."

"I don't wish bad on anybody. I'm just trying to take care of my own."

"You can do that if you want to," he said, limping out the door. "But do that long enough, and someday, if you need help, people might just be looking the other way."

"He's got a lot of nerve," Henny said the next morning when Francis relayed the story of Allen's break-in over coffee at Shorty's. "If I were you, I'd lock that shed up so he can't get in it again."

"I did. Slapped up a big padlock and chain."

Shorty brought over a cellophane-wrapped donut and Francis waved it away. "Got any of those jellies from the bakery?"

"A couple," Shorty said.

"Bring me one—and Henny, too."

Shorty raised his eyebrows. He slid back the glass door from the pastry case and chose two puffy donuts and set them on plates on the counter.

Francis bit deeply into his, making sure he hit jelly on the first strike. Heaven. "I always wondered what these things tasted like," he said, dusting powder off his chin. "Even better than I thought."

Shorty watched him chew. "So things are good?"

"I'm just eating a donut, Shorty. Don't go reading into anything."

Henny coughed. "Got any waffles today?"

"Not ready," Shorty said. "I'd have to mix up the batter from scratch."

"Sounds good. I love fresh waffles."

Shorty frowned and disappeared into the kitchen. Henny rocked on his elbows and leaned in close. "So it's going good."

"I never would have believed it—still don't, sometimes."

"Like I said, it was just your turn. You deserve a break."

Francis frowned. "Now, don't go saying that. You'll scare it away."

"It's not going anywhere." Henny quietly ate his donut. "Forget all that crap Allen said—he's just jealous. Always has been."

"I bet he's right, though. People are watching. They're just waiting for me to fall flat on my face."

"It ain't gonna happen. You're gonna move out of here. I can see it."

"Can't go anywhere—the spring's here. I can't move the damn thing."

"Doesn't mean you have to live your whole life next to it. I see you in Palmdale. In a big white house—"

"Don't talk crazy."

"—maybe with a pond or a pool—"

"I mean it, Henny, you're making me sweat—"

"—and a big car in the driveway. Maybe even a Rolls." Henny took a swig of his coffee. "You sure as hell better invite me over."

Francis swallowed the rest of his donut without tasting it. "I'm so far from that, you don't even know."

"No—listen. You've got a shine on you. I never noticed it before, but that's probably because you're always so close—it's hard to see something when it's right up on you. But I see it now, real clear. It's funny how clear—like it's been there awhile."

Francis withdrew his hands into the cuffs of his sleeves and tucked his head down slightly into his collar. "Cut the crap, Hen."

"The last time we saw it was on Robbie Cutler. You know what I'm talking about. It could be dark as night out and he'd be giving off his own light. It bugged us because we didn't understand it, but now I know what that shine was—I think they call that grace."

Francis dug into his wallet and slapped a five-dollar bill on the counter. "Have another cup of coffee on me, but stay away from the donuts. All that jelly's making you loopy."

"People will see it, eventually—even you. You've been called."

FOR FRANNY'S seventieth birthday celebration, Jackie planned a good old-fashioned summer barbecue in her parents' backyard, with ribs and corn on the cob and slaw. For the cake, she envisioned a triple-layer double-chocolate fudge with dipped strawberries. Jackie wrote in exquisite detail everything she wanted—right down to balloons and noise-maker favors—then handed the list over to her mother, fully expecting her to do the rest.

If Francis had known, he would have done the planning himself. Maybe he would have even booked the banquet room in the Boathouse Café and served a big buffet of steamship beef and flambéed something-or-other. Work was good and steady. They had found their groove, as Marty liked to say. For the first time, they were beating their quotas. Checks were rolling in so fast the branch manager of Mt. Etna Banking & Trust introduced himself to Francis and gave him his personal business card.

"This is my last party," Franny announced, setting a platter of glazed ribs in the center of the Pinkhams' picnic table, which the girls had moved from the kitchen to the backyard so everyone could take advantage of the dry weather and sunshine. "No more birthdays, no more Christmas, no more Easter. I'm tired. Someone else should do it for a change."

The girls lined up on both sides of the table in the exact configuration of their childhood, their spread hips angling for room on the bench. Franny and Larry flanked the ends, while Francis, Anita, and the boys were relegated to a small card table pushed several feet off to the side. Their knees bumped as they picked at the small basket of dinner rolls on their table, patiently waiting for the rest of the family to finish heaping their plates.

"Don't expect me to have Thanksgiving," Jackie said. "There's no room at my place."

Larrie Jr. pried the cap off a bottle of beer with her teeth. "When I move in with Jimmy, we can have it over there."

Franny wrestled the bowl of coleslaw from Billie, whose arm encircled it in a near death grip, and placed a healthy dollop in the middle of her own plate. "I'm not having Thanksgiving at your married boyfriend's house."

"The divorce will go through by then. Her stuff will be totally gone."

Anita cleared her throat. "We could host Christmas dinner at our house, if it that's all right with everyone."

The Pinkhams fell quiet, except for the squeak of plastic knives sawing against Styrofoam plates and the moist chomp of mouths grinding animal flesh. The girls looked at each other from across the table.

"That would be nice, Anita," Franny said. "Thank you."

Larry grunted. "I don't know why we have to talk about this now. Chrissakes, it's half a year away."

"I just want everyone to enjoy today," Franny said, "because after this I'm done."

Marty slit a second roll in half and slathered it thickly with butter. Flynn kicked his legs in agitated rhythm against one of the table legs, making their empty plates and untouched utensils jump along the surface.

"Hey, you know who I heard is getting married?" Rae said. "Miss Pratt and Harvey Comstock."

"Lord knows why he'd buy the cow when he's getting the milk for free," Franny said. "Let that be a lesson to you, Larrie Jr."

"Aw, stuff it, Mom."

Francis turned around and tapped Larry on the shoulder blade. "Dad, pass some food back. The kids are hungry."

Holding a corncob in one hand, Larry picked up a bowl of mixed sweet pickles in the other and passed it absently over his shoulder.

"You can sell that table for double now that Spud ate on it," Georgie teased. "You should sign it for us, big shot."

Jackie snickered. "Are you kidding? We're going to have to hose it down and put it on clearance."

"So business is good, son?" Larry asked.

"We're holding our own."

Larrie Jr. gave him a wink. "Oh, you're doing better than that, aren't you, Spud? Little Marty over there was telling me that business has more than tripled."

"People are still talking about you driving around in that Rolls-Royce," Teddie said. "I wish I coulda seen that myself."

Georgie nodded. "When you get rich, we'll build you a nice house."

"And charge him time and a half," Jackie muttered.

With a sudden start, Flynn picked up his plate and went over to the picnic table, a new suckling wiggling his way to the feeding trough. He wedged his way through the pressed shoulders of his aunts, who paused from their eating to load up his plate. Franny, noting the momentary break, quickly motioned to Marty. "Come on, now," she said. "Come get something to eat."

Anita and Francis never entered the fray, but simply ate the same way they always did at every other Pinkham gathering—by taking begrudged bites off their sons' plates.

"I wouldn't go spending all your money just yet. This water thing's bound to be a fad," Larry said. "What you should have done was stay with wood. Now, *that's* a steady business. People always need furniture."

"They need water, too, Dad."

"Course they do—but they don't need to buy it."

Jackie curled her upper lip. "You better hope this dry spell doesn't last long or you'll be mowing lawns again come next summer."

As soon as the last rib had been gnawed clean, Jackie, Larrie Jr., and Billie presented the birthday cake—an enormous one-layer white sheet cake trimmed with pastel roses and lacy script—Franny's finest work to date. Larrie Jr. and Billie carried the cardboard cake platform at both ends while Jackie supported it from the center. Everyone sang to Franny except Jackie, whose face turned taut and sallow, a hellstorm quivering beneath her skin.

"I told you chocolate," she said, dropping the cake on the table in front of her mother. "Where are the strawberries?"

"For goodness' sake, Jackie, I'm allergic to chocolate. You know that." Franny smiled at the blazing candles. "Now help me blow these out."

As Franny cut her birthday cake, Francis sat back and watched the scene with an internal stillness that approached something like contentment. He let the boys eat their cake and drink their punch, then he leaned across the table and winked. "Boys," he whispered. "It's time."

Marty and Flynn slipped away unnoticed in the middle of all the commotion and returned a moment later, rolling a large ribboned box on a dolly across the back lawn.

"My word!" Franny said as they wheeled the present toward her. "What on earth is this?"

"A box of water?" Jackie snickered. Her eyes were cold.

No one laughed. They stopped eating and stared, looking at the box, then at Francis, then at the box again.

"Well, go on, Ma," he said. "See what's inside."

Franny lifted off the bow and delicately placed it on the table, then ripped the paper down the sides. It was a brand-new color television set.

"Look, Larry—it's a TV!"

Larry smiled. "Would you look at that. Is it color?"

"Course it is. We thought it was about time you had a new one," Francis said. Beneath the table, Anita squeezed his hand.

Franny shook her head. "I was just saying to Dad the other day that it was time we got ourselves a new one. I've been getting those lines across during the news."

"It comes with a remote control and everything. You won't have to get up to change the channel anymore."

"Fancy," Jackie said. "Does it take a crap for you, too?"

Franny ignored the comment and gave her son a kiss on the cheek. "I don't even know what to say, Francis. Thank you."

"You deserve it, Ma." Francis cleared his throat. "Roll it into the house, boys. Let's see how it looks in the living room."

~ Chapter Six ~

The MOUSE DISCOVERS HIS TRAP

It was the morning after the birthday party when the rain returned and Francis Pinkham woke up feeling good about the world. The brief dry spell had left him worried, but the water was back, sinking deep into his ground, replenishing his reserves. He wondered what the spring looked like—if he peeled back the sod and rocks, would he find a hollowed-out bowl of earth filled with water? Or was it as big as a lake, spreading beneath the house and all the way down to the road? Or was the ground porous and spongy, trapping water in tiny little pockets that flowed to the surface via thin veinlike channels? He liked this idea: cells, veins, the pulse of circulation. The spring as a gentle beast hidden in a dark cave, feeding him its blood.

Francis threw back the wedding quilt that covered their bed. The lightness in his heart and mind was thrilling, like the fleeting weightlessness he felt whenever he drove too fast over the railroad tracks on Webber Road. He had made it over the hump of uncertainty, and now, having eased over to the other side, the road ahead was as smooth and sure as Palmdale blacktop. As soon as Mr. Rice returned from Southeast Asia he would talk to him about installing a few more spigots. He'd think about hiring on employees and tripling his output. He'd save for Marty's first semester at Palmdale U. next year, and put a down payment on a brandnew house for Anita. Maybe he'd even buy her a diamond ring.

Anita was in the kitchen, with the morning paper spread across the table. Her lips were white. "Walter Mullen died," she said.

His first instinct was to resist the intrusion. He didn't want anything to spoil this rare moment of happiness, but it was already too late. A small hole had been torn and the lightness that held him up a moment ago was quickly dissipating. "When?"

"Last week. In his sleep."

The obituary showed a young, posed picture of Mr. Mullen—perhaps it was a school photo—with dark hair and eyes so bright it seemed as if they had never experienced grief. The resemblance between this picture and the one of the soldier on the wall of the Mullens' kitchen was startling.

"There's no funeral," Anita said. "It says she had a private memorial for him at Shady Acres last week. I thought she would have at least called."

Right after breakfast, Francis changed into a clean pair of work pants and drove over to Mrs. Mullen's house.

"Mouse, it's so good to see you," she said, giving him a warm hug.

Francis's chest tightened as he walked into the entryway he had been banned from nearly twenty years earlier. On the left was the old coat tree where he had returned the money to the pocket of Mr. Mullen's jacket, a memory of splinter-sharp shame that had yet to work its way out. To the right, through the doorway of the living room, was Mr. Mullen's threadbare recliner.

"I knew you'd stop by once you saw the paper," she said, leading him to the kitchen. "I hope you understand why I kept the service private."

"Of course," he said, just as relieved he didn't have to be there. He took a seat at the kitchen table. The picture of Jasper was down, leaving a ghostly outline on the wall.

"I'm leaving soon—moving to a retirement community in Mt. Etna. I'd like you to go through some things before it all gets hauled off. You can take what you want."

"Don't you think you should wait awhile? It's so soon."

"I've been wanting to do this for years, but Walter wouldn't have it. He hated change. This place is much too big for me." She poured him a cup of coffee from the percolator.

Francis nodded, trying not to imagine how long it took her to walk from the far end of the kitchen, through the living room, and down to the bedroom out back. On the wall next to him, the cat clock's eyes did a concentrated sweep of the room. After all these years, the glittering eyes still struck a chill in his heart.

"Would you like to take that home with you?" she said, noticing his stare. "You seemed so fascinated with it as a boy."

"Thank you—but I don't really have the room."

"Look around. If there's anything you want, take it. It's all going to auction anyway. What about your wife? Is there anything she likes?"

"Salt and pepper shakers—she has a whole collection. I can't say she needs more, though."

Mrs. Mullen smiled. "I think I might have a few interesting ones kicking around in the cupboards. You can see them and decide for yourself." She removed the cat clock from the wall and set it on the table in front of Francis. The tail swept across the tabletop and tapped the edge of his plate. The eyes took a silent read of him and laughed. Francis turned the clock over and ripped out the battery.

"Take the Toro—Walter wanted you to have it. He heard about your water business. He was proud."

Francis's throat squeezed tight, making his eyes burn.

Mrs. Mullen patted his shoulder. It felt warm through the fabric of his work shirt. "No need to keep carrying that around with you, Mouse. You're forgiven."

Francis stood up quickly, his voice raspy. "Where did you say I could look?"

"Start in the living room. I've got lots of furniture."

The living room was exactly as he remembered. There was the old console television; a few end tables topped with doilies and porcelain bird figurines; the old brocade sofa trimmed in mahogany, the cushions still plump and springy as if no one had sat on it since the last time he visited, though the upholstery had paled from the sun. He thought about the saggy old couch in his own living room, and wondered if Anita would think it was an adequate replacement.

He ran his hand along the curved camelback and down the arms. The wood had a tacky feel to the touch and he leaned in to take a closer look. Instead of the deep, silky mahogany he remembered, the wood had taken on a whitish gray haze that reminded him of when Flynn left his bedroom window open during a thunderstorm and his dresser got water-damaged. He scratched a fingernail across the finish. It was soft. Water stains dotted the hardwood floors around the perimeter of the furniture. He went back into the kitchen.

"Did you have a rainstorm in the middle of your living room? Your couch is all wet."

Mrs. Mullen wrapped a pair of cow shakers in a piece of newspaper and stared at Francis uncomprehendingly.

"Your furniture . . . it's water-damaged," he repeated.

Mrs. Mullen looked confused for a moment, then her face lit up. "No, no—that's the protectant."

Francis scratched his head. "Protectant?"

"In case of fire," she said. "It keeps the furniture from burning up. You brush it on." Her hand swept the air with an invisible paintbrush.

He had never heard of such a thing. "Can I take a look at it?"

"It's under the bathroom sink. I just put a coat on the other day so it would be all ready for you."

Francis found his way down a narrow hallway to the bathroom. In the walnut cabinet beneath the sink, he found a clear plastic gallon jug with a paintbrush lying beside it. The label was printed in crude, generic black and white and read: FURNITURE FLAME RETARDANT. There was only an inch of pink liquid remaining in the jug, which Francis swirled around and held up to the light. The pink cap was identical in color and design to the caps he used for his own bottles. He unscrewed the cap and sniffed. Nothing—except for the faint petroleum smell of the plastic. He poured a little of it onto his hand and sniffed. There was no smell. A slow, creeping panic edged along his backbone as he pressed his fingers to his lips. It tasted like nothing.

"Where did you get this?" he asked, holding up the jug.

"I don't know where it comes from. I ordered it over the phone."

A cold sweat broke over his body. "How much was it?"

"I think it was two hundred and ninety-nine dollars for a case—the man on the phone said it was cheaper than a homeowner's policy. I've got a few more bottles in the barn if you want to take some home with you. I don't need it anymore."

Running from the house, Francis could hardly feel his feet hitting the ground. He opened the old creaky side door of the barn and pushed his way inside, past the old Toro, the rusted bedsprings, the oily smells, the accumulation of a long, heartbreaking life. He pushed back the dread that pulsed in his veins until at last he came to it—a sturdy cardboard box with dividers filled with gallon-sized jugs. There were no markings at all, and if Francis wanted to deceive himself, it might have been easy enough to believe that it was an ordinary box that could have come from any-where.

But they were his. He knew.

"WHERE are the boys?"

Anita was making ham sandwiches. Her hands, he noticed, were cracked and chapped, and for some reason that wasn't entirely clear to Francis, it filled him with a deep sense of failure. "In the shed. Why?"

Francis thought about the pink gallons he had stowed behind the seat of his pickup. "They coming in for lunch?"

"I was going to bring some sandwiches out to them." Anita set down her knife. "You're awful pale. Are you coming down with a cold?"

"I'm all right."

"How was Mrs. Mullen?"

"She's moving away." Francis licked his lips. His mouth was as dry as cotton batting. "She gave me the old Toro and some salt and pepper shakers for you," he said, pulling two tiny ceramic cows out of his pocket.

Anita unwrapped the shakers and cooed with delight. "Look at the mail," she said, nodding to the stack on the kitchen table. "We got an-other check today. It just keeps climbing."

Francis flipped through the stack, paying more attention to the junk mail he usually ignored, until at last he came upon the envelope. Just see-ing Rice's name on the return address filled his belly with venom. He opened the envelope and peered inside, careful not to touch the check. It was for nearly five thousand dollars—a staggering sum, yet only a sliver of what Rice was raking in. Francis's stomach heaved.

"Amazing, isn't it?" Anita's complexion had taken on a high sheen. "Marty went and got his application for the fall term. Things are really starting to open up for us."

Francis took a plate down from the cupboard and helped himself to a sandwich. He had no desire to eat, but the repetitive act of chewing seemed to deaden his nerves. "I suppose it was good while it lasted."

"What do you mean by that?" Anita pressed her palm to his forehead. "You're clammy. I think you'd better lie down this afternoon."

"What if Rice decides he doesn't want us anymore?"

"That's just foolishness. I'm going to make you a hot toddy."

"What I mean is, what if the business closes somehow? What if we no longer have this money?"

Anita put a kettle of water on to boil. "It's Walter, isn't it? Going back to that house has you all upset. You've never done well with death. He was an old man, Francis. He had a full life."

Francis shook his head. It felt murky, blurred. "Did I ever tell you about the time Henny and I went to the beach and walked out to the rocks during low tide? We sat there looking out over the ocean for maybe a half hour, all the while the tide was coming in. When we turned around to go back, the water was up to our chests. If we had waited any longer, we might have drowned."

Anita chewed the corner of her mouth. "I'm going to keep an eye on you, and if things don't seem to be getting any better in an hour or so, I'm calling Dr. Shale."

"The spring is like that," he said, pulling her away from the counter and by his side. "We've been looking away for so long that I think it might be too late to go back."

Fear came into her eyes right then, black and damp and dense, smothering her usual light. It was shocking how quickly hope could be extinguished, how it turned her from a Palmdale girl with future prospects to a Cedar Hole housewife locked in endless drudgery. His heart was weighted by the thought of being Rice's pawn, by the bilking of Mrs. Mullen and others, by the shame of allowing himself to be deceived. But worse still was the pain of losing the business that had made him into someone worthy, along with the fear of disappointing Anita once again.

"You don't know how many nights I stay awake worrying," he finally said, losing the nerve to confess.

She touched his cheek. "Worrying never did anybody a bit of good." The kettle shrieked. "Your water's ready. Go lie down on the couch and I'll bring it to you."

While Anita and the boys were working in the shed, Francis sneaked out of the house and drove to the landfill. Seized by the desperate need to make sure Anita and the boys never found out about the scam, he poured out the rest of the water and buried the jugs deep beneath remnants of bathroom tile and a cracked toilet bowl.

"Whatcha got there?"

Francis whipped around to see Harvey Comstock standing directly behind him, with one foot on a stack of bath tiles and his thumbs hooked into his belt. "Just cleaning out the garage," he said, his heart pounding in his throat.

"Plastic goes over there on the left. This here is for toilets and stuff."

"You certainly are the dump expert."

"You spend enough time in a place, you get to know it," he said.

"Speaking of which, how's Delia these days?"

Harvey beamed. "Didn't you hear? We're getting married."

"I thought that was just an unfortunate rumor." He gathered up the pink plastic caps and the crushed jugs and hurled them onto the far side of the plastic pile, far enough to keep Harvey away. "When's the blessed day? My invitation must have gotten lost in the mail."

"Next month. Deelie wants to get married on Robert's birthday. She's a sentimental one." Harvey took out his ticket book and started writing.

Francis's temples throbbed. "Look, Harvey, it's been a rough day. What you got on me now?"

"Improper dumping."

"But I moved it."

"So you never put it in the wrong place to begin with?" Harvey ripped the ticket off his pad and handed it to him. "I don't know what you're boo-hooing about, anyway, Mr. Moneybags. It's all gravy to you."

~ Chapter Seven ~

TRAPPED

The next morning, a deep, throaty growl of an engine rumbled through the house. For an instant, Francis thought a jet had landed in his yard. "What in the hell was that?"

Anita ran over to the kitchen window. "Oh Lord—it's Jackie. She just drove across the backyard." She gnawed on the tip of her finger. "Her face is all red. She looks worked up about something."

Francis sighed. "I bet it's the TV."

"Of course it is. Her eyes got all tough the minute the boys rolled it out."

"I suppose she's mad 'cause we didn't put her name on it."

"Should I call Larrie?"

"No—just give me a minute," Francis said. "I'll settle it."

He ran down the back steps and outside just in time to watch his sister make a halting three-point turn in front of the spring shed, the tires of her truck carving wide arcs into the damp earth. Seeing the truck turned completely around, with its tailgate facing the door of the shed, his first thought was that she had come to steal his water. But the moment he saw her throw the truck into reverse he knew she had something else in mind.

NADINE woke to the sound of the phone ringing. Normally, she would have waited for her mother to answer, but after the twelfth ring, she rolled over and picked up the cordless on her nightstand.

"It's Ainsley. Mr. Holtz just called. I got the job."

Nadine sat up in bed and yawned. "That's really great, Ains. I'm happy for you."

"I can write whatever I want for my first assignment. I was thinking I might interview you about your job at the deli."

"Yeah, okay." She slipped her feet into a pair of fuzzy slippers and poked her head into her mother's room. The bed was made, but several outfits were piled onto the covers.

"I was thinking about interviewing your mom, too, if that's okay."

"You'll have to ask her yourself, but I don't think she's around right now. It's pretty quiet," she said as she began her lazy descent downstairs. "You know, I've been thinking about what you said about how my dad always made the best of a situation. If he could be happy with things here, I can, too, right?"

"Sure. I mean, what choice do you have?"

Nadine took a running start down the hallway and slid along the linoleum all the way into the kitchen, stopping in front of the refrigerator. "What are you doing today?"

"Looking for stories. I want to have a whole list of ideas ready."

That's when she saw the note, pinned to the fridge with an apple magnet:

Morning Hon—
Ran to the store for some eggs. Be back soon.
xoxoxo

"Hey, Ainsley, I gotta go," she murmured. Flashes of her mother's smeary lipstick and Norm's sleepy eyes ran through her head. "I'll call you later."

Nadine hung up the phone and ran out of the house, hardly aware she was still in her pajamas and slippers.

"Hey! Stop that!" Francis yelled at Jackie, waving his arms as he ran across the lawn.

Anita watched him from the screen door. "Don't get too close!" Despite her warning, Francis headed for the six-foot gap between the truck and the shed, somehow thinking in the back of his mind that he could interrupt the momentum of a one-and-a-half-ton truck.

Jackie hit the brakes, but kept the pickup in reverse gear. She stuck her head out of the window and glared at him over her shoulder. "I wouldn't be standin' there if I was you," she said with a slight slur.

Francis held his hands in the air, as though he were surrendering to Harvey Comstock. "Don't tell me Larrie Jr. let you slip a little whiskey into your coffee this morning."

"I wasn't home." Jackie waved her left hand at him, then let it drop loose against the side of the truck. "I kept forgetting . . . paid two dollars' worth of nickels."

Anita was on the back steps now, her hand keeping a safe grip on the railing. "Do you want me to call Harvey?"

Francis shook his head, keeping one eye on the brake lights. "Go back inside. See if you can get Larrie Jr. to come down here and pick her up." He tipped an imaginary beer bottle to his lips to clarify the situation. Anita nodded and disappeared into the house.

He tapped the side of the truck. "Turn off the engine and come out here. Then you can tell me what all this fuss is about."

"Get out of the way first."

"I'm not going anywhere until you come out."

Jackie didn't move. She left the pickup in reverse and let her head flop outside the cab and back against the doorpost, watching him through the side mirror. From his angle Francis could see her slack mouth and the seamless column of flesh made by her chin and neck. The rest of her face was cut off by the top of the mirror. He wished to God he could see her eyes.

"Good show at the party," she said.

"It was just a gift, Jackie. Don't go making it into something big."

"You shoulda put all our names on it, insteada showin' off."

"I didn't think of it." Francis slowly stepped forward and opened the tailgate. Rain snaked down his neck and into the collar of his work shirt. "Larrie Jr.'s coming for you soon. Why don't you come sit out here with me so we can talk better?"

"You looked like a real big shot, getting the boys to wheel it out for you." Jackie knocked her head back against the truck and sighed. "How'd you get so lucky, Spud? You were always such a pansy. God only knows how you manage to keep this thing going when you've got a peanut rattling around in that skull of yours—"

Francis clenched his jaw. "Don't hold anything back, now. . . ."

"—and you never did anything in your life worth anything. *I* should be the one with the water in my yard. *I* should be the one getting rich. Hell, I'm the one that built this damn thing."

Francis glanced over at the house, waiting for Anita to appear behind the screen door, giving him the nod that Larrie Jr. was finally on her way. Jackie, primed by who knows how much alcohol, seemed ready to get into things, and Francis, who was silently stewing about the fresh holes in his lawn and the overt threat to both his spring shed and his person, had half a mind to dive right in there with her.

"Aren't you supposed to be in Palmdale this morning, building a deck with the others? What's got you so worked up that you have to go off and get yourself drunk, then come over here and make a horse's ass of yourself?"

The reflection of Jackie's mouth suddenly puckered. "I'm not an ass—am I, Spud?"

"In my book, anyone who drinks their breakfast at the Left Hand Club and then tears up a perfectly good lawn is a strong contender."

Jackie looked down at the deep trenches that ran alongside her pickup as they filled with rainwater and stared at them blankly, as though for the life of her, she couldn't figure out how they got there. A breeze blew a faint tartness downwind from her. It reminded Francis of the vinegar-soaked shelves in their mother's pantry.

"Don't enjoy your luck too much," she said. "It ain't gonna last. You'll find a way to fuck it up somehow."

Francis looked a second time at the screen door, but still there was no sign of Anita. He felt a sudden, throbbing weariness lodge itself deep in his throat—a fatigue that was both new and familiar, that had been building inside him for years but that only made itself known for the first time just then. The weariness was accompanied by the old maddening hope that Jackie could finally come around, that he could still convince her that he wasn't the total waste of a human being she had always believed he was, that somehow he could do or say just the right thing to make her like him. And after everything, it made him madder than hell that he still cared.

Jackie leaned out of the window a little farther. Her foot slipped off the brake, causing the truck to rock, sinking deeper into the lawn.

Francis's heart slammed against his chest as he jumped back. His shoulder blade made contact with the heavy padlock, radiating a dull pain all the way up to the base of his skull.

"You have a good look on that face of yours," Jackie said as she found the brake again. She laughed a loud, cackling laugh, more shrill than usual. "Don't piss your pants."

"Turn off the engine and get out here."

The loose skin around her throat reddened. Even though he couldn't see her eyes, he knew they were turning red, too. "Don't tell me what to do," she said, revving the engine. "Get out of the way."

"I won't let you do it."

"How you gonna stop me? I'll run you over, too, if I have to."

Francis's thoughts ran thick now, like a herd of cattle, almost too heavy and quick for him to catch. "What if I gave you a cut? I need some more workers—I could hire you on."

"There's no way I'm gonna work for you. Just give me the money."

Anita appeared at the screen door again. "It's going to be a while," she called. "She's got to run to the hardware store." She looked at Francis, with his back pressed against the shed and his hands still in the air, and the creases around her mouth deepened. "Jackie? Why don't you come inside for a few minutes before Larrie gets here? I'll make some more coffee."

"Go back inside, Anita," Francis said.

She went back in but Francis still felt her with him, knowing she was probably watching from behind the kitchen curtains.

"I don't know what you want from me, Jackie. God help me, I've never known."

The blotchy redness had now creeped down the length of Jackie's arm. Her fingers were knotted into a fist, which she was beating against the door panel. "I'm tired, Spud. We can end this. Just move and I'll leave you alone."

Francis took in a slow breath to steady his heart. "I'm not going anywhere."

"Let's make things even between you and me."

"You're gonna have to run me down first."

This answer seemed good enough for Jackie. She took her foot off the brake. Francis gritted his teeth and stared down at the tailgate, wondering if it would do more damage to him opened than closed. The rain was coming hard now, rolling from the crown of his head into his eyes, but he couldn't close them. Instead, he stared down Jackie's white tail-lights, imagining that his will could penetrate the plastic cover and crush the lightbulb underneath.

The engine roared as Jackie hit the gas.

NADINE sneaked into the Superette through the back door. The stairwell was dark and quiet, except for the shuffle of her slippers against the floor-boards. At the front of the stairs, she looked up to make sure the apart-ment door was closed. Nadine moved soundlessly past the meat saws and empty cardboard boxes and edged up to the swinging door leading to the meat counter.

She pressed one ear to the door while keeping her eyes on the second swinging door straight ahead, the one leading to the main floor. Her heart throbbed in fear of Hinckley Hanson's sudden appearance, or worse, an unexpected glimpse of Arnie at the top of the stairs. Even though she wasn't doing anything wrong, her behavior—and pajamas—were decidedly suspicious. Nadine swallowed a gulp of air and prayed that if the time came, she'd come up with a convincing excuse.

On the other side of the meat department door, there were no voices or sounds of any kind. Curling her fingers around the lip of the scratched porthole window, she looked sharply to the right, staying tight to the wall to get a good view of the counter. Bernie wasn't where Nadine had expected her to be—inspecting packages of drumsticks, laughing at one of Norm's unfunny jokes. Norm wasn't there, either. The whole depart-ment was oddly still. A thought, spoken in her father's voice, pressed ten-derly in the back of her mind, telling her to go home, but Nadine ignored it. She moved to the right side of the porthole and surveyed the rest of the department.

On the scale next to the deep stainless steel sink, a piece of butcher paper and two steaks were stacked one on top of each other, waiting to be wrapped. The digits of the digital scale flickered, having yet to settle on the correct weight. Beyond, Nadine noticed the blue door to the meat

locker was cracked open wide enough for Norm to slip in and out sideways. The light inside it, however, was off.

Nadine pushed the swinging door slowly, careful not to let the hinges
creak. With the majority of the early morning customers popping in for
cigarettes and papers, only the front of the store was busy, leaving her to
move freely without the concern of being noticed. She stuck close to the
wall, an area that was always a strain for Mr. Hanson's curved mirrors and
binoculars, and, sliding along with her back to the counter, silently approached the dark locker.

She heard Bernie's voice first. The words were too soft to understand,
but the cadence was rolling and playful, wafting on a tendril of cold air
that licked the side of Nadine's head and tightened her scalp. Norm murmured something next. Nadine was standing in front of the open door,
her skin dimpled by cold, and nudged it wider to get a clearer view. As
the light seeped in, midnight ebbed toward dusk—allowing Nadine the
full vision of her mother giddily pinned between Norm Higgins's lips
and a hanging side of beef.

Bernie blinked as the light hit her eyes. Nadine enjoyed the wide-
eyed shock that reflected her own horror and the withering mortification
that hollowed her cheeks.

"Nadine? Honey?"

She could have yelled, screamed, cried—for every feeling of disgust
and embarrassment was available to her at that precise moment—but her
mother's history of thriving on reaction kept her from indulging in a display. Silence and indifference were the weapons that injured her mother
the most. With a supreme stubbornness of will, Nadine glared dry-eyed
at her mother and Norm, seeing in them and through them, her mouth
upturning with the decided lack of surprise. They couldn't fool her. They
weren't fooling anyone.

"Nadine, please . . ." Bernie pushed Norm's hands off her and took a
step toward the door. Nadine's coolness began to flail; her mouth curdled. Unwelcome tears sprang forth. She covered her eyes with her fore-
arm, and before her mother could get any closer to see, she slammed the
locker door shut.

~ Chapter Eight ~

ESCAPE

Nadine caught Kitty Higgins on the steps of the library, just as she was unlocking the door. "Dear girl! What are you doing running around town in your pajamas? You're all wet from the rain."

"You have to help me, Mrs. Higgins. I have to get out of here," she said, arms crossed and shivering.

Kitty stared deep into her eyes. "What did she do to you?"

Nadine winced, thinking back to the scene in the locker. She wondered how cold it was in there. "Can you bring me to the train station?"

"All right," she said. "But you shouldn't go like that. Is it safe to go home and change?"

Nadine nodded.

"Put some clothes on, and shoes. I'll be there in five minutes."

"COME ON!" Francis yelled.

The truck began to move. Tightening every muscle, he steeled himself for impact. The hot breath of the truck's tailpipe burned his legs. He shifted in the mud, his work boots sinking deep enough to form a suction around the sole. He wouldn't have been able to run even if the thought had entered his mind. Instead, his only thoughts were of Anita, who was watching from the house. He closed his eyes and silently willed her to move away from the window, just in case something happened that could haunt her forever.

He felt nothing. How strange, not to feel any pain. It almost made him giddy. A thick spray hit his face, soaked the length of his torso. Was it blood? He pushed the tip of his tongue against his lower lip for a taste. Mud.

When he opened his eyes, Francis saw the wheels spinning. The tires found their teeth and the truck crawled forward, gaining an inevitable, terrible momentum farther and farther away from him. For half a second, Francis thought he was capable of throwing himself down in front of the truck if he truly believed it would have been enough to stop her. Instead, he fled to the safety of the back steps, while Jackie grazed the rear fender of his own truck and took off, full tilt, down the road.

Anita, who was standing at the screen door, was visibly pale.

"Call Harvey Comstock," Francis said to her as he fumbled for his truck keys. "Tell him Jackie's drunk and headed towards Webber. I'm going after her."

THE CALL came at the most inopportune of moments—when Harvey was in the bathroom, draining the last of his morning coffee. He'd always thought that when the big moment came, he'd be sitting at his desk, hands folded, and not standing in front of a toilet with his fly unzipped. Even worse, the phone rang midstream of what had been nearly half a pot of coffee. Had he realized the severity of the call he would have rushed the process, but since nothing urgent ever seemed to happen in Cedar Hole he assumed the caller was Delia, and that whatever her issue was, it did not warrant the interruption of an eye-closing, head-lolling, full-throttle piss.

He caught the phone on the eighth ring.

"Cripes, Harvey, that place of yours is no bigger than a postage stamp," Anita Pinkham gushed into his ear after identifying herself. "WHAT are you doing in there?"

"I was in the bathroom."

"Jackie was over here a minute ago, drunk. Francis was going to drive her home but she took off in her truck before he had a chance."

Harvey sat on the edge of his chair and watched a buzzing gray haze explode behind his eyes. Blood rushed from his deflated bladder all the way up to his head. His hand ran the perimeter of his service belt, searching for his regulation notepad and pen.

"Did you see where she went?"

"Toward Webber Road. He took off after her."

"He shouldn't have done that. You should have called me right away."

"I did."

"Do you know I could cite him for speeding?"

"Well, Harvey, I'll be sure to tell him that when he gets back," Anita said flatly.

Harvey sighed. "There's no need to be snippy, ma'am."

"Yes, there is," she cried. "You need to get out there and stop her before she kills someone."

The coffee kicked in his veins. His pen twittered across the top page of the blank notepad in a meaningless configuration of stars and squiggles and a fluffy, two-legged goblin with wide eyes and a gaping smile. The situation, while it lacked the glamour of a bank robbery, still had the unpredictability of inebriation coupled with the excitement of a car chase. Not to mention the added bonus of the involvement of Jackie Pinkham, whose recklessness nearly guaranteed Harvey the possibility that his service revolver would finally get some use—even if only to put a few slugs in her rear tires.

Despite all this sudden turn of events promised for Harvey, he felt oddly paralyzed—the point of his pen a skipping needle in the scratched record that was his life, tracing the same doodles over and over on his pad for fear that if he moved forward the moment would be over, along with its infinite possibility.

"Harvey? Are you there? Get in your car and follow her!"

Anita's words were the oil Harvey needed to get unstuck; he was suddenly on his feet, pad and pen returned to their respective holsters, squad car keys in hand. "Stay right where you are, Anita."

"I have no intention of going anywhere."

"I'll take care of this."

"You do that, Harvey. We're counting on you."

·   •   •   •

"You can't tell *anyone* about this, do you understand?" Kitty's voice glittered with what Nadine thought sounded like delicious rebellion. "I would get in a world of trouble if the board knew I closed down during the day."

Nadine slumped against the seat with her backpack beside her. She had thrown in her toothbrush, a bar of soap, a towel, a plastic cup, three pairs of socks, a package of cookies, a pocket mirror, four spoons, and the small trinket box from her mother's nightstand. She had packed poorly and greedily, grabbing items as she ran into them—a tube of lipstick from the medicine chest, a wad of paper towels, a handful of rubber bands from the junk drawer. As she mentally reviewed the eclectic inventory, Nadine's heart began to ache. She had forgotten her father's watch.

Kitty looked over at her. "Are you all right? You look a little green."

"Just a little carsick."

"Oh, I'll slow down," Kitty said, letting off the gas. "It's these frost heaves. It's like being on a roller coaster."

"Don't slow down. I'll just crack the window."

Fat drops of rain splattered the windshield. Questions hung in the air around Kitty, but Nadine did nothing to encourage her. Finally, Kitty said, "She didn't hit you, did she?"

"God, no!" Nadine blurted. The look of innocence in Kitty's eyes brought Nadine to the edge of tears. Was she completely unaware of her husband's behavior, or did she simply choose to ignore it? Nadine toyed with her backpack zipper, envious of such an ability—to be able to ignore the imperfect. Was it something you allowed yourself to become blind to, or were you fully aware of the glaring fault, softening your standards until it became tolerable? What about right and wrong? Was it right to tolerate weakness?

"She's so hateful," Nadine said vaguely. "She makes me sick."

"You're a strong girl to recognize your mother's failings—most girls your age would think her behavior was normal," Kitty said. "You've got a lot of your father in you. It's wise to protect that."

Nadine thought about her mother, standing in the meat locker wearing that thin cotton shirt of hers with the short sleeves. She knew it wouldn't be long before Hinckley heard them pounding on the door and let them out. She wouldn't be seriously hurt, only humiliated from being discovered with Norm Higgins. *She deserves it,* Nadine told herself over and over again, every time the low, cold ache of remorse sank deeper into her belly.

Nadine wiped her eyes with the heel of her hand. "I've got a lot of her in me, too. Maybe more."

"I'm sure you've got the best parts of Bernie, whatever *that* might be." Kitty looked down at the backpack in her lap. "So what are your plans?"

"I'm going to visit my aunt in the city," Nadine lied.

"I didn't know Robert had family there."

"It's my mother's side." Nadine began to tremble. In the swift course of a morning she had become not only someone who would trap her mother in a locker, but a liar, too.

"That's good—you'll be with family," Kitty said. "I wouldn't feel right about letting you go off on your own. Does your aunt know you're coming?"

"I'll call her when I get there."

Kitty slowed as she approached the rise leading to the railroad tracks. "Look at this maniac behind me," she suddenly said, watching a pickup come barreling up in the rearview mirror. "Some people just don't know how to drive."

BY THE TIME Harvey arrived on the scene, it was already over. A Palmdale police officer who had been on patrol that morning saw the accident just after it had happened. He immediately summoned the paramedics, the fire department, and a tow truck, set up road flares, and interviewed witnesses. By the time Harvey arrived, there was nothing left to do.

"Apparently, the truck passed the car and then cut right back in at the train tracks," the officer said. "The driver of the car nicked the rear bumper of the truck. The driver of the truck overcorrected and hit the soft shoulder. She flipped right over."

Harvey's jaw muscles pumped with envy. "She was drunk, you know. I got a call."

"That's what her brother said."

Harvey took out his notepad and pen again, discreetly flipping past the doodles he made during his phone conversation with Anita, and made a few important-looking scribbles. "I'd say that it was the truck's fault."

The officer hit him with a deadpan stare. "Well, obviously."

"I'm glad you think so, too. I'll put that in my report."

"Why don't you forget your report for now, Sherlock, and help us with the deceased?"

Down in the gully, no more than a hundred feet from where they were standing, the pickup was lying on its side with the windshield blown out, except for a few crumbles of glass still clinging to the seal around the edges. Jackie Pinkham's broken body was curled around the base of a pine tree.

Harvey's stomach lurched. He looked away, bracing his hand over his mouth. "What else you got?"

"The paramedics are handling the rest," the cop grunted. "Other than that, you can direct traffic—if there is any."

"I'll see what I can do."

The officer crossed the road. Harvey felt an urgent tingle as fear and the rest of the coffee made its presence known. For a long moment, he entertained the possibility of slipping into the tree line and relieving himself in the woods, but the need to appear professional in front of Palmdale's finest overpowered even the most pressing desire to urinate. He imagined himself letting go among the puckerbrush, only to hear the officer's footsteps tramping the gravel behind him, and quickly decided against it. He refused to be caught with his fly unzipped twice on the same day.

Up ahead, Spud Pinkham was sitting on the rear bumper of the ambulance, hands cupping his kneecaps, head bowed low. Light buzzed behind Harvey's eyes. He sipped at the air and ambled, weak-kneed, to the ambulance.

"Have a seat," Francis said, making room on the bumper. "You look pale, Harvey."

"I never seen blood like that before."

Francis kneaded his mouth with his thumb and forefinger. His eyes looked dead—turned off—as though he had absorbed just about as much as a person could handle and refused to take in any more. "It's odd seeing her still," he muttered. "I don't think I ever saw her still for one minute."

Harvey didn't know if Francis's comment required a response. He floundered among the options and made a desperate grasp for the one that rang clearest in his head. "I suppose it's all for the best."

Francis shot him a look of disbelief. "And how do you figure that?"

Harvey sniffed. He had always thought the phrase was self-explanatory and offered a dose of comfort. Never did he expect to provide hard evidence of its truth. "Well, she was trouble. Always has been."

Francis shook his head. "But there was always a chance of a turn-around. At least there was always that chance."

"I don't know," Harvey said. "In my experience, there's good people in this world and there's bad. The good ones tend toward the righteous path and the bad ones always follow their impulses."

"And what about me, Harvey? Am I good or bad?"

Harvey snickered. "I'm not one to judge."

"Please, go ahead."

"All right." Harvey tilted his brim down to stop the rain from dripping into his eyes. "You know, Spud, I've always liked Anita and the boys. We both know I've let a few things slide. But I don't mind telling you that ever since your business got going, you've had a bit of an attitude."

Francis straightened his spine and leaned back against the ambulance. "The business had nothing to do with it. You've had it in for me from the very beginning. I know my sisters made things tough on a lot of people, but all I'm asking is for you to see me the way I am."

Harvey looked away, keeping his gaze trained down the middle of the road so that he couldn't see Jackie's body out of the corner of his eye. He stood up, walked around to the side of the ambulance, and got sick right next to the tire.

"I'm not made for this," he said to Francis, wiping his chin with the back of his hand. "I'm supposed to be helping them over there and I can't do it. I don't want to see that."

Francis gave him a handkerchief. "I need you to do a favor for me, Harvey."

"I don't know that I'm up for it."

"Sure you are. I need you to go tell Anita what happened. I'm sure she's worried sick," he said. "Have her call my sisters and tell them to meet at my house. Make sure everyone knows I'm all right, but don't let them come here under any circumstances. Do you think you can do that for me?"

"That'd be all right."

"Be quick about it. Don't drag the story out and scare her half to death. Tell her I'm fine the second she opens the door."

Harvey nodded. "I understand."

FRANCIS looked around the sides of the ambulance for a paramedic. No one was around. They were all congregated around the car on the other side of the road. The Palmdale police officer was taking measurements on the road. Jackie, who remained curled up and broken in the ditch, struck Francis as lonely, forgotten. The thought of it didn't make him angry, only pensive. It made sense to abandon the dead for the living.

He opened the ambulance door and found a rough wool blanket and carried it with him down into the gully. Truck debris was everywhere underfoot, identifiable pieces flung in surprising directions. The silver knob of the radio had somehow come off and made it halfway up the embankment. The rearview mirror was whole and uncracked, lodged in the crotch of a tree. The beer bottles Jackie kept in the back of the truck made the shortest, most surprising journey, having landed less than a foot away from the rear tire. Pebbles of glass crunched beneath his heels.

He did not look at her face. Instead, he opened the blanket and spread it gently over her, covering as much of her as he could. The blanket came only to her knees. His body was rigid, on alert, until he realized, fully, that she would not resist. He went limp and fell to his knees in a patch of moss. It was the only time she didn't reject him.

KITTY HIGGINS suffered a concussion and was sobbing as a medic tweezed bits of glass from her eyelids. The passenger, a teenage girl, was sitting at the top of the embankment wrapped in a blanket. Francis felt his stomach give way the moment he realized it was Robert Cutler's daughter.

"They take a look at you yet?" he asked her.

Nadine nodded, pulling the blanket tight around her shoulders. Her face was bloated from crying. "I'm okay. Just a little scratched up," she whimpered. "This is my all fault. I made her drive me out here."

Francis sighed. He tried to conjure some words of comfort, but they all rang false. "Well, I suppose that's one way of looking at it. Another way would be to say that I didn't stop my sister from taking off in that truck," he said. Tears continued to roll down her cheeks and Francis wished he hadn't wasted his only handkerchief by giving it to Harvey Comstock. "I suppose if you look deep enough there's something we all can be blamed for."

Nadine wiped her face with a corner of the blanket. "Why are you being nice to me?"

Francis was taken aback. "Sorry?"

"You've always been nice to me and my mother. I don't get it. I thought you hated my dad."

"I don't know about hate."

"But you didn't like him much."

"I'll give you that one," Francis said. "But just because I didn't like him isn't a good enough reason to take it out on you."

Nadine looked down at the ground. "I was always afraid of you, grow-ing up. I thought you'd be out to get me, that those candy bars you left in the bag were poisoned."

Francis's heart sank.

"But now that I think about it, you were one of the few people in Cedar Hole who was good to us," she said. "You never looked down on my mother."

"She always had to put up with a lot."

"From my dad, or everyone else?"

"Both. I suppose your dad's heart was in the right place, but he didn't always go about it the right way." Francis's voice fell away. It was hard to point out one man's failings without calling to mind his own. "Hey, it doesn't matter. It's not like I've always done the right thing."

"Me neither." Nadine shivered.

"Are you all right? Do you want another blanket?"

"No," she said. "I did something really stupid this morning. Can I tell you?"

"If that's what you want to do."

"I want to say it, but I'm afraid you'll tell on me."

"Did you murder someone?"

"No."

"Then I figure that whatever it is I can keep it to myself."

Nadine exhaled. "I locked my mom in the Superette meat cooler with Norm Higgins."

Francis smiled in spite of himself. "That's quite an accomplishment. Are they out now?"

"I don't know—I just pushed the door and ran." Even though she stared straight ahead, the girl seemed to be watching him out of the corner of her eye. "I didn't do it for nothing, though. I had a good reason. I was trying to get away."

Francis sat down beside her in the dirt and stretched out his legs in front of him.

"Now you think I'm a horrible person," she said.

"No—you seem like a sensible girl."

She looked straight at him. "You don't even know why I wanted to leave."

"Doesn't matter. I'm sure you had your reasons," he said. "What's nice is that you have the chance to make things right again. As long as we're breathing, we can fix our mistakes." The jugs he buried in the landfill came vividly to mind.

"But I'm afraid," she said, her eyes welling up again. "What if things don't get better?"

Francis nodded, understanding more than she would know. "It's worth a try, isn't it?"

Chapter Nine

SAFETY VALVES

Harvey dragged himself up the front steps of Delia's house, weary from the events of the day. The living room was littered with piles of old *True Detective* magazines that Delia made him bring down from the attic so she could reread the exploits of Detective Cabot straight from the beginning. Delia was stretched out on the couch, with one of the magazines open on her lap and a half bottle of gin and a full ashtray nearby.

"You're back," she said, throwing her arms around him.

"You heard?"

"Of course—that's all everyone's talking about. That and Bernie Cutler getting stuck in the meat locker with Norm Higgins."

"No."

"Apparently, Nadine found them and locked them in. They weren't in there long—they have one of those inside releases, of course—but when they got out, Arnie saw them with his binoculars and fired Norm on the spot."

Harvey's stomach churned with disgust. "And all the while his wife is in a car accident."

"Wake up, Harvey. It wasn't an accident. She found out and tried to kill herself—that's what happened. And she tried to kill Bernie's little girl, too, for revenge."

"I'm not sure that's quite right."

"Let's hear you come up with something better."

366

Harvey removed his belt, setting it on a nearby chair. It felt good to get the weight off. "It's been a bad day, Deelie. I had to tell the Pinkhams that Jackie died."

"Oh, I bet they were just *wrecked* about it," she said, rolling her eyes.

"More than you'd think." He remembered Anita's fingers digging deep into the flesh of his upper arm as he described the accident. The Pinkham girls—normally so gruff and unflappable—seemed permanently shattered and lost. Rae drifted into the woods alone and didn't come out until the sun had set.

Delia moved a pillow aside, making space for him on the couch. "So tell me all about it. Every last ugly detail."

"No, I don't think so. I need a shower and then I'm going to bed."

"What about supper?"

"I'm not hungry."

"For Pete's sake, Harvey, it's the biggest day of your career and you're going to clam up about it."

He slipped off his shoes. "Jackie flew out of the windshield and hit a tree face first."

"Holy shit."

"Worst thing I ever saw—I don't care to ever see anything like that again," he said. "I don't have the stomach for it. All this time I've been waiting for the big call and now I find out I'm not cut out for it. You should have seen that Palmdale cop. He knew exactly what to do. I just stood there like an idiot." He tilted his head against the back of the couch. "I don't want to do this anymore."

"Don't be pathetic. We're getting married."

"I'll work someplace else. That's all right, isn't it? If I work for Shorty or something?"

Delia tossed the magazine on the floor and poured herself a drink. "I can't believe you'd do this to me."

"I'm terrible at being a police officer, Deelie. Everyone makes fun of me—they don't think I know, but I do."

"That's because you're a pushover. That stupid cell doesn't help, either. *And* you're a quitter." She took a long drink and poured another. "At least you did this to me *before* the wedding."

"I'll do anything you want."

"Stay a cop."

"Anything but that."

"Fuck, Harvey." Delia slid the engagement ring off her left hand and slid it onto the ring finger of her right hand. "I'm keeping this, you know."

To Harvey's surprise, he actually felt relieved. "I can't return it, anyway. It was on clearance."

Delia gave the stack of magazines a vicious kick. "I've had it up to my eyeballs with this place. I'm moving to Palmdale. What did you say the name of that cop was?"

"I don't know," Harvey said. "But I can find out for you."

BERNIE AND NORM drove over to the hospital in separate cars. The decision was mutual and unspoken—made not out of a joint desire to remain discreet, but out of common embarrassment. Norm's kiss had been forceful and without pleasure—an obligatory experiment in novelty, a curious one-upmanship. Bernie kissed back just as forcefully, in sly competition. The flirtation had gotten out of hand.

Out of the car and through the sliding doors of Mt. Etna General, Bernie felt her body tripping ahead of her. Her head clotted in panic, her tongue felt dense and numb and tasted of acid. The sensations were old and familiar, the very same that had consumed her on the morning of Robert's death. Bernie thought she had insulated herself well against feeling them again, but of course there was Nadine. With a child, fear and loss were an inescapable possibility.

Nadine sat in a chair in the waiting room, in a far corner from Kitty and Norm Higgins, who were engaged in a whispered battle. Physically, Nadine looked perfect and whole. Bernie felt herself breathe for the first time since the phone call, convinced that there could be no greater blessing.

Bernie squeezed her daughter tight. "I don't care if you hate it, just hold still for a second."

Nadine didn't resist, even after several moments passed. She buried her face in her mother's shoulder. "You can't see him again."

"We were impulsive. It's already over." Bernie pressed her cheek against the top of Nadine's head. "I keep thinking that if your father had been the one to survive, you'd probably be a much happier person. But I've tried, Nadine. I really have."

"I almost left today."

"I know," Bernie said. "And if you still can't stand me, I have an old aunt in Palmdale that you might be able to stay with. I'd rather have you living at home, but at least I would know you were somewhere safe."

Nadine's hug tightened. Perhaps just knowing she had a safety valve was all she needed.

FRANCIS left the shed locked for the next week, telling Anita and the boys that they were suspending operations until after Jackie's funeral. One afternoon when Anita and the boys were out of the house, he decided to give Mr. Rice a call.

"Mr. Rice is in Costa Rica right now," Janet said. "It's funny that you called—I was just about to cut you another check. I know it's been a few weeks since your last one. Thank you for your patience."

"Keep your money. I'm done."

"Sorry?" Janet cleared her throat. "I don't like your tone, Francis. You're worrying me. I'm sure whatever's bothering you can be straightened out."

"I know what you're doing with the water. I don't like feeling like a chump and I'm not about to do it to someone else."

Janet sighed and started to laugh. "Is that what this is about? Phew! I thought it was serious. Like Mr. Rice discussed with you early on, he sometimes uses unusual strategies for selling a product. He didn't want to tell you right away—he wanted to wait until things were rolling. Until you could see that we could make it another way."

"That's not what I signed up for. I thought I was selling spring water."

"Oh no. We couldn't do that. That water's full of arsenic."

Francis turned on the tap from the kitchen faucet and took a sip to stop himself from gagging. "It's a dirty business you two are running and I want no part of it."

"I'd tread lightly if I were you," she said, the warmth evaporating from her voice. "Mr. Rice wouldn't like to hear you talking like that."

"You tell him to stay away from my family," Francis said. "Or I'll hunt him down."

The line went dead.

"You can sit around drinking coffee all day," Marty said, getting restless, "but I'm going to get some work done."

Francis handed him his key chain. "Pull the truck up to the shed door and start loading the empty water jugs into the back. Get Flynn to help you."

Marty took the keys. "What's going on? Did Rice call or something?"

"No more questions. Just do what I say."

Marty and Flynn went out into the backyard to start loading the empty jugs into the back of the truck. Anita stared out the kitchen window. "What's happening?"

"We have to shut down."

She looked at him, puzzled. "I thought there was plenty of business."

"There is. It's not about that."

"Well, it can't be about Jackie." Her eyes were searching, confused. "I saw you throw yourself between the shed and that truck."

He brushed the hair away from her face. "You've been so good, Anita. I don't know how you managed it. You always had hope when you looked at me."

She recoiled. "Stop. What are you talking about?"

"It's already fading. I think that's the worst of it." His voice faltered. "I'm lucky to have had it as long as I did. God help me, I'd like to hold on to that forever."

"Francis, look up." He refused to meet her eyes. Anita gripped her fingers on the edge of the counter until her knuckles turned a bloodless white. "The numbers aren't straight, are they?"

"Nothing is," he said.

"It was there all along, but I didn't want to know it. There were too many things to look forward to. Marty was going to start school."

"I thought I could keep it up for you—"

"Don't say that. I would have never asked that."

"But I wish I could have done it anyway." Outside, the boys were placing the jugs upright on the flatbed as though they believed they were still going to be filled. Their careful work made his throat ache. "We'll never live in Palmdale, Anita. I'll never be able to buy you a house like the one you grew up in. I won't ever drive a fancy car or know the difference between cheap champagne and the good stuff. I might be able to retile the bathroom one of these days, but new kitchen cabinets will be a stretch." He sighed. "Do you understand this?"

"You talk like an old man."

"There's still time enough for you to meet a man that can do those things for you. Take the checkbook and the boys and go start a new life for yourself."

She shook her head. "I can't believe what I'm hearing."

"Take it. You'll have a chance to have the kind of life you were meant for."

"I don't understand why you're saying these things now. A person can only take so much in one week—" She paused. "Please tell me you're not sick."

He opened his wallet and pressed his last twenty into her hand. "The timing is perfect. Life's collapsing all around us! Might as well jump right in and crush every last piece!"

"You're overtired," she said. "Go take a nap. We can talk after you've rested."

"This is your only chance, Anita. If I back down now, I'm bound to keep you forever."

"I should hope so, you old fool." She took his hands. "Look up at me."

"I can't."

"Look."

Her eyes were still the same.

~ Chapter Ten ~

CEDAR HOLE REVISED

As for Kitty, upon returning from the hospital she packed a small suitcase and moved into the library, sleeping on a cot in the kitchen. Off the record, the Cedar Hole Library Association was not pleased with the move—it increased the building's utility bills and compromised the library's professional integrity—but no one had the heart to give Kitty a rougher time than she already had. Norm stopped by once to bring her roses.

"This is a pretty nice place," he said, crossing the threshold for the first time.

"The floorboards are rotting between the stacks," Kitty said. "The wood feels soft underfoot."

"You take care of all of this yourself?"

"I'm a librarian, Norman. What do you think I've been doing in here all this time?"

While he wandered around slack-jawed, Kitty opened a book of poetry and read enough Keats to help her gather a little poise. Norm let himself out quietly.

When she heard the door close behind him, Kitty opened her mayonnaise jar and took one last, lingering sniff before dumping the contents in the trash. She filled the jar with water and arranged the roses. Then she sat at her typewriter and composed a curt letter to Norm, demanding a divorce.

• • •

BERNIE waited two weeks before doing anything. Remembering her own experience after Robert died, she recalled that two weeks was enough time to get over the shock; just enough time to let the initial furor taper down before insidious fears began to take hold. It was the time when despair tapped you on the shoulder in the middle of the night and the future alternated between a blank concrete wall and a vast, lonely desert.

She had sworn that she would never be like one of those ladies of the Auxiliary, using plates of cookies and casserole dishes to wheedle their way into the lives of the vulnerable, combing for bits of gossip. But now, as Bernie Cutler climbed the steps of the Cedar Hole Library, it occurred to her that perhaps she had misjudged their intentions. Her own reasons were muddled and complicated, falling somewhere between an obligation and a peace offering—a maudlin passing of the torch, an expression of guilt, an apology. But at the core of it all (and the impetus that she supposed drove the Ladies' Auxiliary) was a feeling of shared helplessness. When things turned unfair, Cedar Hole had a strong need to try to make them right again.

Bernie's instrument of choice was a small lemon cake. Straight from the box, nothing fancy, with a two-minute glaze. Anything beyond would be hypocritical, she thought. She checked the faint reflection in the glass and drew up straight, pumping herself with the gall necessary to get through the front door and face Kitty Higgins.

Kitty was sitting at her old pine desk, the one Robert wanted so desperately to get rid of (and upon close examination, even Bernie had to admit it looked shabby), with her nose pushed low into a book. Her back curved stiffly forward and the pallor of her skin tinged toward gray. Heaviness surrounded her, as though she were encased in an inexhaustible sigh.

Bernie placed the cake to one end of the circulation desk and gently rapped her knuckles on the desktop. "Kitty—hi. I heard you were staying here and wanted to bring you something."

Kitty, roused from her reading, gave Bernie a weary nod. "I'd really rather not hear it. If you have any heart at all, you'll leave me alone."

"I'm not here to give you a hard time—really." Bernie pushed the cake toward her. "I know what it's like to be at the center of something. I know how tough it can be."

Kitty stared distrustfully at the cake. "Did you come to see what a mess I am? My suitcase and cot are in the kitchen, if that makes you feel better. I have some underwear soaking in a basin, because I don't have anywhere else to wash my clothes."

"I know you're suffering. And believe me, it doesn't make me feel any better. I know what it's like to lose a husband."

"There's a big difference between having your husband die in an accident and having him ignore you for other women," Kitty snapped. "Norm's always had eyes for anything in a skirt, so don't think you're special."

Bernie took the hit, knowing she fully deserved it. "I lost Robert long before he died, Kitty. He was more concerned with you and the library and anything else going on in this town than he was about his own family. I know what it's like to be neglected."

Kitty closed the book and leaned her forehead into the palm of her hand. "I can see myself hardening. I don't like the idea of it, but I like the way it feels. I don't have to have a stake in everything. I can choose to pull away."

"Then you can understand how it was for me," Bernie said, almost breathless.

"Are you expecting forgiveness?"

Bernie looked at Kitty, who despite her rumpled clothes and sleepless eyes seemed to command an awesome power that made Bernie feel diminished. "At the very least, I'm hoping for some understanding."

"I've never understood cruelty."

"It's only the passing on of a wound," Bernie said. "But it's left me now, Kitty. I won't be bothering you anymore."

"I don't think you could, even if you wanted to." Kitty opened her book and resumed her reading.

FRANCIS rented a bulldozer. All of his sisters were there, along with Henny and Dixie and a few of the neighbors. Anita made lemonade, which Flynn passed around in paper cups. Marty stayed in his bedroom with the door closed, but Francis thought he might come around as soon as he heard the engine start.

"Who wants at it?" he said, jiggling the keys above his head. "Rae?"

She shook her head. "Can't do it to you, Spud."

"Come on—Billie?"

"You don't have to finish what Jackie started."

"She didn't put me out of business. The idea was all mine." Francis climbed onto the dozer and started the engine. "I didn't like the customers. What kind of dink buys pink water?"

He practiced working the levers. The crowd moved back as he moved forward. The first push was the hardest, caving in one corner of the shed and buckling the front door. Anticipation needled his insides, then warmed and spread wide across his ribcage. He backed up and plowed again, one stud buckling after the next until the building was no longer a recognizable form.

"There she goes," Hinckley Hanson said. "I wouldn't have the guts to end it like that."

Henny nodded. "Not many of us would."

Hinckley stepped forward and waved his arms at Francis, motioning for him to cut the engine.

"Say, Spud, don't you think it's time we brought back the Train Festival?"

The crowd hushed, waiting for Francis to speak.

"Doesn't make much sense without the train," Francis decided. "We should call it something else."

"Like what?"

Before he gave them his answer, Francis allowed his thoughts to wander. His mind turned loose and liquid, floating toward the Toro sitting in the garage. Caked with grass and tacky with old grease, the mower had been too long neglected. As soon as everyone was gone, he would buff out the blooms of rust and sharpen the blade.